Buying Time

A novel

Cali Canberra

Cali Canberra

Published by:

Newchi Publishing
11110 Surrey Park Trail
Duluth, GA 30097
770-664-1611

This novel is a work of fiction. Any references to real people, living or dead; and real events, businesses, organizations, and locales are intended only to give the fiction a sense of reality and authenticity. All names, characters, places, and incidents either are the product of the author's imagination or are used fictitiously, and their resemblance, if any, to real-life counterparts is entirely coincidental.

ISBN: 0-9705004-3-2

Library of Congress Control Number: 2003110694

First Edition

Printed in the United States of America

ACKNOWLEDGMENTS

Thanks to my husband for his support and encouragement through my ups and downs of being a new writer.

Thanks to my daughter for being herself and for believing in me. And, thanks to her friends for having names I can use for characters!

Thanks to Ken Lapine for his legal advice, consulting, editing, and inspiration for a major story line.

Thanks to Susan Bellhassen for rekindling our relationship. She was there in the beginning when I brokered my first horse and was there to help me off the ground when Ro (a jet black Quarter Horse) dumped me in the beginning of almost every ride. Thanks for [trying] to teach me grammer and puncuation.,?!-

Thanks to Hallie McEvoy for editing, encouragement and building up my confidence as a writer.

Thanks to all the readers who have enjoyed my books and have made my writing career possible.

Thanks to all of the retailers who sell my books - especially to those that didn't think fiction would sell in their type of store, but gave it a try, regardless.

Cast of Characters

in order of appearance

*(names in **bold** appeared in* Trading Paper*)*

Nick Cordonelli - Developer of L'Equest, an exclusive equestrian development in Kentucky. Client of Vintage Arabians. Background in the Thoroughbred business. Lives in Ocala, Florida and at L'Equest.

Ron McGill - Business manager for Vintage Arabians. Originally from Seattle, Washington, where he still owns a car dealership. Lives in Scottsdale, Arizona.

Dolan Holloway - Marcie Bordeaux's uncle. Lawyer representing Vintage in *Murphy v. Vintage*. Lives in Scottsdale.

Jessica Sellica - Law partner of Dolan, also handling Murphy v. Vintage lawsuit. Married to Turner Lloyd. Lives in Scottsdale.

Greg Bordeaux - Principal: Vintage Arabians, L'Equest and Bordeaux Hill. Lives in Scottsdale, moves to L'Equest.
Marcie Bordeaux - Wife of Greg.
Thomas Bordeaux - Father of Greg & Patrick. Lives in Scottsdale.
Fiona Bordeaux - Mother of Greg & Patrick. Wife of Thomas.
Patrick Bordeaux - Brother of Greg. Head trainer for Vintage. Lives in Scottsdale.

Drake & Deirdre Holloway - Parents of Marcie Bordeaux. They live in Scottsdale.

Ryan Sanders - Movie producer. Horse breeder. Husband of Shawna. Owns a farm in Santa Barbara, California. Lives in New York.
Shawna Sanders - Highest paid television news journalist in the country. Married to Ryan. Lives in New York.

Alec Douglas - Lawyer representing the Murphys in *Murphy v. Vintage*. Married to **Mimi** Douglas, who is also a lawyer. Lives in St. Louis, Missouri.

Morgan Butler - Equine broker/agent. Owns stallion in Santa Ynez, California. Lives in Laguna Beach, California.

Sonia Finn - Wife of George Finn.

George Finn - Greek tycoon. Garment industry mogul. Vintage client. Owns farm in Southern California. Lives in Beverly Hills, California.

Garth Windsor - Lawyer. Works with Alec Douglas. Grew up in horse business. Lives in St. Louis, Missouri.

Davis & Lily Windsor - Parents of Garth. Former Vintage clients. They live in suburbs of St. Louis.

The Scottsdale Arabian Consortium:

Matt & DeAnn Robard- Owns Robard Arabians. Matt owns a television station and DeAnn is heiress to a confection empire. They live in Scottsdale.

Cal Hampton- Leases a farm from the Robards. Full time trainer. Lives in Scottsdale.

Jay & Jane Peacock- Leases a farm from the Robards. Lives in Scottsdale.

Leonard Cannon- Owns Canco Arabians, Scottsdale's fanciest horse farm. Lives in Scottsdale.

Greg Bordeaux

Larry Brown - Top sales person for Vintage. Lives in Scottsdale, moves to L'Equest in Kentucky.

Mike Wolf - Sales person for Vintage. Lives in Scottsdale.

Johnny Pallinto -Vintage client. Friend of Greg. Lives in L'Equest.

Buying Time

Chapter 1

Nick Cordonelli's fist clenched the phone. A blinding narrow beam of sunlight pierced through the leaded glass window overlooking one of the Kentucky bluegrass pastures.

Greg Bordeaux, the self appointed emperor of the Arabian horse industry and a principal in Vintage Inc., had hired Nick Cordonelli, a land developer by profession, to develop L'Equest - his exclusive Kentucky equestrian project.

"The front page?" Nick moaned as his knuckles turned white. His grip on the phone tightened with every word he digested.

"Yes, above the fold. And whoever wrote this must have an insider feeding them information. They know far too much to be speculating," Ron McGill said, calling from Scottsdale, Arizona. As the business manager for Vintage Incorporated, he reported to Nick regularly.

"What else does it say?" Nick demanded as he unrolled the revised blueprints for L'Equest.

Picturing the veins popping out from Nick's temples, Ron skimmed the story, reading notable lines such as: *'In this decade of the 1980's, nothing succeeds like excess. The prices wealthy equine enthusiasts pay for Arabian horses soar every February as a result of savvy marketing, free-flowing alcohol, and headline entertainers like Sammy Davis, Jr.'*

"What's the headline?"

"I told you – it says: *'Trading Paper: The Legitimacy of the Arabian Horse Industry in Question'*."

Nick bit his lower lip hard enough to make it bleed.

"I'll be there as soon as I can. Thanks for letting me know," Nick said, realizing he had some tough decisions to make. When it came to horses, his common sense and business acumen flew out the window.

In hindsight, Nick should have trusted his wife's instincts. On more than one occasion his wife, Louisa, strongly voiced her opinion about Greg Bordeaux and the Scottsdale operation - she thought her husband should be keeping closer tabs on everything there. Nick, already spread thin, didn't feel it was necessary because Ron kept him informed. Most months he traveled back and forth between the Ocala, Florida race-training farm, the California breeding operation and the Kentucky development. Greg insisted that he could handle everything in Scottsdale. Apparently not.

~~~

It was only ten in the morning and Dolan Holloway already felt as if he had spent a full day in trial on the losing side of an important case. Jittery from too much coffee, he couldn't sit behind his desk waiting for the confrontation. He paced in front of his receptionist's desk complaining about the hot weather as she tried to avoid responding to his mood by sorting through files.

Jessica Sellica walked through the door of the law firm's office.

"What in the world were you thinking?" Dolan blurted out.

She didn't respond.

"What on earth did you do?" he sneered as he pounded a fist on the reception desk. The pens and pencils rattled and the tape dispenser near the edge of the desk fell to the floor.

The receptionist rapidly abandoned her swivel chair and went to the copy machine. The clerical staff grew curious. The office suddenly fell silent - the tapping of the typewriter keys ceased - the piped music was abruptly turned off.

"I don't know what you're talking about. And lower your voice," Jessica said, having no idea why he was fuming. All she knew was that her law partner, Dolan Holloway, suddenly appeared a foot taller and twenty pounds heavier in his rage.

"Get into my office," he groaned in a low voice as he hovered over her five-foot-five frame. Then, "You can all go about your own business," he barked at the inquisitive employees.

Jessica didn't cower to him, but she hurried into his office to avoid creating a scene. He followed closely, slamming the heavy maple door.

Jessica had never known him to have a temper. Composed, she lowered herself into the tufted leather chair,
~~~

smoothed her skirt, took a deep breath, and calmly looked him in the eye.

"Do not speak to me that way again. I can assure you that I don't know what on earth you're referring to. If you can control yourself, please feel free to explain what this is all about," she said, playing the roll of the tough legal adversary she was in court.

"Explain myself? You're the one that has the explaining to do."

"Dolan, how many times do I have to repeat myself? I don't know what you're talking about."

"The newspaper article. I know you loathe Marcie and Greg, but how dare you leak confidential information to the press."

"I didn't leak any information. What article?"

"You haven't read the morning paper?"

"No. I haven't. I went for a run early this morning then worked out at the gym."

He threw *The Phoenix Sun* onto his desk in front of her.

She was shocked by the headline: *"Trading Paper: The Legitimacy of the Arabian Horse Industry in Question."*

As an attorney she had plenty of practice at hiding her emotions and speaking off the cuff. She stood up acting completely dismissive.

"Why are you questioning me about this?"

"Why do you think?"

"I have absolutely no idea. I have to say, Dolan, I'm insulted you would even suggest that I would leak information about any case, let alone one involving your niece and her husband. You should know better."

Dolan questioned his judgment. He softened as he spoke again. Nothing would easily diffuse the situation.

"I trust you, but..."

"You say 'but'?"

"But where would a reporter get the information – let alone the headline *'Trading Paper'*? That's exactly what you keep scribbling on your note pad."

"I won't dignify what you are accusing me of with an answer. I'm going to my office to review a file for a hearing this afternoon. I suggest you rethink your position on this and offer me an apology soon, or you can expect my resignation by the end of the day," she told him as if she were speaking to a defense attorney who was proposing a ridiculously low settlement offer.

Jessica grabbed the front page section of the newspaper from his desk then departed in a huff, leaving the door open behind her.

In the privacy of her own office she read the newspaper article. One familiar passage in particular startled her: '*Vintage Arabians creates their own laws - laws that are followed by friendly competitors nationwide. Greg Bordeaux, the principal of Vintage Arabians, has single-handedly convinced some of the wealthiest people in the country that buying horses for record-breaking prices through Vintage's Scottsdale auctions is a status symbol.*'

Jessica couldn't imagine where a reporter could get detailed information about the inside operations of the Arabian horse industry. Suddenly a flashback jolted her. About a week before, she noticed her husband closing her briefcase. When she asked him what he had been doing, he said he borrowed a pen and was returning it. At the time, although it struck her as odd since there were plenty of pens in the kitchen drawer, she didn't really think much of it.

By the time she finished the article, she fumed at what her husband had done. Should she phone him now or confront him in person? Confront him in person. She had to see the expression on his face when she called him on his crime - a crime against the trust in their marriage.

Not wanting to hear more about his regrets of having bought her an expensive horse, Jessica hadn't told him much of what she learned about how Greg and Marcie Bordeaux operated their business, and by extension, how the wheels were kept greased in the elite segment of the horse industry. As it turned out, her husband secretly read the files and notes she brought home and discovered the unscrupulous business practices in the horse business. He was well aware that the information in her possession was cloaked with attorney/client privilege and confidentiality.

She dialed the phone. He picked up on the first ring.

"Good morning, Turner Lloyd speaking."

"It's me. Do you have time to meet for breakfast? I had a great workout. I'm starved," she said, not letting on what she suspected. Surprise would be the only weapon she would have against him.

"If we don't drag it out all morning. How about Café Casino?" Turner suggested.

He wondered if she had seen the article yet. He knew her well enough to be prepared to defend himself at breakfast.

There would be a storm but hopefully it would subside with his smooth explanation - and when he showed her the tickets for Jamaica.

"Sounds good. I can be there in ten minutes. Can you?"

"I'll be there."

~ ~ ~

A few minutes after Greg and Marcie read the devastating headline in the newspaper, there was pounding on their front door. Pale faced, Greg greeted his parents. Thomas rushed in ahead of Fiona, his pulse racing.

"Dad. I - "

Thomas cut him off. "You're not going to believe what happened. I don't know what we're going to do."

"I read it. Let me explain," Greg said.

Too caught up in his own panic, Thomas didn't hear Greg's response. He continued. "Pedro and Manuel accidentally hauled the wrong colts to the reservation. He took Lodzetta's and Lodzrava's colts instead of Lodzteza's and Lodzalot's."

"No way," Greg grimaced.

"Yes. They did. Jose said your phone line was busy so he called us. Your mother and I went to the barn to see if he were mistaken. Jose was right. They took the wrong colts."

"Shit. What are we going to do?" Greg said, ready to collapse on the spot. This was all they needed. Could things get any worse?

For years, the Bordeauxs and other big breeders in Arizona hauled some of their personally owned weanlings to the Indian reservation on Pima Road. The young horses that they hadn't even bothered to name were set free to grow up as wild horses. It wasn't cruel - the weanlings hadn't been spoiled by domestication; they would quickly learn to survive by integrating into the herd that already roamed the reservation. This seemed to be the only humane way to dispose of horses not meeting the caliber they wanted their clients or their competition to know about. Certainly they would never destroy an otherwise healthy horse or send one to slaughter as people in other breeds were rumored to have done with their cast-offs.

"The Beers are going to have our heads," Thomas said, a bead of sweat forming around his hairline. "And I won't blame them."

Ned and Brenda Beers, loyal clients from New York, spent

their way onto the Vintage 'A List' by acquiring elite horses for top dollar. The couple sought their relief from the competitive business world by collecting fine Arabians and taking an active role in their ownership.

"We'll need to come up with a plausible story to account for the missing colts," Greg said. His parents apparently hadn't read their newspaper yet. He'd be breaking the shocking news.

"We have to tell them the truth and offer them fair compensation," Thomas said earnestly, troubled by Greg's reaction.

"No way."

"Son, we have to tell them. When you give misleading information you've lost your integrity. We're a family with integrity."

Shit. Wait 'til he reads the article. "I'll come up with something believable," Greg said, dropping into the kitchen chair.

"We'll tell the truth and pay the consequences. Making money is important, but you can't keep trying to fix problems without owning up to them. You'll get caught in your own shadow."

Greg stared up at his parents who remained standing. "What do you propose?"

Thomas's eyes wandered to the kitchen table. The front page of the newspaper glared at him - a photograph of their farm entrance and a promotional picture from one of the with the headline: *"Trading Paper: The Legitimacy of the Arabian Horse Industry in Question."*

Thomas instantly forgot what he was talking about. He picked up the paper and began reading aloud: *'Greg Bordeaux is obsessed with flaunting his lifestyle. In fact, he lures wealthy equine enthusiasts into his world of the glamorous horse business by encouraging people to follow their hearts by purchasing living works of art capable of reproducing themselves.'*

As her husband read the article aloud, Fiona almost passed out.

Among other serious allegations, the newspaper article claimed that the public image of the horse industry was contrived. Thomas read: *'The manipulations were brilliant. Vintage Arabians creates the illusion that the horses are priceless superstars. Like Versace and Gucci, the Bordeauxs grew to believe the illusions they created - buyers followed along, hook, line and sinker. The Bordeauxs and their clients had to believe the myth in order for them to dole out hundreds of thousands of dollars for horses that were purchased for a fraction of the price not that many years ago. Vintage Arabians' clients validate themselves in the reflected glory of what the Bordeauxs accomplished. I wonder...How many of them know anything about horses?'*

Thomas sat down with the paper and continued reading aloud at his wife's insistence. Fiona worried about how many of the shocking allegations about their business practices were true. In a single morning, the desert calm was shattered. Her faith in what they had been building disappeared faster than a cool summer breeze in Scottsdale.

Thomas allowed the severity of the moment to filter in. This news would rock the genteel world of the horse industry. Vintage Arabians was a magnet to the rich and famous who wanted to escape their ordinary world. Their clients had an ethical tolerance level that Thomas hoped hadn't been crossed.

Greg grimaced as he waited for an eruption. His mother was often emotional. Thomas was normally calm and rational but this wasn't a normal day.

Just as Thomas dropped the paper to the table and began to ask Greg to step outside with him, Patrick barged through the kitchen door having come directly from the training barn.

Waving his own copy of the paper he yelled, "What the fuck is this?" at Greg.

Here was the eruption. Leave it to his hotheaded brother, who was on an ego trip from being a big time trainer, to make a bad scene worse.

Thomas threw his hands in the air dramatically. "Calm down. We just read it ourselves," Thomas said, his stomach still sinking.

Patrick couldn't keep his mouth shut. "Everyone knows you're not the moral backbone of the horse business, but now they know exactly why," he told Greg.

"Shut up. I've got enough problems without your big mouth," Greg almost shouted.

On cue, Marcie and Fiona left the men alone to digress to their childhood antics and to work out the dynamics. The rivalry between the brothers had always fueled Greg's ambition while it stifled Patrick's.

"Call Dolan right now," Greg said briskly to Marcie.

"Okay."

"Let me know when he's on the line. I want to give him a piece of my mind," Greg said.

"Maybe I should talk to him instead," Thomas

suggested.

"You can come to his office with me. I'll talk to him on the phone," Greg said.

Marcie signaled Greg to pick up the kitchen extension while she remained on the line. As she did so, her own parents pulled their car into the drive and hastily carried their folded newspaper into the house, entering without knocking.

Dolan received the call he dreaded. He was surprised it had taken this long. He inhaled deeply, hoping they had gotten the fury out of their systems.

"Stop. I can't understand you when you're both talking at once. I'll come to your house."

"Fine. And bring that bitch with you," Greg said.

"Don't call her that. I don't think Jessica's here right now. I'll be there as soon as I can."

"Uncle Dolan, why did you do this to us?" Marcie asked before he hung up.

He could hear her crying. "I didn't, Marcie. I promise. It wasn't me, sweetie."

"It was that bitch Jessica. We ought to sue her! I knew we shouldn't have let her get involved in our case – not once we found out that cheap bastard Turner is her husband," Greg vented.

"Calm down. I know this is upsetting but we need to think clearly and do damage control as soon as possible," Dolan said.

"Damage control - that's what we need," Greg said not knowing what they could do about the bad publicity that was sure to follow.

"Greg, I understand why you're so upset, but it's critical we formulate a plan to combat the article. You need to be able to refute the claims and sway another reporter onto your side. We need to make it look as if the first reporter printed information lacking any factual evidence. That she didn't do her homework. That she relied on bad information. Let me hang up and come over."

"Okay, Uncle Dolan," Marcie told him.

Greg and Marcie went upstairs to change into presentable clothes and brush their teeth.

Twenty minutes later, Dolan steered his Mercedes into the main entrance of the farm. He shook his head at the flamboyance of the property, thinking that the sophisticated farm flaunted their success. On the surface, the wealth they created for themselves and others in the Arabian horse industry seemed admirable, but being privy to the details of how they achieved the success, he questioned the value of what they had accomplished.

Dolan entered the house without ringing the doorbell. He assumed everyone would be engrossed in heated conversation. To the contrary, when he arrived, the room was filled with people who didn't know what to say to each other. Silence prevailed. Thomas stood fuming with his arms crossed, biting his tongue. Greg had just finished privately admitting to him the extent of the legal problems that led to someone obtaining the information in the article.

Someone had to break the silence. Dolan cleared his throat. Seven heads turned in his direction.

"What's the proper greeting at a time like this?" he said as an icebreaker.

"I don't know," Drake replied dryly. He didn't know what to think of the web that his daughter Marcie had gotten lured into.

"Everyone's acting like I murdered someone," Greg mumbled to no one in particular.

Marcie snuggled up to his side and slid her arm through his as if this proved that at least the marriage was doing just fine despite any bad press.

Drake turned to Dolan. "They didn't want to discuss this with us until you arrived. We want to know what's happening here. Is the article true?"

Dolan looked at Thomas, Greg and Marcie. "Perhaps we should have a few minutes alone," he said, gesturing toward the den.

"Good idea," Thomas murmured almost inaudibly.

Marcie nodded in agreement.

Patrick spoke up. "You don't think they made all this money without manipulating people, do you?"

No one responded.

"Why do you think I didn't want any part of the business?" he continued.

Still no response.

"Didn't you wonder why I only wanted to be a trainer here and to just show the horses?"

Silence.

"What? Everyone thinks I'm too stupid to know how to be on the business end of things?"

Fiona finally spoke up. "Patrick, no one thinks you're stupid. We love you, dear."

He acted as if his mother hadn't spoken. "I could see the handwriting on the wall the first time Greg sold a horse in front of me - when Dad wasn't around, that is. He's just a..."

Thomas interrupted just before closing the den door. "That's enough Patrick. Just stop right now. We'll talk about this later."

"Yes, son, in the privacy of our own home. Marcie's parents don't need to hear any of this. We've all got a lot on our minds right now," Fiona said.

"Your mother is right. The important thing now is for us to understand what is happening. We'll all remain calm," Drake said wearily.

As if there were a choice.

Dolan, Thomas, Greg and Marcie reappeared looking solemn. Thomas sat next to Fiona. Marcie sat next to her parents, facing Dolan and Greg. That way she wouldn't have to see the disappointment on their faces. Patrick leaned against the bookcase, his arms crossed and lips pursed like he had just eaten a lemon.

Greg started. "First off, don't pass judgment and don't jump to conclusions - just take time to understand the motives." He cleared his throat. "Understand - we've always had good intentions."

Everyone stared straight ahead as if watching a live play.

Dolan took center stage. "Let me say that I'm proud of being part of this close-knit family. It's important that we remain bonded at a time like this. Supportive and understanding are the two words that come to mind. We all care about the well-being of Marcie and Greg as individuals and as family members. And, of course, we're concerned about the stability of the business. If we weren't united before, we certainly must become united now."

Fiona could not remain silent. "What can we do?"

Dolan continued. "Thomas. Patrick. I'm enlisting you to develop and pursue a public relations campaign. Everyone needs to know that all of the actions of the farm have been completely honorable and without intent to harm anyone. Fiona, you can help, too. The public sees the farm as a family business. You must all prove to the country - if not the world - that Vintage Arabians will not relinquish its role as the leader in the horse industry. We must stand strong and become stronger. Persevere."

Greg interjected. "We'll spin their story 180 degrees. The reporters need to understand that we turned the hobby of owning quality horses into an investment - a profitable investment - and an activity that can be enjoyed by people of all economic levels."

"As long as you have a lot of money," Patrick said, not caring that it would aggravate his brother and his parents.

Everyone ignored him. They all agreed.

Greg changed the subject,hoping to lighten the moment. "Dolan, you sound like you're making a campaign speech. You ought to be in politics."

Everyone chuckled. No one appeared sincere.

Drake couldn't wait any longer. "You still haven't told us if the allegations in the article are true."

"Dad, believe me. They took everything out of context," Marcie said.

"Was it out of context when the article says that the thieves of Scottsdale all wanted to share the wealth? You know they were talking about the two of you and people like Robard," Drake said, referring to another large breeder in Scottsdale.

"None of us are thieves," Greg said defensively.

"Are the allegations about how you do business correct or not?"

Greg paled slightly. "Well, most of what they said was true in a certain way but..."

"If something is true it can't be taken out of context. Truth is truth," Drake said stoically as he stood up and planted himself beside the sofa.

Greg frowned. "You don't understand. The article only told part of the story. They didn't say a word about the reasons behind what we did. They didn't say a thing about how no one cares how we conduct business because our clients love the horses and they certainly enjoy making a profit from the horses. There are unspoken practices in this industry - people know - they just go along because it's profitable for everyone. No one gets hurt."

Dolan couldn't help thinking. The entire industry that turned a blind eye to Vintage's business practices is what helped create their successful enterprise. Now, the same actions would probably be what would destroy them.

"Yes. That's exactly right," Marcie added as if she were

actually credible.

Thomas looked to the floor, uncomfortable defending their intimate business.

"May I ask something?" Drake said.

"Sure, Dad," answered Marcie.

"Is it true you had shills in the audience at those fancy auctions you put on?"

Dolan spoke up. "Drake, there were not - "

Drake cut in. "This isn't a legal proceeding, Dolan. There is no need for you to control Greg's answers. I want Greg, man-to-man, to answer me truthfully. I'm asking him a question straight out. I want a straight answer."

Greg forced himself to look his father-in-law in the eye. "There were not hired shills in the common sense of the word. All I did was encourage clients to bid up horses - I gave them incentives. And a few other farm owners and I agreed to bid high prices on each other's horses during the auctions we each put on. And a few trainers that wanted to get in good with me agreed to bid high prices. It's no big deal. We did it to get other people to follow along. However, if any of those people had been the highest bidder, they would have paid for the horses, themselves."

"Like who? Robard? Peacock? Cannon?" Drake asked.

"Yes. And a few of their relatives," Greg answered as he looked to the floor.

"So, did you actually buy the horses from each other or was it all a set-up?" Deirdre asked.

"We tried to make it happen that a 'real' buyer ended up with the horse someone else was bidding up. But it didn't always happen that way. Quite a few times, especially in the first several auctions, we ended up being the final bidders."

"What my wife wants to know is if money ever actually changes hands?"

"Nowadays money does change hands, but I have to admit that initially, for the first few auctions with the sales between our small group, money usually didn't change hands."

"So, you were deceiving the public, *'Trading Paper'* just like the article says?" Drake confirmed.

"Sir, you have to understand. We weren't trying to hurt anyone. We did it to get people to follow along. When enough people are willing to pay a certain price range other people are willing to pay the same or more. We created an industry out of a hobby - an investment out of a hobby. There was never an intent to take advantage of anyone. There was never an intent to have others lose money."

Thomas jumped in. "And no one has lost any money. The horses have been profitable for everyone."

"Especially you!" Patrick interjected, directing his comment to Greg.

"Why are you even here as part of this business discussion? You always wanted to stick with training - go train," Greg answered curtly, dismissing Patrick with a wave of his hand.

"That's because I saw how you operated before any of this was big-time. I could see the handwriting on the wall," Patrick spouted as he leaped toward Greg with a fisted hand.

"Calm down, boys!" Fiona demanded.

"Yeah Mom. You better stop me before I beat the hell out of Greg. You think that's the only thing I can do better than him. You think all I can do is fight."

"Stop it, Patrick. You have got to get control of your temper," Thomas said.

"Or what?"

"I don't know, son. Just get control of your temper. We have more important things to be concerned about right now."

Drake changed the subject and addressed his daughter. "Marcie, you weren't part of any of this deceitfulness, were you?"

"Daddy, it isn't deceitfulness. It's just how business gets done."

"Were you part of this or not, young lady?"

"Daddy, I don't really deal with selling to the clients or the other farm owners, but what Greg does isn't wrong. We didn't do anything wrong."

"This article sure makes you two look like common criminals," Deirdre said.

Greg was on the defensive. "They didn't explain why we did what we did. And they certainly left out the part where everyone is happy - in fact, thrilled, with their horses and the money they make - and the parties, and the ego of having the caliber of horses the farm sells and breeds for them. The article didn't point out any of that!"

"I have another question for you Greg," Drake said. "Is it true that you created these stallion syndications just to make an enormous profit? The article says that you buy a stallion for relatively little money, then you syndicate it and make millions at the taxpayers' expense."

Thomas defended their position. "I take exception to that. We are not greedy. Everyone's been profiting. Not just us. We buy incredibly high quality stallions with exceptional pedigrees. We know how to package and market - is that a crime? I ask you - is that a God damn crime?"

Drake wondered exactly how involved Thomas was in the business since Greg was generally the one in the limelight. The article never mentioned Thomas in particular.

"Dad, calm down," Patrick said. Then he turned to Greg and snapped, "Look what you're doing to this family."

"I'm not doing anything to anyone," Greg said. He stormed out of the house without another word.

"I've got to go with him," Marcie said apologetically.

"Listen," Dolan suggested to Drake. "Why don't I answer the rest of your questions and give the two of them time to adjust to this?"

"That's fine. I just want to know what Greg's really done and what in the article was not true," Drake said.

After an hour of Dolan answering their questions, he finally said, "Let's wrap it up for now. I need to spend the rest of the day coming up with a plan to defuse this. Digest what you now know for a couple of days, then feel free to call me with anything else you want to ask or discuss. I know they're your kids, but please, leave Marcie and Greg alone about this. They have a lot of work ahead of them to clear this up."

"I'm sure it was hard for them to face us. It's always harder to face those that you love when you've done something wrong," Deirdre said.

Fiona snapped back at her. "They didn't do anything that harmed anyone. You heard them."

Thomas intervened before the women could say anything they may later regret. "Fiona," he said in a muffled voice, "let's go home. They don't understand our business."

Drake overheard Thomas and said, "We may not have understood your business before, but we're certainly enlightened now. I never would have given our daughter and Greg horses and money to expand the business if I knew what Greg was going to do."

Thomas held back his gut instinct to defend his son. "We're leaving," he told Fiona. "Drake and Deirdre can apologize when they're ready."

"That'll be the day when hell freezes over," Drake sneered.

Chapter 2

Ryan Sanders returned from jogging covered in sweat. With California's unpredictable weather, Santa Barbara could unexpectedly turn hot any time of year, and today was no exception.

"I need running shoes with more traction. The gravel roads are miserable with these shoes. I ended up actually running in the mare pasture so I didn't lose my footing," Ryan told Marty, his Marketing Director.

Marty grinned. "I've got big news to tell you."

Ryan was used to Marty making an issue out of the smallest thing. She was smart, creative - and hard working, but prone to exaggeration.

"Actually, I'm going to shower. I only swung by to get a Perrier on my way home," he said, referring to the business offices and entertainment lounge connected to the California mission style barn. "I'll come back later for the big news."

Marty thought an immediate shower was a good idea but didn't say so. "Fine. I'll tell you about the buzz when you come back. If you want to wait to find out why Greg Bordeaux and Vintage Arabians made the front page of *The Phoenix Sun*, it's fine with me. I've got more phone calls to make." Marty wasn't a gossip. She simply felt compelled, as a courtesy, to spread the word to everyone she knew. People like Marty would have fuel for weeks.

"What?"

"Front page headline story. A long article from what I'm told. The headline says *'Trading Paper',*" she said enthusiastically as if it were good news rather than potentially devastating for the entire Arabian horse industry.

"You don't have the article do you?"

"No. I've just heard about it, but I trust my sources," she said.

"How did you find out?"

"Shawna called here. She said her intern gave the article to her." Marty didn't bother to mention that Shawna asked for Ryan to call her ASAP about it. In Marty's world, that sort of thing was implied.

Shawna, a famous news journalist for a major television network, had an ambitious intern, who was contacted by their network's local affiliate in Phoenix. They knew Shawna would want to read the article.

Shawna then promptly called her husband in Santa Barbara who was not available to take the call. After Marty took the detailed message, she didn't even bother hanging up the phone. She pressed the disconnect button with her index finger and began dialing everyone she knew.

"My shower can wait. Get Shawna on the phone for me. I'll be in my office," Ryan said in a tone generally reserved for his role as a movie director. Without giving it a second thought, he knew the article was bad news.

This is going to be the buzz this weekend around the Adventure Arabians open house, he thought. A prominent farm just a couple of hours away in Thousand Oaks was hosting a huge marketing extravaganza intended to generate enthusiasm for buying Arabians. Instead, the event would become the forum for spreading the negative press about the horse business.

Chapter 3

Alec Douglas finished his morning shower and entered his bedroom. His estranged wife, Mimi, pulled the pistol out of her jacket pocket, aimed and squeezed the trigger. The Walther PPK didn't fire.

Like a deer staring into the headlights in the pitch black of night on a deserted country road, Alec Douglas froze. Mimi squeezed the trigger again. Nothing happened. Alec lurched forward and grabbed the firearm from her trembling hand.

She had no way to know that the pistol's firing pin was broken.

"He wasn't supposed to kill Nathan. He was supposed to kill you," she whimpered.

"What?" Alec asked, flabbergasted.

"It was supposed to be you. Not Nathan."

Jealousy over an affair was one thing, but attempted murder as retribution? Never in his wildest dreams did he imagine a scenario like this. What happened to the women who were satisfied with financially destroying their spouses? What was the world coming to?

Alec guided her to the loveseat and eased her down as she trembled. She crumpled in on herself as he stood back. Still shaken, he wrapped his robe around himself without taking his eyes off of her. She must have stopped taking her medication. What else could he think? She was a brilliant lawyer and a wonderful wife when she took medication to control her battle with manic depression. During their fifteen years of marriage, he had only seen one psychotic episode where she had a break with reality. At that time, they had been in Europe and she had forgotten to refill her prescription - to have enough to last for the duration of their trip. What a roller coaster ride that had been.

"Stay calm. I'm calling your doctor," he insisted.

Mimi melted into the loveseat in complete emotional and physical exhaustion. The trembling stopped, although her lips began to quiver.

"Poor Nathan," she said as she watched Alec dial the phone. "I can't believe what I've done. I have to turn myself in, don't I?" Her bloodshot eyes were remorseful and sad.

It never dawned on him that his own wife would have hired someone to kill him, let alone that Nathan, his law partner, was killed by mistake. Everyone assumed that Nathan's murder was related to a dissatisfied client or something to do with his business dealings outside of the law practice.

Once on the phone with Mimi's psychiatrist, Alec wasn't about to let the doctor know about Nathan or that Mimi had actually pulled a gun on him. Instead, he told the doctor that she had verbally threatened to kill him and that she was off her medication. Alec pleaded with the doctor to treat his wife at their house rather than in the hospital psych unit. The doctor, wanting to please patients who paid his hourly rate without billing a health insurance company, finally relented after Alec promised to allow him to meet with her once a day for the next few days and to medicate her as he determined would be beneficial.

Alec loved his wife. It was his job to protect her, and he owed it to her after what he had put her through with his affair.

Mimi's psychiatrist came to their house, talked with her for almost two hours, and medicated her. He left her to take a long nap. Alec assured the doctor that her only source of stress and agitation was eliminated.

By that evening, the couple agreed to a reconciliation and to seek the help of a marriage counselor. Mimi promised to stay on her medication and to meet with her shrink. Alec swore he would be faithful.

"What would you think of my coming back to the firm?" Mimi asked casually as Alec chopped Bermuda onions for the salad.

Without saying so, Alec had no intention of letting his wife near a knife.

Deep inside, Mimi missed practicing law as much as she had missed the happy marriage they once had. If he didn't want to work with her again, she didn't know how she would feel. She and Alec had fallen in love while she was a law clerk at his firm and studying for her bar exam. When she found out she passed the bar on the first try, he took her out for a night on the town to celebrate - and what a celebration! He not only proposed marriage but also proposed that she work at his firm with him. Technically, he couldn't make her a partner *per se*, because only the "name partners" were partners in the firm. He concocted a unique idea that the other partners agreed to. Alec and Mimi would work together as one unit performing as a team rather than having separate caseloads.

All went well for thirteen years until he was cursed with a wandering eye. It took Mimi two years to find out. Six months ago, the day the 'other woman' sent her pictures of Alec in the buff, Mimi walked away from her marriage and her career. Emotionally devastated, rather than going for therapy, she stopped taking the medication she depended on to live in a rational world. Now she hoped that she could walk back into her old life as if nothing had happened.

Alec thought about his words carefully. He finished rinsing the romaine lettuce and shook the stainless steel strainer trying to buy time. This was his second chance with her. Their first day back together. He couldn't blow it by panicking her. Alec knew Mimi well enough to know that she craved security - the security of a stable marriage, a career, the same friends for years, the same health club for years – stability could have been her middle name. Perhaps that's why he strayed for a while. He needed something a little different.

He poured two glasses of cranberry juice.

She sensed his reluctance to answer her question.

"I can always look around for another firm," she said, hoping not to sound desperate.

"Actually, I'm surprised that you didn't get a job somewhere else when you left me. You love your work, and you're great at it."

Through suppressed tears, her eyes glistened. "I just froze inside, Alec. I was so furious at myself about so many things."

She patted the romaine with paper towels as he sliced the artichoke hearts.

"Furious at yourself? Why? I'm the one you should have been furious with." He started slicing hearts of palm, not wanting to see the pain on her face. "Actually - you were furious with me – furious enough to kill me."

"Thank goodness I didn't succeed. I love you so much. I was angry with myself for being out of touch with our relationship. I didn't even have a sense that you were screwing around at all, let alone for two years. I beat myself up wondering what I did or didn't do that made you want someone else. You know me. I've always had such good intuition about people. Then when it came to us, I was blind."

"That's crazy. I was just a bastard. I'm a lawyer – lawyers are the best liars. We can create believable stories. That's why you didn't know. Don't blame yourself. It was me, not you. You didn't do anything to drive me away. I want you just the way you are. "

"Me, too. I want everything just the way it was – except without your fooling around."

"Yeah..."

"So, can we work together again? We made a great team. I miss it so much."

"Sit down," he said as he guided her by the waist to the tall stool at the kitchen counter. "I have something to tell you."

A lump formed in her throat. He doesn't want to work with me anymore, she thought.

"I'm probably going to have to resign from the firm."

"What?"

He painted the broad strokes of the story – how he

pursued a case against Vintage Arabians - Greg and Marcie Bordeaux - without the authority of his clients, the Murphy brothers. In fact, in direct opposition to the express instruction of his clients not to pursue anything.

"I can't believe you would do that. You know you could be disbarred!"

"Johan paid two and a half million dollars for a horse. I honestly thought that the Murphy's would decide to sue the Bordeauxs once they found out everything I learned about how they do business. I wasn't thinking straight. You were always my anchor and you weren't there. I was just trying to get a jump on the case – I got carried away."

"Carried away doesn't even come close to describing what you did," she said astonished by his admission.

Neither spoke for a minute or two as they sipped their cranberry juice and tried to assess the situation.

Alec spoke first. "I don't know how else to justify it. You left me. I was devastated and lonely. Nathan was dead. The practice was in turmoil over losing him and it was stressful to be involved with the FBI investigation about Nathan..."

"I'm so sorry. I can't believe any of this."

"What I did or what you did?"

"Both," she said, now facing him, studying his expression. "But we already agreed that I shouldn't turn myself in to the authorities. Like you said, if they don't suspect me yet, they probably never will. It won't bring Nathan back - and we both know I'm not a risk to society."

"Let's forget it. I have a new issue to deal with." He rubbed his temples as he thought about his father's words which haunted him when he was under pressure. His father repeatedly told him that his ruthless ambition would lead to his own destruction.

"Does anyone at the firm know how you handled the Murphy case?"

"No. We haven't even had meetings about our caseloads since Nathan died. After you resigned, Nathan ran the meetings and no one else has stepped up - we haven't even addressed that issue."

"Maybe you can settle out of court before anyone knows. How much do you think the Bordeauxs would take?"

"I haven't thought that far. It's only been two days since their lawyer called to inform me they know I don't have the authority to sue them."

"You need to contact them first," she suggested. "Don't give them a chance to make any demands - hopefully, if it's fast and easy they'll accept a reasonable amount of money and get on with their lives."

"The Bordeauxs will probably settle if it's for enough money. Greg has already traded his integrity for money more than once - if it's enough, he'll walk away with a check and stay quiet."

"But what do you think Jordan Murphy will do?" Mimi said. "He might be a bigger problem than the Bordeauxs."

"I'm not certain, but I think Jordan might not bother pursuing anything against me. He was furious when he called, but I think it was more from the shock of Greg telling him what I had done. Now that his brother has died, he may just want to forget everything to do with Johan buying that horse. From what Jordan said, Greg didn't indicate that he was going to pursue collecting the balance due on the mare."

"And Jordan didn't threaten to sue you or report you or anything?"

"He didn't say a word about it. I think he simply wanted to let me know that he found out what I had done. I'm sure his mind is more focused on losing Johan. I don't mean to sound cold, but Johan was so obese, everyone had to know he was at great risk for a heart attack. I can't believe that Jordan was surprised."

Mimi began to set the dinner table. "All we can do is wait it out. Let's don't worry about it now. If he contacts you again, then we'll decide how to handle it."

Alec wished he could have a glass of wine but he decided against it since Mimi wasn't supposed to drink.

He shook his head. "I know this is important, but I don't want to think about this right now. Can we take a few days for us - no business - no problems - no planning? Be together for a few days before we have to face reality again?"

Chapter 4

After leaving the scene at Greg's house, Thomas and Fiona Bordeaux returned to their own home at the far end of the 150-acre Scottsdale farm.

There was a palpable tension.

"I told you we shouldn't have given Greg a free hand with the business," Fiona said.

"What else would he have done for a living? When he decided not to go to vet school he didn't have an interest in anything except for the horses," Thomas snapped back.

She rolled her eyes. "We could have forced him to go to college. To find a real career like everyone else does."

"I don't need this from you right now. Let it go."

"*Let it go.* That's right. Your famous words - *let it go.*

That attitude is the reason everything has turned out this way. You never could control those boys, and you wouldn't let me do anything with them, either."

"Control them? What was there to control? People take their own path in life. Brothers don't have to be the same. They don't have to get along. You have this story book picture of what a family should be and it's just not reality, Fiona."

"You never disciplined either of them. All you ever did was buy their love and affection."

"I did not. I gave them tools to work with."

"Buying them cars for their 16th birthdays, buying them world-class horses to show, then buying this property so they could live with the horses, then the trucks and horse trailers..."

"Just stop it. The horses and the property and the trailers were for all of us. We love this, too, and it makes us a substantial income. It isn't just for the boys," Thomas said forcefully, as he stormed out of the house, leaving Fiona alone to cry.

When the kids were young, Thomas immersed the family in a world of horse breeding, training, and showing. It seemed to be the only thing to help Greg and Patrick get along; they didn't have any other common interests.

Patrick, a reasonably attractive young man, hadn't been likable as a child, and wasn't generally likable now. He was hot tempered and suffered violent tendencies since he was a toddler. He always seemed to blame everything that went wrong on his older brother, Greg. Somehow he found ways to blame Greg for his own poor grades in school. He even claimed that he didn't want to go to college because Greg would always be smarter than he was. Anyway, what was the point?

In his youth, Patrick was socially active - the kids wanted him around because he made them laugh. The problem was, he wasn't trying to be funny - but the other kids didn't know that. When he was a sophomore in high school, he couldn't find a date to the first dance he wanted to attend. Finally, one of the girls he invited was blunt enough to tell him that girls didn't want to go out with guys like him. When he asked what she meant, she just giggled and walked away.

That's when he turned inward and started living and breathing a life of being with horses. He learned to ride when he was six, but started figuring out horse training techniques the night everyone else was at the school dance. Patrick had no desire to learn from professional trainers with experience. He was determined to learn training skills on his own, even if it meant making lots of mistakes. Most of his life he favored the company of animals rather than humans.

Greg, on the other hand, was not blessed with attractive features. In fact, kids nicknamed him 'monkey face' and, of course, his younger brother called him the same thing when their parents weren't around.

Even as a young boy, Greg was intense. Throughout his academic career, he earned straight A's, even in the most challenging classes. He was President of his class, won school chess tournaments, and consistently raised the most money during fund-raising events for the school and their church. At his suggestion, his high school participated in the National Youth Entrepreneur Challenge, winning awards for his unique ideas and plans for implementation. His friendships were always with other motivated students and high achievers.

Greg never dated in high school, although he had an abundance of female friends because he taught the girls how to ride horses and never charged them for lessons. Other than horseback riding, while growing up, it was rare for him to do anything just for fun except play poker with his father and his uncles. It became a family joke that at twelve years old he could keep a straight face, bluffing them and taking their money a dollar or two at a time.

Caroline, the middle child, had always been a gifted rider but left the family business when she married into the Robard family. There were too many conflicts about which family's horses she would compete with so she simply stopped showing. Her husband had little interest in the horses that his parents revolved their life around.

Fiona found Thomas at the only old barn on the property. She knew that's where he would be. He always retreated to that barn when he needed time alone.

"I'm sorry," she admitted as she handed him a carrot to feed Trooper, the dark bay horse he was petting.

The top of the Dutch door was opened in each of the ten stalls. During the day, the horses were stalled inside when it was hot, and turned-out to pasture at night when it was cooler.

He smiled at her. "You think you can buy back my affection with a carrot?"

"It's always worked before. I was so hard on you,

I brought a whole bag of carrots," she said tenderly.

"Okay. For a whole bag of carrots I'll forgive you. I'm sorry, too."

"Sorry for what?" she goaded him.

"I don't know, but I know you like me apologizing for just about anything," he said half kidding...but only half.

Fiona pouted her full lips. "I hate it when you walk out on me."

Thomas scratched the mare's face, then let her take another bite of the thick juicy carrot. "We spent twenty years arguing about the boys - I thought it was over. Let's please stop the arguing. They're men now. We can't control them or even influence them anymore."

"I know, but we don't have to show our support to Greg when we don't like how he's handling business," Fiona said.

"I understand what you're saying but, I've given authority to him."

Fiona sighed almost as loud as one of the horses patiently waiting its turn to be fed a carrot or two. "As his parents and co-owners of the corporation, we have the right to tell him we don't approve of what he does."

"Greg needs emotional support right now. He doesn't need us judging him or second-guessing him. We're his parents. Show him respect. He's a fine boy."

"Man."

"Man. You're right. That's even more reason not to scold him or treat him like a child. I'm proud of how he's taking over for me and building on what I started when he was just a teenager. He's achieving his own success, and he has to be allowed to make his own mistakes - and who are we to know if he's even made mistakes? No one has been damaged by anything either of us has done," Thomas said in their defense.

Fiona looked into her husband's anguished eyes. "You have a good point. It's just that we raised the boys to be honest - not to lie or to mislead or to manipulate people. It seems that Greg has become a master at those things. That's what is so painful to me. It doesn't matter what his intentions were, and it doesn't matter that no one has been hurt. As his mother, what matters to me is that my son has not been honest with all people at all times."

"You're not looking at this from a realistic perspective. Our intentions are the only thing that matter."

At a loss for what to say or think, her face softened.

"The only thing we can do is to agree to disagree. I'll stand by him no matter what I think or how I feel about it. He's our son. I love him."

Thomas ached inside. He felt guilty about his own role in the operation and his thoughts about what Greg had done were completely opposite to those of his wife, but he didn't want to push it with Fiona.

Thomas knew that the cut-throat sharks Robard, Peacock and Cannon were involved, and they influenced his son to go beyond the business practices Thomas had always used when he began luring people into paying escalating prices. That's how successful businesses are built - by thinking outside the box, by strategic planning and controlling situations. Thomas and Greg were always intuitive and knew how to use it to their advantage.

Chapter 5

Patrick didn't mind admitting to himself that he was thrilled to see his brother in hot water for a change. The newspaper article didn't discuss his father - it only used Greg and Marcie's name and the business name of Vintage Arabians. The reporter never wrote that the business was a corporation owned by their family or that Patrick was the head trainer at the farm.

Now that he had fallen in love with Liz, he was more confident in himself and more outgoing. She built him up and made him realize that Greg was not more intelligent, more astute in business, or more resourceful. Liz was teaching him to think for himself and to accept the fact that he did not need to continue to be subservient to his brother. She assured him that he could be more than a trainer at the farm. He knew she was right - he just needed her to encourage him and believe in him.

Patrick was in love. He respected Liz, enjoyed her company and felt like an important and productive man when he was with her. For the first time in his life, he was ready to propose marriage. In fact, he had planned on proposing to Liz that very evening. Now, he wondered if this was poor timing.

Liz was waiting for him at the training barn. She had a mare saddled up and ready to be ridden.

"Here. Take Staccata. I'll ride Breeze so we can talk," she said, anxious to hear what went on at the house.

In one swift movement, Patrick mounted the horse as he took hold of the set of buttery soft leather reins attached to the double bridle. He lengthened the English stirrup leathers, not mentioning it was obvious that someone else had ridden in his favorite cutback work saddle. Normally, he would have thrown a small tantrum to let everyone know how serious he was about the fact that absolutely no one was allowed to ride in his saddle.

Liz looked up at Patrick. "Sorry about the stirrups. I was going to warm her up for you."

"No big deal. Thanks for taking the initiative. Anyone else would have just longed her and put her on the hot walker until I came out," he said, not considering the fact that when he insisted no one ride in his saddle, they couldn't do what Liz did.

She effortlessly swung herself onto Breeze's back without using a mounting block. She ran her slim fingers through her layered dark blond hair which hung just below her chin. Breeze walked off when she felt a gentle squeeze from Liz's leg.

"Tell me everything. What happened at Greg's?"

Patrick made an impulsive decision. "Will you marry me?"

She looked at him in disbelief. Not at the actual proposal but at the timing and setting.

"I know. This isn't the most romantic way to ask you but I just can't wait until tonight like I had planned," he admitted.

Her eyes gleamed and she said, "Actually, I thought you would probably propose on horseback, but I thought it would be on a night ride when we were alone, with romantic music playing in the background and maybe you'd have champagne or something..."

"So, this wasn't a surprise?"

"Don't be silly," she grinned coyly. With the subtlest cue from her inside leg moving back behind the girth, she cantered the horse in a fifty-meter circle around him.

"It seems like you've played all of this out in your head, too. For the last several weeks I've rehearsed the words and contemplated which swanky restaurant we would be in. And now, I've just gone and blurted it out as if it's not the most important thing in my life. I'm sorry."

She held the reins in her left hand, rode up next to him as close as she could get and reached over to put her right arm around him and kiss him.

"Does this mean you'll marry me?"

"Of course," she replied, spontaneously thinking about all of the changes she would implement at Vintage. Greg and Marcie would have a lot of adjusting to do.

Liz rushed home to shower and tell her roommate and best friend Julie the exciting news.

"Congratulations! Now you can promote me to head groom," Julie said seriously.

"I'll be able to do a lot more than that. Not for you of course, but for Patrick and I," Liz told her as she towel dried her hair.

"Not until you're actually married, though. If I were you, I would forget the big wedding you've been dreaming of. Big weddings take forever to plan. Just elope. Especially with everything going on. The newspaper article and..."

Liz frowned. "Don't remind me."

"I know you love him, but timing is everything. You're brilliant. Like you said, you and Patrick need to be active partners in the farm."

"I need to do something before Greg and Marcie blow it and there won't be anything left for Patrick and me," she said as she applied a light blusher to her cheeks.

"Do you think they'll be surprised when you guys make the announcement tonight?" Julie asked, wishing she could be there with the whole Bordeaux gang.

Liz tilted her head, thinking about it. "Probably. I don't think anyone's had time to even think about Patrick and I - how much we're together, or that our relationship is even that serious. I can't imagine Patrick confiding in anyone about us."

In the meantime, while Liz was with Julie, Patrick went to his parents' house.

"Hi there. You're sure here early. We said eight o'clock for dinner," Thomas said.

"I know. But I wanted to talk to you and Mom alone first. In fact, I don't even want you to tell Liz about our conversation."

Fiona was puzzled. "What's going on?"

"Mom. Dad. I proposed to Liz and she accepted. We're getting married," Patrick said nervously.

Dead silence loomed in the air.

"Liz? I didn't know you were that close," Fiona stammered.

"I knew you were dating, but I didn't know it was serious," Thomas added.

Fiona had to speak her mind. "I don't know if this is a good idea. You're the only person Liz has even really dated – with her coming here when she was just sixteen. Her parents probably think you're like a big brother to her."

"What do her parents have to do with anything?"

"Well, they're clients. They sent Courvoisier here to show and stand at stud. Just because Liz insisted on finishing high school at a boarding school here and stay with Courvoisier doesn't mean they thought you two would get involved."

"Her parents know all about us and approve of our relationship," he said in his defense.

"So, they already know you're getting married? Before we know?" Fiona asked, her feelings hurt.

"No. They don't know I proposed, unless Liz called them when she got home. I just proposed today. But they know everything about our relationship and they think it's great."

"Why haven't we known? It's such a shock, Patrick," Fiona said.

"We didn't want to make a big deal before. We've been serious for almost a year now. Exclusive for nearly six months. I love her."

"She's a very nice young woman, " Thomas said, still taken aback by the surprise.

"I love her. That's the important thing. And she thinks I'm intelligent," he said, his voice trailing off.

The room fell silent. It seemed that even the birds stopped chirping outside.

After what seemed like minutes, Thomas finally responded. "Liz can train and show with you."

Fiona interrupted. "Well dear, if she's going to be family, I think it would be wonderful if Liz took an active roll in the business side of the farm. You and Greg are spread too thin.

Larry and Mike really only deal with the buying and selling of horses and breedings."

Thomas cut her off. "We don't want them to do anything else. They need to concentrate on sales."

"I know that," she retorted. "That's why another family member involved in the overall business could be very useful."

"They aren't even married, yet. You're jumping the gun, Fiona."

Patrick stood and listened, wondering if they even remembered he was present.

"I'm talking about once they're married. This will be perfect," she said with enthusiasm.

"You said that when Greg and Marcie got married. You thought she'd be productive, too," Thomas said.

"So I was wrong about Marcie. But it's not like we ever thought that Marcie was smart, or motivated, or even particularly talented. I was just hopeful that she would be an asset to the business."

"I know. It would have been nice," Thomas admitted.

"At least Greg's happy with her."

"Ron - " Thomas started to say.

"Ron? Ron's not running the show. Just because he's our business manager doesn't mean that we're going to do whatever he wants. He's not family. Liz is going to be family. Ron doesn't come down from Seattle nearly as much as you thought he would. I think we should renegotiate the contract with him," she said, going off in a tangent.

"Excuse me, but would you like to know what we have in mind?" Patrick asked.

"Of course," Thomas said.

"Liz still wants to ride, but she really wants to get involved in putting on the auctions. She's got marketing ideas about ways that the clients can make more money - by our selling more horses for them at auction," he said. "And I want to keep overseeing the training and showing, but I want to get more involved in the business."

Thomas weighed his words carefully. "Your brother and I have always handled the business aspects, Patrick. I don't think ..."

Patrick restrained himself. Liz told him to try counting to ten in his mind before he lost his temper. One, two, three, four, five, six, seven, eight, nine, ten.

"I understand your lack of confidence since I've never shown an interest before, but I'm more mature now. I'm getting married to a very capable woman. I have an incentive - an interest now, in keeping the farm successful. I was just being a spoiled lazy bum before - just wanting to ride and show the horses - having no real responsibility to speak of. Before, I wasn't willing to put myself in a position to take a chance of failing. Now..."

Fiona and Thomas were impressed. Liz was obviously a wonderful influence on their son. In the back of his mind Thomas had wondered if Liz was somewhat of a gold-digger, but now he had his doubts about that.

"Did Liz tell you that?" Fiona asked.

"Not in so many words, but she made me realize that that was exactly what I was doing. She made me realize that I'm capable of making good decisions if I just put myself out on a limb. With training and riding, I know I'm Greg's equal, so it's not really a competition between us. In the show ring, the judges just pick who they want, but I know he's not better or worse than me, so it's okay when I don't beat him."

Thomas softened in a way he never had before. "Son, we've told you this all of your life, but you didn't listen. I guess sometimes these things need to come from a woman who is not your mother."

Fiona nodded. As hard as it was, she restrained herself from hugging him. He was never an affectionate boy.

"I think you should get more involved if you have the time. And I think we should let Liz do what she has in mind," she said.

A thought came to Thomas that he couldn't ignore. "We have a problem that I hope we can solve," he said as he tapped his manicured fingers on the wooden tabletop.

"I know," Patrick said.

It suddenly dawned on Fiona. Greg may not approve of this. He was accustomed to having control over everything and everyone.

"Your mother and I are going to have to talk about this by ourselves. You understand, don't you?"

One, two, three, four, five, six, seven, eight, nine, ten.

"Of course I understand. Should Liz and I wait to make the announcement?"

Fiona didn't hesitate. "I think that would be a good idea."

Chapter 6

As trouble brewed with the Bordeaux family in Scottsdale, life was looking better every day for Morgan Butler. After spending years cultivating clients, her equine brokerage business based in Laguna Beach, California, had evolved into her own small breeding program. In partnership with a handful of investors with a fascination for horses, Morgan purchased a dozen high quality mares to test on Ambiguous, a young stallion she had purchased and imported from Sweden.

George and Sonia Finn, originally named Finnopolis,

changed their names when they left Greece in order to assimilate into American society. Gorges Finnopolis didn't want his Greek ethnicity to be an issue as he and his much younger bride started their new life in Beverly Hills, California. Gorges admired George Washington, hence the name change to George Finn.

Now, Morgan Butler was determined to cultivate a relationship with Sonia Finn. A couple of weeks earlier, Morgan had toured Sonia's farm located a half-hour north of Beverly Hills. Morgan didn't have the opportunity to meet her, but Sonia's car was parked at the farm. As a result, Morgan knew to identify the BMW by the license plate holder which said *Big Mares Win* and the plate said *Spender*.

Today, without Sonia knowing it, Morgan stalked her until they had what seemed like a chance meeting at Adventure Arabians' open house in Thousand Oaks.

Morgan parked her leased Jaguar near the farm entrance and waited for Sonia to pull in with her BMW. When Sonia passed the entry gate, Morgan waited a few seconds then followed in her Jag with her car window rolled down as she talked on her car phone. Following the signs, both women pulled into a pasture that was temporarily being utilized as a parking area.

Sonia checked her lipstick and hair before getting out of her car. She spotted Morgan and repressed a grin.

When Sonia stepped out of her car, Morgan said, 'thanks for calling. I'll see you tomorrow' into her phone.

"There's no mobile phone coverage in Thousand Oaks, yet," Sonia said as she faced the stranger's window.

Wordlessly, Morgan blushed and replaced the phone into its car battery sized cradle. Sonia smiled and strolled away.

Morgan quickly caught up to Sonia who had only walked a few yards by the time Morgan had regained her composure. Without another word on the subject of the mobile phone, the women introduced themselves and made small talk as they headed to the presentation arena and found seats together on the bleachers.

"I'm anxious to see the stallions, but I think they'll show the sale horses first," Sonia said.

"Do you think so? Most farms show the stallions first so that you can see the sires of the sale horses – or if the mare is in foal to one of the stallions, you already know what he looks like," Morgan said.

Sonia nodded. "I guess you're right. I've only been to the Vintage presentations. Greg says they do things differently than other farms, so I thought this would be one of those things."

"You've bought a lot of horses from Vintage, haven't you?"

"I guess. My husband, George, handled all of that, but now I'm really getting interested in the business."

Morgan was encouraged. "You weren't interested before?"

"I was so busy with my kids that I didn't get too involved."

"You haven't had horses that long. What changed your mind?"

"The kids got to wanting to go to the farm - they ride every chance they get now that we bought an old gelding they're safe on. It's a great family recreational outlet."

"So now you're enjoying the horses?"

"I love them. I'm over the idea that an inexperienced person shouldn't ride a valuable horse. Our trainer is teaching me so much and now I'm interested in breeding, too. George is more into the show horses, but I love the idea of raising foals."

Morgan was delighted about the direction of their conversation. She couldn't have scripted it any better.

"Who are you breeding to next season?"

Sonia squinted her eyes in deep thought. "I don't know. That's what I'm trying to decide. I really need to do a lot more studying and investigation. When we bought the broodmares, all of them were already pregnant. Some came as three-in-one packages so those breedings for next season are taken care of."

"Why isn't George here?"

"He's away on business. And like I said, he's into the show horses. Don't tell anyone, but we're going to try to buy Crimson Lace at the next Vintage auction."

"Seriously? She's going to go for at least a couple million from what I've heard."

"I know. George wants to set a new record. He says that if Johan Murphy could pay $2.5 million for Love Letter, we can certainly top that for Crimson Lace - she still has a show career in front of her. Greg says she'll win National Champion Park Horse next year."

The live music went from classical to an upbeat tempo.

"Probably," Morgan said, imagining what it would feel like to be able to spend that kind of money period, let alone on just one horse.

"You know, he bid on Love Letter until the bidding was up to $2.3 million. George is kicking himself that he didn't keep going."

Jealousy seared through Morgan's body. "I've heard that Greg puts three qualified bidders in place for each of the first ten lots in each auction. I'm sure George will have his chance on Crimson Lace."

For those who didn't visit the strategically placed open bars, servers began infiltrating the Adventure Arabians' bleachers carrying trays brimming with glasses of wine and champagne.

"What do you mean about putting bidders in place?"

"When the credit applications come in, they do a thorough financial investigation for anyone requesting a high credit limit to buy at the auction - "

Sonia interrupted. "They do more than a normal credit check?"

"I don't know. But I do know that between their current big clients and prospective new heavy hitters, when you all set up appointments to see the horses privately, Greg makes a plan for the first ten lots that inevitably results in record sales."

"What kind of plan?"

"Did you or George ask Greg which are the best horses in the auction?"

"Of course. We depend on his guidance."

"Everyone does. And he counts on it. So, when you ask him, he suggests specific horses. He matches each horse with three big bidders so you all end up bidding against each other, driving up the price."

"Seriously?"

"Yes. I'm serious."

"How do you know this?"

"I dated one of his inside people. He told me, and I trust him."

Sonia was visibly unsure of the reliability of what Morgan had told her. "If that's true, why would Greg only do it for the first ten lots?"

"It sets the tone for the entire auction. By then, everyone who's really there to buy will bid high prices."

"I see," Sonia muttered.

"In the end, people only pay what they are willing to pay. He just sparks the enthusiasm and the willingness, I suppose."

"You're right. Greg never suggested to us how much we should bid on Love Letter or any other horse. It was George's decision to keep bidding. And it was his choice to stop - even if he regrets it now," Sonia admitted.

Sonia excused herself to use the bathroom.

A noticeable number of people sitting in the bleachers turned their heads as if they were watching an ace being served at Wimbledon. Movie producer, Ryan Sanders, accompanied by Bo and John Derek, drew attention causing a small crowd to gather around them. Their appearance caused enough disruption that very few people noticed as Jane Fonda and a friend blended in with the onlookers in the bleachers. Jane was sensible enough to wear a billowy hat and dark sunglasses.

The commotion settled down as quickly as it came about.

Morgan overheard bits and pieces of a conversation between people discussing a headline article about Vintage that was in the newspaper two days before. The next thing she knew, a speculative buzz about the Bordeauxs started among the people in the stands. Sonia had already told Morgan that she only had an hour available to see horses because her daughter was in a ballet recital. Morgan planned to stay around after Sonia left to get the scoop about the article.

Just after Sonia returned from the bathroom, the first stallion was trotted out from the barn as a live quartet played dramatic music. His handler was dressed in silk black slacks and a white linen button down shirt. He looked as if he stepped out of GQ Magazine.

The stallion, Vistion, a lean dark bay without a speck of white, wore a thin black patent leather halter adorned with twenty-four carrot gold filigree. Vistion's neck was long like a snake and his top line was perfectly flat, including his croup.

"What do you think of him?" Sonia asked, referring to the sleek dark bay.

It wasn't professional to knock down someone else's stallion when you were pushing your own. Shc carefully worded her answer. "He's very nice if you like a pretty horse that can trot."

"He does having an exciting trot, doesn't he?"

"Sure, his trot's above level which makes him appear to be more athletic than he really is," Morgan said, unable to keep her opinion to herself. After all, her goal was to do business with the woman.

Sonia looked at her with a questioning expression but said nothing.

Morgan took the liberty to explain herself. "He doesn't have much hock action because his croup is so flat. He can't bring his back end under himself. Of course, a flat croup is what the halter judges look for. It just depends on if you want an athlete or simply a pretty horse. Personally, I like athletes."

"Me, too. But I want one that's pretty, as well."

Morgan had Sonia eating out of her hand now. "Have you heard about my stallion, Ambiguous?"

"As a matter of fact, I have. I didn't realize you owned him. His pictures are beautiful."

"Thanks. He's only a couple of hours away. I'd love for you to come see him. He's standing at Royalty Arabians in Santa Ynez. Maybe I could take you to see him before you make your final breeding decisions."

Sonia listened and nodded as she watched Vistion prance around the presentation ring.

Morgan continued talking, although not rushing her words. "I think you'd be very impressed with him and he'd definitely cross with quite a few of your mares - both by genotype and phenotype."

"You know our mares?"

"Yes. I was at your farm recently and Richard showed me the mares and their pedigrees. You have at least twenty mares that would cross exceptionally well with Ambiguous."

Morgan would earn $200,000 in breeding fees if she could get Sonia to breed twenty mares. Although $200,000 was peanuts to the big players in the horse industry, it was a goldmine to her. She'd do anything to be able to earn that much money in a lump sum. Plus, once she got her foot in the door with Sonia, there would be a chance for ongoing business. Befriending her was a move in the right direction.

Sonia looked sideways at Morgan. "When are you going to Santa Ynez again?"

"I'm happy to go whenever it's convenient for you. Are you available this coming week?"

"Let me give you my home phone number and you can call me. I don't have my appointment book with me. Give me a call tomorrow."

And so it began.

~~~

Alec and Mimi drove a few miles from the house to their favorite seafood restaurant in Westport Village, a quaint upscale area of St. Louis, Missouri. They took their time,
~~~

savoring every moment of being back together. For insurance, Alec ordered a platter of oysters as an appetizer. He wasn't getting any younger and had been through an inordinate amount of stress these last several months. The oysters couldn't hurt, and Mimi would surely see the humor in it even if she didn't say anything.

The evening started out as a romantic reunion. Then, somehow, the conversation swung to business after Alec mentioned to Mimi that he had eaten a fabulous dish called Chicken Maximilian at Macayo's, a well-known casual Mexican restaurant in Scottsdale. The next thing Alec knew, he was describing the beautiful horses and impressive horse breeding and showing operations in Scottsdale. He then went into detail about how Greg coerced people to pay outlandish prices for horses that had been selling for only a few thousand dollars in the not so distant past.

Mimi was engrossed in his descriptions - not merely about the business practices of selling elite horses, but the social contacts and the horses themselves.

"How did you learn so much that quickly about the horse business?" Mimi asked.

"From Garth Windsor," Alec said, and then explained how he met Garth in a round about way from another lawyer they both knew.

"Does Garth have horses?" Mimi asked as the waiter served her seafood cioppino and more fresh baked French bread.

"He grew up riding and showing. Once he was in law school, he didn't have time anymore. His parents not only bred and showed Arabians, but as it turns out, they happened to have been clients of Vintage. When I hired Garth on for this case, neither of us knew. Talk about a fluke and a conflict of interest," Alec said as he was served his garlic infused scampi.

Mimi shook her head. "What happened when Garth realized you two were suing someone his parents did business with?"

"Garth had to tell his parents. As it turned out, all of Davis and Lily's - those are his parents - investments in horses revolved around the Vintage program. They even owned a stallion they bought from Greg."

"What a tangled web we weave," she said.

"To make a long story short, the Windsors were able to sell out their herd for a good price. They sold out just in time - or at least that was the intent. We all thought I'd be taking Greg to court and wiping out his business - or at least his credibility, which happens to be what his big dollar business is all about."

Mimi was amazed by the story. As a child, she collected model horses, each of which she had named. She played with them all day during summer breaks and holidays, and even made them blankets and halters. She still remembered being overjoyed when her father built a barn for her little horses for her tenth birthday. She couldn't count how many times she read Black Beauty and the books in The Black Stallion series and watched the movie National Velvet. Her mother took her to the public library practically every Saturday to find books about girls and their horses. Eventually, Mimi read them all.

Her family lived in the city and didn't have the financial means for her to take riding lessons, let alone own a horse. So when she was in her teens she didn't think much more about the beautiful creatures. Now, her memory was refreshed about a dream she always had - a dream of owning her own horse.

"I have an idea. Let's buy a horse," she said out of the blue.

Alec's eyes widened. He didn't need to say anything before she added, "Not necessarily an expensive Arabian, but a horse! I've always wanted one - "

He interrupted her. "You've never said a word about it in the eighteen years I've known you. I can't imagine you've always wanted a horse."

"Well, I have ! All little girls do. Don't they?" she said with a hint of childish petulance.

"Maybe little girls, but you're a grown woman," he reminded her, chuckling not only at her words but at the youthful delight on her face.

"I can't explain it, Alec. It's like I know that deep down in my gut the dream of wanting a horse never went away - it's always been there - just suppressed."

"Like lots of people forget the dreams they think can never come true," he said, reaching out to hold her hand across the table. His dream was to be in the CIA.

Suddenly Mimi felt ten years younger, full of enthusiasm and youthful energy. "I think I'm going to find out where I can take some riding lessons around here. That's a start."

"Sure," he said, happy to see her positive attitude and looking forward to something so simple.

After dinner, they returned home. Alec told her he

wanted to shower. She knew what that meant - which was perfectly fine with her. As she waited for him, she spotted a stack of thick magazines on the lower shelf of the end table in the family room. They didn't look like the usual magazines they had subscribed to - Fortune, Time, Money, or any legal publications. When she got close enough to read the spines of the magazines, she could see that they were about Arabian horses.

Mimi settled into the beige chintz chair with an inch thick magazine. The photograph of a glistening white horse on the front cover took her breath away. The dim light didn't do the pictures justice, so she turned the three-way bulb to its brightest. Mimi lost herself in another world, turning each page gently. The potent images were seductive.

It didn't take long to see that the farms with astronomical advertising budgets received major editorial coverage. Vintage Arabians was one of the more prominent advertisers. Mimi was sure that must have been the driving reason for Vintage's growth and the mystique for clients buying from them. A client she represented in her law practice was a magazine publisher. He taught her the ins and outs of the business so that she could better represent his company. The more paid advertising, the more editorial coverage the advertiser would receive. She could see why investor-oriented horse owners would be attracted to the strong imaging in the magazines.

Mimi had no idea how much time had passed before Alec returned to the room patting aftershave onto his face.

Ready to be romantic, Alec rubbed her neck. She responded with enthusiasm but not in a way that could have been mistaken as passion. It was evident that she was browsing through the same horse magazines that he had reviewed for the Murphy lawsuit.

"Pretty horses, huh?" he asked casually, trying not to show he had hoped she would be eager to have him back in the room with her.

"That hardly describes it," she answered whimsically. "These are the most magnificent looking horses I've ever seen."

He reached for her hand, assuming the conversation about the horses was over. It was time to enjoy passions of the flesh now.

Or maybe it wasn't. Not for Mimi at least.

"You can buy Arabians that don't cost what Vintage

Arabians charges, can't you?" she asked, totally oblivious to his subtle advances.

His feelings were hurt, but he knew she didn't intend to actually reject him. "I'm sure that people can buy horses for less than the Bordeauxs sell them for, but I don't know a low end price range. That's not what this case was about," he said, not meaning to sound indifferent. It would be a good idea to save this conversation for some other time.

He gently reached toward her, almost forcing her hand into his. In an instant she recalled that this was their evening to reunite - not an evening to talk about horses.

"I didn't see your picture in here," she said as she stood up and wrapped her arms around his waist.

"Why would my picture be in that magazine?"

"The cover says it's the Stallion Issue."

Chapter 7

"Use glass cleaner on that window before they get here," Matt Robard demanded as he eyed the room, making sure everything else was in order.

"Yes sir, Mr. R," said the houseboy.

"Calm down Matt, you're letting yourself get far too upset about this," said his wife, DeAnn. She refused to ignore his cranky temperament.

Matt wiped the perspiration from his forehead. "Don't you tell me to calm down. Why don't you go to Catalina until the dust settles? I don't need you around here telling me how to act."

"Someone has to keep you under control," she said, dismissing his temper for the time being.

DeAnn Speer ignored her parents' protest and their threat to cut her off financially when she married Matt Robard. Three grown children later, she wondered why she hadn't listened to her parents. They warned her about him the first time they set eyes on the man. They insisted he was marrying her for her money – the family fortune, derived from owning the world's largest chewing gum company.

DeAnn fell head over heels in love with a young man who owned nothing more than dreams, ambition, two pairs of slacks and a half dozen shirts. Shortly before their chance encounter, Matt was a ditch digger on his way to fulfilling a dream. While DeAnn was shopping at one of her favorite jewelers in Phoenix, he walked in to make a delivery. Pedaling loose diamonds on straight commission was part of his plan. His long ago lost charm and charisma instantly attracted DeAnn, despite the fact that his clothes were of poor quality and fit, and his shoes were desperate to be polished.

"Matt, at least keep your blood pressure pills handy," she told him as she attempted to hand him the pill bottle.

He turned his back on her and walked away without responding.

"There's not enough ice in this!" he bellowed to the houseman, referring to the iced tea pitcher on the serving cart.

"Stop it, Matt! You are being foul, and I won't have it. I won't tolerate your behavior about this for one more minute," she said, as if she were talking to a rambunctious schoolboy.

"Screw you," he answered as he looked out the floor-to-ceiling glass wall of the family room.

Thick non-glare glass separated the family room from the small barn with skylights and open turnout area. They had money to burn. Why subject themselves to the heat or feel grit or dust when they wanted to see their favorite horses?

Just outside the enormous sliding double barn doors was a pond with a cascading waterfall and floating lilies. A groom walked by leading a beautiful black mare.

"It would behoove you to take a deep breath and begin acting like a gentleman. If you don't, I will call the front gate and demand that they do not allow entry to our guests," she said, now determined to bring him under control.

In the blink of an eye, he contained himself and turned on his charm.

"You're right. I'm sorry. I'm just angry with myself for not having taken control. It was stupid of me."

DeAnn accepted his apology. As always, she acted as if nothing had happened. She peered at her reflection in the glass and patted her silvery blond hair, making sure the hairspray was doing its job.

"As much as you would like to fool yourself, you can't control the world. You expected the families to merge - the breeding operations to merge - as if our daughter and our horses were big business instead of the living, breathing creatures we've been blessed with," she said.

His chin doubled when he hung his head in disappointment. "I never dreamed Matt, Jr. and Caroline would marry. Thomas and I both thought Greg and Meredith would end up together. Even Fiona hinted at it for years. Hell, they grew up together - learned to ride together - started showing at the same time..."

DeAnn laughed for the first time in days. "Until Meredith

realized that her breasts were developing. When that happened the good-looking boys started giving her attention. You were so busy working all the time, but I remember. Practically overnight she started taking an interest in her appearance, wearing a little make-up, fixing her hair, caring about fashion."

He shook his head back and forth. "Yep. Overnight she didn't need to be best buddies with Greg. Nothing was ever the same after that. But, still. I thought she would outgrow her vanity and look at Greg's talent, and his family, and see that we were trying to get them together..."

"We? Oh no you don't! Don't drag me into this. You tried to force them to be together. I'll never forget that trip to Poland you and Thomas planned." She laughed, recalling the purported vacation. "Matt, no one takes their entire family to a communist country to see horses."

The fond memory made him melancholy. "Thomas and I both had the same idea to get them together. It didn't work, but what a great adventure. Two weeks of meeting with the Polish breeding directors and establishing a relationship that ended up being what it is today - all because we wanted to get the kids together." Finally he smiled, which didn't happen that often, lately.

"You got the kids together, just not the two you had in mind," DeAnn said.

"Oil and water."

"Anyway, you and Thomas didn't go to Poland just to get the kids together, and you know it."

He sighed, but didn't respond.

"The two of you wanted to outdo Fred Herrington, bringing in more horses than he did. Both of you wanted to top the pineapple king."

"That wasn't it. You'll never understand me, will you?" he asked, under his breath.

"The day I understand you they'll be burying me six feet under."

How many times had she told him that same line?

"I should have taken control when the Bordeauxs started outselling us and started building their sales center. They took this scheme way beyond what I had ever considered. And Greg's too young to know how to handle himself."

"You're resentful that they're more innovative than you are and that they took more initiative than you did," DeAnn said.

"Bull."

"Admit it, Matt. You always want to be the one people look up to. The leader. But Thomas and Greg left you in the dust."

He thought she would quit talking if he raised his voice. "Shut the hell up."

"Just because you had the idea. If it was really even your idea – you know, I only heard that from your mouth - "

"It was my idea to start getting higher prices for the horses so we could all build nicer facilities and so that - "

DeAnn rolled her eyes. "I've heard your spiel plenty. The point is, even if it were your idea, you wanted Vintage in on it. What you can't accept is that they were creative and had aspirations bigger than yours."

"Bull. Greg's a punk."

"Matt."

"What?"

"I wish you could hear yourself when you get like this."

"Like what? I was there. I led the first several consortium meetings 'til that punk started taking over. But I'll tell you one thing - I know first hand the ideas I had and the plans we made."

He would have rambled on forever. DeAnn interrupted, stood over him, and shook her finger at his face. "That's a perfect example. I clearly recall that after your group met the second time, you told me, point blank, that Greg came up with the idea to call yourselves a consortium. It was at that same meeting Greg suggested that you all develop stallion syndications modeled after the Thoroughbred business. You came home calling Greg a genius."

"That's not the point. I'm saying that he let all of this get out of hand. He took it too far. That's all I'm saying. And now who knows if it's all going to go down the drain."

"You were perfectly happy with everything about this business until the newspaper article. I'm right and you know it," she said, now sitting at the breakfast table.

"After Thomas started letting Greg handle more and more things, I don't know how many times I sat the punk down and told him he was taking the wrong direction and that he would ruin us all. You don't know how many times he went over my head and said he would do what he damn well wanted with his business."

"It's his business. He can do what he wants. Just as you

can. You never invested the money and effort to be able to accomplish what Vintage has. Admit it."

"Bull."

"I think that's Cal coming up the drive," DeAnn told him glad to break the mood.

"Shit. I should have known that Cal would be the first to show up. He shouldn't even be in the consortium."

"Matt. Stop. You and Hampton go way back," she said, referring to Cal's father. "He taught you everything you know about conformation and athletic ability in a horse. The beers you two slugged down out in that desert; if we had a dollar for each one."

"We do - we probably have a million bucks for each one."

"It was an expression. You take everything so literally," she said.

"Cal's never going to make it big. That's my point," he said quickly before Cal made it to the side door of the house. He knew not to bother going to the front door.

"Cal isn't going to make it big because he won't play your games the way you want him to. He's a nice, honest young man. That's why you don't like him. But show him respect out of respect for Hampton," she insisted.

Matt opened the door to greet Cal before he was up the two steps. He offered his right hand to shake as he used his left hand to give a hug. "Good to see you, son. How's your dad?"

"Dad's aching just a little too much, lately. Too many years of being on horseback - and being on the ground."

"Arthritis is shit," Matt said feeling bad for the old man.

"I know. But now he's trying a new medication they're hoping will ease the stiffness. Dad should feel some results in the next couple of weeks."

DeAnn hugged Cal and handed him an iced sun tea in a tall frosted glass with two spoons of sugar stirred in. He took a sip. It was just as he liked it. Cal appreciated DeAnn remembering his preference after all these years.

An entire generation enjoyed sun tea at The Arizona Biltmore - the place for horse lovers. "The Jewel of the Desert", owned by DeAnn's father, Robert Speer, Jr., hosted fun horse shows that exhibitors and spectators would drive for miles and miles to attend. Cal, Greg, Caroline, Patrick, Leonard, Matt Jr. and Meredith would hang out at the Robard stalls guzzling down the sun tea. Robard Arabians always had the set-up that included unlimited sun tea, candy and snack foods for the kids and teens, and free-flowing alcohol and appetizers for the adults. That was before the big barbecue every evening after the show.

The Robard family knew how to be hospitable - they went all-out and never treated Cal or his parents as second-class citizens just because they didn't have much money. And Hampton was the trainer of choice for everyone important. He barely had a pot to piss in, but he knew his horses and taught all of his affluent clients anything they wanted to know. Hampton practically raised Cal and the Robard and Bordeaux kids on horseback. In turn, they treated his family like their family. The Robards even took a dozen or so horses to Catalina during the summer for the old man to train without being in the Scottsdale desert heat.

They also took all the kids making a summer camp on the island. The whole gang had fun on the adventure driving to California to take a private ferry from the Los Angeles Harbor in San Pedro to Catalina. In the circles they traveled in, no one was impressed that DeAnn's family owned the entire island. Nor were they impressed when the Hearst and Kellogg families visited.

"Have a seat, Cal," Matt said.

"Thanks Mr. R. But, I'd rather look at your bronzes if you don't mind, sir."

The Robards collected bronzes of horses by Remington and other artists they admired.

"Make yourself happy."

"How's business going for you, Cal?" DeAnn asked.

Cal beamed. "It's great. I don't get the prices you do, but I can't complain. I sell everything I want to sell and get offers on those that I don't want to part with quite yet. A man can't ask for much more."

"Sounds wonderful. I'm glad you're happy," DeAnn said honestly.

"By the way - Lori and I are finally tying the knot," he said, without as much enthusiasm as would be expected.

DeAnn offered a bittersweet smile, sensing Lori had finally pressured him to make the commitment.

"Whoever thought you would marry your high school sweetheart?" Matt said.

"She did, I guess. Anyway, we're engaged but haven't set a date. Lori's living with me at the farm again. That part's good. She's back keeping the clients happy and back doing the books and mailing out the sales lists and videos. The clients all love her - that's important. She has a way of getting the rich people to pay their bills, when all I could get were promises that the checks would be put in the mail the first of the month," he said, almost as if it were an arranged marriage that he would learn to live with.

"Don't jump into anything," Matt advised him.

"No sir, Mr. R, I won't. I've thought long and hard about this." He took a gulp of his drink, and then added, "Speaking of thinking a lot, if you have a few minutes after this meeting, I'd like to talk to you privately, if I could."

"Sure," Matt said, wondering if Cal was going to ask him for money. Cal never had asked for a dime before, but if he was planning on getting married perhaps Lori convinced him to ask.

Matt had invited Cal into the consortium hoping that if things worked out as planned he could make Cal rich. At least in comparison to how his family had always lived. All Cal had to do was go along with the consortium, let them come to his auctions and bid up horses and throw in a few phony sales to establish the value of his horses. But no - Cal didn't do anything. A straight arrow who would probably end up filing for bankruptcy by the time he was thirty-five.

Before Cal had finished his sun tea, another car drove up outside the house. Along with Ron McGill, the business manager for Vintage Arabians, Thomas, Greg and Patrick Bordeaux filed out of the car. Matt and DeAnn were thrown off-guard. They had only expected Thomas and Greg. Seeing Ron and Patrick, Matt was surprised that Nick Cordonelli wasn't with them as well. Then again, Thomas probably didn't even know Nick pumped cash into the business to resolve the tax problems that Greg had gotten them into.

Greg had approached Matt for help, but Matt refused, suggesting that he find a silent partner in the business. After all, that was how Matt had gotten his big break in owning a television station. Matt and his silent partner had a prearranged buy/sell agreement. As soon as Matt could, he bought out his partner so that he would have ultimate control again and reap all of the benefits.

Matt wouldn't put it past Greg and Ron not to even tell Thomas that Nick practically controlled the purse strings and had incorporated the business for everyone's protection. A couple of years before, at dinner one night, Thomas had casually mentioned that Greg had been given powers of attorney from him and Fiona, and for Patrick. Thomas was attempting to demonstrate how much he trusted Greg's judgment and business acumen, but at the same time he seemed embarrassed. In retrospect, he realized his son manipulated him into giving him the power of attorney.

DeAnn greeted the gang as they paraded past her in pecking order: Thomas, Greg, Ron, and then Patrick. Matt approached Thomas, shook hands, and led him to the far side of the room to talk privately. Greg felt uneasy about the elders talking alone.

Matt got right to the point with Thomas. "Greg isn't packing today, is he?"

"Packing?"

"Yeah."

"What do you mean, packing?"

"He carries that goddamn gun to most of our consortium meetings, and I make him leave it at the door if he admits to bringing it."

"Greg doesn't carry a gun," Thomas said, having never given it any thought.

"He certainly does."

"What kind?" Thomas asked suspiciously.

"I don't know. I barely know a .22 from a machine gun."

"My son doesn't carry a gun, Matt. I think I would know."

Matt drew in a deep breath and puffed his chest out. "He certainly does carry a gun. I gave him the name of the dealer he bought it from."

Thomas still didn't believe him. "Why would Greg buy a gun?"

"He's been packing it for a couple of years that I know of. He jokingly said that he needed protection from a pissed off client. I don't know why he keeps it on him."

Thomas was completely dumbfounded. He wanted to ask Greg about it, but not while they were at the Robards.

Next, Jay and Jane Peacock showed up toting a crystal vase brimming with fresh flowers.

"Good to see you, DeAnn," Jane said handing her the arrangement.

"You too, dear. Thank you for the flowers - I didn't even expect you. This is a day of surprises," DeAnn said, glancing in the direction of the Bordeaux men.

"I know what you mean. But after the article, I think we all need to get involved. Don't you?" Jane said.

"I suppose. Personally, I don't think that one little article is going to do much damage. Of course, Matt disagrees with me," DeAnn confided.

Jay chimed in. "I think that if we all act quickly, we can diffuse any negative..."

Matt and Thomas joined everyone else when the room became too crowded for a private conversation. Thomas interrupted Jay, reaching out to shake his hand. "It's been a long time," he said as he looked down a good eight inches to Jay's face.

"Jane and I were just talking on our way over. We would love to have you and Fiona over for lunch. You should see how big the boys have gotten already," he said seeming completely oblivious to the fact that he was the only short man in the room.

"Give Fiona a call," Thomas replied. The Peacocks didn't really expect Fiona and him to dine in that rented mobile home they lived in not fifty feet from the barn, did they?

The Peacocks leased their land and the facilities from the Robards. The land, which fronted Scottsdale Road, had been in DeAnn's family for years before anyone lived out that far toward Cave Creek. The buildings were nothing more than prefab steel and prefab stalls. The business offices looked like something at an industrial park.

Still, Thomas thought, Jay and Jane acted as if they were on the same level as his own family and the Robard family. Sure, the Peacock family had money in California from the transportation business, but it didn't matter; Jay would never see a dime of it. Jay's parents disowned him when he lost his license to practice law. No one knew how it happened, but the rumors sure flew around Scottsdale. Jane was nice enough, was certainly beautiful, and had a pleasant personality, but no one could understand what she was doing with Jay.

Finally, fifteen minutes late, Leonard Cannon waddled in. No one noticed at first, because they were looking through the window into the barn. You don't go to Mr. R's and not make a big deal about looking through his window and admiring his horses from Poland. Mr. R was just about as proud of his window as he was of his kids and his champion horses. Anyone could see his attitude improve when people would compliment him on his idea to be so close to his 'babies,' as he called them. If you didn't imply that he was a genius to think of the idea and actually build the window, he seemed like a depressed old man living out his life in solitude. It was much better to let Mr. R think you admired everything he did.

Leonard Cannon cleared his throat to let everyone know he had arrived. Better late than never. No one was about to say a word to make him feel uncomfortable. It was common knowledge in the consortium how ruthless Leonard had been to numerous breeders with fine horses, including the Langs and the Grays, when they spoke out against him. If Leonard wanted anyone to fail, he made it happen without so much as a second thought.

Leonard's father, a prominent entrepreneur who crafted shrewd investments in land throughout Phoenix, Sedona and Flagstaff, had advised him to make everyone believe he was the wealthiest man in the consortium. It worked so far. In reality, the funding for his elaborate farm on Bell Road had actually come from private investment bankers and oilmen from Texas. They were confident that within a decade the land would be prime for commercial development. In the meantime, it wouldn't hurt to utilize the land. They built the most spectacular farm in Arizona, profiting from imported Russian and Polish breeding stock. Tax deductions galore, they all agreed. None of the investors minded being silent partners with Leonard under the condition that they could visit the farm whenever they pleased.

Simultaneously, the group turned around when they heard Leonard Cannon clear his throat. Nine phony smiles appeared at once.

Never a man to mince his words, Leonard said, "I didn't expect this many people. I suppose I should have brought my father and wife."

Perhaps it was an attempt to be funny.

Leonard chose the sturdiest armchair as the others collectively held their breath. The last time the consortium convened, Leonard's chair snapped like toothpicks beneath his bountiful frame.

Now that he had arrived, the meeting could begin. Greg looked at his father. They had discussed the probability that Greg would be blamed for everything. He needed to remain calm and appear to be in control in order to maintain his respectable position in the consortium. He didn't want his father speaking for him, although the emotional support wouldn't hurt.

Patrick was another matter. Greg had no idea why his father insisted that Patrick come, but this wasn't the time to question him. Patrick didn't know anything anyway. Ron, on the other hand, was instrumental in most of the major business dealings, and Greg was glad to have him at his side. Ron was an uncanny judge of character and business opportunities. Greg respected his insight and feedback in most business matters. Ron's perspective of the meeting would be important.

Before anyone had a chance to speak, Matt Robard started. "So Greg, you've certainly caused us a lot of problems."

"You've really screwed things up for everyone," Leonard added.

"No kidding. If I told you once, I told you a hundred times - you can't push the envelope with every sale you make, Greg. Look what you've done. I've had it with you," Matt said.

Thomas held back. He had promised he wouldn't get involved and that he was only coming to show family unity.

Greg blinked hard, corrected his posture. "I don't need you to criticize me. To work all of this out, I need everyone's support."

"We're here to find out what the hell happened. How on earth did the press get their information?" Jay said.

Jane glared at her husband. He had agreed not to shoot his mouth off and here he was doing it before anyone else had a chance to speak.

Leonard Cannon interjected before Jay and Greg got into their usual pissing match. "Of course we want to know how the press got their information, but I think the rest of us need to distance ourselves from you and your operation."

Thomas couldn't remain silent. "Distance yourself? That's not what you need to do. You need to show support. There's no way that our customers will buy the idea that the article didn't tell the full story if everyone distances themselves from us."

Leonard shot back. "I'm damn well letting people know that I don't have anything to do with you anymore."

"Me, too," Matt said. He hadn't thought about it before.

The Vintage crew couldn't believe what they were hearing.

Ron put in his two cents. "That's going to screw things up for each and every one of you. It doesn't matter that the reporter only emphasized Greg's name and farm. The article talks about our consortium and what it did to inflate the prices. The people who matter certainly have no trouble knowing that the consortium is all of you. They aren't idiots."

Jay couldn't help himself. "Your clients must be idiots or they wouldn't be doing business with you."

Thomas didn't give Greg a chance to respond. "Okay. This is enough. I know this is a tough thing, but don't you think it would be better to get productive instead of pointing fingers and making threats?"

"Good idea," Ron said.

No one spoke for a few moments.

Greg broke the silence. "We need to decide how to combat the article. My lawyer suggested we develop a plan to convince the public to think the reporter had an ulterior motive and printed a story that had not been thoroughly investigated."

"I'd love to see you bullshit your way out of this, Bordeaux," Jay said.

Greg glared at him. "That is exactly what happened. The reporter definitely printed the story before she checked any facts or heard our side of how we operate the industry. As far as an ulterior motive, it must exist, but I have no idea what the motive would be."

Matt couldn't keep his opinion to himself. "I know part of it. That reporter happens to be Kevin Kincaid's daughter."

Ron McGill interrupted Matt. "Who's he? I've never heard of him."

"He owns Diamond Ranch off Pima Road - over by the reservation. Made his fortune as a pioneer in the electronics field. Until we came along, his operation was the only fit place within five hundred miles for a horse to live. Kincaid and his men buy and sell Thoroughbreds and Quarter horses for prices even Greg would wet his pants to get. They breed 'em, train 'em and sell 'em. For years they were one of the only places people knew about to take riding lessons and buy horses. Hell - half the ideas we implemented were things Kincaid told me they do in the Thoroughbred and Quarter Horse business. He bragged about it every time he could get within ten feet of me."

Leonard chimed in. "I know what you mean. He's been trying to get my family to buy from him for as long as I can remember. You know, he was President of the American Horse Council for years – the stories he told dad and me. He knows what he's talking about. He could spend days telling us crooked things that go on in other breeds."

"Why would his daughter trash our business when her own father is in the horse business?" Ron asked.

"I'll bet you my last dime that they're furious that we've built an incredible industry with Arabians. Kincaid might act like he's kidding, but he's always claimed Arabians are useless lawn ornaments - and now look what we've accomplished. They want to destroy us and this is how they plan to start - with that article," Matt said.

"That makes sense," Thomas said.

Everyone nodded in agreement, absorbing the enormity of the situation with stone faces. DeAnn was the only one who had already known what Matt thought and she agreed with him. She wasn't too concerned about just one article, but he was the one in the media business and he insisted the one story was just the beginning.

Patrick shocked everyone by speaking up next. "So, what do we do now?"

Greg didn't give anyone else a chance. "Matt, you own a television station. You can do a prominent news story that destroys their claims. Maybe even do a special segment about the horse business in general. Cover all the major breeds and put a little extra slant about how great Arabs are."

"I've thought about that. But I've never tried to influence the news staff or the programming. I only deal with the network and the finances," Matt said.

"It's crucial. You're the only one that has any influence on the media - we need you to do this. It's for your benefit, too," Ron told him, as if no one else were in the room.

He thought for a moment. "I'll try to get something done later today," Matt said.

Leonard addressed Matt. "We should sue the newspaper if they don't print a retraction."

"A retraction based on what?" Matt said.

"They didn't investigate any details. There was nothing positive about what we've done," Leonard said.

Greg jumped in. "He's right. Force them to print a retraction."

"I can't force them to do anything," Matt said.

The publisher owed him a big favor. Maybe this is how he would call it in. He would have to give it some thought. If Matt and DeAnn lost all the money they had put into the horse business, it wouldn't matter. He could only call in the favor once with the publisher.

Chapter 8

Four days after the Adventure Arabians open house, Morgan met Sonia at the Hamburger Hamlet on Beverly Drive off Wilshire Boulevard, in Beverly Hills.

As they waited for their salads, Morgan went through her personal written evaluations of twenty-five of Sonia's mares. Morgan described the attributes that she felt Ambiguous would contribute through either corrections of faults, or duplications of the mares qualities or a combination of each. Morgan also justified the proposed pedigree crosses by showing her pedigrees and pictures from auction catalogs and printed advertisements of other horses with very closely related pedigrees.

Sonia was impressed with Morgan's approach and research. She had already inquired about breedings to various stallions owned by prominent farms throughout the country. Not one person gave her program any personal consideration. They simply attempted to sell her breedings or stallion syndicate shares.

"What do you think of how Farroah is producing?" Sonia asked, referring to the stallion imported from Poland by Ryan Sanders.

Morgan didn't hesitate to answer. "When he's bred to the right mares, he's one of the best stallions out there. They've been very selective about what mares to cross him with. Of course, when a farm doesn't need to make a profit, I'm sure it's easier to be selective."

"You don't think Ryan Sanders cares about making a profit?"

"No more than you do. He makes plenty of money in the movie business, and obviously his wife is rolling in money," Morgan said, referring to Shawna, network televisions highest paid news journalist.

"I met with Dan and he showed me Brighten and Farroah. He said that since Brighten was syndicated, there were no breedings available to him."

Morgan wasn't convinced. "He probably meant their farm didn't have breedings available. Usually, you can buy a breeding from one of the syndicate members directly."

"Dan made it clear. Anyone who had breedings for sale this season has already sold them, and it only took a couple of phone calls. He said that if I'm interested for next year, he can probably find a few people I can work with."

Morgan was curious as to whether or not Dan said these things in order to sell Sonia breedings to Farroah. Morgan didn't think Ryan Sanders was motivated by profit, but she realized that the business did need to generate cash flow, and Dan, his partner and trainer, was expected to bring in buyers for horses and breedings. Most trainers at large farms also handled the sales. Because Dan was a business partner with Ryan in the horse operation, he would have added incentive to sell breedings not owned by the Brighten Syndicate members.

Just after lunch was served, Sonia's mobile phone rang. Morgan blushed at the recollection that she had tried to show Sonia she owned the new technology of a $3000 mobile phone.

When Sonia answered the line, she grinned and winked at Morgan, as if to let her know she found humor in Morgan's embarrassment.

Sonia's nanny called to let her know her daughter wanted her mommy; the child had come down with a fever. Sonia apologized to Morgan for canceling their trip to Santa Ynez, but promised to reschedule as soon as she could. Disappointed at the postponement, Morgan gave Sonia the pedigrees and notes.

~~~

Alec left Mimi to sleep in. He was anxious to get to his office while he still had one. Who knew how long that would last? He hoped that Dolan Holloway hadn't contacted anyone in his firm about what he had done. Hopefully, he could try to deal with it privately. Now that he was back together with Mimi, it would be more important than ever to keep his partnership at the firm so that they could work as a team again.

Alec's secretary handed him eight messages - including one from Dolan. Before returning the call, he wanted to draft a settlement offer, just as he and Mimi had discussed.

As far as he knew, there was no precedent to guide him. He doodled as he contemplated wording. He knew the dollar amount they were prepared to offer, but composing the offer was an entirely different matter. Without admitting guilt or wrongdoing, he had to identify the reason that an offer was being made so that the Bordeauxs couldn't accept the money and then come back and sue him regardless.

Mimi woke up with the scent of roses floating through the air. Alec had bought her a dozen red roses early that morning and left them on her nightstand next to a note: *Went to work. There's fresh coffee ready and a fruit plate with an apricot Danish wrapped in the refrigerator. Love you, Alec.*

She yawned and stretched and wondered how long the romance would last this time. When she sat up in bed, she swung her feet around to put on her slippers, but there were none. That reminded her, she would need to arrange to move her things back to the house. And, to call her divorce attorney. Those services were no longer needed.

In Alec's dresser, she found an oversized soft cotton shirt to wear. Usually, he threw his robe in the hamper after wearing it only once or twice as if it were a bath towel. Mimi wondered
~~~

if he still did that since she wasn't there to do the laundry.

The phone rang.

"Hi sweetie," Mimi said.

"I'm sorry. This isn't sweetie. Is Alec available?" the man asked.

"No. Sorry about that. Did you try him at his office?"

"Yes. They said he wasn't in."

"Would you like to leave a message?"

"Sure. Tell him that Dolan Holloway called. Please, ask him to call me as soon as he can."

She swallowed hard and contemplated what to say next. "Dolan from Phoenix?" she said, then immediately regretted it.

"Yes. I'm the Bordeauxs' attorney."

"Ah."

"I'll try him at his office again, but if I don't reach him, please let him know about my call," he said.

"I've got your name written," she said, out of a lack of anything better to say under the circumstances.

Immediately after hanging up the phone, she dialed Alec's direct number.

"Thanks for the flowers and the breakfast," she said as she paced the small kitchen.

"My pleasure. You were fantastic last night. I mean, it was so nice to have you back and..."

"That's enough. I know what you mean. I love you too - that's not why I'm calling," she said quickly. "Dolan just called. I wanted to give you a heads-up in case you weren't prepared to have a discussion with him yet."

Good old Mimi. Always thinking like a lawyer.

"I appreciate it. I can't seem to write a word for this offer. Maybe I should just talk to him. I hoped that I would be contacting him first. It's probably too late," he said.

"Why don't you call him right now and act as if you didn't know he tried to call you already. It's worth a try."

His secretary signaled him and said that Dolan was on the other line.

"Too late. I better take the call. I'll let you know what happens."

"Good luck." She wanted so badly to come back to the firm to work with him.

"Hello Dolan. This is Alec. How are you?"

"I'm fine, and you?"

"As good as could be expected under the circumstances."

Dolan cut to the chase. "I suggest that you consider your options within the next day or so. The Bordeauxs are very anxious to sue you, but I've convinced them to give you ample time to make them a settlement offer. He wants to report you to the disciplinary counsel and file suit."

Alec made a split second decision.

"What's the weather like in Arizona?"

Dolan was caught off-guard. "Not a cloud in the sky."

"Actually," Alec said, "how about if my wife and I come to Scottsdale? We could meet and hash this out. I really don't want my law firm involved in this."

Chapter 9

After his meeting with the consortium, in his home office, Greg listened to the messages on the answering machine: Ryan Sanders called to say he heard about the article and was sorry it would be causing more grief. George Finn called to say he had mailed in his credit application for the upcoming auction, but wanted to talk about a cash discount. Dolan called to say that Alec Douglas was coming to Scottsdale to discuss a settlement. Nick Cordonelli left a message saying he had heard about the article. He said he was coming to Scottsdale and didn't know how long he would be staying. Fiona's message said that she wanted Greg and Marcie to come talk with her and Thomas when they wouldn't have to rush out. She didn't say what it was about, except that it was important. That was odd - his father hadn't said a word, and they had just spent the morning together.

Greg paced like a caged animal. Reflecting about the house of cards he had built, his heart pounded in his chest so hard his eardrums felt the pressure. He knew that if he couldn't finesse the mess he was in, it would open a real Pandora's box.

Once his heart rate normalized, he went to the kitchen hoping to find coffee left in the pot. Marcie was on the phone canceling her weekly manicure and massage appointment at the day spa. She wouldn't be able to relax anyway, so what was the point of taking the time to be pampered?

"My head is just about ready to explode," Greg said after she hung up.

"Sit down. Let me rub your shoulders."

"Sounds good."

She bit her lower lip, and then asked, "Are you ready to tell me about it?"

"I don't want to talk about it. But I'll tell you one thing - those guys are a bunch of ungrateful assholes. I do what we all agree to do, then when it backfires, they blame everything on me."

She kneaded his tight shoulder muscles. "Honey, I know you don't like talking about things sometimes, but maybe it would help you right now. Please, don't shut me out."

"I don't want to discuss it," he said, not telling her that he had heard rumors that she had been confiding their problems to a groom. That was all they needed. He couldn't teach her class, and money didn't buy common sense.

Marcie didn't respond. If she pushed too much, he would not only emotionally retreat from her, but he would physically pull away also. She couldn't bear that right now.

"Do you want to go upstairs for a while?" she suggested as she ran her fingers through his hair, ignoring the natural oiliness.

"Marcie, I can't. I've got too much on my mind."

"Maybe it will relax you. You need to let go," she said, not wanting to make it sound as if it were only about passion.

"I can't."

She took a deep breath. "Just because you couldn't last night or this morning doesn't - "

He didn't let her finish. "I didn't mean literally. I meant that I have too much to think about right now."

"Okay," she said softly as she kissed the top of his head still ignoring his greasy hair.

Marcie poured some fresh squeezed lemonade and took it out to the pool. Feeling left out and lonely, she sat at the edge dangling her feet in the water. Greg always shut her out when he was concerned about anything important and when he had problems he didn't want her to know about. He sometimes acted as if she didn't even exist. At least this time it wasn't that bad.

If only they had had a child that she could love and nurture. She knew she had a good life, but what was marriage without a child? Hopefully she was pregnant from the night they were celebrating that Johan Murphy was dead - or should she think: celebrating that he wasn't suing them after all - yes, that sounded better.

Greg opened the French doors and called out, "I'm going to my parent's house, then to the barn. See you later."

"Sure. I'll be out in a little while to ride. Do you want me to work anyone in particular?"

"Doesn't matter to me."

"Fine," she said with an emptiness to her voice.

She found it unbearable when Greg was down. When he was up, she was up. It was as if she couldn't have her own set of emotions. Her mother told her that was what love was, but Marcie didn't think it really should be that way. Especially in these modern times when women were supposed to be so strong and independent.

Marcie swam laps in the pool to relieve some stress. When her shoulders couldn't take another stroke, she floated to the shallow end of the pool to use the steps. As the sun dried her, she tried to get her mind off their problems by reading the new Cosmo magazine. Unable to concentrate, she showered to rinse off the chlorine, then dressed in her riding breeches and a new blouse.

When she approached the training arena, she was stunned to find Greg riding a mare and using a long whip on her. The first time she saw him smack the horse hard enough to leave a welt she assumed the mare must have done something absolutely terrible to warrant the punishment. Then, after a moment, she realized her husband was punishing the mare just because she wasn't staying on the right lead.

"Stop it!"

Startled, Greg turned toward her voice. It was obvious he didn't see anyone else around. His face was beet red and his knuckles were white from his tight grip on the reins.

"Get off of that horse right now," she screamed.

He halted the horse and dismounted.

The poor mare was lathered up with sweat and shaking from fear.

Marcie took the reins from him, loosened the girth and walked off with the mare, stroking her neck to let her know she wasn't going to be hurt any longer.

Greg saw the mare was limping on her back leg. He felt horrible seeing the mare's heaving flanks and for treating an animal that way, especially now, knowing she couldn't stay on the right lead because she was hurting. What was he becoming? He wondered how Patrick lived with himself, always in a hurry and taking training shortcuts. That meant forcing horses into submission in order to get them to do what he wanted.

Marcie handed the mare over to Julie without mentioning that Greg had been riding the horse. "Can you remove her tack and give her a linament bath? Don't put her on the walker when she's clean. Just tie her in the stall to dry. She's had enough work today. And wrap her legs. She's sore."

Julie immediately spotted the welts on the mare and assumed that Patrick had gotten out of control again. She would use plenty of mint mouthwash, then hemorrhoid cream, on the welt marks. It had been quite a while since she had seen any signs of Patrick's temper. She'd have to tell Liz to talk to him again. They thought he was over taking his problems and frustrations out on the horses.

Marcie stormed back to the arena rehearsing in her mind the words she planned to yell at her husband. She spotted Greg sitting in the dirt, leaning against the fence. Once again, he didn't know she was watching. In fact, he didn't really think about if anyone at all was around. His head was in his hands and tears cascaded from his eyes. He hadn't seen her yet, when unconcerned about the surface, he rolled onto his side and curled up into a fetal position.

She ran toward him. He didn't hear her steps in the sand. When she was within arms reach, he abruptly sat up.

"Get out of here. Just leave me alone."

"But Greg..." her voice trailed off.

"Get out! Just get out! Get out!"

"You need help. Please talk to me," she pleaded.

He turned his back toward her, embarrassed and humiliated to have been found in such a vulnerable position. He just wanted to be alone.

Tears streamed down her face. In a panic, she drove one of the golf carts to her in-law's house.

Fiona answered the door. "Why are you knocking? You know you don't have to knock."

When Fiona saw Marcie in tears, she put her arm around her and led her to the living room.

"Marcie, this is nothing for you to cry about. Everything's going to be fine, dear."

She looked at her mother-in-law curiously. "Fine?"

"Yes. Liz will - "

Thomas walked in. "What's going on? Why are you crying Marcie?"

"I, I, I wanted to tell you what - "

Fiona interrupted her. "I was just telling her that everything would be fine."

Thomas took her chin into his hand and gently lifted her face to look at him. "Marcie, don't feel threatened by all of this. I know it will be an adjustment, but this is a family business."

She stood, looking confused. "I don't know what you're talking about. Let's start over. I came here to tell you that I think Greg is having a nervous breakdown. He won't talk to me."

"Are you two having a fight? Sometimes when he's mad, he just won't talk," Thomas said.

"We're not having a fight. I found him whipping a horse he was riding. I yelled at him to stop, then took the horse away. When I got back to the arena, he was on the ground in a fetal position and crying."

Fiona gasped. "Oh my God - I can't believe this."

Thomas stormed out the door.

Fiona didn't want to be the one to tell Marcie, but under the circumstances she had to.

"Dear, we told Greg we wanted to talk to both of you together."

"He didn't tell me."

Fiona stroked Marcie's hair in a motherly manner. "Well, Greg came to talk to us. I have no idea why he didn't bring you. He said he wanted to keep it private, even though he didn't know what Thomas and I wanted to discuss."

Marcie felt lonelier and more left out than before, if that was even possible. "Why does he shut me out?"

"I don't know. It's just his way. Both of the boys do it. Thank goodness Caroline's not like that."

"I can't stand it. He knows I want to be there for him, but he just shuts down and withdraws," she said as the tears poured.

"The reason he's so upset is because Patrick and Liz are getting married."

Marcie interrupted her. "That's great. Why would Greg be mad about that?"

"Because we told him that we're going to divide the business differently - with everything happening and all."

Marcie's eyes widened. "Differently?"

"Yes. You and Greg will own a third of the business, we're giving Patrick and Liz a third, and we're keeping our third," she said as if there was no budging.

Marcie stood up and backed away. "You can't do that. We already own sixty percent. Patrick's just a trainer - he's only entitled to ten percent, and that's only because he's family. You can't take it from us," she yelled.

Now she realized why Greg was so distraught: Nick Cordonelli's financial interest in the business. Other than Ron, no one else knew - not even Thomas and Fiona or Dolan and Jessica.

From the very beginning of the partnership, Nick and Greg insisted that Nick's actual involvement and interest in Vintage Incorporated, the holding company for all of the Vintage related assets, be completely confidential. The only thing people were to know was that Nick purchased some horses and stallion syndicate shares from the farm, and he was handling the development of L'Equest in Kentucky.

Ron, Greg and Marcie were to be vague about their actual business relationship with Nick. Nick warned them that he would force them to buy out his interest before the agreed-upon buyout date, if, without his consent, it was ever disclosed that he had infused capital into Vintage Incorporated. They needed his money to pay the Internal Revenue Service. Nick insisted that Greg obtain the powers of attorney from his parents and his brother before they formed the corporation, and before he funded the payment for the enormous taxes owed by the sales company.

"Please calm down," Fiona said gently.

"You're saying that you plan to do this against our will?

You can't do it."

"We don't need your permission," Fiona said, truly sorry for how all of this was happening.

"Greg won't agree to it," she screamed through the tears.

Fiona remained calm, as if she dealt with hysterical people all of the time. "Marcie dear - Patrick and Liz very much want to be part of the business. Thomas and I owe them that. This all started as a family business. It was never meant to be just for Greg."

"You can't..." she sobbed.

"Oh, Marcie..."

"You can't do this," she yelled as she stormed out the front door.

Chapter 10

"Patrick is here to see you," the receptionist announced to Ron through the speakerphone.

"Send him in."

The two lead salesman for the farm, Larry Brown and Mike Wolf, were in their respective offices on the phone. They were doing damage control with some clients who had committed to buying but hadn't signed contracts or sent money yet. The walls were thin, making private conversations impossible.

"What did you want to talk about?" Patrick said as he waltzed through Ron's doorway. He thought it was odd that Ron would call him in after they had already spent time driving back and forth to Matt Robard's earlier.

Ron stepped out from behind his huge oak desk, which encompassed almost half of his moderate sized office. He put his arm out, directing Patrick back out the door. "Have time for a drive?"

"Not really, why?" Patrick said, distracted.

"It's important," Ron said. He guided Patrick outside where at least they could be alone.

"I really should be working horses right now. How much

time do we need?"

"It depends. We definitely need privacy though. Are you sure you can't take a drive?"

"I can't right now. How about if we check the horses in this pasture? I haven't done it myself in a while," Patrick suggested, referring to the pasture closest to the sales office.

Ron thought for a moment. It was a dry, hot, windless day. If it were up to him, he'd prefer the air conditioning. Could this wait? No.

He needed to talk while he had the nerve. "All right."

Patrick could sense Ron's uneasiness. "Just say what you have to say."

Ron relaxed his hands on top of the white three-rail fence. Other than the distant silhouette of pregnant mares, the horses were too far away to see. He gazed into the starkness of the monotonous tan dust bowl of a pasture, not really looking at anything in particular. Ron shared Greg's love for Kentucky: the lush bluegrass, enormous trees, honeysuckles, fireflies and the relaxing chirping of birds. He wished he was there now.

"What do you think about the direction that Greg's taken the business?" Ron asked.

"It doesn't matter what I think."

"Of course it matters. You're a Bordeaux."

"A lot of good that does me," Patrick said, disgusted.

Ron understood the feeling, but still he asked, "What do you mean?"

"You know what I mean. Greg owns the majority of the business. Not me. Even though my dad wants to restructure everything."

Ron was taken aback. "He wants to restructure?"

"Yeah. Liz and I are getting married. She wants to get involved in the business, and my parents think it's a great idea. Plus, after all that's going on right now, they think big brother can use more help - from family, that is."

Ron muscled his jaw back and forth as he reconsidered what he planned to talk about. Thomas hadn't said a word to him yet.

"Congratulations on the engagement."

"Thanks."

"So your parents want to restructure the business?" Ron asked as he unconsciously wiped the gritty dust off of his face.

"That's what they said when I told them I was getting married."

"Is that what you really want?" Ron asked, afraid to hear the answer.

"I don't know. All I'm really thinking about is whether I want to fight with Greg about Liz and me actually being involved in the business aspects of the company. I doubt that I have the inclination to fight him to get more than the ten percent I already have."

"I can make it happen, if you want it," Ron said. "I should say - we can make it happen."

Patrick looked curious as a cat.

"Patrick, don't flip out - because I really don't know where to start," he said, then swallowed hard before telling Patrick the entire sordid story.

Ron tried to read Patrick's reaction, but his face was as still as a rock.

Then, Patrick's eyes narrowed. He studied Ron's features as he had never done before. "You're serious?" he said, not believing what he was just told.

"I'm serious as a heart attack."

"Dad said the car dealership was just an investment he made."

"Look," Ron said, " the point is, if you really want to get involved in the business, your engagement is perfect timing."

"Why?"

"Because we need to protect ourselves. Greg is screwing everything up. We need to take over."

"I don't know enough to take over, and you have to admit - you don't know shit about horses," Patrick said. "And Greg won't let us take control from him."

"Not knowingly. And he doesn't really have control."

"Yes, he does. My parents gave him power of attorney. And he made me give him a power of attorney."

"I know," Ron said, "but Cordonelli bailed the farm out of a tax problem. He bought controlling interest in the business. He's supposed to be a silent partner, but believe me, he's not going to stay silent anymore."

"Cordonelli?"

"Fifty-five percent of everything except L'Equest."

"Shit!" Patrick said with a huge grin on his face.

"This makes you happy?"

"Sure. My brother's a jerk."

"I know you and Greg don't really have much in common, other than liking horses, but I didn't know you felt so strongly," Ron said.

"How do you know about Cordonelli's financial interest?"

"I helped arrange it. That's another long story. Anyway, there are other things we need to talk about."

"What were you saying about our taking over the business? Greg will never let me - "

"One step at a time," Ron said confidently.

"You don't understand. I always wanted to be part of the business - the business end of the business - not just training and stuff."

"You and I can take advantage of the problems that are going on now. It's ideal timing for you to get on Cordonelli's good side."

"Why do you want to do this?"

Ron chose one item from his list of reasons. "Let's just say Greg rubs me the wrong way."

"You two act as if you're a great business team," Patrick said surprised.

"Act."

"Aha, it's just an act?"

"Now it's an act. It didn't start out that way, but now it is," Ron admitted.

"So, he doesn't know you have a problem with him?"

"No. But now I really want to put him in his place," Ron said.

"Why?"

"Because I'm entitled and he's become arrogant. And he's backstabbing clients. He uses them, chews them up, and spits them out as soon as he's wrung every last dime he can get out of them. Until Cordonelli got involved, I'm the one who went out and got most of the big-time buyers. I find them, get them excited about getting involved with horses, with Vintage, the whole nine yards. Then, Greg eventually screws the whole thing up, even if the clients don't know it yet."

"What do you mean by, 'until Cordonelli got involved'?"

"Well, he's the one who gets the really heavy hitters. Not that many bought much yet - he's working on turning them over to me. He's stroking them, and then I'll get them and put the hook in. Unfortunately, your brother will end up with them after me, and he'll put the screws to them."

"So what do you propose?" Patrick asked, completely forgetting why they were outside in the desert heat.

"Are you sure you have to work today? I think we should go for a drive."

"Your car or mine?"

The wheels were set in motion.

~~~

Thomas couldn't imagine Greg having a breakdown. Marcie was prone to exaggeration. Nevertheless, he rushed to the riding arena. His son was nowhere to be found in the arena, any of the barns, or the offices. Perplexed, he returned home and reported to his wife.

"Did you check the Prevost?" Fiona asked. The last time he went ballistic he hid in the motor coach.

"How many times do I need to tell you - you don't pronounce the *st*? It's Prevo."

She was getting aggravated and her voice showed it. "Who cares? I pronounce it how it's spelled. Is that all you have to worry about right now? How I say Prevo?"

"No. I've got plenty of other things to worry about, thank you. I'll go check the Prevost though. I didn't even think about it."

The coach was parked at the far side of the property, back by the tractors and trailers. Out of sight, out of mind.

Thomas opened the motor coach door without knocking. Certainly Greg wouldn't have neglected to leave a $500,000 coach unlocked.

Greg was startled and speechless when the door unexpectedly swung open. He stood in his briefs, his hair damp from the shower. Aftershave lingered in the air. A fresh pair of pressed jeans and a clean Ralph Lauren polo shirt sat neatly laid out on the bed.

"Good, you're all right. Marcie was worried," Thomas said, not letting on the he and Fiona were worried also.

"I'm fine now. Just give me a second to finish getting dressed."

"Take your time. I just wanted to check on you. I better get back to the house and let your mother know that everything's fine," he said. He wanted to ask what really happened in the arena. Instead he added, "I'll let Marcie know that you're okay, too."

"Thanks. Tell her I'm sorry."

"Just so you're all right," Thomas said as he lowered
~~~

himself out the door onto the hydraulic steps.

Thomas reported to his wife. Fiona called Marcie to tell her the news, and she offered to stay with her until Greg returned home.

Now that Marcie knew Greg was fine, she wanted time alone to sort out her feelings. Why hadn't Greg taken her to his parent's house earlier? Why didn't he at least come home and tell her about Patrick and Liz? There wasn't a thing she could do when he was in a mood like this. She wasn't about to storm in on him in the Prevost. He obviously didn't want her around. Emotionally drained, she cried herself to sleep on the couch in the middle of the day.

~~~

Alec and Mimi checked into the The Pointe Resort late in the afternoon. Alec unpacked their bags while Mimi browsed through the brochures about various tourist attractions in Arizona.

"I know we're going to be spending a considerable amount of money on this settlement, which isn't a pleasant thought, but I'm excited to be here. I've always wanted to see the Grand Canyon and Sedona. Scottsdale is gorgeous, too - for a vacation at least," Mimi said, not sounding worried about meeting with the Bordeauxs and their lawyers.

Alec smiled at her from across the room. "I feel the same way. It's strange. You would think this would be more stressful."

Mimi smiled. "I guess we're calm because this is a new beginning for us. This is like a honeymoon."

He nodded in agreement.

"Open the drapes so we can enjoy the view," she suggested.

He pulled back the drapes, catching a glimpse of a familiar looking man strolling down the winding path. There was something about his demeanor, the way he had his hands in his pockets that seemed so familiar.

Alec opened the French doors and stepped outside. "It's comfortable out here. Want to join me?"

"Sure. How about if we order room service? Maybe a cheese and vegetable platter?" she suggested.

"Garth and I went to a great happy hour buffet when we were here," Alec said, referring to when they took the depositions
~~~

of Vintage Arabians' clients.

Mimi examined her hair and make-up in the mirror. "Let's check it out."

"You look great."

They found their way to the last available outdoor table with a view of Camelback Mountain. Surrounded by palm trees and potted flowering cactus, they were refreshed by the artistic paddle fans circulating the air. An acoustical guitarist strummed away in the background. Alec faced several women wearing revealing swimwear in the hot tub.

The waitress took their beverage order and offered to prepare them plates from the buffet.

Mimi said playfully, "I think we can help ourselves, thank you. My husband and I need to switch seats anyway. I'm sure he'll prefer the view of the sunset."

The waitress grinned. "Your iced tea will be waiting when you get back. Let me know if I can bring you anything else."

At the buffet, Alec spotted the man he had seen walking past their room. He nonchalantly walked to the opposite side of the buffet table to get a closer look. Alec couldn't place the familiar face. It would probably come to him in the middle of the settlement negotiations.

Back at their table, Alec sampled the gazpacho. "Maybe it was just wishful thinking to say they might settle for two hundred grand."

Mimi tried her chili relleno. "I was thinking the same thing. What you did was just about the most unethical thing a lawyer can do. If I were in his shoes, I wouldn't settle for that little."

"I need to decide what my law license is worth. That's what it really comes down to. If I want to keep practicing, what's the price I'm willing to pay if push comes to shove?" he said, ready to scarf down his shrimp and artichoke quesadilla.

Mimi looked stunned. "Are you saying you might be willing to give up your career?"

"I've thought about it. To be honest, I'm not that happy being a lawyer anymore."

"Since when?" she said, still absorbing his statement about considering giving up his career. She reluctantly nibbled on her crab stuffed mushrooms.

"I don't know. I can't pinpoint a date if that's what you mean. Do you mind if I have a margarita? Would it bother you since you can't drink?"

"Go ahead."

He signaled the waitress. She promptly took his order.

Alec looked flustered. "I can't believe you're coming back to me and having to deal with this right off the bat. I'm sorry."

"Don't worry about it. But, you have to decide if you really want to continue practicing law. I want to, but I think it's because I loved working with you so much. I don't know if it was all about the law itself. Maybe it was just our teamwork."

"Yeah. That could have been it. I think I was happy being a lawyer when we were a team. Maybe I stopped enjoying it when we split up. Everything was different."

She dipped a chip into the guacamole. "Could be."

When the waitress delivered his margarita, Mimi asked for a coffee with cream for herself.

They threw around ideas about their future. It all boiled down to the actual amount the Bordeauxs would be willing to settle for. They agreed to play it by ear.

Later that evening, by the light of the hot tub, Alec saw the familiar looking man again.

"Do you recognize him?" Alec asked his wife, as he nonchalantly directed his gaze toward the stranger.

"Who?"

"That guy in the hot tub. I've seen him a couple of times, but I can't place who he is."

She looked over casually. "I can't tell with the steam. Why don't we go in and join him. We don't have to say anything."

"Good idea."

Back in their room, they agreed that the man was Bob Crane, the star of Hogan's Hero's, a television show they both watched when they were younger.

"He's still a handsome man. I'm surprised he was alone," Mimi commented.

The next morning Alec and Mimi woke up early and took a drive around Scottsdale. They were enthralled to see ranches almost everywhere. Quarter Horses, Thoroughbreds, Paint Horses, and Appaloosas. Eventually, they found their way down Scottsdale Road, where they discovered several Arabian farms. Mimi was impressed, although she couldn't actually see many horses from the street. The only exception was Patriot Farms, the least impressive of all of the facilities within view of the road. The farm didn't look ostentatious; there was no architectural styling to it.

Then, they found Bell Road, where the major farms, including Vintage Arabians, stood in all their glory.

"Look at this place..." Mimi commented in awe, referring to Canco Arabians.

The spectacular entry rivaled a world-class resort: tall white pillars, custom rod-iron fencing, a guarded entry gate and a bigger than life-sized bronze sculpture of a rearing horse.

"This must be the farm," Mimi said, "on the back cover of that magazine. The one with the copper colored horse standing next to the reflecting pool. That fountain area is probably the reflecting pool. What other farm would have pillars like this?"

"You're probably right. I think the ad said that the stallion was from Russia, if I'm remembering correctly."

"Could be. I can't imagine what it must be like behind the gates..." she trailed off, daydreaming aloud.

Alec tried to curb her enthusiasm. "I'm sure it's just as spectacular. We'll never know."

"Can't we go in?"

"What's the point? We would never buy a horse that would cost what they must charge. They can't have a facility like that, and then sell horses for a couple thousand dollars."

"I know, but it would be fun. I'd like to see it just out of curiosity. We obviously can't go to Vintage Arabians," she said pleadingly.

~~~

Greg was in no mood to explain the scene in the arena. And, he didn't look forward to the repercussions of his overnight disappearing act. At daybreak, he hoped to avoid facing Marcie until he'd at least gotten a strong cup of coffee.

Too bad. Marcie had been waiting up half the night. She sat at the kitchen table scanning the morning newspaper looking for another article about them - hopefully a retraction.

"Sorry," he said, looking toward the tile floor rather than at her.

She didn't respond verbally, but her angry expression was impossible to deny. The coffee was brewing and so was she. He poured a glass of orange juice, not knowing what to
~~~

say, or if he should say anything at all. Wordlessly, he unwrapped a new pack of graham crackers and ate a few as he looked out the window toward the glistening pool.

She cleared her throat hoping to solicit a reaction from him.

"I'm going to change shirts. I'll be down in a minute," he said tentatively, still avoiding eye contact.

Greg continued to avoid her for two more days by staying in the barns as much as possible. They hardly spoke during dinner and he went to bed early without going through their usual evening routines.

The following morning, Marcie found Greg in the kitchen drinking coffee and reading *The Phoenix Sun*. Wanting to start on a fresh note, she ignored his recent mood swing.

"Do you want to go out to breakfast before the meeting?" She held her breath waiting for his delayed answer.

"I'm going alone," he said, studying the stock reports. His tone magnified the distance growing between them.

"I'm coming," she said after having rehearsed this foreseeable scene in her mind for half the night. "The settlement is for both of us and Dolan is my uncle."

Greg weighed his words. "I don't need you there glaring at me if I lose it with Jessica again."

"Please, Greg. Drop it. Jessica apologized profusely. I'm sure it took a lot of guts for her to come here and plead with us," Marcie reminded him.

"I could destroy her career. The only reason I'm not pursuing legal action against her is because of Dolan. I'm assuming he's being honest when he said that his firm would be liable for her actions."

"It wasn't Dolan or Jessica's fault. They didn't know Turner was snooping around, let alone that he'd call a reporter. Thank you for letting this go. I know it was a tough decision."

Greg shook his head. "Like I said, I don't want to hurt Dolan. And, their waiving our legal fees will help us some. I hate to think about what our bill would have been."

"Do you think Jessica's really going to divorce Turner over this?" Marcie asked.

"She said she was. Who knows?" he shrugged.

"I feel so bad that our problems may be the cause of her divorce. Hopefully she just said that so we would realize how horrible she felt about what happened."

"He's an ass. She ought to divorce him," Greg said.

"It's their business, not yours. I'm worried about what you're going to say to her," Marcie said.

"Why don't you just go alone then? I really don't give a shit anymore. I've got other things to deal with."

She spoke slowly. "Damn you. What did I do to you? Why are you treating me this way?"

"Okay, we'll go together. If we don't, it will show a sign of weakness," he conceded.

Marcie was flustered. "I'm not just talking about this settlement meeting. I'm talking about everything. What are you hiding from me? It seems like my whole world has been turned upside down totally out of the blue."

She desperately wanted him to turn around, take her into his arms, and assure her that everything would work out.

"Grow up. Not everything is about you," he said as he looked her in the eye, shook his head, and wondered why they were even married.

"Greg, I'm begging you," she said, determined to keep her cool. "Just tell me what we're going to do. Your parents told me they talked to you about dividing the business differently. They can't do it. What about Nick?"

He ignored her question.

At Dolan's office, to everyone's surprise, Greg took control of the meeting that was intended to be a settlement negotiation. It didn't last for more than five minutes. He was soft-spoken and to the point.

Alec and Mimi left the conference room in shock.

"He was completely unreasonable. He's playing a mind game," Mimi told Alec when they were alone.

"The Bordeauxs can't think that there is any possibility that I could or would pay them $5 million," Alec said. "Even Dolan and Jessica looked surprised."

Mimi shook her head in disbelief.

Alec wondered what their strategy was. "At least they didn't threaten to report me to the disciplinary counsel immediately. It was strange how lethargic Greg was - saying I should give his demand some thought and to weigh the consequences of not settling."

"Does Marcie ever talk?" Mimi asked.

"I haven't been around her very much. Most of the work

done was in investigating the industry and deposing Bordeaux's clients," he said as he started the car. "Come to think of it, Garth said that when he first met Marcie, she looked at him strangely for a while. It made him feel uncomfortable, although he couldn't put his finger on it."

"Strange how?"

"He said he couldn't explain it, except for that she couldn't take her eyes off of him at first. Then, he kept catching her looking at him for no apparent reason."

"That's odd," she sighed.

"By the way - if I am able to continue practicing law, I'd like for you to meet Garth. If you approve of him, I think we should bring him on board full-time. I'm very impressed with his work and his instincts. I think you will be, too."

Mimi smiled. "I trust your judgment. I don't need to meet him. Just hire him if things work out."

"You're sure?"

"Yes. We can always use another good associate."

"I was thinking he could work directly with us on our cases. I trust him."

"Fine."

Greg began to leave Dolan's conference room before anyone had a chance to saying anything. Dolan would have read his clients the riot act if Marcie weren't his niece.

Marcie wouldn't let Greg off the hook. "What the hell was that all about?" she demanded of Greg.

"I told Alec what I think I deserve."

"Uncle Dolan and Jessica were supposed to do the talking. We agreed to hear Alec's proposal. You're being a jerk. They're never going to settle if you expect $5 million."

Greg walked out, giving the impression that he didn't care if Marcie joined him or not. Too embarrassed to have Dolan drive her home, Marcie followed her husband. If Dolan had driven her home he would want to know why Greg was acting that way. She didn't even know herself, so how could she explain it?

Dolan decided to write a letter stating that he was withdrawing of their counsel.

Chapter 11

Mimi looked at her notes. "Cal Hampton isn't at his farm today, but the woman who answered the phone invited us to stop in and browse around. She said she could give us a sales list, but no one is available to show us specific horses until tomorrow."

"Okay. What about Patriot Farms?"

"We can come any time," she said.

"Dean and Brian Pondergrass said that they put on the big auctions and they do business with some big investors. There must be something to the operation. Maybe it's more impressive inside than from the road," Alec said.

"Let's go to Patriot and then play it by ear. Maybe they'll tell us other places we can go."

Fifteen minutes later they drove down the long narrow driveway lined with four-rail black board fencing. As they drove in the parking area, a plump blond woman darted out of the barn to greet them. She wore frayed cut-off denim shorts, a dirty tee shirt, and old sneakers stained from mud and manure.

"Hi! Are you the folks who called just a little while ago?" she asked.

"Yes, I'm Mimi, and this is my husband Alec."

"Nice to meet you. I'm Sherry. Just park over there," she said pointing to an area under one of the few shade trees.

"Excuse the footing. We're getting more gravel brought in. This can be like a flood plain - we're constantly battling to keep the parking area usable."

"No problem. Are you the owner?" Alec asked.

The woman smiled. "No, not yet."

"You're buying the place, Sherry?" Mimi asked, just being friendly.

"No. I didn't mean that. I just meant that someday, somehow, I'm going to own my own farm," she said, wiping the grime and perspiration from her face using the corner of her shirtsleeve.

Mimi and Alec hid their disgust at her action.

"Keep working hard and saving your money. Maybe you can get yourself a little place out in the country where the real estate is reasonable," Alec said, trying to be as friendly as his wife.

The dark roots of Sherry's bleached blond hair showed when she bent down to retie her stained shoelace. "Actually, I think I'll just marry a filthy rich widower. Plenty of those come around here, and I can clean up pretty damn good when I want to."

"Ah, good plan," Mimi said, kidding back with her.

"Anyway, let me call Jane and tell her you're here. She's the owner."

Just as Sherry walked away, an attractive man appearing to be in his late twenties or early thirties approached them. He wore nicely fitted designer jeans, a pressed short sleeve button down shirt, and clean leather shoes.

"I'll take care of them," he told Sherry.

Mimi and Alec introduced themselves.

"My name is Robasz. Excuse my accent. I'm from Poland. I'm learning better English."

"You're doing great," Alec told him, looking out into the

flat and barren pasture. It wasn't picturesque like the ads in the magazines.

"I was imported to the United States by Mr. Jay Peacock, along with the Polish National Champion stallion, Goderrett," he announced with pride.

"Pardon me?" Mimi said.

"Let's go inside and see some horses while we are speaking," Robasz suggested as he led them to the closest barn.

They followed him to a large stall with a small chestnut stallion. The symmetrical white strip on his face and nose was beautiful to an uneducated eye.

"This is Fire Warning - the first Champion stallion that the Peacock's trained and showed. They are very much proud of him. Do you like?"

Mimi and Alec looked into the immaculate stall. The fluffy pine shavings were deep and aromatic like a lumberyard. A sparkling clean water bucket was filled to the brim in the front corner of the stall.

"We don't really know anything about horses yet, but he sure is a nice looking animal," Alec answered.

Robasz nodded, not showing enthusiasm for the horse, but not wanting to sound disrespectful. He took several steps backward toward another stall as he spoke with the demeanor of a tour guide.

"This is the stallion that gave me the gift of coming to your country. This is Goderrett," he boasted with pride.

The dark chestnut stallion stood tall and proud in his stall, with his head hanging out into the barn aisle.

"He's breathtaking!" Mimi said.

"Yes, he is," Alec added with genuine enthusiasm.

"May we pet him?"

"Oh, sure. He loves people. Just don't put your hands by his mouth. Stroke his neck and move slowly," Robasz said, smiling from ear to ear.

Goderrett anticipated carrots. When he realized that none were forthcoming, he retreated to the far side of his stall and turned his tail toward them.

"Would you like to see him out?"

Mimi grinned. "Can we?"

A dark brown leather halter with 'Goderrett' engraved on the nameplate hung on the brass hook outside the stall. It was far enough away that the horse couldn't reach it.

"Oh, sure. I'll bring him for you," Robasz offered.

Goderrett snorted and started to push his way out of the stall. Robasz lightly tapped him on the chest with a dressage whip. The horse dropped his head and backed up three steps, showing respect. When the halter was fastened, Robasz stood at his left side to lead him out. Goderrett lit up like a strobe light in a dark room. His nostrils flared. His tail flipped over his back. Robasz gently bumped the lead rope which was attached to a wide stud chain padded with Vetrap. After a single light reminder bump of the chain, the stallion relaxed enough for Robasz to permit him to exit the stall. In just a few short steps, the stallion tensed his muscles and danced with his feet as if he were walking on air. The magnificent animal was clearly conceited.

Goderrett obeyed Robasz as he led him in a large circle in the barn aisle. His movement was as fluid and graceful as it was powerful and masculine - especially when he gazed outside and snorted, calling attention to himself. The four horses on the hot walker looked at him immediately as if they were in the military and had been called to stand at attention. To their dismay, they could only stop for a brief moment. The mechanical hot walker kept them moving in a fifty-foot diameter circle at a speed of two and a half miles per hour.

"Do you like?" Robasz asked, breaking the spell the stallion had cast upon them.

"My heart stopped a beat, he's so beautiful," Mimi said.

"Yes. He looks like a fine strong specimen," Alec said, not knowing where the ridiculous words came from.

"Oh, sure. He is the best stallion to come out of Poland. He could not come here without me. The director of the stud farm would not sell him unless I provide for his food and care the remainder of his life," he said proudly.

"Wow," Mimi said, dumbfounded.

"Oh, sure. I was imported. He was imported. Soon, I will go back and bring my wife here. Then she will be imported too!"

"Thank you for allowing us to see him out of his stall. He's even more beautiful when you can see his full body," Alec said.

"Yes. Sure he is. Would you like to see him turned out? That is when he is at his best. Goderrett is a superstar athlete."

Alec and Mimi didn't know what the term 'turned out' meant, but they told him they would enjoy seeing the stallion turned out. Robasz directed them to follow at a safe distance as they headed toward an enclosure with soft sand and sturdy six-rail fencing.

Robasz led the stallion into the enclosure, closed the gate behind him, and removed the halter. Goderrett pivoted on his hind legs to move away, then reared in the air and struck out with both front feet as his tail whipped over his back. He walked on his back legs for several steps before he hit a lick at a trot, taking each step with an offhanded confidence. Mimi could visualize him humming to himself.

The stallion had an insatiable curiosity about everything going on around him as one eye remained on his handler. With a subtle hand gesture from Robasz, Goderrett took off cantering the perimeter of the large oval ring. Robasz stayed in the middle, confident that the horse that appeared wild would not harm him. After a few minutes of the stallion cantering, then trotting, then kicking up his back legs as he swung his hips to the side, Robasz said a single word in Polish. The horse stopped on a dime, faced his handler, and dropped his head, showing his kind expressive eyes. Robasz, bursting with pride, calmly walked three steps toward the magnificent creature. When he turned to face the guests, the horse rested his chin on the Pole's shoulder and gave him a gentle nuzzle.

"This is World Champion Goderrett," he announced, as if there were a crowd.

In the background, Sherry had stopped cleaning the stall she was working on so that she could admire the stallion she saw several times a day. He never failed to take her breath away. Sherry daydreamed of owning him one day.

Jay and Jane Peacock strolled over to greet their guests and introduce themselves. When Alec heard their last name, he held back a chuckle. Peacock was the animal he thought of when he saw Jay strutting as he walked toward them. Jane didn't seem to belong with Jay. Jane, whose smile could have been in a toothpaste commercial, reminded Alec of a petite Ali McGraw, the star of the hit movie 'Love Story'. She looked like the All-American girl, with just a hint of sexuality thrown in. The Peacocks were dressed in designer sportswear and they both wore tasteful, expensive gold jewelry. Alec assumed that they owned the Porsche and the Mercedes in the drive.

"It's warm out here. Would you like to come inside? Our boys are napping and I need to hear them if they wake up," Jane said.

Alec and Mimi didn't know what she meant when she said inside, but they accepted the invitation.

Jay thanked Robasz and invited him to join them - an offer which was declined without explanation.

"Very very pleasurable to meet you," Robasz told the guests.

"And you, also. Thank you for showing us the horse," Mimi responded.

The Peacocks led Alec and Mimi to a doublewide mobile home. The Douglas' had never been in a mobile home before. It was immaculately clean, tastefully furnished and decorated, and smelled of baby powder and fabric softener.

Within ten minutes, Jay told them the history of their experience in the horse industry, claiming that he was so successful he had walked away from a lucrative law practice in Southern California. He said that he had made so much money from breeding and raising Polish-bred Arabians, he was compelled to make it his livelihood. It was too good to be true, the way he told the story.

Jay said they were leasing the Scottsdale facilities while they built their own grand farm in the heart of the Kentucky bluegrass. It was their opinion that the Arabian horse industry would move to Kentucky once people grasped the fact that lush grass and wide open spaces were much healthier than the sandy ground and the climate in Scottsdale.

Jay explained that for years he had visited the Polish government- owned stud farms to study their breeding program and buy horses for his clients. He claimed that his clients were essentially investors who loved horses and the tax deductions associated with horses that are purchased with the intent to make a profit.

"How would you like be the first to see our new video?" Jay asked them, making it hard for them to refuse.

"Sure," Mimi and Alec reluctantly said at the same time.

Jay inserted the video in the machine, bragging that he paid $50,000 to have it produced. He said it would be well worth the money - so many people invested in their stallion syndications based on videos and their impeccable reputation. Surely, the brand new video with new footage about Arabians throughout history and Arabians in Poland would stimulate more business than ever.

As the beginning credits ran on the video, Alec thumbed through each of their four brochures with photographs glued inside. He wondered why the photos weren't printed in the marketing piece, especially since the paper was high quality, and the covers were foiled, embossed and die-cut. Johan Murphy had brought Alec full color brochures from a few different farms, including Vintage Arabians.

The sun reflected too much glare on the television to see the video, and the toddlers woke up crying. As a result, Mimi and Alec were able to escape the doublewide. Jay attempted to get their names and phone numbers, but Alec changed the subject quickly and inquired about restaurants.

"Jane was fine, but Jay reminded me of a used-car salesman," Mimi said as they drove away.

Chapter 12

"I've raised the bar for this operation and taken us to new levels. This is what you do to pay me back? Turn us into criminals?" Nick Cordonelli sneered.

"It might sound scandalous but it's not criminal," Greg lied. Dolan had made it quite clear that their actions were criminal.

Greg was drained and the meeting wasn't over. It had taken two hours to explain what had happened with Johan Murphy and Love Letter, the Pondergrass brothers, the lawyers, and the fallout of so many clients being deposed.

"What a mess," he said, shaking his head. "We're going to lose so much business, and we're probably going to get sued by the deposed clients. And now Johan is dead. You've really screwed up, Bordeaux."

"We're not going to get sued by any clients," Greg assured him. "I've already handled it. Everyone who was deposed signed confidentiality agreements. In exchange, they'll be compensated with unlimited breedings to Vintage owned stallions or stallions we own syndicate shares in. We're also giving them free board for the mares being bred for whatever time period it takes the mares to conceive and be checked sixty days in foal. And of course, they won't be required to pay off their contracts on the horses purchased at the auction."

Nick frowned. "Shit. That's better than the exposure of being sued, but we're going to feel the financial consequences. It's going to hit us hard. We count on their money for board and what we earn selling them breedings - plus, now we'll have to pay off their bank notes on the horses that were financed through the lenders. I can't believe you haven't said a word about this. Besides the legal exposure, all of these things alter the numbers for the business by at least several million dollars over the long term."

Greg looked at the floor, feeling guilty. "I should have told you. I'm sorry."

Nick was disgusted. "I don't know if the things you've done are criminal or not, but I don't want my name associated with anything scandalous and you know it."

"Your name never came up Nick. Not even with our own lawyers. I promise."

Nick was Greg's shortcut. His money machine. He had to keep him happy.

"By the way," Greg continued. "When I found out we weren't going to collect on the payments for Love Letter through Johan, I called George Finn to see if he still wanted her. He bid on her up to $2.3 million at the auction. It looks like he'll probably buy her."

"For $2.5 million?"

"For the balance due. Johan paid twenty percent down and has made one payment," Greg clarified. "Finn wants to think about it. You know him, he'd rather have been in the limelight at the auction, paying that kind of price for a horse in public, with camera's flashing in his face."

Nick felt better at the prospect of at least still having Love Letter being paid on. "Get Finn to buy her," he said as if it were no big deal.

Ron stuck his head through the door. "You still busy?"

"Come on in," Nick said.

"I've got some good news and a proposal for you, Nick," Ron said.

"What's the news?" Greg said, glad to be out of the hot seat.

Ron beamed. "I sent the contracts for L'Equest to a lawyer I read about in Fortune magazine. He specializes in Truth-In-Lending Act violations in real estate transactions. Anyway, he says we've got a reasonable claim against Tony Valdachelli personally, his holding company, and the Japanese investor that owns the note on L'Equest."

Nick perked up. "What kind of claim?"

"To be honest, I don't really understand the terms he was using, but he said there are some gray areas that he can bring to the lenders attention. It should be enough to force their hand at letting us pay off the note and get them out of the picture."

Greg sighed with relief. "What's the lawyer get out of it?"

"We can either pay an upfront fee of twenty-five grand, or pay fifty percent the amount saved if the lawyer works on a contingency. Obviously, in our situation, we'd go with the upfront fee. The law firm writes a letter stating their findings about the Truth-In-Lending Act violations and the other contract issues. Then, they'll follow up and handle a settlement agreement that will allow us to pay off the note without prepayment penalties or other fees."

"Let's do it," Greg said.

"Wait a minute," Nick said. "Where's the money going to come from to pay off the note?"

Ron was quick to answer. "That's where you come into the picture again, Nick. We need you. And this is perfect for you."

"I wouldn't hesitate if it were in Ocala. You know that. I told you when I bailed you out of the tax problems I didn't want anything to do with L'Equest except to act as a developer. You're just like any other paying customers," Nick said, referring to the exclusive Kentucky equestrian development.

"I understand that was your intent," Ron said. "But, we don't know how else we can do this without your becoming a partner in L'Equest also."

"I can't keep penny pinching," Greg told Nick. "I had to make a sale to the Zellers just to start on the stallion barn. It's going to continue like this if we can't get the funding we need to build everything at once. You can see that."

"That's how these things go sometimes," Nick said. He'd seen it a hundred times over.

Nick's clients often lacked the resources to build what they envisioned. Nick was shrewd enough to collect the majority of his developer fees up-front. His own income was fixed regardless of client's building budgets being tightened.

"Come on. It's just a little more of your money and your credit," Greg said lightly as if they were talking pennies.

"It's not just 'a little' and you know it. Plus, like I told you when I saw your plans in the first place - you don't have enough land for it to be profitable," Nick said, referring to the two thousand acres.

"How much do you think we need?" Ron asked, now sitting down and prepared to take notes as if it were new information.

"Everything surrounding what you already own – at least six or seven thousand acres. Vintage East alone should be about seven hundred acres to handle the breeding operation. The sales center should be on more acreage than what's planned. You need more land to sell clients – at least seventy tracts," Nick said.

Greg had heard Nick's opinion before, but this was the first time he really took it seriously.

"I'm sure you're right. Are you in?" Ron asked.

Greg held his breath, hoping for a firm 'yes'. He desperately needed Nick as much now as he had before.

Nick tapped his fingers on the desk. "Let me run some numbers and call my money people. I'll let you know."

Although Greg wasn't surprised, he was disappointed about Nick's lack of commitment. Greg looked out the window toward the gravel parking lot and small sandy paddocks, longing to bask in the rolling bluegrass hills of Kentucky.

Ron and Nick exchanged sly grins - everything had gone just as they planned. Greg was none the wiser.

Nick had wanted ownership and control in L'Equest ever since he and Greg chartered a helicopter flight to see an aerial view of the property. Nick knew all along that the project would cost far more to develop than Greg projected.

When Greg proved to Nick that he had some funding and was totally committed to the development, Nick's strategy was to get paid the up-front developer and contractor fees. Then, Nick manipulated Greg into practically begging him to be a partner in order for the grand project to proceed. Nick had no idea that Ron's motive and goal was to push Greg out of his position in the horse operation and the land development.

"How much time do you think you'll need to decide?" Greg asked as he fidgeted with the sterling silver letter opener on the desk.

"I'll let you know as soon as possible. I'm sure I'd want a buy/sell agreement on this deal if I do it."

"Fine. No problem," Greg said.

Ron paced the office as a thought formed. "We need some Japanese investors to buy land."

Nick agreed. "If we do this together and get the amount of land I'm planning on, we should go after them. They love to buy land in the states - there's nothing left in Japan. Start some networking," Nick said to both of them.

"Actually, Johnny Pallinto could probably help us. His father has contacts in Japan," Greg said. Then as an afterthought, he added, "I ought to talk to him about building in L'Equest."

Nick perked up. "That name sounds familiar. Johnny Pimento. Johnny Pimento. Where do I know that name from?"

"It's Pallinto. He was a client of Canco," he said, emphasizing the word was. "Johnny drank more than he should have during a Canco auction and bought some Russian mares for top dollar. He claims Leonard Cannon made him an offer - if he paid green cash under the table for the horses, Leonard would let him in on Mussalot when they were ready to get him out of Tersk Stud in Russia. Supposedly, Johnny went to the farm the next day with a briefcase full of cash and they shook hands on the deal about the stud. Then, when Mussalot got here, Leonard claimed they never even discussed it. Of course, that's Johnny's story. Who knows?"

"Oh yeah. I remember now. Johnny's the tall fat guy who sweats a lot. He came to my Ocala farm with his father years ago. Made quite an impression on me even though they didn't buy any horses. I remember seeing him listed as a buyer at Canco in one of the magazines," Nick said.

"I don't recall what he does for a living," Greg said.

"His family is in the nursing home business. They have dozens of them," Nick said without hesitation.

"Is that profitable?" Greg asked.

"Seemed like it. His dad wanted me to invest in a few

locations. I didn't ask him to, but he sent me a prospectus. Too much government regulation for me. I told him thanks, but no thanks."

Greg nodded and tried to remember how it came up about Johnny's father having contacts in Japan.

Nick continued. "Try to sell Pimento a big parcel. His family has the money. I'm sure you could get him to build a first-class operation. He's got the quality of horses to warrant it."

Greg nodded again, hoping the conversation would continue on a good note.

His mission accomplished, Ron excused himself, pleased with how the encounter went.

A few moments passed when the pallor hung in the air again. Greg shouldn't have stopped talking.

Once again, Nick's face turned solemn as he boiled under the surface about the newspaper article and the problems with the Murphys, Vintage clients being deposed, and everything else that had transpired without his knowledge.

"I don't know how we got off track," Nick said. "I need to weigh my options."

The color drained from Greg's face.

"Options?" He was well aware that his fate hung in the balance of what Nick would tolerate.

Nick, sitting behind the massive desk, pursed his lips - his index finger tapped a crystal paperweight with a horse embedded in the design. He wondered how Greg had kept the problems with Johan a secret from Ron.

"If it weren't for my bailing you out, you'd be bankrupt and probably in jail. Did you think I was going to hand over that kind of money without expecting to be kept informed?" He raised his bushy eyebrows to emphasize the question.

Greg swallowed hard before answering. "I had no alternative but to take your money. I know that. I've thanked you. And I said I'm sorry for not keeping you informed."

Striking a deal with Nick improved his odds for the business to grow exponentially. Two years ago, there had been a remote possibility that Greg and his sales team could have sold enough horses to pay the enormous past due tax bill, but he wasn't confident it could be accomplished before his father and the public discovered their financial predicament.

Greg lacked sophistication, but he didn't lack ambition. He had spent all the Vintage Incorporated cash reserves on buying two thousand acres of undeveloped woodlands and pasturelands in LaGrange, Kentucky. Until he invested in land, what had felt like an endless stream of money from the Scottsdale and California operations began flowing into the simple basics of land development in Kentucky. The stream went dry. In less than two years, Greg borrowed from one bank to pay back another.

Eventually, he was strapped for cash to the point he was unable to pay the taxes. By the time everything on the farm was leveraged and payments were late, he finally went to Ron and confided to him that he was a drowning man. Ron arranged restructured payment plans with the banks and approached Nick, a client of theirs.

Nick, a land developer and racehorse breeder by profession, arrived in the nick of time. Thanks to Ron, Nick bought a financial interest in Vintage Incorporated, that included the Scottsdale real estate and all business assets and inventory of Vintage Arabians and the sales company. In addition to the credit line and cash Nick infused, he contributed his farm and horses in Ocala. Once business arrangements were worked out, the undaunted team, led by Greg, remained the major force in the industry without anyone knowing any of their dirty laundry.

Nick stood. "When you approached me with your proposition, you swore you didn't care about making money. You said you just wanted to stay in the horse business."

Greg's face flushed. "But you - "

Nick spun on his heels and faced him. "Don't you interrupt me, Bordeaux."

"But - "

Nick glared at him. "If you interrupt me again, I'm out of here. So is my funding and my credit. And you can be sure that I won't bail you out of L'Equest."

"Screw you. I have every right to defend myself."

"Screw me? Every right? No - you don't have any rights with me unless I tell you that you do," Nick said as his lips pursed and his thick chest puffed out.

Greg nodded and kept his trap shut.

"The problem is Bordeaux, you got greedy. Remodeling that house in Equestrian Manor - it's still not finished. Then you buy a $500,000 motor coach without asking me and you start wearing fur coats. You look like a fag – I don't know if you think you're impressing people - "

This time Greg had to speak his mind. "You're the one who insisted I should create an image of success - of having money to flaunt. Marcie picked out that coat for me. People know I'm not a fag."

"When I told you people are attracted to people of wealth, I assumed that you would consult with me on what you had in mind. Only a handful of people will know about the motor coach or the Equestrian Manor property - it's in a gate-guarded community for God's sake. You need to have things that everyone can see."

"I can't have something just for me? Me and Marcie? You can't tell me where to live."

"I can and I will," Nick said. "Sell that place. Consult with me from now on. You're not going to burn through money unless it's for things I approve of."

"You're a silent partner," Greg said defensively.

"The day we met you didn't have two nickels to rub together. All you had was a herd of horses and not enough buyers for the prices you were establishing. Now banks are loaning money, buying notes from you, and the client base is growing - you know it's because of me and only me."

"I recognize that. But you agreed to be a silent partner," Greg said.

Greg certainly wasn't going to remind Nick that it was really himself, his father, Ron, and his sales staff - Larry Brown and Mike Wolf - that were making the majority of the actual sales.

"I agreed to be silent in the public's eyes. Not yours. I control the purse strings from now on. You'll still have your luxuries, but I'll let you know what's appropriate."

"You said I would be in control of everything unless I screwed up," Greg reminded him.

Nick remembered the conversation quite well. And remembered not to put anything about control in the contract.

"You've screwed up. And big time," Nick reminded him.

"I haven't screwed you."

"Not directly, but you screwed up with this Johan Murphy character and with this newspaper article."

"You were completely aware of how we sell horses," Greg said. "Just because you're not aware of every single detail, it doesn't mean you were kept in the dark. Half the reason I do what I do is to give you the financial returns you're demanding."

"The returns we mutually agreed to," Nick said with an obvious coolness.

"Fine. I was backed into a corner. I admit I agreed to the returns you demanded."

"If you don't like the turn of events with me, feel free to exercise our buy/sell agreement. Come up with fifteen mil and I'm out of your life. Do what you want when I'm not involved," Nick said.

"This is going too far. I want to be partners with you. You know that. We do great together and we have the same vision. Let's just step back and calm down."

"I'm fed up. Really. I'm just fed up with your presumptuous and arrogant attitude. We might have the same vision, but we're not on the same wavelength. Just buy me out."

"I can't buy you out right now and you know it. You're acting like this because of the newspaper article. Everything was just fine before."

"I looked at our contract this morning. I suggest you do the same. I've got a strong case for legally being able to force you to buy me out or to force you to simply walk away from it. I'll keep quiet and allow you to disappear without embarrassment," Nick said.

Greg pounded his fists on the desk. "Are you crazy? I'm not walking away ever - let alone at this point in the game."

"I've had it with you, Bordeaux. I hope you're not out of options. You've got a year."

Chapter 13

"What we need is our own limo and full time driver," Nick said reflectively.

Greg was afraid to ask Nick if his demand to be bought out had simply been impulsive. For now, it would be prudent to assume he had the burden to buy out his partner. After yesterday, he was about ready to chuck it all and flee to a deserted island.

"A limo sounds good to me. It'll impress clients," Greg agreed.

"You need to think positive. Think ahead. Make plans for a bigger future. We need to show the public that we're strong and the future is brighter than ever," Nick said enthusiastically, as if his demand twenty-four hours earlier had never been made.

"I agree," Greg said.

"By the way - I'm meeting with Matt Robard later."

Greg wanted to protest but didn't dare. For the time being, he intended to walk on eggshells.

Nick stood up, signaling that Greg should leave him alone.

Greg opened the hand-carved door and dropped his chin toward his chest as he left.

"I'm meeting with your father, too," Nick said to Greg's back as if it was incidental. He knew it would drive Greg wild.

A sharp searing pain pierced Greg's stomach. He turned around abruptly. "That's not necessary. He thinks you're a good client that I let use the offices when you're in town. The only thing he knows is that I hired you to manage the development. He's never even asked the details of our business relationship. Please, just leave my family out of this."

"I can't anymore. People need to know we have staying power. Alone, you're vulnerable. It's not a sign of weakness to be in business with men of influence. You'll still have control over which horses to buy and sell, and the breeding and marketing methods. Like I told you when I got into this with you - this can be a much bigger business than you imagine, but you can't accomplish anything without my public backing and without my contacts."

"Do you have to tell my family about the tax problems?" There was nothing he dreaded more.

"No. I'll avoid that. Nevertheless, I won't remain a silent partner. I was going to tell you this before all of the problems happened, but I wanted to talk in person and there wasn't opportunity until now."

"You wanted to do this before the shit hit the fan? Why?"

"I've been cultivating some very important people, trying to get them into the horse business. Politically powerful people. Each of them is on the verge of making a commitment if I'm visible to some extent. They don't want it to appear that a trainer brought them into the industry."

Greg was offended and intrigued. He wasn't just a trainer. He was Greg Bordeaux. This time he was finally smart enough not to respond.

"I shouldn't be telling you this yet, but I'll trust your discretion. Darrel Desmond and Alfred Nale are both ready to do something on a larger scale. Your father has gained their respect and has started forging a very good relationship with them. I've got others, too. This is just the beginning. I've been working on these people for quite some time."

"Won't they be scared away by the bad press?"

"I'll deal with it. Just do what I say and we'll get them into this and make everyone plenty of money."

"How much are they talking about spending?"

"We haven't talked about specific dollar amounts, but they'll be buying their own herds, operating their own business, having their own trainers and advisors. We're just going to get them started."

"Building farms in L'Equest?"

"No. Southern California. Desmond already owns a couple thousand acres with cattle on it. He'll use part of the spread for his horse operation. Alfred Nale will probably keep his collection of horses with Desmond - they have other investments together - you've heard of Proxy Petroleum, haven't you?"

"No," Greg said. "I don't know the name."

"A huge petroleum company and they have - "

"By the way, Finn left a message saying that he's sending a new credit application for the auction. I've got him convinced that the only way he's going to make a big splash in the industry is to buy Crimson Lace for a record price."

Nick hated how Greg always interrupted him, but he ignored it this time. "Is Finn the guy in the schmatte business?"

"Yeah. He's who I said will probably buy Love Letter."

"Sell him a big tract in L'Equest, too."

"He already owns a farm in Southern California, not far from his home. That's fine. He's willing to pay big bucks for horses - and at public auction. He and his wife are glitzy and have already spent at least a few million with us just to get a feel for the business. Believe me. They'll put in millions more."

"Keep stroking him. We can't lose clients like him," Nick said.

"Finn's wife and Marcie get along great," Greg lied. "That helps."

"That's another thing. You've got to keep Marcie away. I've heard she has a big mouth."

"Marcie? No, she doesn't," Greg lied again.

"I'm telling you. Don't confide in her. She doesn't have any discretion. Keep her busy with something that will keep her out of the barns and away from the business."

"Like what? The Equestrian Manor mansion is almost finished. We're supposed to move in a couple of weeks. She'll be with the horses every day."

"Move her to Kentucky. Design your own house and barn. You've got five hundred acres everyone has to drive past. Name it Bordeaux Hill or something, so it will be obvious that you own the estate. That'll keep her busy working with the architect and interior decorator there."

"I want my wife with me. I already travel too much. I don't want to be away from her more."

"Your marriage is your business," Nick said. "If you want to be married to a stupid bimbo, that's your right, but keep her away from the business. I can't get any blunter than this."

Greg hated his wife being called a bimbo, but he'd heard it behind his back plenty of times. "I'll see what I can do. Maybe I can start working out of L'Equest soon. Bring the team there - other than when we need to show the horses for the February sales.

"Work it out."

"I will," Greg said.

"I'm meeting with your father this afternoon. And, in the next day or so I'll meet with Patrick, too. You need to at least have the appearance of a united family. Your father needs to be more visible again."

"Patrick is marrying Liz. You might want to bring her in on the meeting - apparently she has some great marketing ideas. With everything going on right now, I haven't had time to talk with her about it yet."

"What's your opinion of her?" Nick asked.

"She'll be valuable to us," Greg said. "She's a hell of a lot smarter than Patrick. I'll tell you that. And he doesn't seem to be rough with the horses lately - that's due to her influence. I think we should hear her ideas and see how we can utilize her."

"Fine. We need more good people. A couple more trustworthy people working in sales, and definitely more trainers to train and show," Nick said.

"Speaking of that - I've been thinking the same thing about needing more trainers. Patrick and I are spread thin. The apprentices don't know enough to turn out a finished product. I really don't have time to train much and I can't show all of the horses that the clients want me to. You know, some of them won't let Patrick show their horses, and even if they did want him, each of us can only ride one horse per class. We're too big now to accommodate everyone."

"Have clients complained?" Nick said.

"Quite a few are getting pissed off that they spent so much time and money on training and qualifying shows. We've had to create excuses for not showing at the last minute. Plus, some of the horses were sold with the promise we would show them at Scottsdale or the Nationals. Now, we have to make up some bogus story. They're catching on and getting aggravated."

"We need more trainers who aren't wet behind the ears."

"Right," Greg agreed.

"Do you have anyone in mind?"

"I'd really like to snatch up these two brothers from California. Have one here and one in Kentucky. They pretty much know what they're doing and they have good instincts with horses and the public."

"Why would they want to work under you then?"

"I can convince them they have a lot to learn," Greg said arrogantly. "I'll tell them they need to apprentice with us for a couple of years. If they'll fall for it, we won't need to pay them that much. We'll offer them commissions on sales to lure them in."

"Are you talking about those two kids from Santa Ynez? Eric and Adam Stanton?"

"Yeah. Do you know them?"

Ron had suggested them to Nick, but Nick couldn't reveal it to Greg. "They already own their own farm. They wouldn't walk away from that."

"Their mother owns it. I'll get them to walk away. Don't worry about it. They're dying to be in the big time - especially Eric. They want to cut their teeth with me. I let them catch-ride quite a few times, and they let me know they don't plan on working for their mother forever. They handle the sale horses for the auctions, too. It's obvious they don't want to stay at their hole-in-the-wall farm in Santa Ynez. They want the limelight and we can offer it to them."

"What's their mom going to say?"

"Who cares? They're adults. They have their own lives."

Nick shook his head. Greg took the Grand Champion ribbon for cold-heartedness sometimes.

"I'll call them when I get a chance," Greg said.

"Fine. I'll get with you after I talk with your father and with Robard."

Greg ached to insist on being at the meetings. "You don't mind if I join - "

"If I wanted you there I would have told you to be there," he said before Greg could continue.

Nick was set in his ways. Greg had learned when to push and when to hold back.

"Right. You're the mastermind and I'm the iron wall. How could I have forgotten?" Greg said impulsively.

"One year. Fifteen million."

Chapter 14

Alec and Mimi spent the morning speculating about why Greg wanted to meet them at their hotel without his lawyers present. They had mixed feelings about the proposal, but agreed to the meeting regardless. As Mimi had pointed out, it wasn't their responsibility to advise Greg on how to handle his own business affairs.

There was a soft knock at the door.

Mimi unlatched both locks and opened the door without asking who it was, assuming Greg was early. To her surprise, it was Marcie. She walked in as if she owned the room, and sat down at the small breakfast table near the glass doors that led to the patio.

"Please don't tell Greg I talked to you without him," Marcie said.

Mimi and Alec exchanged glances, then looked back at

Marcie without responding.

"He would be furious if he knew I was here," Marcie said. "He's got so much to deal with right now - he's under so much pressure. You have no idea what we're going through because of all of this. I'm hoping that I can get him to be more reasonable with you."

Mimi and Alec simply nodded, wondering what this was leading to.

"Go on," Mimi said.

"I had no idea that Greg thought you would settle for five million dollars. I can't imagine that you have that much money, and I doubt that Greg thinks you do either. I guess he thought he would just scare you or something. I don't know."

Alec spoke up. "No. We don't have five million dollars and don't have a way to get that kind of money."

"I understand. He's just not thinking clearly," Marcie said.

Mimi sensed that Marcie seemed to be looking for sympathy. Why on earth she thought they would be sympathetic to her situation was beyond Mimi. It was better to let her spill her guts if she were that naïve.

"Go on," Mimi said.

"If you would do a favor for me, I'll convince Greg to lighten up and settle for next to nothing - just to be rid of this and go on with our business."

Alec let Mimi do the talking, woman to woman, at least for now. Marcie seemed to have the delusion that she could befriend them.

Out of curiosity, Mimi asked, "What kind of favor?"

"Well, with all of this pressure and problems, Greg and I aren't getting along very well. He's moody and he started ignoring me. I'm worried that he may divorce me," she confided.

"Marcie, we can't help that. I'm sorry," Mimi said as if she cared.

"I know it's not your fault, but maybe I can help you and you can help me. I still have a lot of influence over my husband even if we're not getting along. I'm sure I could convince him to let you off light. But I want something from you first."

She's watched too many poorly written movies, Mimi thought. "What do you have in mind?"

"Pay me money on the side that Greg won't know about. If he kicks me out he'll be ruthless. I know him. It will be a nasty divorce and he'll fight to keep every penny for himself. I'll need money for a good lawyer and money to live on. Believe me, I don't want a divorce - I love him, but he's so emotional sometimes I don't know what he'll do. I need to protect myself."

Mimi and Alec looked at each other, both knowing they wouldn't commit to anything without talking with each other alone first.

Mimi said, "How much did you have in mind?"

"For me, or for a settlement that I'll get Greg to agree to?"

"Both."

"How about a million each?" Marcie said, as if it were Monopoly money.

Mimi didn't hesitate to answer. "No. I think you need to leave now. We're not interested."

"But that's less than the five million!"

"Yes, it is. But it's still way out of line and we don't have the means to pay two million. If Alec loses his license to practice, so be it. I'm a lawyer too, and I can practice with Alec in the background. We'll be just fine," Mimi said.

Marcie wasn't a businessperson. She didn't know how to handle herself, but she didn't know it. She had always lived vicariously through Greg and enjoyed being the kept wife.

"Make me an offer. Tell me what you can give me that Greg won't know about. And tell me what you'll give in a settlement. Lets get this done and over with."

"First off, I'm sorry to be the one to tell you this, but Greg should be here any minute. He wanted to meet us without you, too," Mimi told her.

Marcie's eyes widened, her heart wounded. Before she had a chance to gather her thoughts, there was a knock on the door.

Mimi opened the door to the patio. "You should go out right now if you don't want Greg to know you were here. We won't tell him."

Marcie was speechless. She picked up her purse and slipped out the patio door.

Alec let Greg into the room.

"Thanks for meeting privately with me," Greg said.

"Sure. Where's Marcie?" Mimi asked.

"Getting a manicure."

"Have a seat," Alec said, gesturing toward a chair with the utmost civility.

Mimi and Alec sat next to each other on the loveseat.

Greg cleared his throat and crossed his leg. "I'd like to get our situation resolved. I have a lot to deal with and I want to get past this."

The leather and metal caught Mimi's eye. Unable to divert her attention from Greg's ankle, a lump formed in her throat.

Alec smiled, looking eye to eye with Greg as if they weren't in a conflict. A courtroom skill. "What do you have in mind?"

"This is confidential?" Greg asked.

Alec nodded. "Sure. If you want it to be."

"I'll drop the whole settlement demand if you'll do a favor for me," Greg said, unsure of how to word his request.

Mimi's eyes were still plastered on Greg's ankle. Didn't her husband see the gun? He was carrying on a conversation while Mimi's heart pounded.

Alec nodded again. "What do you have in mind?"

"Do you know how to set up a system where I can hide money? You know, build a nest egg on the side, in case I ever need it?" he said, worried about how it sounded.

Greg and Marcie sure make a pair, Mimi thought.

"Like a secret bank account?" Alec asked.

"I don't know. I guess."

Alec thought for a moment. "How aggressive would you anticipate someone would be if they wanted to try to find hidden money?"

"I have no idea. Right now, no one would be looking for the money. I'm planning for the future. For a worst case scenario in the future," Greg confided.

"How far in the future?" Alec asked.

"I don't know. It's just that when the whole problem with you and this bogus lawsuit came up, it made me realize that I need to have a way to hide some money so that I'll have something to fall back on if I ever need it."

"I understand," Alec said.

Mimi didn't like the idea of helping Greg, but how else could Alec respond? The man came to their room, made sure his gun was visible, and asked for a favor. She hated the threat. But, if Alec went along and Greg was a man of his word, which may not be likely, it would keep Alec's career and their financial status as is.

"How much do you think you would contribute to the account annually?" Alec said.

"I have no idea. I don't have anything to speak of to put in right now. Maybe twenty, thirty thousand to open it up," Greg said as if it were pocket change.

Alec thought for a moment before he spoke. "What if we open a business account rather than a personal account? That way, you could funnel money to that business. I think it would be the easiest and safest way to hide money and assets in a way you would have easy access to it."

"Yeah. That's a good idea," Greg said. "Do you know how to accomplish it?"

"Not in a way to keep things hidden. But I can find out. I've got a couple of lawyer friends in Ohio I would feel comfortable asking for advice. I know they have clients they help that way. Give me a week or two."

"Fine. As I said, I'm just thinking about the future," Greg confided.

Mimi couldn't resist. "You want Marcie to have access to the money also, don't you?"

"No. I don't. No one is to have access except for me," Greg answered without contemplation.

Alec thought there may be a snag. "What about Dolan and Jessica? They're expecting us to enter into a settlement agreement."

"I'll tell them I've decided not to pursue anything against you because even though you've caused so many problems, you've actually taught us a lesson - and that was priceless. They'll go for that. I'll play out the whole scene acting as if I'm remorseful. Don't worry about it. I'm sure they don't want to deal with our legal problems anymore."

Mimi and Alec nodded in unison.

"I'll call you when I know anything concrete about how to proceed," Alec said.

"So we're settled up then?" Greg said.

Mimi's legal mind was set in motion. She ignored how threatened she felt by his gun. "If Alec wants to do this, it's fine with me, but I'm warning you. If you ever try to come after us about this, or anything else, I'll leak everything Alec knows about how you do business to the press. I swear, I'll leak everything - and including giving your deposed clients' names and contact information."

She must not know about the article in *The Phoenix Sun*, Greg thought. "I'm not going to pursue anything against Alec."

"Good. I hope we can trust each other on that. And

thank you," Mimi said to Greg.

"For what?"

"For not going for the jugular," Mimi said honestly, forgetting for the moment about the gun.

"I'm not as bad as you thought?" Greg asked.

She didn't respond as she recalled the gun. Alec ignored the question and escorted Greg back to the lobby.

When Alec returned to their room, he found Mimi crying and visibly shaken. "What's wrong?"

"I can't believe you're so calm," she muttered.

"Calm? I'm ecstatic! This is going to be swept under the rug and we'll go about our lives. What more could we hope for under the circumstances?" he said, a huge smile spread across his face.

"What about the gun?"

Alec became worried. "A gun?"

"Yes. I think he was threatening you - like the Mafia does - they ask for a 'favor' nicely, but they're threatening to kill you at the same time," Mimi said, still shaken.

He wondered why her medication wasn't working. "He didn't have a gun. Perhaps we should call your doctor."

"I'm not imagining it. He had an ankle holster with a gun. I saw it when he crossed his leg. You didn't see it?"

Alec's expression showed that he didn't believe her.

"I swear Alec. He had a gun."

Tears rolled down Marcie's cheeks as she walked toward the poolside café. A man followed her without her knowledge. He kept his distance - she was obviously distressed.

Marcie found a table away from the other hotel guests. She ordered a glass of wine and a hamburger with fries. She couldn't bare to go home and face Greg, or be around anyone she knew for that matter.

The stranger casually strolled in her direction and sat down leaving an empty table between them. Intrigued, he couldn't resist staring. She looked sad and lost. Just perfect, he thought.

When she had finished her meal, Marcie glanced at the familiar looking stranger. He winked. She blushed but didn't look away. In an instant, the waiter appeared at her left side and asked her if she would like anything else. Before she could respond, the stranger hovered at her right side.

"How about another glass of wine?" the stranger

suggested.

Marcie recognized his voice, but couldn't place it. "Sure. That sounds like a good idea if you'll have one with me," she said.

He sat down as if they were old friends. "Great. Bring us a bottle of Chardonnay."

Marcie couldn't believe she was doing this, but she felt so vulnerable she didn't stop herself.

"I know you from somewhere," she said.

His gut wrenched inside. A long successful career and hardly anyone ever remembered who he was anymore.

"Can't place it?" he asked.

"No. But I know your voice."

"Picture me in a hat and a bomber jacket," he suggested.

"You're Bob Crane. I'm sorry. I'm just so upset right now that I'm not as sharp as I usually am," she said.

"I thought you looked upset. I saw you exit the back door of that hotel room," he confessed.

She felt uneasy and flattered at the same time. Had he been following her?

"You saw me?"

"I was walking down the path when you stepped out the door so quickly. You caught my attention the way you lingered then snuck away."

"I guess that would look strange," she admitted, looking down at her empty wine glass.

"I'm kind of a Peeping Tom myself," he said as he gave a sly wink.

"Peeping Tom?"

"Well, maybe that's not the best way to put it, but I do get curious and watch people - watch what they're doing - their mannerisms, you know. I guess it comes from acting school. It's how actors learn to get in character."

"So, you probably listen to private conversations, too?" she pried.

"When I can. I'm just curious about other people. What they have to say. What they think about. I'm studying life. It's hard to explain."

She smiled for the first time all day. "Actually, I understand. I watch people and listen to them, too. We have a set-up in the lounge at our farm where clients think they have privacy. But really, we have a two-way mirror behind the bar so we can watch them - and it's wired so we can hear them.

Usually I'm the one behind the mirror and my husband will excuse himself to his office or out to the barn while the clients are left alone. They have no idea what's going on."

"Why do you want to listen to your clients?"

"My husband sells expensive horses and stallion syndications. He concocts a bunch of different kinds of investments in the horses. So, I listen, hoping to hear people talk privately about what horses they really really want. If they're really in love with a particular horse, he can get them to pay more. Or, sometimes I hear them talk about their finances, how much they have to spend, or whatever. I don't know. Plus, sometimes they talk about what a jerk my husband is and I can let him know what they really think of him. But, mostly, it's to try to find out how my husband can get the most he can out of them."

Bob raised his brows in amazement. This woman was sure talking freely to a complete stranger. "How do you know they'll talk in the office?"

"We don't. But it's likely. It's not expensive to do. What costs the most is paying the guy that bugs their hotel rooms and listens in."

"What?" Bob said, amused.

"Sometimes when we have somebody really really rich that's looking at horses to buy, we pay this local guy to bug their room and report back to us what they're saying about buying horses or anything that might concern us. It's kind of expensive, but it pays off," she said with no remorse.

"Man, I never thought about people doing anything like that."

"Well, it goes on in investment companies all the time," she said.

He wondered whether or not to believe her. Perhaps she was just trying to impress him by sounding exciting and mysterious. He decided to change the subject.

"May I ask why you were crying? You looked quite upset."

"I'd rather not talk about it. I'm having some marriage problems."

The server delivered the bottle of wine. He filled her glass, which she guzzled down in record time.

"You might feel better if you talk about it," he said as he refilled her glass.

"It's private. I don't even know you. It's just that my

husband is going through business difficulties, so now he's shutting me out."

"You're in the horse business?"

"Yes. I said that, didn't I?"

Marcie tasted a sip of wine and didn't set the glass down, as if she were preparing to drink it as quickly as possible.

"Yes. You did say that. Why won't he talk to you? You seem like you're very easy to talk to."

"I think I'm easy to talk to. But, really, this is private. I don't want to spill my guts to a stranger."

"I understand," he said. "Sometimes it helps to talk to someone who you won't ever see again though."

"I'm not comfortable. It's just that he doesn't even want to make love anymore. He's so preoccupied. I really shouldn't say anything. I'm sorry." She closed her eyes and took a deep breath, as if cleansing her mind. Then, another long sip of wine.

Bob took her hand in his. She didn't resist. "You know that means your marriage is over, don't you? If he won't make love to you, he's probably got someone on the side. You can't trust him. Believe me. I'm a man. I know how men operate."

"I can't believe Greg would be with another woman. In fact, I know he wouldn't."

"I hope you're right," he said, not wanting to crush her.

"I'm sure I'm right. I just don't know what to think when he has meetings with people behind my back, like today."

"Why don't we go back to my room? We can talk about it there, in private," he suggested.

"I'm married. I can't do that."

"He's getting ready to leave you. Or kick you out."

"Do you think so?"

"I'm not trying to be cruel, but face it."

Alec and Mimi entered the restaurant from the lobby. At their request the host led them outside to have lunch near the pool and waterfall. The Douglas' spotted Marcie, crying and drinking wine, with Bob Crane's arm wrapped around her. A few minutes later, they saw Crane sign the guest check and then he walked away with Marcie. Mimi resisted the impulse to follow and see if Marcie went to Crane's room.

Chapter 15

"Shit. I can't believe this."

"What?" DeAnn asked.

"It's on the front page but below the fold. He promised it would be on top," Matt fumed.

Last night a courier delivered a draft of the proposed newspaper article for Matt's approval. He approved every word of the splashy exposition which read like a glorified ad about how wonderful the Arabian horse industry is, and, in essence, retractions to the previous front page article about them.

"What's the lead article?" DeAnn asked.

"That actor Bob Crane was found dead in his hotel room at The Pointe," he said, as if the news wasn't shocking.

"Murdered?"

"They don't know. I can't believe this. He assured me the article would be the headline."

"Someone famous died for unknown reasons in Scottsdale. What else could he do? He had to make it the lead story. Your story is still on the front. Everything will be fine."

Matt threw the paper on the floor and took his coffee out to the barn without saying another word.

DeAnn grabbed the paper. The article reported that Crane's body was discovered at eight o'clock the previous evening when the maid entered the room to turn down his bed. The police interviewed hotel guests. Currently there were no real leads. A number of people who were interviewed by the police and the newspaper reported seeing a crying woman leave his hotel room late in the afternoon. No description of the woman was available.

~~~

Alec and Mimi checked out of the The Pointe immediately after Greg left their room. They ate lunch in the hotel restaurant where they saw Marcie with Bob Crane. Shortly after, they drove the rental car to the Grand Canyon to spend a few quiet days in Arizona before returning to St. Louis. They agreed to make this time together a second honeymoon and celebration that their problems were over. It was time for a new beginning with a bright future. Mimi said she was feeling well, her medication was working, and an appointment was scheduled with a marriage counselor.

Alec turned on the car radio hoping to hear a weather forecast. Several songs played before the news aired. Stunned, they listened to the story about Bob Crane's death and the speculation about whether it was a murder or a suicide. One reporter speculated that Crane may have accidentally killed himself in an attempt to get attention from the public. Another reporter said that Crane had been to several local bars and talked to strangers about his failed acting career and how he couldn't get an acting job once Hogan's Hero's went off the air. People who called the radio station to talk about their encounters with Mr. Crane all said that he seemed depressed and talked about how miserable his life had become. Still, the medical examiner hadn't determined if he was murdered or if it were a suicide.

"What time did we see Marcie with him?" Alec asked.

"I don't know. I didn't pay attention."

"Maybe we should contact the police," he suggested.

"Marcie couldn't kill someone. I know I don't know her, but I can't imagine she could kill someone. It's just a coincidence. Let's stay out of it."

"You're right," he said, not completely sure he was in agreement with his wife about if Marcie was capable of murdering a man in cold blood. After all, Mimi had tried to kill him.
~~~

Chapter 16

Nick changed the subject. "To be honest - I was surprised Robard was actually able to pull off getting the newspaper to print another article. I'm pretty confident it will diffuse most of the damage done. Especially since the reporter was fired," Nick said.

"I loved the opening of this new article," Ron said.

Nick grinned. "It is memorable. I have to admit it." He picked up the paper and read aloud: *"A man is more than the worst thing he's ever done. Greg Bordeaux, the ringleader of the Arabian horse industry in Scottsdale, has one purpose and one purpose only - to make his clients' money trading in the most spectacular horses in the world. The Bordeauxs are always looking to the future. It's their approach to life, which is only natural for breeders of elite, rare and collectable horses."*

Ron couldn't be more pleased with the article. "Hopefully the word will spread about this article as quickly as it did about the first one. We can't just assume that everyone will see the good press. Greg might be the guy on top, but you know he has rivals and most of them don't know their place in the food chain of this business. They see him as being flush with cash and spending lavishly on himself while he takes clients to the cleaners."

"That's another reason to go public with my involvement in the business," Nick said.

"I agree," Ron said. "But it's going to be a tough call how to announce it - what to disclose. Do you make it seem like you just bought your interest or do you disclose that you've been involved for as long as you have?"

Nick tented his fingers on his desk. "I'm not sure. I've thought about it quite a bit after Desmond and Nale said there was no way they would buy from a glorified trainer. When I told them that I'm his partner, and that I'm actually the one in control, they did a one-eighty."

"Because you're a developer and the horses are what you do as a hobby?"

"Sure. That's a legitimate reason for them to feel secure. To them, I'm credible. A kid who grew up with horses and was funded by his family isn't."

"Right," Ron agreed, drawing out the word as he was still absorbing Nick's point of view.

"If I act like I just got in, it will make it look as if I'm bailing him out. If I disclose how long I've been in, then it will look like he was too arrogant to let anyone else know that he needed funding and outside business expertise."

"Do you want my personal opinion?" Ron asked prepared to give it regardless of Nick's answer.

"Of course. That's why I have you."

"I think we need to meet with Thomas again now that he knows about your involvement and what's really at stake here. I'm not sure he really digested the situation when you told him about bailing Greg out. Thomas is a man with a lot of pride and dignity. I doubt if it ever entered his mind that Greg had been spending beyond his own means. He wasn't raised that way."

Nick chuckled. "He may not have been raised to overspend, but he was obviously raised with a silver spoon in his mouth."

Ron grinned. "That, I don't deny. The point is - Thomas deserves to be part of what you decide to do with regard to disclosure. Especially because he's agreed to be more active and visible again."

"It's my money and my line of credit."

"We both know that's not completely true, but that's neither here nor there," Ron said in a subdued voice.

Nick ignored the comment. "I don't need Thomas telling me what to do."

"I'm not saying you should let Thomas dictate to you. I'm saying that he's had some time to digest the shocking news, including the reason he was manipulated into giving Greg his power of attorney. Give him the courtesy of allowing his input.

This is his life, his sons, and his horses."

"No. I'm not going to let him influence me. This is too critical. I'm a father myself – I know he'll - "

Ron became more assertive. "His input could help you make the right decision for what's in your best interest."

"No. I'm not discussing this with anyone else."

Ron stood, trying not to have an aggressive posture. "You're being close minded and it's only going to harm you. Every time you act so controlling about everything it gets you into trouble."

"Don't bring up the Thoroughbred business again. I'm tired of hearing about it."

"When you act like this, you needto be reminded."

Nick furrowed his brows. "What's with you?"

"My gut says that Thomas should be in on important issues. How you announce your financial interest and control is critical to the potential success or failure of the entire operation."

Nick gave the idea time to sink in. "Which way do you think I should do it?"

Ron didn't hesitate. "I think you should tell the truth about when you got involved. Make it clear that you continue to support the Bordeauxs – that you're looking forward to a future brighter than ever. Otherwise, someone will find out the reality, including the tax problems - and think you and Greg were deceptive. This isn't something that should be shrouded with mystery. You know how rumors can start to swirl and end up out of control."

"What if people start asking why no one knew before?"

"Tell them you didn't want to distract from the talents of the Bordeaux family. For you, it was strictly a love of the horses and an investment. That's really why you did this. We both know it."

Nick shook his head. "I don't agree. People will think Greg betrayed their trust, leading them to believe he accomplished everything on his own."

"He and Thomas did accomplish everything on their own – more or less. All you did was put up money. No different than a bank. No one says a bank contributes to anyone's business success."

"I've guided Greg in directions he never would have dreamed of. You know I'm more than just a money man," Nick said, annoyed.

"Ultimately, Greg decided what to act on. That's really the issue. Not whose idea or input or who funded it. He carried out the ideas that made the most sense to him. He came up with his own ideas, too."

"You have a role in the success of Vintage - and what about Larry and Mike? You've all contributed significantly."

Ron sat down again. "I know. But Thomas and Greg found them, and now they mentor and support them. Thomas and Greg pretty much give me free rein, not out of laziness, but because they know they can trust my judgment and integrity."

"Still," Nick said. "I don't want to let people know how long I've been a partner. It will show more confidence if we portray it as if I decided to become his partner in spite of the Trading Paper article and all of the fallout. That's how confident I am. Yeah - that's a wiser approach. That's what I'm doing."

"I don't agree," Ron said assertively. "Why don't you wait a few days to ponder this? A few minutes ago you said you didn't know what you wanted to do. This sounds like an impulsive decision that I think you'll regret."

Nick rolled a cigar between his fingers. "No. I need to go with my gut. I'm saying I just put up my money in spite of everything going on right now. It'll sound good."

"It will sound how it sounds. The truth is the truth - but like everything else, the truth is going to require good lighting if it's going to look attractive."

"The only untruth that I'm going to tell is the timing of when I got involved. Either way, we weren't going to discuss the tax problems. That will show weakness. Either way, when we tell about my partnership, it will be to show I believe in Greg and his ability to create a lucrative business."

Ron gritted his teeth as he controlled himself. "If you do it the wrong way people will know you're bailing him out. They can't think that. Or know that."

"You're overreacting."

"This is the horse business," Ron reminded him. "Anytime anyone screws up, it's an opportunity for someone else to stand on the corpse and look taller. Remember the kind of people we're dealing with in this industry."

"You're really overreacting."

"Why do you even bother asking me?" Ron asked in a tactful manner.

"Only a fool wants to hear the echo of his own voice."

~~~

Years ago, when Nick was young and cagey, through opportunism, he subtly finessed his way into a prominent Thoroughbred farm in Lexington, Kentucky.

Using gamesmanship, the first thing he did was make sweeping changes in the staff and the direction in which the farm had successfully been operating. He launched into a flurry of high-stakes purchases, including buying interests in top ranking racehorse studs.

His goal was to muscle his way into the Kentucky horse world. He had always wished he were a Kentucky blue blood rather than an immigrant who arrived in the U.S. with only the clothes on his back.

Nick spent the farm's money and burned up its line of credit. Then, to generate operating capital, he lured in dozens of people who knew nothing about horse racing. He warned them that the stakes were high and emphasized that so were the odds. That was enough for his conscience. His buying sprees emptied the pockets of millionaires who dreamed of glory on the track.

While trying to buy respect with top Thoroughbred breeders by bringing them buyers, he made a healthy commission from every sale. The farms took his clients' money and compensated Nick financially, but they didn't respect him any more than they would a common man off the street.

Never one to drink a mint julep, Nick was rough around the edges, but couldn't admit it to himself. He made catering to the moneyed elite his primary goal in life. He thought that if he made millions, he would be accepted. His millions turned out to be pennies to the fabled aristocracy of the Lexington high society. Nick never had enough money of his own, but he didn't let that be an obstacle. When he took control of the Thoroughbred farm, he wanted acceptance so badly he could taste it. He always found a way to get more money. He thought that he'd eventually breed another Seattle Slew and reap the rewards, but before he could, the well went dry.

Nick fled to Ocala vowing never to set foot in Lexington again. He couldn't bear the humiliation of encountering anyone who ran in the circles he once tried to fit into. He iquidated his Thoroughbred operation and replaced them with Arabians - they didn't race at the same time on the same tracks, and the owners in the different breeds rarely mingled together.
~~~

Chapter 17

Matt and DeAnn invited Thomas and Fiona to dinner at The Arizona Biltmore. They apologized for not seeing them socially for quite some time. The Bordeauxs were glad for the invitation - they had debated whether or not to suggest that they meet privately.

"By the way," Matt said, "Cal stayed at the house after the consortium meeting. He wants out of the consortium and wants to buy the property he's leasing from me."

Thomas sighed. "I didn't know all that much of what was going on with the consortium before the newspaper article. From what I've seen, Cal hasn't really participated in the group anyway."

"No, he hasn't. He doesn't have the balls - " Matt began.

DeAnn interrupted him. "Don't talk like that. You're just upset because he has values. He cares about the horses more than the money, just like it used to be back when the horses were simply for fun. If you ask me, you old coot, you could learn a lesson from him."

They all laughed, then she added, "His father taught you everything you know about horseflesh. Let Cal teach you about being ethical."

"Bull," Matt told her. "Anyway, the real issue isn't so much that Cal didn't participate in bidding up horses or claiming higher prices than he really gets - the real issue is that he knows what we've done. He's been in the inner sanctum."

Thomas and Fiona were uncomfortable with how lightly Matt took the situation, but they didn't want to make waves if they didn't have to.

"Well Matt, old boy - if I were you, I wouldn't sell him your property. I'd give him the grant deed to the land he's on and hope he keeps his mouth shut - imply an unwritten understanding. Call it a wedding present," Thomas suggested.

"I'm not giving him twenty acres of land on Bell Road. Do you know what that's going to be worth?"

"Hell, Matt, what's the difference? You own so much land around here. You've known Cal since he sucked his thumb - we all have. He's an honest, hard working guy just like his father. Give him the land, you cheap son-of-a-bitch," Thomas told him seriously.

Fiona chimed in. "We all know that we bought this land for next to nothing. Especially you two. You were here before us. I don't even want to know how much money you made from selling us our tracts."

"They're right, Matt. Give it to Cal. We don't need more money or to pay the taxes on the sale of the land," DeAnn said.

"If word gets out that I gave Cal the land, then that asshole Peacock is going to try to manipulate me into giving him the land he's on."

"No, he won't. Peacock's conniving, but he wouldn't be that bold - plus, even though he's small time compared to us, he's been an active player in your consortium. He's got nothing to hold over you that he's not guilty of himself. He's just not dealing with as much money as you," DeAnn said.

Matt quickly grew tired of the razzing. "Okay. So we'll give Cal the land. That's settled," he said as he haphazardly slammed down his drink glass, causing some of it to splash on his shirt cuff.

They nibbled on crab stuffed mushrooms and escargot appetizers while they talked about Caroline and Matt Jr.

Sometimes it was easy to forget they were related through marriage since there weren't any grandchildren, and Caroline and Matt Jr. lost interest in the horses. They kept to themselves and created their own world that rarely included the family.

By the time their steaks were served, they were back to talking business.

"I don't think any of this bad publicity is Greg's fault, but I want to assure you that I'm going to help straighten everything out," Thomas said.

"Like how?" Matt asked.

"I'll cut back on the hours I spend at the weight loss clinics, and I'll become more active in the horse business again. My visibility will put a respectable face on the industry."

Matt was put off that Thomas had insulted him and insinuated that it was his fault the industry wasn't as respectable as it once had been. Surprisingly, for a change, he kept his mouth shut.

"You're active enough. You consult on the breeding decisions and make most of the final decisions about which colts to geld and which ones to keep as stallions," Matt said.

"I mean, more active about business plans and putting on the auctions, and furthermore, to be visible to the public and our clients."

"Furthermore, furthermore..." Matt said under his breath.

Thomas ignored him and went on to explain that Patrick and Liz were getting married and that they were going to become active in the business aspects.

"I can't believe Greg will go along with that," Matt said, now using a serious tone. He had mixed feelings about it, but it wasn't his family to control.

DeAnn squeezed Matt's leg under the table, as if to say 'don't get involved'.

Matt chuckled and slugged down his drink like a drunken longshoreman. "Shit! What did Marcie say about all this? She's a little..."

"Control yourself Matt," DeAnn said through clenched teeth as she kicked him.

Fiona couldn't help but replay in her mind how upset Marcie was when she found out.

Matt spouted off more. "You don't know her the way we do. She acts like the sweet little daughter-in-law around you. She pulls more strings than you know about. That little girl has your son wrapped around her little finger so tight."

Fiona didn't like to admit it, but she knew Matt was right. The man sure did speak his mind. He always had and he always would. She supposed that owning a television station was the perfect investment for him. He liked to make a splash about everything and everyone.

The cocktail waitress replaced Matt's drink. She knew the kind of service he expected. The Robards were regulars, and old Mr. R was a generous tipper.

"That perky skinny little girl is with your son for one reason and one reason only. His horses, his property, and his money. Oh yeah - and - she loves to be looked up to as 'Greg Bordeaux's wife," Matt continued, not caring who heard him. When he thought about it he laughed aloud until tears came to his eyes.

That's four reasons, you idiot, Fiona thought.

Thomas cleared his throat, stood, and looked at DeAnn who was turning beet red. "Get him under control by the time I'm back from the restroom."

DeAnn mouthed the word sorry to him and meant it.

The waitress cleared their steak platters as Fiona followed her husband. Neither of them used the restroom. Instead, they talked about how out of line Matt was and that his drinking problem seemed worse than before.

"Now I remember why we stopped entertaining them," Fiona told Thomas.

"I didn't forget. DeAnn has her hands full. I don't know why she puts up with him."

"Surely not for the money. She could buy and sell him ten times over," Fiona said.

"She's just a proud woman trying to live with her mistake, I suppose. We ought to get back to the table," Thomas said. Then, he saw that DeAnn had her hands full still. "Actually, let's wait a minute."

At the dinner table, Matt began slurring his words and he rambled on to his wife. "That Marcie wouldn't be with Greg if he didn't have prestige and money. You know it and I know it. Thomas and Fiona know it too. You all are mad because I speak my mind, that's all."

DeAnn grew furious. "Stop it right now or we are all leaving without you."

"Go ahead. I don't give a shit," he said.

The waitress started to serve him another drink. DeAnn refused the drink on Matt's behalf, then asked the waitress to bring him a cup of strong black coffee instead. "Hot enough to burn his mouth so that he'll shut up," she added, winking to the waitress.

Matt rolled his eyes but didn't object. There was no point when DeAnn had her mind set.

"I'm going to signal them to return to the table. You start behaving this minute, you old coot. If you don't, you'll be sorry. Believe me. You'll be sorry."

Her last words sobered him up. That tone of voice always got his attention. Unfortunately, she couldn't use it too often - like reprimanding a dog - he's got to know when to take it seriously enough to pay attention.

"Okay. I get it. I'm just saying, that pretty little thing..."

She dug the pointed heel of her shoe into the top of his foot near his ankle where he was sure to feel it.

"I guess you could say you're putting your foot down. I get it. I'll stop talking about the little tramp. I promise." A split second later, his phony toothy grin erupted as if they had been having a stimulating evening of hilarious conversation.

Thomas and Fiona saw the coast was clear when DeAnn signaled them. Her expression looked helpless and apologetic at the same time.

DeAnn eased the tension. "That's wonderful - Patrick and Liz tying the knot. What a nice looking couple."

Matt sipped his coffee and stroked the linen napkin in his lap acting as if he hadn't almost created a scene.

"Hopefully she'll be an asset to us," Fiona said.

"I think she will," Thomas said.

Matt couldn't contain himself. "Another gold digger."

DeAnn was about ready to strangle him. "Stop! Why on earth do you think all women are gold diggers?"

"You are, too," he said to her while staring into his lap.

She straightened her almost perfect posture and exaggerated her speech. "Oh, yes. It's common knowledge that I married you for your money," she said sarcastically.

"I was a diamond broker when you married me," he said with pride as he sat up taller, having realized that he was slouching over the table.

"Who cares?" DeAnn spouted off, just as she always had when he brought it up.

"Just don't you forget that I worked my ass off most of my life. I never took a dime from you, Miss Speer," Matt said, drawing out her maiden name. He always loved that she took the Robard name when they married. He didn't want to be thought of as a gigolo.

"You're right about never taking a dime. Regardless, I'm worth more than you. Always have been. Always will be. But I can tell the truth - it's my family's money - they earned it. Not me. At least I know it and I can tell the truth," DeAnn said, putting him in his place.

"You pretty little thing. You know you married me because you knew I was going to make it big..." he said as if he were still drinking.

"Get over yourself. The world is not about you," Thomas finally chimed in, hoping to break the tension between Matt and DeAnn.

"Noooo - tonight the world is about your family and all the problems Greg caused just because he's too damn stupid to play his cards close to the vest," Matt said.

Fiona stood up. "Come on Thomas. We're going home. DeAnn, would you like us to take you home?"

DeAnn stood up. "Actually, I'll follow you in our car. He can use our suite tonight. Let him sleep it off."

They still had a suite from when DeAnn's father owned the resort.

All three left before Matt knew what hit him. Not phased, he signaled the cocktail waitress over and told her to keep the drinks coming. He patted her on her tight little rear end and slipped her a hundred bucks from his engraved gold money clip.

Outside, as they waited for the valet, DeAnn profusely apologized.

"I can't believe you have to live with that man," Fiona said.

"I don't know why I do. He's getting worse all the time."

"Do you want to stay with us tonight?"

"No. He doesn't lose his temper anymore. Too old and slow now, I suppose."

They all thought back to the times when DeAnn and the kids would come to their house for protection. No one wanted to continue the conversation about it if she weren't in danger any longer.

"Well, how about coming over for some coffee?" Fiona offered. "I can't imagine you want to go straight home."

DeAnn looked worn. "Can we get together another time? He's just drained me for tonight. Not just what he actually says, but what I'm worried he's going to say," she confided.

"Sure. You take care of yourself and call us if you need help," Fiona said out of an old habit from years ago.

The valet pulled up in the Robard's Rolls Royce. As always, DeAnn seemed ashamed of the outlandish luxury that Matt had insisted upon. Still, she had to get home. Once in the driver's seat, she adjusted it all the way forward and sat up as tall as she could in order to see over the steering wheel.

Thomas and Fiona slid into their Mercedes and let out sighs of relief before either of them spoke. It was exhausting being with Matt - they had forgotten how difficult he could be sometimes. Years ago, DeAnn and the kids being together with the horses is what made their social scene pleasurable.

The Bordeauxs drove without speaking for a few minutes and then Fiona said, "If Patrick and Liz are going to be dealing in the business aspects, maybe we should let Ron go."

"No. We're not letting Ron go. I don't mind if you want him to be here more, or want him to account for his time when he's not here, but that's as far as I'll give on this issue," he said.

Fiona shook her head. "I don't understand why you don't think that with you, Patrick and Liz getting involved, it won't be enough. That's three of you to one of Ron."

"Ron's a business manager. We need him," Thomas said.

"He's a glorified farm manager who sells horses, too," Fiona said.

Thomas controlled his agitation. "He may have started out as the farm manager, but he's legitimately our business manager now. Just because we have corporate advisors and Nick's involvement, it doesn't mean Ron's not in an important position. The work he does is crucial. We couldn't operate without him."

"I don't really understand everything he does, I guess," she conceded.

"Plus, who brought us some of our biggest clients? Ron did."

Fiona made a face. "A few big clients, and sometimes I wonder about their money," she said.

"What do you mean?"

"You don't think it's odd that some of our biggest clients are in the 'concrete' business?" she said.

"Road construction and bridge building is profitable. They're all very nice people. And according to Greg, they don't question much of anything that he does. They're ideal clients."

"What about the ones that are in heavy construction, commercial building, all those rough and tumble trades? It makes me a little uncomfortable," she said.

Thomas laughed at her. "First of all, Ron was brilliant to target market them. They make a lot of money, and they don't act or talk as if they're the most astute business people in the history of the world. They're all down to earth with money to blow on horses."

"Why can't we have more doctors or other white collar professional clients? I'd feel better about that," she said.

"Ron says, everyone selling investments hits up the doctors and white collar people. There's too much competition, and overall they like more conservative investments."

"He doesn't even know much about horses," Fiona reminded him.

"I know. But business sense is business sense, and knowing how to cultivate investors is an art that can be applied to anything with a profit motive and tax advantages," he replied.

"I don't know. Surely..."

"You're just trying to come up with reasons to criticize him and it's not very clever. Besides, you ought to get to know some of the clients and judge them for who they are instead of thinking you know what someone will be like based on their profession."

She smiled. "Green is green, I guess. Who am I to say?"

"That's how you need to look at it. Green is green and good credit is good credit."

"Sure," she conceded.

"Speaking of credit, if it weren't for Ron, we wouldn't have Citibank or Majestic Savings in Ohio buying our notes. Our cash flow is radically improved from the arrangements he made."

"Keep Ron. I won't say another word."

Chapter 18

Morgan and Sonia finally made it to Santa Ynez. Sonia fell in love with Ambiguous the moment he strutted across his pasture when Morgan called out his name.

"Ambiguous has every quality a breeder looks for - perfect legs, correct conformation, flaring nostrils, refined ears pointing forward, a high set muscular arched neck, and a vibrant proud demeanor at every gait," Morgan told Sonia as she climbed over the white four-rail fencing to be in the pasture with her pride and joy.

With each animated step, the stallion's muscles rippled and his veins pulsated as if he had a testosterone overload. He was dynamic and flashy, yet had kind eyes that showed he loved people.

It was obvious Morgan and Ambiguous shared a bond. Sonia saw Ambiguous had his left eye glued on Morgan's every move - he nickered at her the entire time he pranced around, eagerly obeying her subtle body signals and quiet voice commands. To Sonia's surprise, Morgan asked Ambiguous to canter in a circle around her and then called for him to halt by pointing to the ground a foot in front of her. The stallion did as asked. Morgan sat down in the grass and Ambiguous nuzzled her hair as gently as a kitten.

"He's fabulous. I definitely want to breed to him. Of all the stallions I've seen, he's the first one I've been smitten by like this," Sonia said.

"I thought you'd feel that way. Between his phenotype, genotype, and personality, he's a dream horse."

"What's phenotype mean?"

"The way he's put together - his conformation, structure, musculature, the entire physical picture. Genotype is his genetics - his bloodlines."

"I knew genotype but I hadn't heard of phenotype before. Anyway, yes, I definitely want to breed the twenty mares you recommended."

Morgan imagined what it would feel like when the check cleared - two hundred grand in stud fees from one client would be a first for her. Now that she owned her own stallion, all of the money from the stud fees was her profit. Until now, she had only sold individual breedings for ten thousand each, which was great, but a twenty breeding package would be a dream come true. Morgan had only paid $85,000 for Ambiguous, and bought him on four-year terms. Doing business with Sonia Finn, especially selling her twenty breedings, would surely catapult Morgan into the higher echelon of players. She wouldn't be considered big time yet, but it would give her a leg up and added credibility. As an agent or broker she had sold expensive horses to clients, earning a twenty percent commission, but this was a completely new arena, having her own stallion, and next year, her own foals to sell. As of today, life was turning around for Morgan and she basked in the glory of it all.

"Can you mail me individual breeding contracts for each of the mares on the list?" Sonia asked.

"No problem."

"If some of the pregnant mares that came with breedings for next season foal babies I don't like, I'll consider them for Ambiguous also," Sonia said, referring to the three-in-one packages that Greg had sold them.

Morgan hid a huge grin. "I would appreciate that. I think we'll enjoy doing business together."

"Me, too."

The women had a late lunch in Santa Barbara and stopped at Jedlicka's. It was one of Morgan's favorite tack stores, because the owner, Si, was so nice and made his customers feel appreciated. The closest tack store in El Toro, near her own home in Laguna Beach, was owned and managed by a guy who was rude and nasty to her.

Morgan drove Sonia back to her home in Beverly Hills. Sonia invited Morgan in for a cappuccino and tiramisu.

After small talk, Morgan asked, "Can I get a deposit today?"

"No," Sonia said regretfully. "It will have to go through my husband and our business offices. I'm sure George will want to look over the contract."

"I understand. If I have the contracts to you by the end of the week, when do you think I can get them signed and get the deposit?"

Sonia began to feel pressured, but she didn't say so. "As soon as possible. George travels a lot, and I don't know his schedule."

"My breeding contract is a standard contract. Don't you have the authority to sign - "

Sonia cut her off. "I said I would breed. Please, just relax."

Morgan could taste the money. The twenty percent deposit alone would be forty grand and she didn't want to take a chance of Sonia changing her mind on a whim. Hopefully, if she pays the deposit, Sonia wouldn't be willing to walk away from the obligation. Suing someone just wasn't done, regardless of a contractual commitment. If someone didn't want to breed to your stallion they shouldn't have to. It was one of the unwritten rules in the horse business.

"How about if we simply hand write a quick letter of intent now?" Morgan suggested.

Sonia felt Morgan was about ready to cross a threshold, but she liked her regardless. In addition to the time they spent at the Adventure Arabians open house and at a few lunches in between, they had spent four hours driving back and forth to Santa Ynez and had gotten to know each other quite well. Sonia had confided in Morgan about her personal life because she was so easy to talk to and was quite compassionate.

"If you don't trust my word, maybe we should just remain friends and not enter into a business relationship."

Morgan's pulse raced. "No. I'm sorry, I didn't mean to get pushy. We don't need anything until we do it the way you need to do it."

"Fine. Just send me the contracts when they're ready."

~~~

"What did Greg say when you confronted him about Nick telling you everything?" Fiona asked Thomas.

"He said he was out of options," Thomas explained.

Thomas struggled to make a complicated situation easy for Fiona to understand. The accountants told Greg there wasn't enough positive cash flow to keep pumping money into Kentucky.

Fiona sighed. "Greg obviously set his sights on something well beyond what he was capable of. I told you all along that the boy didn't live with reality in his head. He never did, growing up - all his big dreams - thinking he could do so much."

"I wanted the kids to have dreams and goals," he said.

"I still don't understand how it came up that he was pouring money into Kentucky instead of paying the taxes. How could he have done that? All of us would have lost everything. How could he have risked everything just to build another farm?"

Thomas frowned. "I'm disappointed that after everything that's happening, he still wanted to keep it from me. I don't remember how it surfaced. I assumed that he knew Nick told me everything. Apparently Nick had agreed to keep it from us - then had a change of heart."

"Is our boy just outright greedy and selfish?"

"No," Thomas said. "He just has big dreams and it costs money to fulfill them."

"If it weren't selfishness and greed, how else, without a second thought, could he put everyone in jeopardy? It breaks my heart, but I can't think of any other reason he would have done it."

"Like DeAnn said - he just lost his way without realizing it. He tried to expand too quickly and without enough experience or assets to accomplish what he wanted to. The good news is that Nick bailed him out and things are on track. Everything will be fine."

"Except that we don't know our own son," Fiona said.

"We know him as much as any parent knows their adult children. He's got a good heart. He hasn't hurt anyone, and all the clients who have the desire are making money. Just because he had too much pride to confide his growing pains doesn't
~~~

mean he's not a good man with a bright future."

"Matt thinks Greg's in over his head. Don't you think his opinion matters?"

Thomas shook his head. "He had too much to drink as usual. He didn't know what he was saying."

"DeAnn and I talked on the phone for a long time about this. She made me promise not to tell you, but Greg asked to borrow money from Matt to pay the taxes."

"That son-of-a-bitch turned him down? After all of the land we bought from them and all the money they make from the horses because of what Greg and I created? Matt's got a lot of nerve. No wonder DeAnn didn't want me to know. Obviously he didn't either, or he would have said something by now. That lowlife!"

Fiona was nearly in tears. "I'm starting to feel like everyone important to us has been betraying us - Matt, by not even telling us that Greg was in the dire situation; Greg, and everything he's been doing; and Patrick not telling us about how serious he was with Liz until he decided to marry her. Who knows what else people have been keeping from us? I don't know how much more I can take."

"Honey, you're blowing this out of proportion. Successful business people go through struggles and have to resolve unexpected obstacles all of the time. Greg's no different from anyone else successful. It's just that we had no idea what was happening. That's what hurts you. But Fiona, we did give Greg the reins to run the business as if it were his own. He had no fiduciary duty to tell us details. I'm sure he didn't want to disappoint us or worry us when times were shaky. I'm sure the reason he didn't tell us things was because he wanted to protect us from needing to worry, not lack of respect."

"On a conscious level, I know you're right," Fiona said. "Nevertheless, he's hurt me deeply by keeping so much from our and by risking us losing our land and our home over the taxes."

"Perhaps he would have eventually come to us if things had not worked out with Nick or another outsider. He just has too much pride," Thomas said.

"Even if he came to us, we don't have that kind of money. He spent and spent and spent, putting all of us in a vulnerable position."

"We need to get over it. Everything turned out fine. He needs our support now, not our criticism. Please, Fiona, don't make him feel guilty. He's going through enough right now."

"Matt said if he doesn't start operating out of Kentucky by his own doing, the consortium would find ways to make things unpleasant for him here," Fiona said.

"I know he said that, but what on earth could he really do?"

Fiona felt helpless. "I don't know, but when Matt and Leonard get upset they make things happen that no one quite understands. What about the Grays and the Langs? Matt and Leonard didn't want them around, and now they just stay in the background as quiet as can be."

"They can't just make him go," Thomas said as if it were fact.

"If they want to make his life miserable here, they will. I don't like it any more than you do, but Matt's a controlling ass."

"I'll suggest that they go to Kentucky until the dust settles. Greg loves it there."

Fiona concurred. "Nick would rather be able to keep a tight rein on him. It's Marcie who will probably resist the move."

"She'll be fine. She's outgoing when she wants to be. She'll make friends."

"Apparently that's the problem - a loose mouth and little sense of style."

"She dresses just fine. Designer clothes and shoes," Thomas said, recalling how Ron repeatedly said that Marcie is the ultimate symbol of nouveau riche.

"I mean personal style and etiquette. Charm. Other qualities you can't name but you know she doesn't have."

Chapter 19

"You're not going to believe this, but I just saw Mikos and I think he may have seen me," George said, calling from the Cayman Islands.

"No way," Sonia said. She dropped the menu request she was writing for their chef.

"I swear. I saw him in a coffee house with some other man."

"You couldn't have."

"It was him."

"It couldn't have been. It must be his look-alike," she insisted.

George shook his head, still stunned. "I know it was him. I'm absolutely sure. I waited and followed him down the street to a hotel."

"Are you crazy? Why would you risk his seeing you?" she said, her heart racing.

"I had to know if it was really him. I was careful."

"I don't know what to say."

"I'm going to find another hotel at the other end of the island. I can't risk running into him."

"Can't you charter a flight home right now? Just get off the island."

"I still need to get to the bank. I can't leave yet."

Sonia had mixed feelings. "I'm worried. Be careful."

Later that evening, on the opposite side of the island, after checking into a small hotel, George found a remote restaurant to have dinner. His back was to the door and he wore a straw hat.

"Gorges Finnopolis," Mikos said as he moved toward the table.

Instinctively George turned in the direction he heard his given name called from. Of all the people in all the places, he thought. I'm in the Cayman Islands for God's sake.

George slid his chair back. "Mikos. What a small world."

"It is a small world Finnopolis," Mikos said.

George flushed as beads of perspiration formed around his mouth and hairline. Mikos's deep-set dark intense eyes looked just as they had before George fled Greece.

"What brought you here?" Mikos asked.

"Hiding money from the IRS. America is a wonderful country, but our taxes! How about you?" George said, hoping to sound as if he were just kidding and hoping that Mikos would let the past be in the past.

"Can I join you?" Mikos said as he pulled out a chair before hearing an answer. No one said "no" to Mikos.

George motioned the cocktail waitress.

"What'll you have?" the waitress asked.

"Something strong."

In a flirtatious way the waitress said, "Should I surprise you?"

"No. I'm surprised enough tonight. Bring me a tall Tanqueray and tonic."

The waitress smiled and headed for the bar.

"Let's cut to the chase, Gorges."

Shaken by his short conversation with Mikos, George chartered a flight home the next day after he did his banking.

Before he had a chance to unpack or call his office, Sonia reminded him that she needed him to sign twenty contracts for breeding to Ambiguous.

"How many times do I have to tell you? I don't want you to breed to a stallion I haven't even seen," he said.

"I've put off Morgan so long that she probably thinks I'm stringing her along."

"That's her problem. I've got my own problems," he said.

"Don't act like this."

"I've got too much going on. That's why I didn't want to get involved in a breeding operation. There are too many decisions and there's so much more to learn. With show horses, they've already got a record. I just decide if I want to keep showing them and who will show them."

"I'm learning about pedigrees and breeding. Morgan's

taught me a lot. I don't need you to learn anything. I'll take responsibility," Sonia said.

"Who is Morgan Butler anyway? All you've said is that she's a broker and owns Ambiguous."

"She's a nice woman. I've become close friends with her and I don't want to screw her around. Just sign the contracts and give me a check or go see Ambiguous. I know you'll be as impressed with him as I am."

"Don't start with me. I've got enough on my mind," he said, and then backhanded her across the face.

Sonia bolted out of the room crying. His horseshoe shaped gold and diamond ring cut her cheek, making it bleed. She could feel the swelling already. Her face barely had time to heal from their argument the previous week. At least the bruising on her back didn't show. It was impossible to hide it when he hit her in the face.

George answered the ringing phone as if nothing happened.

"George?"

"Yeah," he said gruffly.

"Hey, George. How the hell are you?" Greg said.

"I'm fine. How about yourself?" he said in a friendly tone when he realized it was Greg Bordeaux.

"I'm okay. I've been meaning to call you for a while. Are you going to be home for the next week or so?" Greg asked.

"Most likely. I never know with my schedule. Why?"

"I'd like to talk to you about a business proposition. Can I fly out next week?"

"You still have the jet?"

"Two of 'em," Greg said.

"Sure. Just call first and make sure nothing's changed."

"Great. I'll let you know when I'll be there."

George cleared his throat and ignored Sonia returning to the room with a bag of frozen peas pressed against her cheek.

Sonia tried to gain her composure. "We've got to go to counseling. I'm not going to take this anymore."

"I'm not going to a shrink."

"It doesn't have to be a shrink. Just someone who specializes in this sort of thing."

"All you need to do is learn not to push me. Is that too hard to get through your thick head?"

Sonia looked at him, afraid to answer.

"I'm asking you a question. Why can't you learn your

place? I give you everything. I ask very little of you, and then you go and push me until there's nothing I can do but slap you. Still - you don't learn."

"They aren't slaps and you know it. You hit me and throw me around. And even if it were simply a slap, a real man does not treat a woman like that."

"You better learn to appreciate me and learn to stop pushing me or you'll see what abuse is."

"I'm not going to take this anymore. I swear George - I don't care about your money. I just want you to treat me the way a woman deserves to be treated."

"For someone who claims not to care about money, you sure spend it like it's water. Jewelry, clothes, cars, the country club, spa treatments, servants, a chef. I could go on and on. You had nothing before you married me. Now look at you. And you push to spend two hundred G's on stud services because you made friends with some woman whose horse you like."

"I'd rather be broke again. Broke and never hit by you or any other man."

"You may just get your way if you keep mouthing off at me."

"We need help. Please, let's get help. For the kids sake."

"You need help. Not me."

"Bastard."

That was the last straw. He shoved her against the marble countertop, then punched her in the stomach. She doubled over in pain and then vomited on his shoes. He slid off his shoes and kicked them at her.

"That's the last time you'll touch me. I swear. The last time."

The last time she had said those exact words, she yelled them to Mikos's younger brother, Milam. The next night, George slit Milam's throat. Hours later, George and Sonia were on a plane heading for California and the alter. George hadn't returned to Greece, even for his father's funeral.

He walked out of the room as if they had only had a minor argument. It infuriated her even more.

~~~

The Vintage jet landed at the Van Nuys Airport where Greg rented a Cadillac Seville. Twenty minutes later he pulled into the driveway at the Finn residence in Beverly Hills.
~~~

As Greg walked through the entry door he took in the expansive open floor plan - his eyes widened in amazement. He had never seen a house like this, let alone a multi-million dollar home. The children's crayon drawings and finger painting projects were Scotch-taped directly onto the canvas of original oil paintings. Dolls and toys were scattered everywhere. Magazines and books were haphazardly piled on sofas and on the Steinway grand piano. Paper plates with cookies and candy dotted the coffee table and the end tables. Loud music echoed in the background from the children's rooms where giggling and shrill screeching escaped the closed eight-foot doors.

Greg couldn't believe how the Finn's lived. The clutter the two live-in housekeepers had to clean around was incredible. They were like trailer trash living on the hillside in a gorgeous home filled with elegant furniture and collectable artwork. Their gentleman's farm, only a half hour away, was neater than their home.

Because of interruptions from the kids, it took a couple of hours for Greg to explain to George that he needed a new partner or a loan to buy out Nick Cordonelli.

"Sounds interesting. Very interesting," George said.

"One last thing. You would need to sign on the bank notes and establish a line of credit for the businesses in your name."

When Greg showed George the financial documentation he brought, George glanced through the information, then fanned himself with the papers.

"The fifteen million is a possibility, but I don't know if I would want to swing the rest of the obligations. You're talking a lot of money that I'd be at risk for if things didn't work out."

"What's not to work out? This is a great industry. I'm just in a little bit over my head without Nick's participation."

"A little over your head?"

"Yeah."

"My idea of over your head is different than yours," George said smugly.

"Are you saying you won't do it?"

"I can't give you an answer on the spot. I need some time to analyze this. I understand if you think you should pursue someone else - if you haven't already."

"I really don't want other people to know," Greg admitted. "I'd rather give you some time to decide. Can you let me know in a couple of days?"

"A couple of days for this kind of commitment? No way. Even if I didn't have my own business to run, I wouldn't be able to study your proposal and analyze the whole scenario in only a couple of days. If you make big decisions like this so fast, maybe that's why you're in this kind of a predicament."

"It's not a predicament. It's an opportunity for you to latch onto something that's a once in a lifetime opportunity. Most people would be flattered I gave them the opportunity."

"That might be how you see it, but I look at it like you're up shit's creek and you want me to paddle you to safety."

"I'm not up shit's creek just because I need funding. Anyway, let me know as soon as you can. Nick wants to know I'm working things out."

"Fine," George said. "By the way - do you know that stallion Ambiguous?"

"Never heard of him."

George handed him a black linen folder with the Ambiguous logo printed in gold foiling. "Here's pictures of him and this is his pedigree."

Greg glanced at the pictures and scanned the pedigree. "Never seen him. His pedigree is good. Why?"

"Sonia wants to breed twenty mares to him."

"Why don't you breed to our stallions? We've got plenty to choose from, and if we become partners, you won't need to pay for the breedings - we'll make free breedings part of the deal. Forever."

"Sonia likes the idea that Ambiguous isn't far from our farm. The mares could be hauled during their heat cycles to be covered and then return to our farm. She wants the mares where she can see them easily whenever she wants to. And the kids have fallen in love with the horses and being out in all the open space on the farm. We built a playhouse and got them a trampoline out there. They love it."

"I'm glad everyone's enjoying it. But still, you'd only need to ship your mares to Kentucky for a few months. You're already going to be doing that with the mares you bought in the three-in-one packages," Greg reminded him.

"I know. I told her. Still, she said that's even more reason to keep the rest of them close to us."

"I've never seen that stallion, so I really couldn't comment. But regardless of his quality and his pedigree, the foals aren't going to be eligible for the Medallion Stallion program or any of our auctions."

"I was under the impression that if we bought the mares from you, their foals would be eligible for your auctions. I'm sure you told me that. It was the only reason we bought from you."

Greg stumbled on his reply. "You must have misunderstood."

"I didn't misunderstand. Your brochures even state it."

This wasn't the first time Greg had to address this with a client. "If you read the wording, it clearly says that if you buy mares or fillies from us and breed to stallions that we endorse, then your foals will be eligible - and the mares themselves are eligible for resale through our auctions."

"That's not how we understood it. Sounds to me like you want a monopoly on your client's horses," George said, trying to sound diplomatic.

"Not at all. But can you imagine what it would be like if we had a mish mash of bloodlines - "

George wouldn't let him finish. "Ambiguous has the same bloodlines as your stallions. There are a lot of stallions out there you don't endorse who aren't in the Medallion Stallion program and have the same bloodlines as yours. Polish horses are all from the same genetic pool. You don't have a corner on the market, although I can see that's exactly what you're trying to do."

"You're wrong. We simply want to stand by and support our client's programs. To do that, we have to adhere to strict guidelines that encourage our clients to work together - "

Again, George wouldn't let him finish. "In other words - you require your clients work together."

"We don't like to think of it that way, but yes, I'll admit that's what it really boils down to. On the same token - don't you see that's the only way we can operate?"

"Why would it be the only way you can operate?" George said, willing to be open minded in considering Greg's answer.

"When people spend money with us, we have an obligation to support them and keep recycling the money that flows through the business. If we allow outsiders to benefit from our auctions and other marketing programs - and by outsiders I mean people who haven't spent money with us or our clients - then they benefit rather than our own clients being rewarded."

George thought through the explanation. "Okay. I can see that. You've got a perfectly good point. I can see that."

"Good. So you understand how things work."

"Yes. I do. But I don't like that I was misled - "

This time Greg didn't let George continue. "We've never intentionally misled anyone. Sometimes people hear what they want to hear and don't bother reading what's in writing."

"Let's drop it. It's a moot point now."

"I just don't want you to think I took advantage of you. That's all."

"You've convinced me. Let's just drop it. Now that I know the foals wouldn't be eligible for your auctions, I'll keep that in mind. Nevertheless, we don't intend to sell many horses anyway. We still may want to breed to Ambiguous so that Sonia can have her way."

"That's fine, but I don't even know who owns that stallion."

"Somebody named Morgan Butler. The Butler Agency. You've never heard of her?"

"I've heard her name, but she's a nobody. You need to associate with the big players - even if it's not Vintage. You can't just go by the stallion's quality and pedigree - or even how great of a sire he might be. You've got to do business with the right people or you'll lose your ass in this. I thought you understood."

"Don't preach to me," George said. "Tell Sonia. She's the one who wants to breed to him. And now she's become friends with Morgan."

"Is Sonia home? I'm happy to explain how the industry works to her."

"No. She's playing tennis at the country club or something. I don't know when she'll be back. I'll tell her what you said."

Greg wiped lint from his slacks. "She can call me any time. I'll set her straight."

George hesitated before he decided to broach the subject. "By the way, did you ever hear anything more about Johan Murphy?"

"The FBI interviewed all of us and they went through our bank accounts with a fine tooth comb. We told them about Jordan calling and informing us that Johan was dead. I haven't heard anything since. I guess they didn't know he was dead until we told them."

Greg looked out the bay window in the family room. He was amazed that this multi-million dollar home sat on a postage stamp sized lot and overlooked the back of four other houses and the sides of each of the next door neighbors. He wondered why anyone would live like that by choice. George made enough money that he could live anywhere he wanted. Why in such a crowded area? Just to say he lives in Beverly Hills? It didn't make sense.

"I'm going up to Santa Ynez in the morning to check on the operation there. Do you want to come along?" Greg said.

"Maybe. Let me look at my schedule before you go."

"We don't need to take that long. I just want to pop in and remind the staff someone's checking on them."

"You lease that property, right?" George asked.

"Yeah."

"Don't you stand stallions there?"

"None that you'd want to breed to. Those stallions are really entry level. We're just testing them on average mares. Your mares are too good to breed to the stallions at Vintage West," Greg said.

"I appreciate your candor."

"If you come with me, we can swing over to Royalty Arabians and see Ambiguous. That way, when you tell Sonia that she shouldn't breed to him, at least you'll have already seen him," Greg said.

It didn't slip by George that he had never mentioned the stallion was at Royalty, let alone in Santa Ynez. Greg obviously knew more about him than he was leading on.

The next evening George returned home from his trip to Santa Ynez. He informed Sonia that he was seriously considering buying out Cordonelli and told her what it would entail.

"If you want. It's up to you," she said. "What did you think of Ambiguous? I love him."

"He's fine, but we're not going to breed the mares to him. Greg said we would have free breedings to any Vintage owned stallions or stallions they've syndicated if I become his partner. There's no sense in buying breedings to any other stallions if I go through with the deal."

"But this is about the latest we should be breeding for this season. Why can't I just breed to Ambiguous this season? Morgan said the vet can inject the mares with progesterone to make them cycle on a schedule that the stud can handle. We can start shipping them in a few days. I don't want to lose this season," Sonia pleaded, hoping she hadn't pushed him too far again.

"I don't want to hear another word about it."

Tears formed, but Sonia held them back. "How soon will you decide if you're buying out Nick? If you don't do it, then I can breed, right?"

"I said I don't want to hear another word about it. By the way - keep your trap shut about our maybe buying out Cordonelli. Greg doesn't want his situation getting around."

The next morning Sonia called Morgan.

"George went to see him without me?"

"Yes," Sonia said. "He called Royalty and they told him he could come by any time and that they'd be happy to show him."

"They weren't supposed to do that," Morgan said. "I like to present him myself. I'll have to talk with the manager there."

"George said the manager showed your horse, but he also pushed several of their stallions too."

"Seriously?"

"Yes. I thought you'd want to know," Sonia said.

"I do. Thanks. I'll definitely be having a serious discussion. I like to present Ambiguous myself because our relationship impresses people, but the other reason is because it's not uncommon for farms to show or push their own stallions. It's not fair. I spent the time and money to get people there for my benefit, not the farm's benefit. I already pay them almost eight hundred dollars a month for board, and they make money on handling fees. They shouldn't be trying to steal my clients or prospective clients, no matter how subtly they're doing it. That really makes me mad."

"I understand."

Morgan calmed down enough to get back to business. "At least George saw him. Can you get the contracts signed and get a deposit check? I'm happy to come to your house today and finalize this."

"I'm sorry, but George didn't like Ambiguous. He said we can't breed to him."

"He didn't like him? Why?"

"He wouldn't say. He's got a lot on his mind. And Greg was with him, so who knows what his influence was."

"Greg Bordeaux was with him?"

"Yes," Sonia said as she reminded herself not to disclose

that Greg wanted to be partners with George.

"Why?"

"I don't know. He didn't say, and they didn't want me there."

Morgan wasn't about to comment about him not wanting her with him when he saw Ambiguous. "I thought the show horses are for George and you were dealing with the breeding."

"Look, I'm sorry. But there's nothing I can do. George earns the money and the final decisions are his. Believe me, if it was just me, I would have worked with you the first time I saw your horse. I love him. I really do. It's not personal. It's just not in my control."

"Sounds like you have a great marriage..." Morgan said, her thought trailing off.

"Please don't talk like that. I had nothing when I met him. Now I've got everything I've ever dreamed of and more."

"Including being afraid of your own husband."

"I obviously shouldn't have confided in you," Sonia said. "I thought we were friends. Has all of this just been business to you?"

"No. Of course not," Morgan said. "But you shouldn't live in a relationship where you're afraid of your own husband and where in one breath he says the breeding operation is for you and then he won't let you do what you want."

"It's our way. There's nothing else I can say."

"I feel sorry for you. That's all I can say."

"Give me some time," Sonia said. "If I can change his mind..."

"From what you've told me about him, you won't change his mind. He wouldn't let you survive even trying to get him to change."

"Now you're exaggerating. It's not like he's ever put me in the hospital. He just has a short fuse."

"Sounds to me like you married him for the money."

"I love my husband."

"I think you love the money more. You didn't know how he would be when you fell in love, but now you know him and put up with it for the money. It's obvious, Sonia. And it makes me sick."

"How dare you talk to me that way!"

"I'm sorry. It's just that if he weren't around, you could do what you wanted."

~~~

The last words Morgan had spoken resonated with Sonia. She took the kids back to Greece to stay with her family and contemplate the kind of father she had given her children. Was this a life they should be exposed to? The kids were getting old enough to realize that George had been rough with her, and who knew if it would get worse. In one phone call her life could change. She could be free of George if she really wanted to, but how bad did she want it?

~~~

George's business was full of headaches as usual. One of his fabric suppliers had gone out of business, creating a huge problem at his factory in Mexico. Now he needed to locate a similar fabric in the mass quantities he needed that could be delivered in time to have the dying process completed and the blouses sewn. If he couldn't deliver to the Target distribution center on time, he'd lose a multi-million dollar sale, and his contract with the company. A serious virus struck factory workers at the Guatemala sweatshop and more than half of the workers were unable to do their jobs. If that continued, he'd lose his contract with Izod, too.

The garment business was getting tiresome. It seemed the only time he enjoyed himself was when he was with the horses and his kids. If he wanted to, he could simply liquidate his garment business and focus on the horse industry. He loved his horses, and it seemed to relieve the stress if you had enough money.

For three long weeks, George ruminated about the idea of getting out of the garment industry and going into partnership with the Bordeauxs. His business lawyer and his tax advisor had given him their opinions: proceed with caution if you go against our advice.

In the interim, there was no word from his wife, Sonia. George ignored the seven messages from Greg and the two that Morgan had left for Sonia.

Eventually, George called Greg and agreed to meet him at the house the next afternoon. Greg was relieved. Nick had been putting more pressure on him every week.

Shortly after George hung up from making plans with

Greg, the phone rang.

"Is Sonia in?"

"No. She's not. Who's calling?"

"Morgan Butler. Is this Mr. Finn?"

"Yes it is. You can call me George. By the way, I saw your stallion. He's nice. Sonia loves him. I'm sorry it didn't work out for her to arrange breedings."

"I got the impression from Sonia that you didn't like Ambiguous."

"You must have misunderstood my wife. I like him but I don't think we should breed to him."

Morgan's voice cracked. "May I ask why?"

"Sonia's out of the country, so I suppose I can tell you without ruining the surprise for her. I'm buying a stallion from Vintage. A stallion we can breed most of our mares to."

"As a surprise for Sonia?"

"Yes. An anniversary gift."

"Which stallion?"

"I don't know. I haven't talked to Greg about it yet. He's coming to the house tomorrow afternoon. You know him - he'll have a perfect stallion to sell me when he knows I'll write him a check on the spot," George bullshitted, hoping to get Morgan to leave them alone.

~~~

With no regard for small talk, George got to the point. "I'm sorry, Greg, but I'm not going to be able to help you."

"Why did you have me fly out here? I can't believe you strung me along, got me out here, and then just say you can't help."

"I wanted to tell you face to face."

Greg was flabbergasted. "What for? You think that makes you a man? Telling me face to face after you lead me to believe that you'd get the money I needed - "

"I never led you to believe that I would do your deal."

"Yes you did," Greg insisted, knowing it wasn't true.

"I didn't even return your calls. You're irrational."

"I can't believe you're doing this to me. After everything I've done for you."

"Everything you've done for me?" George asked, flabbergasted by Greg's attitude.

"I sold you some of our best horses. Some of the best
~~~

we've ever had. I don't give just everyone the chance to buy the cream of the crop."

"First of all, I paid top dollar for those horses - you didn't do me a favor. I've had consultants tell me that half the horses you sold me weren't worth the money it would cost me to feed and train them for a year - "

Greg wouldn't let him continue. "That's bullshit! Who told you that?"

"That's not the point. The point is, I never questioned you or tried to get out of my contracts on those horses."

"Tell me - who told you that I screwed you? I have a right to know."

"A few people. One's the director of the horse center at Cal Poly Pomona College of Agriculture. He's very well respected," George said, referring to the most important person at the W.K. Kellogg Arabian Horse Center in Southern California. "I certainly think his opinion is of value."

"He's full of shit!" Greg said.

"I trust his opinion. He's got no vested interest in the horses. And, given that he was elected President of the International Arabian Horse Association, he must have the respect of plenty of people."

"He's a past-President," Greg said, as if it mattered. "Anyway, he makes his living from negative evaluations and low appraisals. He's only at Cal Poly for the credentials - they don't pay him much. And he rarely tells people they've got outstanding horses or they've paid fair prices. He wouldn't have a consulting and appraisal business if he did. No one would refer clients to him."

"All I'm saying Greg, is that I gave you the benefit of the doubt."

"I can't believe you even questioned the prices you paid," Greg said incredulously. He acted as if he had never uttered those words in his life. If he were counting, this probably would have been at least the hundredth time the very same words rolled off his tongue.

No one was going to talk to him like that. "I've got every right to have my own horses evaluated," George said in a raised voice. "You've got a lot of nerve trying to make it seem as if I've done something against you. You're a real piece of work, Bordeaux."

Hearing himself called Bordeaux instead of Greg reminded him of Nick. "I'm sorry. You're right. But please, will you please reconsider buying out Nick?"

George didn't hesitate to answer. "No. I can't. I've got my own problems."

"Money problems?"

"No, but things I need to deal with," George said, growing agitated.

Greg remembered Ron telling him that the garment business was full of swindlers that screw people like Finn. George must account for those losses as a normal part of doing business.

"If it's not money problems, why can't you just write me a check? Why can't you just buy out Nick? I'll let you take any horses you want. Just get me the money. That's all I ask."

"I said no and I mean it."

"Why is everyone against me?" Greg asked emotionally.

"I'm not against you. I've got no grudges. I just don't have time to deal with this."

"What kind of time do you need? Just write me a check. We can deal with the paperwork and the banks when you have time. Please, don't make me beg."

"I can't deal with it right now. This just isn't practical."

"How about just making it a loan then?"

"You'd never be able to pay it back. That wouldn't be wise for me to do."

"It's just pocket money to you," Greg said.

"You've got your problems and I've got mine. We all go through ups and downs in business. Sometimes you have to lose everything to appreciate things."

"It's not only Marcie and me that will lose everything - my parents will too - and everyone that works for us will lose their jobs."

"When you play with the big guys, you have to learn how to lose big time. It's part of the fun. Part of the challenge," George said, repeating the words he had heard from competitors.

"What can I say or do to get you to do this?" Greg said, a sick feeling overcoming him. Nick insisted that he couldn't invest in L'Equest unless Greg found someone to buy out his interest in Vintage.

"Nothing," the Greek said. "Nothing at all. Like I said, it's not personal. I've just got my own problems to deal with right now."

"Is it something you'll consider when you have the time?

I need to know that there are some options out there."

"Don't count on it. You really should pursue another avenue."

George trailed behind Greg as he left the house and got into his rental car. When Greg turned on the ignition he didn't speak. What could be said when the world was falling in all around him?

George walked back to the house. As he opened his front door two bullets seared through his back and one lodged in the base of his neck severing his spinal cord. He was dead before he hit the ground.

Chapter 20

Not knowing her way around Beverly Hills, Morgan Butler left her house a half hour early to play it safe. She was unintentionally one of the first to arrive at the funeral service. She didn't plan on being early, but definitely hoped to be there before a large crowd had gathered, so Sonia would be sure to see her.

When Morgan saw the closed casket she was relieved. The few times she had to view a dead body it gave her the creeps and she had nightmares for weeks.

"Morgan. Thank you for coming," Sonia said, giving a hug, although not close enough to wrinkle her gray Channel suit.

Morgan worked at bringing a tear to her eye, but it wouldn't come. "I know we haven't known each other that long, but I wouldn't think of not coming to offer my sympathy and support."

"Thank you. You don't know how much it means to me. Will you sit with me? My mother's health isn't good and she couldn't fly back to be with me when I got the news."

"I'd be happy to," Morgan said, "but what about your friends?"

"I only have three friends from the country club and they're all together at La Costa. They probably don't even know about George."

Morgan raised her brows. "LaCosta, the spa?"

Sonia nodded, not showing any signs that she had been crying. Her eyes were clear and her make-up perfect.

"I'm sure you can call them. They aren't in seclusion and they're less than two hours away. Would you like me to call?"

"I don't want to bother them. They go on a retreat there every few months – girls' time away from their husbands. I don't like the tiny meals and all the exercise. It's not my thing."

More people began wandering in. Employees, a few bankers, and executives from the country club dotted the chapel and were easily identifiable - they stuck out like a sore thumb wearing conservative black clothes. The rest of the attendees at the memorial service could have just as easily been on the guest list for a gala event in the horse business. They ran the gamut: people George bought horses from, trainers, and people who simply knew of the Finns and wanted to be seen with the in-crowd. The implication would be that whoever was there belonged there. George wasn't going to sit up in his coffin and point out the people he had never met and ask them to leave. Sonia wouldn't know who belonged and who didn't, nor did she care.

Morgan knew the majority of the people, at least by recognition, if not knowing them personally. Sonia only recognized a few people in the horse business.

"Please, will you tell me who they are if they start coming toward me?"

"Sure," Morgan said. "I think most everyone will come to console you. Isn't that what people do at funerals?"

"I guess. I've never been a widow. I've only been to my grandfather's funeral. I wish I weren't here."

"I know. You shouldn't be a widow at your age. I feel so bad for you."

Sonia tugged at her Channel jacket. "I simply mean I wish I didn't have to be here. I'd rather stay at home and reflect on everything in the privacy of my own home."

"Sonia, you can cry here. People won't think less of you. You don't need to hold it in until you get home."

"I don't need to cry. I don't want to be here."

"I'm sure you cried all the way from Greece to California. You're cried out. I understand."

"No, you don't understand. Who is this coming toward

me? They look familiar."

"Matt and DeAnn Robard from Scottsdale. George bought a mare from them at their auction last year. You were there. I saw you. I remember it was the first time I had seen you and George in person. Before that night, I had only seen your pictures in magazines."

"I hated those pictures. Every time George won the bid, a camera was there in our face snapping a picture. He loved it. I thought it was ridiculous. Sometimes I think he bought horses just to get his picture in the magazines."

Morgan smiled with slightly closed lips at Sonia's candor.

DeAnn spoke quietly. "Mrs. Finn, we're sorry for your loss. Please let us know if there is anything we can do."

"Thank you for coming. You're very kind."

This went on for almost an hour.

Sonia's eyes lit up and she hadn't a notion to hide it.

"Morgan - look. It's Ryan and Shawna Sanders. I can't believe they've come," she said as if the funeral were a social event.

"Maybe Ryan was already in Santa Barbara. I wouldn't have thought that Shawna would fly in from New York," Morgan agreed.

"I suppose it's not the right time to talk to them about this, but I've always thought that my life would make a fabulous movie - or at the very least, an interesting story on a show like 60 Minutes. Now that my husband has been murdered, my story would be even more fascinating."

Morgan was taken aback. "You're right. It's not the time to talk with either of them about it."

When Sonia realized that the Sanders seated themselves without coming to offer condolences, she did little to hide her aggravation. More people filtered in and paid their respects, very few of whom Sonia personally knew. Morgan continued to tell her who was approaching so that Sonia could attempt to be gracious.

Sonia quickly tired of the charade.

"Should we sit down?" Morgan asked.

"Yes. Let's do," she said as she looked toward the back door. Then, "Wait."

The Bordeaux clan arrived.

"I see."

"Let me talk with them first. Go ahead and sit down

next to our purses. I'll be there in a minute."

Morgan did as Sonia asked, but wished she could have stayed by her side when the Bordeauxs gave their condolences. Hopefully, they would at least see her sitting with Sonia. The mere act of sitting with her at a time like this would be perceived as their being close friends. Maybe that would move Morgan up a rung in the ladder of people who haven't made it to the top yet.

Morgan was using her handheld mirror, checking her lipstick when Greg Bordeaux approached her.

"This works out well for you," he said.

She stood up to look him in the eye. "Pardon?"

"You wanted those twenty breedings for your stallion and now you've got them."

"Excuse me?"

"I was with George when he went to see Ambiguous. I'm sure Sonia told you that George didn't want to breed to him. Now, it's Sonia's decision. Congratulations."

Morgan turned beet red. For once in her life she was speechless.

While Ryan Sanders thought his wife, Shawna, was using the restroom, she had actually slipped out the side door of the chapel to talk to her investigators.

"Jamie," Shawna said, "try to sit directly behind Mrs. Finn if you can. Listen for anything, even if it seems inconsequential right now. Pay attention to her demeanor. If anything she does or doesn't do seems out of place, make a mental note of it."

"I can't believe my first assignment is at a funeral," Jamie said.

Nicole laughed. "I had to dig through a dumpster on my first assignment. Hopefully Shawna won't make you search the casket when the chapel is empty."

Shawna smiled. "Everyone has to start somewhere. I'll let the two of you flip a coin if I decide the casket needs searched."

"Thanks," Jamie said.

"Nicole - mingle as much as you can and see if anyone acts like they actually knew Mr. Finn well. If you find someone, be discreet and try to find out if he had any enemies."

"A man doesn't get murdered at his front door without having enemies," Nicole said. "Hopefully I can figure out who to talk to. I've got a job interview set up for Thursday at his corporate office. I'm sure I'll be able to dig up some dirt there, if I get hired on."

"That's my girl," Shawna said.

Erin approached. "I talked to Richard and he didn't know of any enemies."

"The farm manager?" Jamie clarified.

"Yeah. But when I talked to one of their housekeepers, she said that Mr. Finn was unusually worried when he came back from his last trip to the Cayman Islands," Erin said.

Nicole wanted in on a good source. "Maybe I should try to talk to the housekeepers, too. It couldn't hurt."

"That's fine. Just don't be obvious that you're on the job," Shawna reminded her.

Nicole rolled her eyes, then caught herself. "I'm sorry. I didn't mean to be disrespectful. I'll be nonchalant."

"Erin, try to sit where you can hear the Bordeauxs if you can. With Greg being the last known person to see George alive, you never know what he might say," Shawna said hopefully.

"Do you think he's stupid enough to say anything that could be construed the wrong way or that would incriminate himself?" Jamie asked Shawna.

"Probably not. But he's so arrogant, who knows?" Shawna said.

Nicole and Shawna already spoke extensively about the history of the Bordeauxs in the horse business and Shawna's short time spent with him. "I wouldn't put it past him to say anything."

The women were blindsided by Ryan. "I can't believe you're here with investigators," he said to Shawna.

"Ryan, please. This is legitimate news."

Nicole, Erin and Jamie took the cue to give the couple privacy.

"I should have known you didn't come just to be supportive of me."

"You barely knew the man."

"Still," Ryan said. "I thought you were here to make an appearance as my wife, just as I'm here to make an appearance as a fellow equestrian."

"I'm here for both."

"Right," he said, disappearing as quickly as he came.

Shawna followed her husband. She spoke in a hushed voice. "I'm sorry, but this is news, and it might make a good story. My staff is investigating his business and what the garment industry is like. It's known to have its share of dirty dealings. Trish has already come up with a lot of interesting information about the illegal things that go on. And she found out he banks in the Cayman Islands."

"Fine. I'm just disappointed that you didn't even bother to mention it to me. You could have at least given me the courtesy of letting me know your agenda."

Ron used the pay phone at the Beverly Hills Police Department. "Be glad you're not here. You're not going to believe this."

"What?" Nick said.

"After the funeral services, police detectives were waiting outside the chapel. They asked a few people to go to the station for an interview - including Greg," Ron said.

"Greg?" Nick said as he dropped his glass of ice water.

"Yeah."

A lump formed in his throat. "He's not a suspect, is he?"

"I don't know. Apparently the detectives asked Greg, another man we don't know, and Morgan Butler to meet them at the station. From what I understand, the police told the widow that based upon tracing the phone records, these people may have been the last to talk with George. They won't tell Thomas anything except that they needed to question a few parties."

"Who's Morgan Butler?"

"Some small-time broker. I guess she knows the Finns. She lives an hour or so away from them, from what I heard. During the service she was like honey on a jar next to Sonia. Greg pointed her out to me and reminded me who she is."

Nick was stunned. "Do they think one of them murdered Finn?"

"I would imagine it would be the only reason they would be questioned since there were no witnesses," Ron said. "You heard the news reports with me. Has there been anything new in the media?"

"I haven't paid attention. I'm dealing with lots of business issues."

Ron nodded. "I understand."

"Why on earth would they think Greg would have killed him?" Nick asked.

"We found out that he was killed right after Greg left his house."

"Greg was at his house that day? I thought he was there

a few weeks before."

"He was there the day of the murder, too. He met with him thinking they were going to be able to strike a deal for Finn to buy you out," Ron explained.

"I didn't know he went back. I thought he was just buying time when he said Finn was seriously considering it."

Ron was concerned about other things. "Thomas and Fiona are a major wreck right now. I wish I could do something more than assure them that there's no way that Greg murdered anyone."

The blood rushed from Nick's face. "Greg doesn't have that stupid gun on him, does he?"

"I don't know. I didn't even think about it," Ron said. He had told Greg to dispose of it where no one would find it, because it wasn't registered.

"I told him to stop carrying that gun everywhere. I hope he left it at home. Do you think I should call Marcie and ask her?"

"No. Don't get her all worried. We haven't called her. Greg can tell her about the nightmare himself when everything's over with," Ron said.

"But what if he's got the gun on him? It's a concealed weapon. I don't even know if it's legal to carry it in California. Do you think they'll search him?"

"I have no idea, but I doubt it. He doesn't have an attorney with him. I don't know how these things work."

Nick paced the office. "Shit. What if Greg's got the gun on him, and it's the same kind of gun that was used to kill Finn?"

"You know Greg didn't kill anyone. Even if he's got the gun, they'll be able to tell that it wasn't fired and the ballistics doesn't match."

Nick relaxed. "That's true. I suppose it would actually be a good thing if he's got the gun on him and he can prove that it wasn't fired - assuming that it's not a problem he's carrying a concealed weapon."

"Right," Ron said. "What I'm worried about is any possible bad press. I hope his being taken in for questioning doesn't make the news. They won't tell the story accurately and it could hurt us worse that the Trading Paper article."

Ron returned to the waiting area. Fiona was alone crying, unable to remain calm.

"Where's Thomas?"

"A detective wanted to ask him a few questions," she said,

gesturing to a glassed in office.

Even from a distance they could see Thomas looking nervous and his face turning pale.

"What could the cop be asking him?" Fiona said.

Ron didn't know if Fiona was aware of Greg having a habit of carrying a gun. "I have no idea. I wouldn't worry about it."

Before they had a chance to continue, another detective asked Ron to step into an office.

"I'm Detective Harman. I just have a few questions for you."

"Sure. I don't know anything though," Ron said.

Harman looked at his fingernails then, said, "Do you know if Mr. Bordeaux owns a hand gun?"

The blood rushed to Ron's cheeks. "A gun?"

"Yes. A gun. Do you know if Mr. Bordeaux owns a gun?"

Ron stumbled on his words. "Which Mr. Bordeaux are you referring to?"

"I was referring to Greg, but you've got a point. Do you know if either Greg or Thomas Bordeaux own a gun?"

"Greg does. I don't know about Thomas."

"What kind of gun does Greg own?"

Ron shrugged.

"Please answer the question."

"I have no idea."

"You've never seen it?"

"I've seen it, but I don't know what kind it is. I don't know anything about guns."

"Did you see Greg handling the gun?"

"I've seen him slip it in and out of a ankle holster dozens of times. Seen him put it in his desk drawer. Seen him put it in his glove compartment. Other places too, I suppose. I've never really thought about it."

Harman nodded. "You see your employer handle a gun on a regular basis and you've never thought about it?"

"Never given it a second thought," he said too eagerly.

"You are both businessmen, correct?"

"Yes. We're involved in the horse industry."

"Can you think of a reason why your employer would need a gun for his profession?"

"No."

"Any personal problems that may lead him to feel safer if he's carrying a gun?"

"Not that I know of."

"Do you care to speculate about why your employer would carry a gun?"

"No. I wouldn't. May I ask a question?"

Harmon smiled and leaned back into his chair for the first time during the questioning. His nod was his answer.

Ron leaned forward and spoke in a low tone. "Is Greg a suspect in Mr. Finn's murder?"

"Should he be?"

Greg, Thomas, Ron and Fiona didn't speak while they were in the police station, but the moment they got into the car they began talking all at once.

Greg's voice was the loudest. "I can't believe these people are questioning me."

Thomas raised his voice over the others. "Did you have a gun on you?" he asked Greg.

"No."

"Good. Detective Kasten asked me if you own a gun. I told them that I was not aware of it if you did. I was a nervous wreck that you might have it with you," Thomas said.

Fiona began crying again. She didn't know her son owned a gun and she couldn't imagine why he would - let alone why he would ever carry it.

"Detective Harman asked me the same thing," Ron said.

Thomas and Greg spoke at once, saying the same thing - "What did you say?"

"I told the truth," Ron said.

"Big deal. I don't have the gun anymore anyway," Greg said.

Thomas was pleased. "Where's the gun?"

"I threw it away."

"Threw it away?"

"Yeah."

Thomas thought it sounded odd that anyone would simply throw a weapon away. "When?"

"I few weeks ago."

"Son - you're saying you suddenly up and decided to throw a gun away?"

"Sure," Greg said.

Ron sat back, listening to the stressed banter, laughing

inside at Greg.

"Why? Why now?" Thomas said.

"It was stupid to have. I didn't want it anymore."

"You don't just throw away a gun. Anyone could find it and use it or sell it. Are you nuts?" Thomas said.

Greg threw up his hands. "It seemed like a good idea at the time." It was Ron's idea, as Greg recalled.

Skeptical, Fiona finally interjected. "Where did you throw the gun?"

"In the ocean."

"When you were in California?" Thomas said in disbelief.

"No - the ocean in Arizona."

"I'm not kidding around," Thomas said.

"Neither am I. You and Ron always said I shouldn't be packing. Nothing pleases you two sometimes."

Fiona was getting aggravated. "Greg - we're trying to understand you - trying to help you."

"I'm sorry, Mom. I'm under a lot of stress. I've got to find someone to buy out Nick, and now I've got the police questioning me in a murder investigation. Give me some slack, would you?"

"What did you tell the police when they asked you about your gun?" Thomas said.

"I told them I don't have a gun anymore."

"That's it?" Ron said.

"When they asked questions about my relationship with Finn I told them everything. That's what we spent the majority of the time talking about.

"Surely they asked you more about the gun," Ron said.

"I told them if they wanted to talk about the gun I once owned, I wanted a lawyer to represent me."

"Good thinking," Thomas said.

"I don't know about that," Ron said. "I would think an innocent person wouldn't care about having representation."

The men hadn't noticed that Fiona was in the passenger seat, crying. What was happening to their lives?

"That's not the case," Greg said as if he were experienced in this sort of matter.

Thomas felt his blood sugar dropping. The stress on his system was catching up with him. "I need to eat."

Fiona glared at her husband.

"What? I'm starving. We can still talk about this, but I

need to get something in my system."

"Me, too," Greg said.

"Police are questioning you people and all you can think about is food?" Fiona said.

Greg wished his mother hadn't come to California. "It's not all we can think about, but we're starving."

"Fine. Find a restaurant," Fiona said. "But please - don't talk about this where anyone could possibly hear you. This is bad enough without my needing to be worried about being embarrassed in a public place."

Greg was getting annoyed. "Why do you always think people are listening to us? Like they have nothing better to do or think about than listen to anything we say."

"Leave her alone. This is difficult for everyone," Thomas said.

"I'm just saying - she's always so worried that people listen to us. She doesn't even want anyone to overhear her talk about her grocery list. It's ridiculous."

Thomas looked at Greg sharply. "Stop it. Stop it right now."

They pulled into Junior's Deli on Westwood Boulevard. The men got out of the car. Ron opened the door for Fiona. She refused to join them. There was no point in arguing with her.

"Here's the keys if you want the radio," Thomas said.

"Thanks. I'll just crank up the radio and dance on the hood - celebrate my life."

They ignored her comment.

"We'll bring you a sandwich," Thomas said.

"Don't do me any favors."

"Mom - please - this is hard on all of us. Please stop making everything worse. I can't take it. I really can't."

She swung her legs out of the car and stood. Greg was short enough and she was tall enough that they almost met eye to eye.

"You can't take it? You can't take it? You're the one who has caused this living hell for everyone!"

With that, her tears began again.

Greg slammed his own car door and stomped off in a huff. This was bad enough, but in a few hours he'd be telling Nick the latest. That wasn't going to be a pretty scene either.

Chapter 21

Greg retained a criminal attorney after returning to Scottsdale. His lawyer warned him that although no charges were filed, he most certainly was one of several people under investigation for the murder of George Finn. When Greg told the police that he had planned to leave for Kentucky, they told him to stay accessible in the event that they had other questions, as the investigation remained open.

Fortunately, Greg's newest problem didn't make the newspaper or make it into the horse world's rumor mill.

Even with Greg's added complications, surprisingly, Nick granted Greg an extension of time to buy out his interest in Vintage.

It's amazing how much can be accomplished when a team of capable people are determined.

After returning to Kentucky, within sixty days Nick, acquired his interest in L'Equest and arranged for the additional financing through Aetna. He oversaw the expansion for what ultimately became a 7000 acre equestrian development.

Ron permanently left his car dealership in Seattle in order to work full time for Vintage. Other than flying in for quarterly meetings, his efficient staff would take over complete operations of his business. As it was, for the last few years, he was rarely at the dealership, and generally, things ran smoothly.

Patrick and Liz had an impromptu wedding ceremony in Maui. They stayed in Scottsdale to manage the training program and show string.

Greg and Marcie sold their Equestrian Manor home and moved into a client guesthouse at L'Equest, while construction began on Bordeaux Hill Farms. Renovation s began on the hundred-year-old tobacco barn, transforming it into a horse barn. They added amenities, including an indoor arena. The new mansion would be showcased on five hundred acres of prime L'Equest land that bordered the hundred acres Johnny Pallinto purchased.

Johnny started construction at the same time as Greg and Marcie, and they all became close friends. Johnny joined

Greg, Nick and the Vintage sales team at the stallion barn lounge or the conference room for coffee and pastries most mornings. He was warmly regarded and treated like one of the family.

Liz began producing the auctions for the next Scottsdale February sales. She worked with the professional photographers, graphics designers and printers for producing the marketing materials, the ads, and the auction catalogs. She selected the caterers decorators, and limo companies, and hired the private air charter company to fly in the heavy hitters. Too bad everyone that worked under her or around her thought she was a bitch who felt entitled to be treated with respect, just because she was now a Bordeaux. It was "her way or the highway" once she and Patrick were married.

As a direct result of the media blitz that included back covers, inside front covers and spreads in the equine magazines and a lavish display at the U.S. Nationals, Vintage held its own as an icon of the industry.

It was indisputable that Vintage was the best financed operation in the Arabian breed.

Unlike the Thoroughbred industry with people of unimaginable wealth and high society, Vintage filled a niche for moneyed people who had a passion for horses they could enjoy being around and admired for their beauty.

For hundreds of affluent Americans, top-notch Thoroughbred race prospects and proven racehorses were too expensive. According to the scripted sales pitch used by Arabian marketers, Thoroughbred racing was much riskier than owning Arabians. The Quarter Horse market thrived, but many affluent people weren't attracted to the western attire for horse or rider. Hunters, jumpers, dressage horses and Grand Prix horses had their own specific market that even the Bordeauxs didn't fully grasp.

Wealthy people looking for ways to spend their money had a place to do it, thanks to Vintage Arabians and to the glorious 1980's, with its attractive tax benefits for horse ownership. People were induced to pay escalating prices for no rhyme or reason, other than having Greg or Thomas make a recommendation. The Vintage sales team worked with gusto. The Arabian market flourished as if the *Trading Paper* article never existed.

Horse enthusiasts in every breed were buying as if the stream of money would flow forever. Vintage got more than its fair share.

Chapter 22

The following year the Bordeauxs were flying without wings. They effortlessly convinced existing clients and new clients that it was buying time. Buying and selling horses for record prices became an emotional entitlement. Because of a new wave of prosperity, money flowed almost as steadily as water from a faucet.

To prepare clients for the Scottsdale auctions, the sale barns were show rooms that projected the dream. Vintage hosted buyers' seminars packed with people who were eager for the transition from fantasy to reality. Whether at auction or by private sale, everyone who attended the seminars would be buying horses. From behind a pedestal with a microphone, Ron spoke about the Vintage incentive programs. A tax attorney spoke about the deductions and depreciation schedules for the three classifications of equine investments. The attorney also explained the various forms of ownership, including the advantages and disadvantages of limited partnerships, syndications, co-ownerships, trusts, and various other forms of ownership.

The glamorous auctions were more incredible than ever. Liz and Greg were equally passionate about the production details that would ultimately impress their audience. The stage lights had to be a particular shade of red, which wasn't an easy task, but the team insisted on perfection. The wrong shade would make the horses blend into the stage set rather than highlight their beauty. Liz felt strongly about red lighting because it inspired energy and spending. Greg agreed.

Vintage loved what was extravagant and better than normal, and they attracted buyers who loved the same. Women dressed in Christian Dior, Givinchy and Versace evening dresses were part of the verve in the auction productions.

The mares were presented on stage with live music, expressing a sensuality, strutting flirtatiously and provocatively. They were neatly shaven, oiled and sparkling with a hint of glitter. They wore elegant gold halters, as handsome men in silk tuxedos finessed them like runway models for the audience.

Celebrities were seen in the audience and performed as entertainment, but through clever marketing, Vintage made the first few lots of each sale the biggest celebrities. As always, after the auctions, the horses would become Vintage's walking billboards for years to come.

If a buyer wanted to say 'I'm here' - they bought at least one horse for a record price and several other horses for prices that would boost the statistical averages. The extravagant purchases were publicized in magazine editorials, brochures, advertisements and future auction catalogs. Clips from bidding would be highlighted in future marketing videos.

All five lavish auctions achieved spectacular results - seasoned Vintage clients were delighted that their consigned horses sold for record prices. The IRS would be satisfied, too, because the owners claimed they were in the horse business with the intent to make a profit.

The Vintage Sales Company, the auction entity, charged a 20% sales commission on over $35 million of horseflesh. From that, they netted a 10%-12% profit after production expenses.

For Vintage, the real profits came in after the auction,

in both Scottsdale and Kentucky. Unsuccessful bidders and people who weren't able to qualify to get a seat bought farm owned horses by private treaty. So far, they had done $15 million in sales and the month wasn't over. Additionally, as agents for their clients, they sold at least $5 million worth of horses, again, earning a 20% commission.

~~~

It was a spectacular day in Kentucky bluegrass country when Greg pulled out of the car dealership driving his new Mercedes. In that moment, all in the world was right. Nick had given Greg yet another extension of time to buy him out - sales were beyond all expectations. The pressure was still on, but it wasn't as intense. Over the past year, as Nick had demanded, Greg kept Marcie away from the barns and the clients. She seemed to adapt well to the lifestyle of being the wife of a Kentucky gentleman. The detectives in California hadn't contacted Greg for over six months, although the Finn murder hadn't yet been solved.

Greg sounded the horn of the new Mercedes as he pulled into the circular drive of Bordeaux Hill. Marcie motioned him to come inside. Hanging on the wall of the dramatic marble spiral staircase was a life-size oil painting of Marcie with a generous bust-line and cleavage, wearing a low-cut pink satin gown and high heel silver shoes.

Greg's eyes widened. How would he ever invite anyone into their home? In reality, Marcie was so flat-chested she scarcely needed a bra. Even if Marcie resembled the painting, it was atrocious to own, let alone to hang at the focal point of their main entry.

"What do you think?" she asked with a sparkle in her eye.

He shuddered. "I'm speechless."

"In a good way or a bad way?" she asked.

"You know me well enough not to have to ask."

"Good. I'm glad you love it as much as I do."

Marcie and a professional decorator traveled throughout the country acquiring just the right pieces. There was no way the decorator could have approved of the painting, Greg thought.

"I've got to go. Nick and I are meeting the photographer at the Lear. We're doing a photo shoot of me in the new Mercedes parked in front of the jet with Nick holding one of the yearling
~~~

show horses."

The picture would be used in advertising promoting the Kentucky Yearling sales scheduled during the U.S. Nationals in October. Advertising in equine publications, The Robb Report, and investment oriented magazines was slated to start in June.

"Let me get your J.R. hat. That will make the picture perfect," Marcie said, referring to a hat she bought him. She boasted that he had the same power and influence as J.R. Ewing from the television drama Dallas.

"I don't think they'll let me wear a hat."

"Okay," Marcie said. "I'll see you tonight."

"Go ahead and eat dinner without me. We're having a meeting. I have no idea how late we'll be."

"I can bring everyone some fried chicken and the fixings," she offered.

"No, thanks. We hired two chefs."

"What do you mean?"

"We hired chefs to work in the guest house and in the sales office."

"I didn't know," she said, her feelings hurt.

"Sorry. I thought I mentioned it. Anyway, they'll prepare our dinner, so don't bother. Thanks, though."

"Can you call me when you're going to eat? I'll come join you."

"It's a working dinner. You just stay home and relax. I'll try to see you before you fall asleep," he said.

After the photo shoot, before the sales meeting convened, Greg drove around L'Equest. The land development was a separate business entity from Vintage East and the other Vintage locations. Although the sales of horses and breedings were outstanding, the development was not on target with projected costs or sales.

Greg drove around the perimeter of the sales center that cost $6.5 million to build. The original budget had been $2.5 million, but Greg had pushed Nick to approve his flamboyant upgrades, including an enormous bar. They argued about the issue because the development was situated in two different counties. Before Nick bought his interest in the development, Greg decided that for ease of road access and traffic patterns, the sales center would be built where it now stands. What he didn't know was that it was in the dry county where liquor couldn't be sold. Greg pushed and pushed Nick for the upgrades, saying they would make back the overage in a few auctions and that they gave away the liquor anyway. Nick disagreed about spending so much on the sales center knowing they would lose special event and facility rental contracts since they couldn't sell alcohol.

Greg manipulated Nick into signing off on the upgrades by claiming to have a pending deal for almost $5 million with a client planning to get out of the Saddlebred business. In reality, the man existed, but not as a potential buyer. He wanted Greg to join him in breeding Saddlebreds to Arabians and creating a new breed registry and prize money system.

As Greg cruised L'Equest, he was disappointed that there weren't as many 'sold' signs on the parcels as he had hoped by now. He wondered if they had priced the land too high. When Greg confided his concern about it to Johnny Pallinto, he said he thought the property was priced fairly. Of course, Johnny tended to be more liberal with his money,as he didn't earn his own fortune.

Barry Hamsen, a client from Denver, snatched up the original dozen parcels of land that comprised the development. On the company's behalf, he discretely bought the land under different names for an average of $1,000 per acre. Now, it was selling for $8,500 to $15,000 per acre. Certainly, the sophisticated buyers realize the cost of building roads and bringing in utilities was substantial, especially because they had to bring in water lines. Before he bought the land, Greg didn't know they couldn't drill wells into the rocky earth.

Greg trusted Nick about the current value he put on the land, just as Nick trusted Greg about the values he put on the horses. Still, there was always that nagging feeling - for both of them.

By the time Greg drove past Vintage East's $7 million breeding complex, he decided to voice his concerns about the development to Nick.

Nick sat planted at the head of the solid mahogany conference table. He was organizing stacks of reports when Greg walked in an hour early and slid out a chair, making himself comfortable.

"Can I talk to you?"

"Sure," Nick said, preoccupied. "What's on your mind?"

"I know we need to sell property, but I'm having second thoughts about letting the Rye's buy, if they're really going to build the facility their proposal calls for."

The plans called for cheap Colonial styling, barns built of cinderblock, and mesh metal stall doors and panels.

Nick had been thinking the same thing, but the potential income was foremost in his thoughts. The Rye's were prepared to buy 75 acres for $1.2 million.

"It's not the image we had in mind," Nick said wearily as he rifled through the papers.

"It's not fair to clients who built quality facilities with attractive architecture. The Rye's place would downgrade the entire development. And, my father will have a fit."

Nick grimaced. "I know. But we need the money. We're losing our asses right now."

"I understand."

"The problem is - if we approve their design proposal, there's no way we can require new buyers to build to the caliber we want," Nick said.

"I wouldn't want their design anywhere, let alone on the corner parcel they want. I've walked the property and there is no way the buildings can be set back out of view. With the flow of traffic the way the roads are laid out, half of the people who come here will have to drive past that parcel. I think we should tell them their plans don't meet our standards."

"I agree. You tell them and I'll back you up if they call me," Nick said.

"Me? You're the developer – you tell them."

"You're an owner, too. I'm not going to be the one to tell them that their plans are too tacky to use in our slice of heaven. This wouldn't have happened if we had done this project in Ocala, like I had wanted."

Greg ignored the reference to Florida. "How are we going to handle this then?"

Nick shrugged. "Send them a letter. Our contract states that approvals and denials need to be put in writing."

"That won't make it any more comfortable to deal with. They'll be insulte, and they'll want to debate it because our criteria are not detailed in any recorded covenants."

Greg had always thought it was a mistake to have vague guidelines about what constitutes quality, but he knew better than to tell Nick.

"If we lose the land deal are we going to lose any substantial income from horse sales, too?" Nick asked, although the two were separate enterprises.

Greg had already thought about this. "I don't think the

Rye's will buy many more horses from us, but they'll be an asset as a satellite boarding facility."

Vintage East needed more full-service satellite farms offering boarding. Although Vintage owned plenty of land, it was cost prohibitive to build enough barns and pastures to accommodate all of the horses their clients were breeding and raising. Their solution was to convince L'Equest property owners to build facilities large enough to maintain their own horses, and where they could generate income from boarding horses owned by other Vintage clients.

Vintage clients who did not own property in L'Equest wanted a safe place with impeccable care for their mares and foals and a place for the horses to grow up. It was in Vintage's best interest to keep client horses in the immediate area so that when they came to visit their own horses they would hopefully stop in and look at sale horses and stallions to breed to in future breeding seasons. Keep the money flowing.

"I understand," Nick said. "But how do we turn down their plans without insulting them?"

"Maybe I should meet with them and feel them out about how firm they are on the design and play it by ear."

"Try to get them to change their plans so that we don't lose the land sale," Nick said, as if Greg didn't already know.

Nick had other pressing things on his mind that he would be discussing during the sales meeting. "Try to make it work. We're so over budget, the money will help."

A third of the seventy L'Equest parcels were sold or under contract. Unfortunately, most of the owners didn't want to make their facilities available for boarding, even though clients wouldn't be on their property that often. During breeding season, a shuttle horse trailer from Vintage East went to the participating farms and picked up mares to be bred and delivered them back to their homes after the process had been completed. It wasn't much trouble for the farms, but so many of the initial land buyers simply didn't want the hassle of billing their boarders and keeping them informed about their horses' well-being. Besides - the financial incentive that Greg and Nick pushed wasn't a reality. There was no way any L'Equest land owner could generate enough income to pay for the additional labor, barns and pastures - let alone the land at up to $15,000 per acre. Egos played a big role in their refusal to be a boarding facility, also. Even Johnny Pallinto wouldn't do it as a favor to Greg. Consequently, it was important to try to work things out with the Ryes.

Natalee, the receptionist, peeked her head around the door and caught Nick's attention. He waved her in, and she handed him a few message slips, which he read.

"Why does Maggie Stanton keep leaving me messages? Maggie told Natalee you won't return her calls, and that's why she wants to talk to me," Nick said with genuine concern.

"I told Eric to tell her that we're not buying her mares. She's mad as hell," Greg muttered.

"What are you talking about?"

"Don't worry about it. I'll handle it."

"She's calling me. I want to know," Nick said as he glanced at the wall clock to make sure there was time before the meeting.

After the success of the auction season and the profits generated from the private treaty sales, Greg didn't feel like he was skating on thin ice anymore. He decided to tell Nick the unabridged truth for a change.

"Okay. It's a little complicated, though."

"Go on," Nick said, dreading what was about to come. Anytime Greg called something 'complicated' it turned out to be something Nick didn't approve of.

Sales from horses and the auctions were exceptional, but Nick was tiring of Greg's antics and concerned about how often Greg flirted around the edge of laws and ethics.

Greg told the Stanton boys to think of him as Santa. If they believe in him, the profits will happen. Adam wasn't so sure the opportunity to move to Vintage would be a wise move - a lot of trainers thought Greg was a snake oil salesman. Eric wanted the resources they would have at their disposal if they signed on.

"You know that I sold the Stanton's Home Run, right?"

"I still don't understand that one. Why would they want to buy a young stud if they were going to make the move to work for us?"

"I sold them the colt before I offered them the positions. I wanted them to buy Home Run first. I budgeted the money generated from that sale to pay their salaries."

"What did they pay?" Nick asked without telling him it was a cleaver idea. No need to encourage him.

Greg almost said a million dollars for a half interest. "We sold him for $500,000. I got $100,000 down payment and they have four annual payments of $100,000 each, plus 10%

interest. We didn't sell the note."

"Why not?"

"Because when I hired them, I figured that we'll be paying them the same amount we'll be bringing in from their annual payment - basically, the way I look at it, their Mom is paying them each $50,000 a year to work for us instead of her," Greg chuckled. "Plus, we get the interest income!"

Nick didn't think this made sense. "Aren't we on the short end of the stick? You sold a $500,000 colt and - "

Greg cut in abruptly. "Home Run's not worth more than $100,000 max."

Vintage didn't have much money into the colt, because they bred him and owned several syndicate shares of his sire, Lancelot. His dam had already paid herself off ten times over.

"That's what I thought when I saw him as a yearling," Nick agreed.

"Dad and I each had an impossible time trying to get a hundred grand without guaranteeing that we would sell syndicate shares in him - which we weren't willing to do. Then, the Stanton's said they were looking for a two-year-old colt that was good enough for them to show at halter and syndicate. They wanted to make enough money from the stud to at least pay the farm off for their mom. Home Run was perfect."

"Perfect? What do you mean? We just agreed he wasn't worth more than a hundred grand."

"That's their problem. In Santa Ynez, they stand Artistople at stud for his syndicate. They sell plenty of horses and they do pretty well in the show ring. They can't sue me for misrepresenting Home Run's value - they're in the business and know how the market works. They aren't relying on me at all. Plus, they wanted to syndicate him themselves to establish their own leadership. It was perfect."

Nick stared blankly into the distant pasture and wondered if Greg could sleep at night with that much greed running through his veins.

Greg actually sold a half interest in the colt for a million dollars and was getting half of the money, less commission, paid out for the syndicate shares. His secret profits were being socked away into the rainy day bank account that Alec Douglas and Garth Windsor arranged for him. The Stanton brothers knew what Greg was doing on his own behalf, and agreed to participate on the condition that they would be assured that at least two mares in foal to Home Run would go through a Vintage auction each year.

"Now that they work for us, isn't their owning their own stallion and syndicating him a conflict of interest with our operation?" Nick asked.

"What they make, they make. Don't be greedy. I'm not worried about it," Greg said, his eyes looking toward the carpeting.

"I saw their marketing package. It's more impressive than anything we've ever done."

Prospective clients received padded royal blue satin presentation books with the Home Run logo embroidered in gold colored thread on the front. Inside, glossy color photos of Home Run; his sire, Vintage-syndicated Swedish National Champion Lancelot; and his dam, Gwynettla, along with other famous horses in his pedigree. Printed on parchment paper were two pages about the historic significance of his bloodlines, two pages about show ring achievements and sales prices of horses in his pedigree, two pages about the Stanton's dedication and experience in the horse industry, and five pages that covered the financial issues associated with the syndicate shares.

Details were provided about the $250,000 shares that included three breedings per year, payment schedules that were stretched over five years, offering great leverage for tax benefits, a sample schedule of payments and tax deductions, and a ten year spreadsheet showing profit projections. In smaller print, the customary disclosures warning investors no guarantees were being made with the offering.

"The more sizzle the better when a colt's not outstanding," Greg said. He and dad invented the game.

"He won the futurity halter class at Scottsdale. He can't be that mediocre."

"We paid for it. He didn't win it," Greg said as if it were commonplace.

"Is that what you needed the $30,000 cash for? You never did say."

"Yeah."

"I still don't understand why Maggie is calling either of us," Nick said.

Greg rolled his eyes. "I promised Eric that I'd seriously consider buying her herd of mares for $300,000 if they would jump ship with her and come to work for us."

"Why did you do that?"

"They said they couldn't put their mom in a bind by

leaving. She had just bought the mares a couple years before and just finished building their facility. Eric and Adam knew most of their clients would leave, and she would be without enough income - even if she could get another trainer or two to lease her stalls for their own training operations."

"So you said you would buy her mares?"

"Said I'd seriously consider it - apparently they told Maggie that I was doing it for sure. Now she wants to get paid and wants us to come get the mares so she doesn't have to keep supporting them."

"So do it. Buy them and resell them to a client even if we don't make a profit. Just keep your word."

"I don't want the mares. I thought I could pawn them off on the PenDenno's, but they don't want them either. I guess they've learned more about horses than I thought. When I showed them the video they practically laughed at the idea."

"If Maggie needs the money, just buy them."

"No. I didn't sign a contract. I don't want those mares."

"Greg, when you do these kinds of things, it reflects on all of us."

"She's not going to tell anyone. It would make her and her sons look like poor business people. It would be more embarrassing to them than what it's worth."

"Just buy the mares," Nick insisted. "It's the right thing to do. You can't leave that woman in dire straits and take her sons from her."

"She'll be fine. Her ex-husband is rolling in money. He'll make sure she's taken care of. Don't worry about it."

"It's not his responsibility. It's yours. You implied a commitment."

Before they could continue the heated debate, it was time for the scheduled meeting.

Chapter 23

Five men, dressed in starched button down Ralph Lauren Polo shirts, pressed dark blue jeans, and polished soft leather shoes, filed in after Liz who was dressed in a feminine version of the same.

Nick remained at the head of the conference table. Greg perched himself at the opposite end, thinking he was at the helm. Thomas sat to his left. In the middle sat Larry Brown - director of sales, Mike Wolf - a sales associate who worked primarily in Santa Ynez and Scottsdale, and Patrick and Liz, who sat next to each other. Ron melded into the chair next to Thomas and imagined the day when he would control the growing empire – the day that all eyes would be on him rather than Greg and Nick.

Each participant brought notes and reports they personally compiled. Lorraine, Nick's assistant, distributed spiral bound documents prepared by the corporate office in Scottsdale, then sat in the corner at a small table prepared to take notes.

Nick spoke. "Our numbers are outstanding, thanks to everyone's hard work. As you know, we did $35 million in consignment auction sales, and over $15 million in farm-owned horses right after the auction. Thank you."

Larry reported his sales for the past year to have totaled $9.7 million. Only $300,000 less than the previous year, and that was only because a good client was stalling him on a pending transaction. Mike reported his sales to have totaled $3.2 million, his best year to date. Ron reported his sales as $5.3 million. Ron noted that Eric Stanton had recorded only $435,000 in sales. He added that Eric sold twenty shares in Home Run, reminding Nick that Vintage wouldn't see a dime of that money. Happy to have added to his secret bank account, Greg didn't comment.

Finally, Greg referred to a computer generated report. "My sales totaled $9.8 million."

He had to show that he sold more than Larry. Of course, no one in the room knew that, through clever manipulations, he had secretly amassed another $3.5 million for his rainy day account.

Thomas cleared his throat, picked up a typed piece of paper, and acted as if he were actually reading. Everyone knew he had the figures memorized, as they all had. "I sold $890,000 in individual breedings and $4 million in stallion syndicate shares."

"How much did we make in commissions on client owned private treaty horses?" Ron asked.

"Just over a million," Nick said.

"Break out the scotch," Larry said to no one in particular.

Mike poured himself three fingers and passed the bottle to Larry. The bottle made its way around the table, except to Liz who had gotten a diet cola from the fridge.

"Let's get back to business," Thomas said.

No one spoke, knowing that Greg expected to share his thoughts first.

"I want to produce the first U.S. auction for the Polish Government in Scottsdale next year. I'll have the breeding directors from the State Studs select thirty-two horses that I have final approval of. They send them to us for the better part of the year, and let us get them in the kind of condition we present our horses in. We market them like we've never marketed anything before. The sale will make history and make us a bundle. Liz can go all out with the production, the catalog, and the advertising. The Poles won't need a dime. We'll deduct the cost to fly the horses here, and deduct all the expenses for board and conditioning from the proceeds of the sale. How can they say 'no'?"

Thomas knew Greg was going to present his idea at this meeting. "We'll make history with the concept and the prices. We should support the Poles - help them make money after all the money we've made from their horses."

Larry hadn't heard a thing about this until now. He was quick to react. "We're not a charity organization. If you want them to have more money, spend your own and buy their horses for top dollar. Don't risk company profits to help them."

"We won't lose a dime. We'll make money, and we'll cause a stir. Maybe we can even charge for seating at the auction," Greg said.

Larry stood abruptly and planted his knuckles on the table. "You're out of your mind. There's only so much money out there to buy our type of horse. We need to support our own clients. We have hundreds of high quality client-owned horses that don't make it in the auctions. You can't take the money out of our clients' pockets after they've lined ours," he said, trying not to provoke Greg or Thomas. He was surprised that no one else had voiced an opinion yet.

Ron tried to diffuse the escalating tension. "How much do you think we would average for each lot?"

"I think we could reasonably get $450,000 per lot if we play off the idea that this is the first, if not perhaps the only, sale of horses owned by the Polish government in the United States," Thomas said.

"I agree," Greg said.

Nick calculated the total figure - $450,000 times thirty-two. "That's $14.4 million. The 20% commission is almost $3 million bucks."

Larry poured another two fingers of Cutty and gulped it. "You'll be making a huge mistake. Almost $15 million out of the pockets of our clients will be a big blow. We need to circulate the money among our clients. The Poles will never buy from us. Every dime that gets spent on those horses will be lost forever. When we sell our clients' horses, it comes back to someone in the industry in one way or another - very often back to us."

"You're talking in circles," Greg told him.

"I understand what he's saying, and I agree," Ron said.

"Me, too," Nick said.

"You agree with Larry?" Thomas asked Nick, wanting to clarify if he simply understood what Larry was saying, or if he merely concurred.

Nick cracked his knuckles. "I agree with Larry. He's right about the money, and we're in this for the money."

Patrick rarely spoke at the meetings unless it was about training issues. He startled the group when he finally chimed in. "Speaking of ways to make more money - if Greg will just lower his standards for selection, we can make a lot more money in the Medallion Stallion incentive program. I can get at least another fifty stallions in at just the two Medallion level."

Liz had wanted to speak up and say that she too agreed with Larry, but this was only the third meeting she had been invited to attend, and had never responded to anything controversial before.

"Not everything is about money," Thomas said.

"Not everything in life is about money, but this business is all about money, so long as the horses are cared for properly. We spare no expense for their care and treatment, which is an additional reason to make everything as profitable as possible," Nick told Thomas.

"I've never thought of you as a greedy man before," Thomas muttered.

"I'm not greedy. I'm just smart enough to not be so emotional about this business. Numbers are numbers, and it takes a lot of dough to pay for everything we've set out to do – including this development."

"I understand," Greg said. "But the publicity will be phenomenal. It will pay off in future years."

"Pay off how?" Larry wanted to know.

"It just will," Greg said.

No one had bothered asking Mike his opinion about the potential auction, and he didn't offer one.

"Hopefully, there will be more years with these high prices," Nick finally said.

Everyone looked at him as if he were off his rocker.

"My accountant said there are rumblings about a proposed new tax legislation."

The mood around the table turned increasingly serious.

"I haven't heard anything about it. What are they

proposing?" Ron said, raising his eyebrows a little too theatrically. He didn't want it to be known that Nick and he had already discussed the topic.

Nick explained what little he knew about the proposed reform. During the heated discussion about the devastating consequences of a tax reform being adopted, the Cutty bottle was passed around the table at least three times. Everyone felt anxious except Greg. He couldn't imagine any such thing would pass in Congress. Too many politicians and influential wealthy taxpayers owned and leased horses they were writing-off. They wouldn't let a bill like this pass in a million years.

Thomas suggested they adjourn the meeting. No one would be able to focus on anything else until they had time to absorb the possibility of Congress destroying a viable industry.

Nick asked everyone to meet in a couple of days to discuss goals, growth plans and budgets. For now, he was anxious to talk with his advisors and find out more about the proposed new tax laws that could adversely affect their business.

That evening, Ron found Thomas in the stallion barn picking wilting leaves from the foliage in the cast-iron planters surrounding the Koi pond. Thomas felt at peace listening to the horses munch on the remnants of their sweet smelling alfalfa. A trickling fountain echoed in the background. Inhaling the combination of fresh hay, aromatic cedar footing and horsehair helped him think clearly.

"I thought I'd find you here," Ron said.

Thomas' visitor didn't surprise him. They often were on the same wavelength and ended up at the same places by coincidence.

They sat together on one of the slatted wood benches listening to the stirring sounds - water being slurped, a soft greeting whinny, a circling stallion looking for the exact spot he wanted to lay down, another one rubbing his tail against the polished wooden stall door.

"I'm glad you came," Thomas said.

"Everything all right?"

"I suppose."

"Anything you want to discuss?"

Thomas contemplated his answer then said, "In confidence?"

"Of course," Ron said.

"I'm concerned that Greg doesn't want to consider the consequences of the tax reform. And I'm worried about the idea of producing an auction for the Poles. I don't know how to tell Greg that I'm against it."

"You said you supported the idea."

"I loved the concept before I heard Larry's reaction. He's right about our needing to recycle the money amongst our own customers. And now, learning there may be a tax reform...it could destroy this business."

Ron knew the answer to his question before he even asked. "Can't you just tell Greg 'no - we're not doing it'?"

Thomas stood and slid his fingers into his front pockets. In the middle of the atrium, he pivoted around slowly looking at each of the beautiful stalls, then up toward the three-story gazebo roof with skylights.

"Can you believe this stallion complex - this work of art - a hundred and twenty thou a stall?" Thomas said.

"If Greg designed it, I believe it."

"Please don't talk that way. You know I helped him design it, and we deserve a barn like this. We worked hard for it. It's our mark on the horse world."

'A flamboyant waste' Ron thought. "That's a lot of money," he said instead.

Thomas looked away. "It's all relative to what you make. In theory, a few syndicate shares paid for this work of art," he said referring to the stallion complex.

Despite his curiosity, Ron never had bothered to question how much was spent on the solid brass top rails that enclosed the gazebo-style round pen outside. Regardless of the cost, it was incidental to the whole Vintage East property.

"Paying a hundred grand for the bronzes in the entry was a bit much," Ron said.

"You don't understand the importance of first impressions."

"Yes, I do. That's what the intricate stone walkway and elaborate landscaping and urn planters leading up here are for - first impressions."

Thomas sighed, resigned to the fact that Ron didn't relate to the extravagances necessary to enjoy life to the fullest. After a long silence, he slid open a stall door and scratched Wise One on his withers.

"Winds of change are blowing again," Thomas said

intuitively.

"I couldn't agree more. Do you want to talk about it?"

Thomas slid the stall door closed, eased his hands back into the front pockets of his jeans and strolled from stall to stall, looking into each horse's expressive dark eyes as he spoke.

"I may have made a mistake turning the reins over to Greg. He's a brilliant businessman, a mastermind in his own right, but at times I think he just wasn't ready."

Ron nodded in agreement and let Thomas continue.

"My son has a heavy weight on his shoulders even when things are going incredibly well. I shouldn't have burdened him so soon. At the time we talked about my stepping back from operations, we didn't realize the industry could become what it has. If we only knew the pressures..." he trailed off.

Ron had Thomas where he wanted him. "I probably shouldn't tell you this, but Greg's told me more than once that he feels an overwhelming obligation to please you. It's difficult on him."

"When did he tell you this?"

"A few times over the years. Usually when he knows you'll disagree with something he wants to do, or when he and Patrick get into an argument and he doesn't want you to know about it," Ron said.

Thomas nodded and crossed his arms. "We're like every family. We have conflicts that churn beneath the surface."

"I know," Ron said. "And I think Greg feels like the luckiest man in the world - and simultaneously feels like a fly caught in a spider's web."

Greg had never really thought about whether he actually wanted to enter the family business. Thomas simply opened the door for the boys and Greg walked through.

"When ideas like this sale for the Poles surface, I know he doesn't want to be operating under my thumb and feeling as if needs my approval or support, but deep inside, I know he wants it," Thomas said.

Ron took a deep breath. "He has the utmost respect for you. We all do."

The stress intensified - deep wrinkles around Thomas' eyes were accentuated. "Sometimes when we completely disagree on something, I can see that look on his face – that look he had as a boy when he felt the stinging feeling of helplessness."

"Greg doesn't want to cause conflict, but we both know

him – he thinks he's always right, and he's going to do what he damn well pleases," Thomas admitted.

Ron nodded. "Sometimes I think the money he raises by selling horses is a psychological substitute for love. Especially in the last year or two since he and Marcie have grown apart."

"I haven't been around enough to see it," Thomas said regretfully.

"I know you don't want to disappoint him by putting your foot down – plus legally, I guess you really couldn't even if you wanted to."

Thomas felt tortured. "Do I advise Greg not to produce a sale for the Poles, especially given the possible crisis with tax reform swooping in before we know it?"

"It's your call. I think you should tell him your opinion, but that's me."

"I need to give it some thought."

Ron offered more advice. "It's not good to have differing opinions that aren't expressed. It's a recipe for disaster if Greg doesn't know what you think and how strongly you feel about it."

Thomas sat back on the bench and rolled his neck in a circle. "Do you think I should object to his idea?"

"Vigorously."

"We both know he can't accept guidance without taking it as criticism."

Ron shrugged. "So what. You still have to voice your opinion. If you let him keep the reins of the business, but don't tell him what you think, the good life for you and Fiona and everyone else depends on his sole judgment and success. That's not necessarily healthy for him emotionally."

"Are you saying I should take control away from him?" Thomas hadn't considered the idea.

"If you think the survival of the business will depend upon it – yes. Take the control from him."

"Nick owns the controlling interest in the company anyway. Taking power from Greg won't do much good," Thomas said.

"You're forgetting two things. One - Nick is demanding to be bought out, and a time will come when he's out of the picture. Second - although Nick has ultimate control, he doesn't want to fight with Greg. Greg's got Nick wrapped around his little finger most of the time. You need to take control now, before Nick, his money and his credit are of no benefit to us."

Thomas could see that he had a lot to consider when he returned to Scottsdale.

Neither of the men spoke as they wondered about the future.

"By the way, Sashan had a bay filly with a white star," Thomas finally said. Fiona had called from Scottsdale to let him know.

It was great news - they had a contract for the unborn foal. If a colt was born, they would be paid $30,000 if he stood and nursed and checked out by the vet to be healthy. If a filly was born, they would be paid $200,000, assuming she were healthy and didn't have too much white on her legs or face. If a filly or a colt were chestnut color there would be no sale.

"I'll bet she's beautiful," Ron said. "Did Fiona shoot a video?"

"Of course."

Fiona always loved foaling out their mares and imprinting the foals. As much as she loved the financial rewards of a large operation, she missed the days when they handled all of the breeding and foaling so she could bond with the babies.

"Sashan has always been one of her favorite mares. I'm glad she stayed in Scottsdale while you came out for our meetings," Ron said.

"She doesn't like getting too involved in the day to day operations anyway. Besides, she's never missed one baby being born from our original mare band."

The Bordeauxs paid only $750 for Sashan, the Polish import. She produced eleven foals, generating almost a million dollars in income. Fiona didn't care about the money itself. It was the lifestyle she loved.

"What does she think of Greg's idea to have a sale for the Poles?"

"She thinks it's wonderful," Thomas said sadly. "But she hasn't been enlightened by Larry's insight and she doesn't know about the tax reform issue. I don't like to bother her with financial details."

Without Thomas or Ron noticing, Greg walk through the ten-foot door when Ron said, "So, are you going to tell Greg that you don't support his idea?"

"What idea?" Greg said, having only heard Ron's question.

Thomas and Ron were startled. Several of the horses

whinnied and threw their heads in excitement when Greg approached the middle of the barn atrium.

Ron looked toward Thomas, not wanting to be the first to answer.

"We'll talk about it tomorrow. Don't worry, son."

"We can talk now. What don't you support?"

Thomas asked Ron to excuse them for a few minutes. Ron went into the lounge-like video viewing room that stood in the middle of the atrium. The artful structure was a half-circular room constructed of smoked glass with etched horses. Plush upholstered seating for ten offered comfort to clients wanting to luxuriate in all the comforts of home. Alcohol and soft drinks stocked the wet bar, and gourmet food was available when clients visited and during open house presentations.

Ron poured himself a Cutty as he tried to listen through the open door of the lounge.

Thomas looked at one of the stallions rather than at his son when he said, "I'm having second thoughts about the Polish auction idea. I want to sleep on it, and discuss it another time."

"Not to be disrespectful, but it's not your decision," Greg said quietly as if he didn't want to disturb the horses.

Before Thomas could respond, Nick walked in.

"What's up?" Nick asked.

"Just enjoying the horses," Greg said.

Ron stepped out of the lounge with drink in hand when he saw Nick.

"Pour me one of those," Nick told Ron.

Ron automatically poured for Thomas and Greg, too.

"Working late?" Thomas asked Nick.

"More or less. I've been on the phone half the day finding out more about this tax reform shit. I saw your cars when I went to leave. Having a meeting without me?"

"Certainly not. We all gravitated here. It's the best place to be after dark," Thomas said.

Nick looked around taking in the beauty of the structure as if he had never witnessed it before. He knocked down his drink. "I guess we've all been absorbed in our little world. Apparently most of the bigger farms have heard at least some rumblings about the tax reform proposal."

"Seriously?" Ron said.

"Yep. I feel pretty damn stupid if you want to know the truth. Each of my advisors assumed I already knew about it," Nick said.

"So what exactly is this proposal?" Thomas said.

Nick told them how the IRS had caught on to the blatant abuses of deductions and depreciation periods for various investments, including real estate tax shelters and equine investments. The IRS wanted to repeal the tax credits, lengthen the depreciation periods and revise the tax loss deductions for everyone who is not an 'active investor' - which meant the majority of the people buying and selling horses for over a few thousand dollars. The majority of people with the money to buy expensive horses, even those that owned their own farms, probably wouldn't qualify as being 'active' in the operation.

"It's going to kill us if this goes through," Ron said.

Unconcerned, Greg didn't respond. He was sure the reform legislation would never pass. Too much money was circulated in the horse industry between all of the people who were employed, and the trades that fed off the industry.

Thomas spoke. "We ought to prepare for the worst. When do they anticipate this is going to happen?"

"Eighty-six," Nick said.

Ron chimed in. "The minute people know, they'll stop buying. They're looking ahead for write-offs."

Greg shook his head and spoke with ease. "All we have to do is make the business more profitable so the tax incentives aren't their primary motivation to buy or continue breeding."

"How would you propose we do that?" Nick said.

"I don't know," Greg said. "But there's got to be a way."

"Let me know when you figure it out. In the meantime, I think Thomas is right. We need to prepare ourselves for the worst," Nick said.

"We can expand our own programs for prize money and get IAHA off their asses - get them to increase prize money for the shows. If people had a good chance of winning enough money to at least come close to breaking even, I think they would still participate," Greg said.

Thomas almost smiled. "He's right. They do love the horses. They won't lose their interest in the horses themselves just because they can't take the write-offs against their other income."

"We need to start reeducating clients and introduce potential clients with a new motivation - stop promoting the tax aspects." Ron said.

Greg was still calm. "People with expensive boats and vacation homes and memberships in country clubs don't expect to make a profit or any income from what they do for enjoyment. We need to turn them around to think the same way about their horses."

"I've got news for you, Bordeaux - no one is going to pay the prices we're used to seeing once it's not quickly depreciable," Nick said to Greg.

Greg nodded. "I know. But we don't really need to get the kind of prices we do in order to be profitable. We can sell the horses for a quarter of what we get now and still make a profit - if we don't go all out on everything as we have been.

Nick felt a little better, but not much. "If it's not too late. We've spent years pushing the tax advantages."

"Right. But, they do love the horses. Let's not forget that," Thomas said.

Ron poured everyone more Cutty. "Loving the horses is one thing, but who's going to need more than one or two horses if they aren't going to make money from them?"

"And who will buy stallion syndicate shares and expensive breedings if they can't make money?" Thomas added.

Greg was tired of hearing all the negative talk and speculation about something he didn't care to accept the possibility of. "I'm going home. See you in the morning."

Chapter 24

Haunted by the anticipation of tax law changes causing the potential collapse of the industry, Thomas hadn't slept for two nights. He was in no mood to be summoned by Nick the first thing in the morning.

Dreading the meeting that he knew had little chance of bearing good news, for the first time in his adult life, he didn't bother shaving before leaving the house. He went so far as throwing on a faded sweatshirt and wearing the jeans he'd worn the day before.

Nick grimaced when he saw Thomas lumbering up the stone walkway to the administration building. It was the first time he had seen Thomas in a less than polished state. Thomas was normally meticulous about his hair and clothes.

"Morning," Thomas said bluntly, watching closely for a reaction.

Nick frowned. "Something wrong?"

"My world might be falling apart. Other than that, no - everything's just wonderful," Thomas snapped.

"Your world isn't falling apart. Don't overreact about this."

Thomas muttered, "I said 'might be'."

"You need to learn to appreciate the mystery of life. If we always knew how things were going to turn out, life would be boring."

"You don't understand. The farms and these horses are our lives. Our family has dedicated our entire lives to building these businesses. We have nothing to fall back on like you do," Thomas said bewildered, referring to Nick's development business.

Nick looked skeptical. "You have your weight loss clinics."

"That's just a side source of income. I don't like that business - I've never invested my heart or time into it to speak of. At least not like the horse business. Besides, the clinics couldn't even support Fiona and me in the lifestyle we're accustomed to now.

Thomas sighed, then added, "I can't imagine Greg or Patrick wanting to work in my weight loss business. They're horsemen at heart. They live and breathe the horse business."

"They would adjust," Nick said. "Very few people in life get to do what they want to do - especially for a living."

"I don't think my boys could cope with a change at this stage of their lives. I hate to say it, but I really don't see their being able to adjust to another profession," Thomas confided. "Especially Greg."

Nick rolled a cigar between his fingers as he repeated the words he had rehearsed over coffee. "Thomas - between the two of us, we've given Greg a free pass in life. I hate to say this - but we may have ruined him by giving him the freedom to avoid making any true personal commitments."

Deep wrinkles around Thomas' eyes were accentuated from the stress. "That's ridiculous - he's the most committed man I've ever met. And I'm not saying it because he's my son."

"You're wearing blinders. He's never paid his own way. He's never struggled one damn day of his life. You started Vintage, and he walked right in without a worry in the world. You gave him everything he needed, including a viable business, assets, money and credit.

"The first time things went sour, I bailed him out of his IRS problem. The second time things got rough, I bailed him out by buying my interest in L'Equest. I'm not going to drown with him."

For once in his life, Thomas didn't know how to articulate what he was feeling. He restrained himself from throwing a sucker punch, but still, the anger showed in his eyes.

"You know he could have never made it on his own," Nick continued.

Nicks words stung. Exasperated, Thomas said, "You didn't do him - or our business any favors. You took advantage of a situation to profit from our growing pains. You came out quite well from supposedly bailing us out, and you know it."

"You're upset. I understand. But you're not thinking

clearly right now. Between Greg being your son and your seeing the future isn't going to continue bringing prosperity, you're emotional. I understand. On the same token, I wanted you to know before I told Greg."

"Told Greg what?"

"What I just told you. I'm not going to drown with him. I refuse to go down with a sinking ship. I've got a lucrative development company I need to get back to."

Thomas locked eyes with him. "You can't just walk away from this."

"I know. I'm not simply walking away. I've instructed my lawyer to draw up a formal demand for Vintage to buy out my interest in both Vintage Incorporated and in L'Equest. Like I said - I wanted you to know first."

"But..."

"I'm not playing around with more extensions. This is serious now - it's not just Greg pissing me off."

"What about - "

"Stop. There's no more buying time. I'm not making another compromise and granting more extensions. I'm getting out of this whole thing, clean and simple. Cut and dry."

"Does anyone else know about this?"

"Louisa. My accountant. My business lawyer. Ron."

"Ron knows? You told Ron before you told me or Greg?" Thomas lashed out.

"Yes. We've worked closely together for some time now. I depend on him for information," he said proudly.

Nick's disclosure felt like a spike through Thomas' heart. The revelation caught him by surprise. For several moments there was nothing but the rise and fall of his chest. He was almost unable to speak.

"Information? You mean you have him reporting what we do in Scottsdale?"

Nick let him vent.

"Like an informant? You think we're doing things behind your back? This is bullshit!" Thomas said, tasting bile in his throat.

Thomas abruptly stood and turned his back on Nick. He stared out the window, bitter at the way he thought everyone was conspiring against him.

"Calm down," he shot back. "You're blowing this out of proportion."

Thomas pivoted back around and looked down at Nick,

his fury not yet spent. "I don't think so. You've sure had us bamboozled. We thought we could trust you. I thought I could trust Ron. What's all this come to?"

Nick repositioned himself nervously. "You can trust both of us. We're not doing anything behind your back, and Ron's not taking sides - he never has."

"He reports to you behind our back. I would most certainly call that taking sides," Thomas said sharply. He dropped himself into the leather chair and rubbed his throbbing temples, feeling like he might throw up.

"He simply tells me what's happening in Scottsdale and California so that I don't have to bother you or waste Greg's time. I have every right to be kept informed more casually than official sales reports."

"You'll have to say more than that to worm your way out of this, Cordonelli!"

Nick raised his voice and glared at his adversary. "Do I have to remind you that I own controlling interest in this business?"

"I'll be talking to Ron. That's all I've got to say. I can't believe how you've gone behind our backs." And I suppose Ron has too, Thomas thought.

"No one has gone behind anyone's back. We just talk about things. That's all. Don't take this so personally. Don't you ever confide in Ron about anything? You two are obviously close to each other."

Thomas grew defensive. "Well, sure. I confide in him sometimes - and I suppose he confides in me. But that's different. I've known him all of his life. And, we're not being all secretive and keeping things from you."

"So, it's a matter of seniority?" he said trying to lighten the mood.

Thomas chewed his lower lip, and then drew in a deep breath. "No. It's not. But it's different. It's not just business. With you and Ron it's simply all business."

"That's your assumption? That Ron and I couldn't have also become friends?"

The concept lingered in the air before either of them spoke.

"This is getting ridiculous. Fine. So you told Ron before you told me," Thomas said, now wondering if the tension between them was unwarranted.

"And before I told Greg," he reminded him.

"Actually - that, I appreciate. It seems that I'm usually the last to know anything important."

Nick spoke softly and admitted, "I never wanted to keep you in the dark, but Greg always put me in a difficult situation. He would plead with me not to tell you things, and when you were staying more in the background and letting him run things, it just seemed like I should do what Greg wanted. It always bothered me though - if that makes any difference to you."

"I'm sure it was awkward. We've all been in awkward business and personal situations with this being a family enterprise until you came along - and the more that Ron got involved. Fiona says we're almost like our own *Peyton Place*, and she doesn't know a fraction of what goes on, or the dynamics between everyone."

Nick couldn't have agreed more. He nodded. "You and I are the same generation. That's what's been the most difficult. When Greg didn't want you to know things, he made me feel as if should abide by his wishes because you put him in charge."

"What kind of things have you kept from me?"

"I don't suppose there's any point in not being open with you now. I'll be out of here as soon as my lawyer has the paperwork ready."

Thomas had almost forgotten.

"Go ahead. Tell me. What can be any worse than what's happening now?" he said, leaning back into the chair and stuffing his hands into his pockets.

Nick leaned back in his chair and rolled his eyes. There was only a moment to decide how candid to be.

~~~

Thomas, Ron and Nick agreed to give Greg a taste of his own medicine for a change - let him be the last to know. The following Monday, a formal demand would be on the table when the accountant would have the final buyout figures.

When Nick was ready, the Vintage group spent a grueling ten straight hours in the conference room guzzling coffee and nibbling finger food prepared by the Vietnamese chefs.

They plotted the coming year, assuming the tax reform bill would be passed even though Greg ignored the entire concept. Regardless, all four of the Vintage locations would need to generate as much revenue as possible, as would the L'Equest development.
~~~

What began as an exchange of ideas grew into a plan for the business having a new sense of purpose. Although Greg didn't see it, the next year could be the last opportunity to generate a profit from the horse industry. For that reason alone, an expanded strategy took shape - one with a clear mission and focus of what the business would evolve into in order to be saved from doom.

"I don't think we should discuss the tax reform issue with anyone, even if they bring it up," Ron said gravely.

Thomas had his own idea. "If they want to talk about it, we should claim we know insiders in Congress that have assured us the bill will not pass - therefore, we personally are not concerned."

"That's a perfect response," Ron said, determined to make a mint while they could.

Larry was undecided about how to address the issue. Selling high-caliber horses was a unique form of entrepreneurship, but he had always sold horses with the utmost integrity. If clients wanted to wined and dines, to enjoy swanky equestrian facilities and offices, then they surely realized that, as buyers, they would pay the price. Most Vintage clients smelled of money, and were bright enough to recognize the Ponzi sheme as the entertaining charade that it was.

"I have an idea that might generate a lot more sales and instill confidence in buyers," Larry said.

Greg furrowed his brows. "Confidence?"

"Right. You know, eventually everyone is going to talk about the reform. I agree with Thomas. We should act as if we're not concerned. In fact, we'll buy mediocre quality horses from people in order to give them an opportunity to upgrade," Larry started.

"Set up a fund to buy horses we don't even want?" Ron asked. It sounded so absurd he almost started laughing.

"No. Not to actually buy horses we don't want - to get people to upgrade," Larry tried to explain.

"I don't get it," Greg said.

"Here's the idea: we offer to evaluate their horses and breeding programs at no charge to them. We explain that we want to support their efforts, and that while we're traveling around looking for horses to buy for clients, we're also happy to visit them and give our professional opinion - "

Greg interrupted. The goofy sly grin on his face made him look five years younger. "Then, on their turf, we'll say their horses are good, but they would make more money if they allowed us to sell them a horse or two – to upgrade and be able to utilize our expertise and be eligible for our auctions and for the Medallion Stallion program. We hook them in their own backyards instead of trying to get them to come to us."

Ron looked unimpressed. He studied Larry for a moment before deciding to keep an open mind.

Larry elaborated. "We go a step further. We evaluate their horses and tell them we have the perfect horse to fit into their program. A horse to compliment and upgrade what they already own. Then, for example, we price a mare at $100,000. The person would probably say they can't afford it, or they don't have room, or time to take care of another horse. So here's the hook – we tell them we'll take their horse as a trade-in for a $25,000 credit toward the purchase - and that we think we're getting a bargain for $25,000."

"Genius!" Greg said, smiling for the first time in days. "They know they don't have much money in the horse we're saying we value at $25,000 or more – so, if they buy a mare we price at a hundred grand, they think they'll make a killing from her babies. Genius."

Ron grinned. "I thought the car business was slick. This is great. The beauty of it is that on their taxes they'll probably be able to show they made a sale for $25,000. It's beautiful."

Nick studied Greg's face and fought the temptation to speak out.

"So what do we do with the trade-ins?" Thomas asked, admittedly impressed with the idea.

"I know some guys on the East coast who will buy mediocre horses for a couple grand. The horses will go to good homes and end up as nice family pleasure horses," Larry said.

"Fine. That would be fine. I'm sure we can pick up some that I could test the young studs on too, just to see what they can do," Thomas said.

"You'll need to be careful about what mares we're letting them upgrade with. We have to make at least a forty percent profit margin after commissions and relocating the trade-ins," Ron said.

"That goes without saying," Larry agreed.

"We'll prepare a special categorized list that meets our criteria for the circumstances. There are thousands of people out there that will definitely qualify as active owners by the IRS - people with backyard farms following everyone in the big time.

We'll have a good market there," Ron said.

"I agree. What about existing clients that only bought one horse from us or a breeding, and they have a couple other horses at home? They'll be prospects, too," Greg said.

"We need to try to sell them breedings to upgrade their breeding programs - put them in the big leagues," Thomas said.

"Naturally," Ron said.

"We all go on the road then?" Mike Wolf finally said.

"I think we should. I've been itching to use the Prevost again anyway," Greg shot back.

"Who's payin' the expenses to do this?" Mike asked Ron.

After Ron hesitated, he said, "We'll give you an expense account and a budget. If you go over, it's your money unless you start generating some big bucks."

"That works," Mike said. "Would you care if my dad worked on this scheme, too? He's not handling retirement too well, and I'm sure he'd love to dabble in Southern California. There wouldn't be any travel expenses for him."

"No problem. Just make sure he knows the sales lists inside and out and that he's at least seen the videos of the mares. Tell him the final contract acceptance is by me," Nick said, forgetting that he wouldn't be around.

"Another way we can generate more income is by raising our handling fees," Thomas said.

At one time, the profit from the stud fee covered the labor costs for the breeding process. Greg came up with the idea of a handling fee - clients didn't question it. When mares are brought to the farm for breeding, the mare owners pay a fee to handle the mare and a foal at her side. This has become commonplace since most stallion owners don't own their own facilities, and there are labor costs involved in handling the actual teasing of the mares and the breeding process.

Because technology required a state-of-the-art breeding lab, they also charged the stallion owners a handling fee. No one complained when they saw the skill and physical risk involved in handling the teaser stallion, the skill involved in cleaning the breeding stallion, and the breeding process itself.

It was never disclosed, even to Thomas and Nick, when the wrong mare was mistakenly bred to the wrong stallion.

"I've been thinking the same thing," said Ron. He had looked at their actual costs, and they weren't making much profit on handling fees. "I think we can get away with raising it another hundred bucks for mares and five hundred for stallions commanding stud fees is over $7,500."

"Good idea. But make it negotiable," Greg said.

"Like everything else," Ron concurred.

"What about the Medallion Stallion program? Patrick's idea of lowering the standards would raise more money," Larry suggested.

"We can't give them Medalions and the sane benifts.What would the stallion owners get out of it?" Thomas asked.

Larry had already given it a lot of consideration. "We'll give them a quarter of a page in the stallion promotion catalog - put their color photo, pedigree, stud fee, and contact information. Their names and what city and state they reside in will be listed in all ads for the Medallion Stallion program. Their offspring can be eligible for prize money still, but we'll start a separate program for that category."

Ron wasn't convinced it was a good idea. It really diluted the concept of horses being the caliber Vintage wanted to endorse. "We'll take the idea under advisement. Thanks for thinking of it."

Larry started to say something, then thought better of it. Whatever he had to say would do nothing to advance his cause when Ron said he'd take something under advisement. He'd talk to Greg or Thomas some other time.

Greg searched Nick's face, wondering why he hadn't really spoken on any important topics. As he watched him, something nameless grew in the pit of his stomach. He sat up rigidly in an attempt to clear his mind of negative thoughts. It backfired. Instead, he grew more anxious. Grew more aware that his partner was evaluating every word he said and every gesture he made. He pretended it didn't bother him, but he found himself loathing Nick to a degree that even shocked him.

Chapter 25

Thomas and Ron drove to the sales center knowing they would find Greg checking out the footing for the pathways and the holding area between the barn and the indoor stage. If the footing wasn't just right, the horses wouldn't feel good jogging into the building. They needed a non-slip surface that wasn't too deep or too shallow. It only took a few minutes from the time a horse left its quiet stall until it would be paraded stage as if it were in a beauty pageant. Its mental attitude and physical comfort could mean the difference between tens of thousands of dollars. An interested and enthusiastic acting horse that felt good enough to jog on the stage would always sell for more than a slow walking, quiet horse. Pizzazz was the secret ingredient. A company out of Lancaster, Pennsylvania shipped two truck-loads of recycled ground-up rubber footing for Greg to evaluate. If Greg liked it, he would put it in all of the barn aisles, each of the arenas and round pens, and use it as the footing in the hot walker enclosures.

"I like this. What do you think?" Greg asked his father and Ron.

"Looks good," Ron said. In his opinion the footing was the least of their worries. Soon, Greg would realize the same.

"You'd need to try a mare with a baby at her side on it first. See how the baby reacts. It does look good and there's no dust," Thomas said.

"I've got a trailer on the way over. I'm having Kim bring a mare and baby and a rambunctious yearling. Between the two, we'll see how they react. If it does well, she'll bring whichever stallion is the most excitable."

Ron wasn't one to mince his words. "We've used regular shavings for years. If you like this new footing, what's it going to cost?"

"I didn't ask. If the horses move better, they'll sell for more, so the price of the footing is a moot point."

Thomas knew what Ron was thinking - Greg hadn't fully accepted the reality that profits were more important than ever, from this day forward.

"Ask the price before you order. And clear it with me," Ron said.

"With you? I don't even clear things like this with Nick. I'll do what I damn well want."

Thomas put his hand on Greg's shoulder. "Things are changing - starting today."

A few minutes later, the three men sat on imported Italian outdoor furniture on the sales center's veranda. Thomas flipped the switch for the cascading water to flow into the pond that had a small island in the center. At the edge of the island, stood a life-size bronze of a mare drinking and her foal grazing. The stone paved veranda and pond overlooked the Vintage East stallion barn in the distance.

Greg cleared his throat. "What's changing?"

"Life," Ron said bluntly.

"Son, we need to work towards the most profitable year the business has ever experienced, but at the same time, we're going to have to radically reduce our overhead and stick to a tight budget."

Ron didn't give Greg a chance to respond. "We can only buy the necessities - no more extravagant purchases or spending. It starts today. Everything gets approved by me from now on."

Thomas waited for an explosion. Greg simply looked to the clear blue sky and shook his head.

"Do you understand what we're telling you?" Ron said after Greg had remained silent.

"I'm not deaf," Greg said, looking away.

"Don't get smart-mouthed," Thomas said.

"I'm not responding, so I don't become smart-mouthed. You don't want to hear what I'm thinking."

"Tell us what you're thinking - without losing your temper," Ron said.

Greg leaned forward and tapped his fingers on his thighs. "Fine. I'll tell you what I'm thinking. I'm thinking that you work for me - I don't work for you," he said to Ron. Then, to his father, "I'm the one in charge. I know you have a vested interest, but I'm in control."

"That's where you're wrong, son."

"Wrong? Oh, because of Nick. Yes, I suppose that it's both Nick and me who are in control. If there's cutting back to do, we'll decide. Regardless, it won't be Ron, and it won't be you, Dad. I'm the one who's taken us this far - don't forget that."

"Vintage's success has been a team effort - don't you forget that," Thomas retorted.

"A team effort with me at the helm for its most successful years," Greg said proudly.

"If that's how you see it son, - fine. The point is, things are changing from this moment forward."

"That's a load of - "

Ron didn't let him continue. "Would you like us to tell you why we're right and you're wrong? Or would you like Nick to tell you?"

"What are you talking about?"

Ron grinned as he looked off in the distance toward the parking lot. "Speak of the devil."

Thomas and Greg looked in the direction that Ron faced.

"Should we tell him now or wait until Nick's here?" Ron asked Thomas.

"Tell me what? What's this game you're playing?"

"It's not a game anymore, my friend," Ron said. "The jig is up. You're no longer in control. I'm sorry, but I'm in charge of the business until you find someone to buyout Nick's interest. He's serious this time. He's not giving any more extensions, and his lawyer sent a formal demand in writing.

Nick's going back to Ocala, and he put me in charge."

Greg absorbed the news without so much as a blink.

"I'm serious," Ron said forcefully.

"Bullshit!" Greg slammed a fist on the table.

Nick read the body language of the three men - the shit hit the fan. He laughed to himself. Part of him wanted to be the one to tell Greg, but he was glad Ron and Thomas had done so. Greg wouldn't have taken him any more seriously this time than he had the last two times. Unfortunately, if Nick had told Greg, it would be like the boy crying wolf, even with a formal demand.

"Nick. I'm glad you're here," Greg said.

"Are you?"

"Yeah. They're teasing around, saying you bailed and put Ron in charge. What a hoot..."

Nick pinched a cigar between his stubby fingers and squinted his eyes from the sun. "It's not a joke. I've had it with you and this sinking ship."

"You can't be serious," Greg said. "We've had our best year ever. Things are only going to get better. Why would you want to bail now?"

"Haven't you been listening to anyone besides yourself?"

Ron interjected. "The tax law changes are coming, whether you want to admit it or not. We're won't have much time to make a killing. We've got to make what we can, while we can. We have to pay down our debt."

Greg shook his head in disbelief. Why was everyone turning on him when things were going so well?

"Why do you want out before the reform is in place - if it even passes?" Greg asked Nick, looking him straight in the eye.

"I've got a lucrative development business in Florida I should concentrate on. Taking my time for something that's going to go belly up would be stupid."

Thomas swallowed hard before he spoke. "We're not going belly up. There's just not going to be the same level of profits we've enjoyed. We'll still be in business. But, of course, I understand that you want to get on with your own life. And to tell you the truth, I'll be glad to get this back to being a family business again."

"I'm glad you think of me as family, Thomas," Ron said, wanting to assure himself that he wouldn't be let go after Nick was bought out.

"I hope you can find a way to raise the money without needing to bring in another outsider. Honestly, I really hope you can," Nick said.

Greg couldn't believe what he was hearing. He had completely forgotten about the footing, and the mare and foal that Kim had been letting graze nearby as she waited for him.

"You're actually putting Ron in charge?" Greg asked in complete disbelief.

"Yes. I'm out of here as soon as Ron's caught up on everything he'll need to know."

Greg gritted his teeth and said, "Why didn't you give it to me?"

Nick held back a laugh. "To you?"

"Yes. It's my business."

"That's where you're wrong. It's where you've always been wrong. You think you're the boy wonder of the horse world - and that no one else contributes. That's precisely why I didn't put you in control. I don't trust your decision making abilities right now."

"So why not give control to my dad?" Greg said in spite of the pressure and the insult.

"He wouldn't take it."

Greg looked at his father in disbelief. "He offered you the control and you wouldn't take it?"

"No. I wouldn't," Thomas said. "I'll work in an advisory position only. I hope that for once you'll listen to me and stop thinking you're always right. I trust Ron to balance things."

"Because you think of him as your third son. Yes - we've heard it a million times, but this is going overboard. Turning down Nick's offer to give control to Ron. Are you senile?"

"Don't talk to him that way," Ron said.

"Of course you'd defend him," Greg said to Ron.

"I'm not going to miss scenes like this," Nick told them.

"We're just talking. It's not a scene," Thomas said, trying to lighten the moment.

Nick chuckled. "You're right. I've seen worse. Especially when Patrick's in the middle."

Greg didn't think it was funny. "Does anyone have an objection to my personally buying out Nick's interest? I'm not going to bother if you're going to fight me on it."

"Your mother and I will always retain our interest, and so will Patrick, but we'd never fight you on trying to buy out Nick on your own. We simply assumed that you'd need to bring in an outsider again."

Greg acted as if it were a simple challenge. "Let me see

what I can do. I understand Ron's in charge of operations for the time being, but as long as I have your word that you won't fight my efforts regards to me trying to personally raise the money, I'd sure like to try."

"Fine with me," Ron said reluctantly.

Thomas concurred, unsure of whether he was proud of his son or weather the idea was a recipe for disaster.

Nick suddenly remembered why he had come to the sales center after all. "Not to change the subject, but Greg, you got a call from Detective Harman in Beverly Hills. He said he's the lead investigator in the Finn murder case. He wants you to call him right away."

"I don't know if I should. Isn't he supposed to go through my lawyer?"

"I have no idea. It's not like you've been arrested and you're out on bail. Call your lawyer and ask him," Nick suggested.

Thomas turned pale. He had hoped they finished with that chapter in their lives - the chapter where Greg was under suspicion for murder.

Later that afternoon, Greg met with Sally and Jesse Rye at the parcel of land they wanted to buy. They walked the property, talking about where different structures could be placed based on wind patterns, water drainage, shade and the summer heat.

Greg studied an anthill to avoid eye contact. "You know I like both of you. And you're great clients. I want you to know I appreciate your business - but, I have to tell you - Nick isn't going to approve your plans as they're designed."

Sally Rye looked at her husband and said, "I told you they wouldn't think it was nice enough."

"I'm not spending more money. I can get the cinderblocks from my brother for next to nothing. I'm not building with wood or buying those pre-fab stalls," Jesse said.

"What about a stone façade on the exterior?" Greg said, offering a compromise. "Get rid of the pillars and spend the money on the exterior."

"Sally already thought of that. I checked out the cost, and it's prohibitive," Jesse said. "I'm not interested in building a showplace."

Sally smiled. "Our place will be functional and clean. That's all that should really matter - that, and that we'll have trained staff to take impeccable care of your clients' horses."

"Nick says he won't approve it. I'm sorry," Greg said, knowing they needed the money.

Jesse wouldn't waiver. "Not very many people will even see our farm. You said yourself that clients would seldom see their horses. What's the difference how our place looks cosmetically?"

Greg acted embarrassed. "Nick thinks it's not the image we want for L'Equest. It's not me. I agree with you, but there's nothing I can do unless you'll make radical design changes."

"So he's prepared to turn down a $1.2 million land sale because he doesn't like Colonial architecture and cinderblocks?" Jesse asked.

"I know - it's crazy," Greg said, shaking his head.

Sally really wanted a farm here. "There's nothing you can say to change his mind?"

Before Greg had a chance to answer, Jesse said, "What if I grease the wheels with some extra pocket money for you? Would that make you push any harder on our behalf?"

Greg didn't answer.

Sally could see Greg contemplating whether or not to take the bait. "How about it? You can make a little something on the side if you'll convince Nick to approve our plans."

"I thought you said that building the property as designed would be your maximum budget. If there's room for leeway, put the money into upgrading the façade," Greg suggested.

Jesse shook his head. "No. That would cost too much. How about if we give you fifty grand in green cash, if you can get Nick to sign off on our plans as they are?"

The men shook on the deal. Greg felt confident he could sway Nick and pocket some cash along the way.

Within an hour of leaving the Ryes, Greg went home to make an important phone call.

"Is Alec available?"

"May I ask who's calling?"

"Greg Bordeaux."

"One moment please."

Before Greg had time to open his can of Pepsi, Alec was on the line.

"Did you get the last statement Garth forwarded to you?"

Alec said.

"Not yet. I haven't gone to Louisville in a couple of weeks," Greg said. He kept a post office box under another name, just as Alec and Garth had advised.

"I thought you were calling to find out why there was money missing from the account. Garth said he forgot to put a note with the statement."

"Money missing?"

"Not actually missing, but I assume you've kept your own records of your deposits. I had to pay taxes, so there's that much less in the account."

"I see," Greg said. "Thanks for thinking of the details."

"Actually, Garth thought of it. So - what can I do for you?"

"My criminal attorney is bear hunting in Canada and can't be reached. One of the detectives on the Finn case called me directly because he couldn't reach my lawyer. I wasn't available - he wants me to call him back. Do you think I should?"

Alec didn't like the idea of advising him about this. "I don't know. Ask Dolan. He's a criminal lawyer. Call him."

"We're not really talking anymore."

"Why?"

"He said he wanted to distance himself from me. Not Marcie, but me."

"Hmm."

"What about his partner, Jessica?"

"No way. We don't talk," Greg said without further explanation.

"Have Marcie call Dolan. It's a simple question."

"I'll just call the detective. It's not like I'm guilty - there's no way I could incriminate myself."

"Only you know," Alec said.

"You think I killed Finn?"

"I didn't say that."

"You didn't need to."

"You took an offhanded comment the wrong way. I apologize."

Greg's temper flared. "That wasn't an offhanded comment. No one says something like that if the thought's never crossed their mind."

"I don't think you killed Finn."

"Then why did you suggest that I get the best lawyer I could afford?"

"I was just trying to help. I gave you my professional advise. That doesn't mean I think you're a murderer." A crook, yeah, a murderer - I doubt it, he thought.

"You're an asshole. I'll talk to you later."

Alec knew Greg would get over it. "Hold on. While we're on the line, I wanted to let you know that one of the last checks you sent bounced."

"Bounced? Which one?"

Alec had Greg's file on his desk. "The one from Brazil for $100,000."

"It must be a mistake. The Da Silva's own diamond mines," Greg said.

Alec winced, thinking Greg had been conned. "There are no diamond mines in Brazil. Diamonds come from South Africa."

"His diamonds aren't for jewelry. They're industrial grade. They use them for tools, like saw blades, drill bits - things like that."

"Oh. Well, anyway, Garth put it in for deposit again just in case it was simply a matter of timing for funds clearing. I'll let you know what's going on as soon as I find out if the check clears or not."

"I'm sure the check will clear" Greg said without hesitation.

"The Ritona's check cleared," Alec confirmed. "What was their hundred grand for?"

"My commission on the sale to the Da Silva's."

"What's the Brazilian's check supposed to be in payment for?"

"It's a buyer's fee," Greg said. "For the package of mares that the Ritona's owned."

"I didn't even know Vintage had clients from Brazil," Alec said as an afterthought.

"Vintage doesn't."

"What do you mean?"

"I don't run anything I do in overseas sales through Vintage. I keep the commissions and mark-ups for myself."

Greg had been developing a small client base in Brazil, Chili, Italy, England and Belgium. He sold the foreigners horses through the company Alec and Garth formed. Greg's mark-ups and commissions on those sales never went into Vintage accounts. All money was funneled through his rainy day account. His U.S. clients agreed to keep their transactions a secret from other people in the business. In exchange for their silence, he would accept one horse into a Vintage Scottsdale auction and one yearling into the Kentucky Yearling Sale.

~~~

Ron urged Greg to meet with the detectives without a lawyer present. He joined Greg on the trip to offer moral support.

"Mr. Bordeaux, thank you for coming," Detective Harman said.

"Did I have a choice?"

"Of course."

"I've really got more important things to do."

"More important than clearing your name?"

Greg wondered if it was a trick question. "What can I answer that I haven't answered before?"

"What's your relationship with Mrs. Finn?"

"I told you, I have no relationship with her. I doubt that I've exchanged five full sentences with the woman. I've only met her casually after one of our auctions where George bought horses."

"I just want to make sure. I didn't know if you've thought of any other encounters."

"There haven't been any other encounters."

"What's your impression of Mrs. Finn?"

"I don't understand your question."

"I'm sure she must have made some impression on you. What was it?"

Greg thought about it. "I guess it crossed my mind that she married a man so much older than she was. I didn't give it much thought - it's common among wealthy people. My wife is twelve years younger than I am, and no one gives it a second thought."

George was at least twice Sonia's age.

"Did George ever indicate that he had marriage problems?"

"I told you before, he never spoke about his personal life. Why are we discussing the same things again? I've got better things to do."

"I appreciate your cooperation, but we have more questions. It's a matter of procedure to see if you've recalled anything new."

"Fine. Let's get this over with."
~~~

"I understand he may not have specifically said he was unhappy, or said she was unhappy, or that either had a lover, but can you think of any circumstance in which any type of conflict was discussed?"

Greg gave the question serious thought. "I don't know that you'd call it a conflict, but Sonia wanted to breed twenty mares to a stallion he didn't want to breed the mares to."

"When was that?"

"Right before he died."

"Before he was murdered."

"Fine. Before he was murdered."

"How did it come about that George made you aware of their conflict about the stallion?"

Greg told him the unedited story.

"Do you think Sonia would kill her husband - or have him killed, just so she could breed her mares to that stallion without an argument?"

"Of course not. That's ridiculous."

"Maybe it wasn't ridiculous to Mrs. Finn. Maybe she couldn't tolerate him always being in control. She indicated to us that she was rarely free to do as she pleased."

"I can't imagine her murdering him over something like that."

"Do you know if the Finn's had an open marriage?"

"I have no idea."

"Did George ever hint at the thought that either he or his wife had a sexual relationship outside of their marriage?"

"No."

"Did George ever show a temper around you?"

"No."

"Did George ever indicate that he was abusive to his wife?"

"No. How many times do I need to tell you - I don't know anything about their personal lives."

"I'm sorry Mr. Bordeaux, but sometimes people don't realize what they know about someone."

"Do you suspect Sonia of the murder?"

"We can't say right now. We discovered she was having an affair, and, she wasn't in Greece for as long as she had said. She spent three days with her lover here in California."

"Was she here the day he was murdered?"

"Yes."

"Still," Greg said. "Why would she kill him? She had

everything any woman could ever want."

"She says he was abusive with her - but she also says she didn't kill him and she doesn't know anything about the murder."

"Do you believe her?"

"We're still investigating."

"Am I still being investigated?"

"You're still, as we say "a person of interest," but we haven't come up with anything new."

"Then why am I still a suspect?"

"You were the last one to see him. You had motive. You had means."

"I had no motive and I had no means."

"Mr. Bordeaux - I don't move in the circles that you do. I acknowledge that fact. But anyone would see that you could be angry enough to kill Finn. He turned you down for a business deal which would potentially save your business, or cause you to go bankrupt if the deal didn't go through. That's motive. And we know you owned at least one gun."

Greg had the right to remain silent, but not the ability. "That's bullshit! I told you myself that I was trying to get him to buy out my partner's interest in our business, but there's no way I would have gone bankrupt. Just because I was disappointed he said no doesn't mean I'd kill him. I didn't kill him."

"You just happened to throw away your gun during that same trip?"

"Yes."

"Let's continue this interview making the assumption for now that you didn't murder Mr. Finn. Can we?"

"Fine."

"What do you know about Morgan Butler?"

"All I know is that she's a broker, and she owns her own stallion."

"Is she close friends with Mrs. Finn?"

"I have no idea."

"I understand Mrs. Finn did in fact breed her mares to Ms. Butler's stallion."

"I wouldn't be surprised."

"Why do you say that?"

"I told you before. George and I went to see her stallion because Sonia wanted to breed to him."

"And you convinced Mr. Finn to say "no" to Sonia?"

"I don't know what he said to Sonia. He obviously didn't go into partnership with me. I didn't get his business. Or Sonia's after he died."

"And that made you angry?"

"I don't know. I suppose I drove away from the house upset, but I also thought there might be a possibility that he'd change his mind about the opportunity I presented him."

"Why would he have changed his mind?"

"I'm saying it was a possibility," Greg said with an attitude. "Rich people are fickle. Sometimes they say they'll buy something and then back out of the deal. I've had more than a few big deals go through after a client has turned me down."

"Did you have any hint from him that he wasn't absolutely certain that his answer was a final answer?"

"I suppose so. I was rushing him for a decision. I wanted to tell my partner, Nick, that everything was taken care of. And, I needed to get on with other business. Then, George said he had problems to deal with that weren't related to money. He indicated that the amount of money wasn't the issue."

"Fifteen million bucks and using his line of credit wasn't an issue?"

"No. It wasn't. The problem was me getting too pushy to get the deal done - and, like I said, he had something else going on, so he couldn't give the decision process his full attention."

"All right. Let's get back to Ms. Butler."

"I don't know anything more than what I've told you."

"Would you be willing to wear a wire and meet with her?"

Greg raised his brows. "What do you mean? Why would I meet with her? I've only met her once for a brief moment at George's funeral. I don't even know if I'd recognize her."

"Do you think she would meet with you?"

"I'm sure she would if I had a good premise for a meeting. What's this about?"

"We're hoping you'll cooperate regarding a lead we have. If we had another alternative, we wouldn't have bothered you."

Greg left the meeting at the police department feeling hopeful. He and Ron checked into the Sportsman's Lodge after Greg lost the argument about wanting to stay at L'Ermitage Hotel. To Greg, it was bad enough they were staying at the Lodge,but Ron insisted on sharing a room with two double beds to save on expenses. When Ron refused to let Greg order room service, Greg was annoyed.

"I've got a few phone calls to make," Ron said. "I'll call Morgan and set up a meeting. Why don't you go to the concierge and find out where we can get a good meal for a decent price."

"Fine. I'll see you in the lobby when you're finished."

Ron called Ryan Sanders. He was surprised to get right through on his direct line. They had only spoken a couple of times before, so he was glad Ryan remembered who he was.

Ryan got to the point. "So - what can I do for you?"

Ron spoke as if they were old friends. "All of us at Vintage want to play a practical joke on Greg. His parents are even in on it. I was wondering if you know how I could find an actress that looks like Morgan Butler."

"What's your joke?" Ryan asked out of curiosity.

Ron was ready with an answer. "We're going to produce a mock ad campaign that says Greg is leaving the horse industry to pursue other interests. We're announcing that Morgan Butler is replacing Greg at the helm of Vintage - that she'll be evaluating horses for acceptance into the Vintage auctions, and she'll be Director of Sales and Marketing. It's going to be hilarious!"

"I'd love to see his face," Ryan said. "But really, you only need a model for something like that. Not an actress."

Ron laughed nervously. "Actually, we're going to make a video too, where the actress is already working with us - a joke still, of course."

"I see. It sounds like fun. If you think Greg won't be mad at a practical joke like this," Ryan said, "I'll be happy to help."

"He won't be mad. Most people don't know him well enough to realize he's actually got a great sense of humor. I'd appreciate your help."

"I'll call Karla, a casting agent I work with in Santa Monica. I don't know this woman you're talking about. Did you say her name was Morgan?"

Ron smiled to himself. "Right. At Finn's funeral, she was with Sonia most of the time. Do you recall seeing her?"

"The woman with dark brown hair, about five-foot-five, medium build, right?"

"Yeah."

"Great," Ryan said. "I actually have access to a picture of Morgan and Greg together," he said without explaining that

Shawna had brought investigators to the funeral.

Nicole, Shawna's ambitious intern, took pictures of everyone she could at the funeral. A week later, after Shawna's team found out Greg and Morgan were suspects in the murder, they sorted through the pictures and found one with Greg and Morgan talking. Shawna brought the picture home to show Ryan - it was interesting that the two suspects spoke to each other. They agreed it wasn't likely that Morgan ran in the same circles as the Bordeauxs or the Finns.

Dumbfounded, Ron wondered why Ryan would have a picture of them, but he didn't dare question it. "What do I do from here?"

"Give me a couple of days. I'll call Karla when we hang up, and I'll overnight the picture to her. Do you have a number she can reach you at?"

After wrapping up the details with Ryan, Ron found Greg having a beer in the lounge that could be seen from the hotel lobby.

"Morgan's out of town for a few days or so, according to her housekeeper," Ron told Greg.

"I'll call Detective Harman and let him know," Greg said. "I've never been to San Francisco. How about if we fly up there tomorrow and stay a couple days while we wait for Morgan to get back in town?"

Ron knew that idea wouldn't work. "I'd like to stay here and relax. Why don't you go on your own? I'll bet some quiet time to think about the future would be good for you. Rent a car and drive - see the coast for part of the way. Highway 101 is beautiful. You can stop in Monterey and Carmel, too."

"That does sound like a good idea," Greg admitted. "I can't remember the last time I've had time alone, other than on the jet. You sure you don't mind?"

"Not at all. I think it would be good for you. Just check in by phone and I'll let you know when I reach Morgan," Ron said.

"That sounds good. Will you call Nick and tell him we don't know how long we'll be away? He probably expects us back in a couple of days."

A week later, Greg and Ron flew directly to Scottsdale from California. They had to tell Thomas and Fiona the good news in person. This would be one less thing for them to stress over, and it may be one of the last times they'd be able to use the jet for personal reasons as they were cutting back on expenses.

Dinner reservations for Mancusos at The Borgata were arranged for seven that evening.

While Ron talked with a friend he ran into at the bar, Greg let the maitre d' seat him at a booth for four. He ordered a bottle of wine recommended by the sommelier, Escargot Bourgogne, Oysters Rockefeller, and Capraccio di Manzo appetizers before his parents arrived and before Ron joined him.

Thomas and Fiona weren't themselves. The problems had been taking a toll on them and it showed. Their faces were drawn, their postures were slightly slumped, and there was little deliberation in their strides.

"Cheer up," Greg said as a greeting.

"Do we have something to be cheerful about?" Fiona asked.

"That's why I invited you here," Greg said.

"I was afraid it was more disturbing news," Thomas said. He half expected to need to bail his son out of jail - if they even granted bail in a murder case.

"All my problems are over in regards to the Finn investigation."

Thomas sighed with relief. "It's about time. What happened? I can't believe you were there so long."

Ron answered before Greg had a chance. "They put a wire on Greg and we met with Morgan Butler - "

Thomas interrupted. "The woman who owns Ambiguous?"

"Right," Ron said without remorse. In times like these, he had to be cunning.

"Let him finish," Fiona said.

Ron sampled the wine. "We told her we were interested in her coming to work for us in the sales department - that was the premise for the meeting. She jumped at the opportunity to meet, although she did make it clear up front that she would still need to market her stallion, just as the Stanton's are with Home Run."

"Go on," Fiona said, anxious to hear the meat of the story.

"Ron and I wanted to enjoy a beach view, so we went to dinner in Laguna Beach at Las Brisas - it's near where she lives, and we knew she'd probably want to drink margaritas, which would loosen her up," Greg said. "We told her that we needed someone like her, who could convince a guy like George, to breed to her stallion rather than continue doing business with us."

Ron continued. "She didn't say so, but she was flattered we wanted to hire her. Eventually, we got her to talk about Sonia. Before our food came, she drank a couple of margaritas, and a third one with dinner. Then, she wanted to sit at the patio bar and have another round. We only drank club soda, by the way."

"You were trying to get her drunk?" Fiona said, disappointment in her tone.

Greg didn't answer her. "Anyway, Morgan's got a loose mouth and not much sense. She bragged about becoming great friends with Sonia, and claimed she could probably get Sonia to start doing business with us. Then, she starts telling me about how George had gotten increasingly more abusive with Sonia in the last year before he was murdered."

Thomas was surprised. The Finns seemed so happy together. "Really?"

"That's what she said," Ron reiterated. "So, then I asked her if she thought Sonia murdered him to stop the abuse."

"What did she say?"

Ron continued. "She didn't give her answer a moment's thought. She said, 'I know Sonia didn't murder him' - so, I asked her how she could know for sure."

Greg interjected, "Then she guzzled down the last half of her sixteen-ounce drink and said, 'Trust me. I know she didn't kill him'."

Thomas couldn't believe it. "And all of this is being heard by the cops?"

Greg nodded and smiled. He was obviously off the hook.

"Yep," Ron said. "So finally, to make a long story short, after she drinks a Keoke coffee to supposedly sober up, she asks both of us if we would ever kill someone for money? I tell her I didn't think so, but you never know - I just said that to get her to keep opening up to me. Greg didn't answer!"

"I didn't answer because I didn't want to take the chance of what the cops might think," Greg said defensively.

"So, anyway," Ron said, "she drinks a second Keoke coffee and finally spills her guts and tells us that she killed George to protect Sonia from future abuse and so that Sonia would buy those twenty breedings."

Thomas and Fiona's eyes widened in disbelief.

Fiona almost choked when she said, "You can't be serious! She actually confessed?"

Greg laughed. "You'd have thought that two-hundred

grand was like two-hundred million the way she said it. But, seriously, it seemed like she did it just as much to protect Sonia as she did it for the money."

"You're serious? She actually came out and said she murdered him?" Thomas said, flabbergasted.

"She's not a smart drunk," Ron said.

Fiona never envisioned a conversation like this. Still absorbing her son's involvement, she had the clear mind to ask, "Were you there when they arrested her?"

"They didn't arrest her, yet," Greg said. "Our meeting was for gathering evidence. I think the police are going to use the recording to get a search warrant for her house and then arrest her. I'm not sure."

"So you're cleared now?" Thomas asked Greg.

"Yes. But I'll have to testify in court."

Ron acted as if he had a revelation. "I wonder if she were trying to set you up when she did it. She was obviously waiting outside his house while you were there."

Greg nodded. "The cops think that's just what she had in mind. The phone records show that she called the house, so George probably told her he was meeting with me."

"Do they think Sonia put her up to it?" Fiona asked.

"Harman said they'll definitely be investigating it further. He said they'll probably offer Morgan a deal if she'll testify that Sonia put her up to it. All I know is, I'm glad this is over, and that life will be back to normal."

"Cheers," Thomas said.

No one at the table thought that life was going back to normal, but for tonight, they all wanted to pretend that Greg's problem was the only problem.

After the long story and the appetizers, Fiona ordered the Seafood Provencal, Thomas ordered Lobster Fra Diavolo, Ron ordered Veal Scallopini and Greg ordered Chateaubriand, feeling like he could finish off his entire meal.

Chapter 26

Garth Windsor visited his parent's farm for the first time in weeks. It seemed strange for him to see only three horses on the property that had once been a profitable breeding and showing operation. There would no more watching foals romping in the pastures, or young horses for his father to start under saddle. As beautiful as the landscape was, there was a void without the herd of horseflesh. In the past, whenever he visited his parents, he was lured to the smell of the barns.

"When you went to Brazil, did you go to Da Silva Farms?" Garth asked.

Davis smiled at the memory. "No. We tried, but we couldn't get an appointment. Apparently their farm is by invitation only. We did go to a couple of farms in Sao Paulo though," Davis said, referring to when he was a commercial airline pilot. He and Lily were international travelers - free airfare was one of the benefits of working for the airline. They toured at least one Arabian farm in each place they visited so they could write-off all of the other expenses for the trip.

"Did you know the Ritona's when you were doing business with Vintage?" he asked casually.

"We know who they are. We never really talked to them," Lily said.

"I thought maybe some of their clients knew each other," Garth replied.

"We were introduced to them once, and of course, we know who they are through their ads, and that they've had quite a few horses consigned to the Vintage auctions," Davis said briskly, glad to talk a little about when they were in the horse business. He missed it desperately.

Lily saw the sparkle in her husband's eyes. She reached her hand over his and gave a gentle squeeze.

Garth fiddled with his cloth napkin. "Do you think they would tell me if a check cleared from Da Silva?"

"I have no idea. Why?" Davis was obviously curious and looked at his son with a question in his eyes.

Garth wasn't inclined to say why he was asking.

"What's this about?" Lily said before Davis could.

"I can't tell you. It's in regards to a client," he said truthfully.

Davis closely watched for Garth's reaction when he asked, "Didn't you say that your practice with Alec and Mimi wouldn't handle anyone in the horse business?"

"More or less."

"What does that mean?" Lily said.

"I said we weren't going to take on any clients who wanted us to represent them in the horse business."

"That's a response crafted by a lawyer avoiding an honest answer," Davis said, aggravated. He paid for law school so his own son could avoid answering his questions?

"Sorry."

"You look sorry. So why do you want to know about the Ritona's?" Davis pushed.

"I can't tell you why. Just forget it."

Lily went to the kitchen before she said something she might regret later.

Davis tried not to sound agitated. He controlled the tone of his voice the best he could manage. "Why did you bother asking in the first place?"

"I shouldn't have. Never mind."

"Look, we haven't been in contact with many of the people we knew through the horse business, but if there's something you want me to find out, I will," Davis conceded.

"Are you sure?"

"Yes. Your mother and I have *enquiring minds that want to know*," he said, referring to a long-standing family joke about the *Enquirer* tabloid. "I won't ask anything else. What can I do to help you?"

Lily rejoined them after overhearing that there wouldn't be an argument. She slid slices of fresh blueberry cobbler in front of the men and offered a genuine smile.

Garth didn't hesitate to take a bite before anyone had a chance to say anything else. "This is great, Mom. Any leftovers I can take home?"

"Sure. I'll wrap it before you go. And don't forget to remind me - I have strawberry preserves for you, too," she said.

"What do you want me to try to find out?" Davis asked Garth, dying of curiosity.

"Can you just see if there's any talk about the Da Silva's having any financial difficulties?"

"Sure. But I can't imagine that anyone in the U.S. would

know."

"Da Silva wrote a check to a client of ours, and it bounced," Garth said, offering a tidbit without disclosing that Greg Bordeaux was the client.

"I'll get on it in the next couple of days," Davis offered.

Lily asked Davis to help her with the coffee and creamer from the kitchen, a clear signal that she wanted to talk with him alone. They quickly agreed this would be just as good a time as any to tell Garth what they had waited to tell him. After all - this was a Friday afternoon, and if he was upset about their announcement, he'd have the weekend to calm down.

"Where's the coffee?" Garth asked.

Lily answered. "It's brewing. I forgot to turn the coffee machine when I was in there for the pie."

Davis cut to the chase. "There's something we've been waiting for the right time to discuss with you, and we'd like to do it now."

"Sure," Garth said, assuming it was about their will or a trust account. He was surprised his parents hadn't discussed it with him before.

Davis told their only child that he actually had a half sister - and the circumstances of why he never knew before. Lily remained relatively calm, although tears intermittently dripped down her face

Garth was shocked, and he ached for his mother's pain, but at the same time, he was thrilled to have a sibling.

"Have you ever tried to find her? I can help. I know I can," he said enthusiastically. A moment after the words came from him, he added, "You do want to know where she is - how she is, don't you?" Then, he stammered, wishing he hadn't blurted that out either. "I mean, if you don't want to know, I understand, but if - "

Davis interrupted his stumbling son who didn't know how to handle the situation. "We know who she is and how to reach her, but we haven't done it yet. We'd like you to be with us. We want to talk to her as a family."

"How..."

This time Lily filled in the blanks. "We talked to her adoptive parents during the time we were selling the herd. They said she was fine, but they didn't want us contacting her until she and her husband were over the hump of some business problems. They wouldn't tell us her name until a couple of months ago."

"Why did you wait so long to tell me? Don't you want to meet her?" Garth said, an octave higher than usual.

Davis put his hand on Lily's knee as they braced themselves for Garth's reaction. Lily took a deep breath. They hadn't discussed which one of them would actually place the final piece of the puzzle they were laying out for their son. When it became painfully obvious that they each hoped the other would tell, Davis finally blurted it out.

"Marcie Bordeaux is your mother's daughter."

"Marcie?" Garth grimaced, recalling how she had looked at him so curiously when they met.

Lily moved to where she could hug him. "It's a small world, isn't it?" she said with the ghost of a smile. Lily had always liked Marcie - what little she knew of her at least.

"This isn't by chance a bad joke, is it?" Garth said hopefully.

Davis was stunned by the suggestion. "It's nothing to joke about."

"I know. I know. It's just that once again, there's a complication," he said, still shocked.

Davis shifted in his seat.

"I know it's going to be strange and shocking when we tell her, but I wouldn't call it a complication. You said the lawsuit you and Alec had initiated was dropped. There shouldn't be any complication."

Garth raised his brows. "We're going to have to think this through. There's something *I* need to tell you now."

Lily's heart dropped out. She couldn't imagine what he was about to say that could compare to their announcement.

"Go on," Davis said thoughtfully.

Garth masked his concern about disclosing confidential client information again. "Greg came to Alec saying he wanted a nest egg in case he ever lost everything. He agreed not to pursue legal action against Alec, if Alec would agree to form a company Greg could funnel money into. Of course, Alec and Mimi jumped at the opportunity. Our firm has been assisting Greg in hiding money from Marcie, his parents and everyone involved in Vintage."

"This is a convoluted situation if I've ever seen one," Davis murmured.

Chapter 27

Within a month of Ron taking over for Nick, Greg and Ron started butting heads for the first time in their lives. Thomas interceded by calling Nick before the situation escalated.

"Greg's wasting time writing a five year plan. And, he still won't face reality by cutting back on spending. He flew in a blacksmith from California to trim three of the club-footed horses. He claims that this is the only guy that can straighten their feet. Apparently, he's used him in Scottsdale on quite a few young horses. Anyway, Ron is trying to assert his power, but Greg acts like it's a joke," Thomas reported, calling from Kentucky.

Nick was disappointed, but not surprised. "Goddamn him. He better not keep flying horses from Kentucky out to Scottsdale just to get them to Patrick quicker."

"I've tried talking to him, but he won't listen. He says he wouldn't have gotten anywhere if he weren't a positive thinker."

"I can't picture him writing a business plan at all, let alone a five year plan. He's usually the one who wants to do everything by the seat of his pants," Nick said.

Thomas agreed. "I know. I asked him if he had a bank or an investor that wanted the information."

"That's the only explanation I can think of, now that you mention it. What did he say?"

"He wouldn't answer me. He told me not to worry about it. I don't know what to do," Thomas said truthfully.

There was a long silence on the line as Nick reflected on the situation.

Nick cleared his throat, and said reluctantly, "I suppose I could come back to Kentucky a couple of days a week."

"I think it would make a big difference if you think you could swing it. Greg needs to concentrate on finding a way to raise money to buy you out. He's wasting time and energy being counterproductive dealing with Ron."

Nick was agitated. "I'll get back as soon as I can."

"I'm sorry."

"The worst part is that I lost twenty bucks to my wife. She bet me Greg would do something to provoke me to return," Nick said lightly.

"Fiona bet me fifty dollars," Thomas admitted.

"Will you let Greg know what's going on?" Nick asked.

"Sure. Hopefully your return will get him back in line."

"It damn well better. Like I said, I've got to get back to my own business. I can't baby-sit your son."

On impulse, Thomas said, "Greg may appear confident, but he's actually crying out for help. I don't think he can cope with an outsider having control, whether it's you or Ron - but at least when you're in control Greg understands that you financially paid for the privilege. Greg probably resents that Ron doesn't have a stake in anything, yet he's being more aggressive than ever."

"Aggressive in what way?"

"Ron told him he won't approve the auction for the Poles. Greg's furious."

"Ron's doing the right thing," Nick said. "It's time to buckle down and earn more profits while we can."

"I know. I've reminded Greg, but then the two of us get

in an argument, too."

"Tell both of them about our conversation and that I'll be back as soon as I can. This has got to be resolved," Nick said, annoyed.

"I understand. We all have a lot at stake, including Ron in his own way," Thomas said without further explanation.

Nick knew better than to ask what the reference to Ron meant. "I will tell you one thing - I'm absolutely serious this time about being bought out one way or another. If I need to have my hand in the business in the interim, I will, but only to protect my own investment."

"That goes without saying."

A week later, Nick showed up. He found Thomas, Greg and Ron entering the gate to a pasture where wildflowers bloomed and clusters of horses grazed patches of clover.

"Hold up!" Nick yelled out of his car window.

Ron turned. "We didn't expect you until tonight."

"I caught an early flight," he said, referring to a commercial airline rather than using their own jets which were expensive to operate. "Let me change shoes, I'll join you."

Greg was actually glad Nick had arrived when he did. He'd already argued with Ron, saying they should wait until Nick arrived before discussing this long-term problem.

Nick entered the pasture, then leaned against the four-rail black board fencing. The vast expanse of the lush emerald green grass and huge trees dotting the gently sloping hillsides never ceased to amaze him. It was a welcome contrast to Ocala and Scottsdale. Even the air smelled cleaner here, and the blooming honeysuckles permeated his every pore.

Why did nature's incredible blessing of gorgeous horses and picturesque land all have to revolve around money? Mother Nature certainly never intended for only those that could profit, or those that could withstand business losses, to be the chosen people to reap the pleasure of this kind of life. Yet, that's how it was, and no one would ever change it.

In Vintage's quest for expansion and financial gain, their farm almost single-handedly helped the rich get richer and further divided the horse enthusiasts into haves and have-nots. On days like today, when there wasn't a cloud in the sky and the gentle breeze swept over Nick's olive skin causing the slightest tingle of a chill, he felt guilty that people without his financial advantages couldn't enjoy such a simple pleasure.

"I'm glad you're here," Greg said to Nick.

"What a day," Nick said. "If they could all be like this."

"I love the desert sunsets in Scottsdale, but they can't compare to the vastness of this place - and the quiet. Sometimes I can hear my own heart beat when I'm out walking the fields here," Thomas said. He knew the calm wouldn't last.

Ron picked up the pace of the walk without anyone noticing. Before they knew it, they stood at a rippling creek where at least a dozen two-year olds were either drinking or standing in the shade under the solid tree cover. If it weren't for the yellow identification bands around their throatlatches, it would have been a picture worthy of a magazine cover.

Greg pulled the typed list out of his back pocket and cross- referenced the number to match the filly's identification tag. "This is a Lancelot daughter out of a Lodz daughter, with a tail female line to Skowronek."

"She's gorgeous," Nick said.

"That's the problem," Greg said economically.

"Problem?" Nick asked, bewildered.

"Tell me - how many beautiful horses do you see here in front of you?"

Nick scanned the area and then looked closely at each horse. "They're all stunning. Some more than others, of course, but I think they're all exceptional."

"Right," Greg said. Then he put paper from his list in each hand, threw his arms in the air as he lurched toward the largest cluster of horses, making as much noise and movement as he could.

The group bolted, tails high in the air and heads tossing as they snorted and played.

Thomas looked over the youngsters. "They can't trot and they don't have the hock action they need. They're pretty, but not athletic." He had thought about this for the past few years but never brought it up with anyone, including his sons.

"And they're nightmares to train under saddle. They aren't athletes, and they don't want to work. These Lancelot horses are nothing like the Lodz get. We're supposed to be performance horse breeders and trainers. Between our own horses and our clients' horses, we've got hundreds of horses that can't move worth a damn," Greg said, hoping not to insult his father.

In Sweden, Thomas pushed for buying Lancelot to breed to the Lodz daughters. They needed an outcross bloodline, and

Lancelot was both beautiful and athletic. Unfortunately, his sire, dam and full siblings didn't have any of the qualities that Lancelot did. The Bordeauxs bought all of them and sent them away. It was as if they disappeared into oblivion, yet no one discussed it.

"So, we'll start a halter horse division," Nick said reasonably.

"Patrick and I are riders. We specialize in English and Park. So does everyone that works the horses. We only show a handful of halter horses. You know that."

"Hire the Pondergrass brothers and their assistants," Nick suggested.

"They've got their own successful operation. They don't want to work for anyone else any more than I do - and they don't need to," Greg said, knowing the point wouldn't be lost.

Ron chimed in. "We've got plenty of other performance stallions standing at stud. We'll breed them more."

"None of them are producing like Lodz did," Thomas admitted.

"Lodz built us. He made us who we are. Who the American performance horse is. Or now, maybe I should say 'was'," Greg said disappointed.

"We've got great horses," Nick said.

"That's what we tell everyone, but the truth is in our face - in our pastures," Greg pointed out. "It doesn't matter what the public thinks right now. We haven't been producing athletes - it's going to catch up with us sooner or later."

"What are we supposed to tell the people who paid $75,000 a share?" Thomas said referring to their first stallion syndicate where they sold seventy-five shares in Lancelot.

Greg grimaced. "I don't know. But we can't keep breeding horses like this. We'll ruin the breed. We made a commitment to preserve the integrity of the Arabian horse, and now we're going to destroy it if we keep up like this."

"People have millions invested in our breeding program between all the mares and stallions and their boarding and training expenses. What do we say? 'Sorry - let's change directions - we were wrong'?" Ron said, visibly upset.

Greg didn't have an answer, but he knew they couldn't continue going down the path they started years ago.

Unfortunately, by the very nature of horse breeding, because of the eleven-month gestation cycle and the years it takes to raise a horse and attempt to turn it into a performance horse - the business was a huge gamble. Aside from the cost of producing the animal, the cost of finding out you made a mistake was enormous. The consequences could be devastating when such a large breeding program failed to achieve the desired results. To compound the problem, these are living breathing animals. What do you do with them when they don't work out? It's not like other business inventory - you can't simply put in warehouse storage or destroy it.

Thomas defended his breeding decisions. "It's not like we haven't produced any athletes. We've got more winners out there than anyone else in the business."

"Fool yourself all you want. We've also had more horses to choose from. You must realize that in proportion to the numbers we've produced - we've failed to create a truly great performance horse not sired by Lodz," Greg said. "I'll bet you anything that any of the Lancelot horses who are good performance horses won't stay sound, in the long run."

Thomas was sickened by the thought, but he knew his son was right. "The other stallions may work out," he said hopefully.

"I haven't seen one that's producing consistently like Lodz did," Greg said. "Sure, each of the stallions has sired a few great horses, but the odds aren't good. It's not good breeding and not good business. The public is going to catch on, and we're going to lose our reputation and prestige for breeding winners."

"You could promote more Arabian racing on major tracks," Nick said, intentionally excluding himself from the future.

"They may be able to race. They don't have an elevated or extended trot to waste their energy or slow them down. The big problem is - most of them don't have strong hocks and they'll likely break down early, even if they do make it through a successful racing season. Look at their top lines. Most of them are like tabletops. Pretty to look at, but they aren't going to move under themselves, at least not for long."

"You're talking overall. Some of them would be good racing stock," Thomas said.

"But that's not our business, except for Nick in Ocala," Greg snapped without intending to.

"So, what's your solution?" Nick asked Greg.

"I don't have a solution as to what we do with these horses, but we need to buy proven performance horse sires. We need to go out and buy the best Lodz sons that we can. And to look for outcrosses that are proven. We can't keep speculating. It's going to catch up with us."

Ron looked at Greg sharply. "I told you. We need to sell horses for as much as we can - not buy horses, let alone expensive stallions."

Thomas frowned. "Greg, we've all agreed that we need to take advantage of this next year to make as much profit as possible in the short-term, so we can survive. If the tax reform doesn't go through, then we can look at changing our program. For now, we need to exploit what we've got."

Nick was relieved that Thomas took a stand. "I won't approve any purchases whatsoever," he said with a steady calm. "I don't care about the long-term at this point. I respect that you do. As an equestrian, Greg, that's the responsible thing. But we're business people and we need to concentrate on the bottom line."

Greg was defeated for now, but when Nick was out of the picture, he'd do what he thought was right. He vowed to disassociate himself from the third and fourth generation second-rate herd and start over with a new harem of mares and stallions.

One way or another, he'd get a fresh start.

Chapter 28

The next year was like mining gold. Admirers envied Greg, thinking everything he touched turned to gold. Clients looked to him for direction as they treated him like a God. The façade continued to make Vintage clients feel like unspent money represented missed opportunities.

If only the overhead for Vintage and L'Equest wasn't so daunting.

Appearing as confident and carefree as ever, the Vintage crew traveled the country implementing their business plan of selling more horses and breedings than ever.

From a distance, outsiders thought Vintage was flying high. No one had any inkling that Vintage was desperately struggling to pay down debt for L'Equest, the failed equestrian development, as they attempted to accumulate cash reserves for the lean years to come.

Greg spent his life reaping the rewards of wealth, power, respect and prestige. By now, he was no longer aware of how ordinary people lived.

Still, it didn't make up for his marriage slowly deteriorating. Greg and Marcie were rarely together. When they did spend what should have been quality time, she was painfully aware that their bond was broken. Marcie's use of alcohol increased, especially at the lavish parties they hosted for clients. It got to the point where an employee was paid to stay near Marcie at social events, so that when she drank too much, they could take her away before she became an embarrassment. When Greg tried to talk to her about the growing problem, her only response was: 'If we could have a baby, I'll sober up and be a good mother and wife.' He still didn't want a child, and she wanted one more than ever. The lonelier she became, the more she drank.

All this time, Nick increased the pressure on Greg - tempers would often flare. Greg would threaten to walk away from it all and leave everyone hanging - he thought the operation was nothing without him in the limelight. Nick would threaten to use all income to pay off the business loans and mortgages for which he had co-signed, leaving no money for salaries or to operate the business.

Greg was unable to raise enough money to buy Nick out on his own, and was unable to find a partner to replace him. The ensuing arguments about Greg's supposed efforts would lead to rage and then soon be forgotten.

Eventually, Greg learned to stay out of the line of fire from Nick.

As time went by, as a result of Nick's influence, Greg had less and less regard for his clients' best interests and the best interests of the long-term breeding goals.

During one of Nick's weak moments, Greg convinced him to authorize the auction of horses for the Polish government by saying that if the market was going to collapse anyway, it really wouldn't matter if the money wasn't recirculated in the American market with their own group of clients. Vintage would make their twenty percent commission regardless of who the consignor was. It didn't take much for Nick to relent.

Greg thought the Polish Reaction auction may be his last big hurrah - he was determined to make it memorable. Liz went all out on the production and promotion for all of the auctions, and the Polish Reaction Sale was unforgettable. It would surely go down in history, regardless of what happened in the future. The sale of thirty-two horses in the Polish Reaction Sale generated incredible enthusiasm and unfettered spending. The horses sold for an average of $560,000, which was incredible, especially because the majority of the mares were aged and wouldn't have many more years of foal production.

The other auctions that season set record prices, generating almost $50 million in sales.

For the most part, Greg reluctantly did as he was told, squeezing as much profit as possible from each transaction and each client.

He worked more vigorously than ever, just in case his cohorts were right about the impending tax reform and its potential impact. Sometimes he found himself actually hoping the reform would destroy the high end of the horse industry. He could blame the failure of the Vintage breeding program on the economy, rather than the fact that the generations they were responsible for creating were deteriorating, not improving.

Chapter 29

The following year, competition for buyers was fierce as the number of qualified buyers slowly diminished. Jealousy and greed among industry insiders spread faster than weeds in the spring. The impact of the October 1987 stock market crash occuring during the U.S. Nationals didn't help.

At the February Scottsdale show, the auctions and the U.S. Nationals, Vintage's major competitors took advantage of meeting Vintage's heavy hitter clients. They made it common knowledge that Greg bled the wealthiest clients over time, if he couldn't do it all at once. Either way, it was a consensus that when Greg was finished with a client, the client would be a dried up corpse.

Greg continued to funnel money into his rainy day account. He wasn't about to walk away from his life's work penniless if everything fell apart.

Alec and Mimi took a sabbatical from their law practice to travel around the world. Garth took on their caseload, including overseeing Greg's fictitious business. Garth and Greg talked frequently on the phone as more deposits came in.

Garth convinced Greg to let him invest his money in a start-up technology business. The enterprise was gearing up to market a futuristic communication system that utilized home computers and telephone lines. Greg wasn't quite sure what Garth was talking about, but he trusted him to invest the money. Garth assured him that it would be liquid with ninety days notice. According to Garth, when the company went public, the return on investment would quadruple. If the start-up didn't go public by the time Greg needed his money, the company would return 100% of his principal.

~ ~~

In October of 1988, the day after the U.S. Nationals in Kentucky, the skies were gloomy and so was the mood around the Vintage office.

The Yearling Sales that took place during the show were a disaster. Very few private treaty horses were sold, and only a dozen or so breedings to the stallions went under contract for the following season. Not one stallion syndicate share sold.

Greg meandered into the office as if he was told to drop in at his convenience, when in reality Nick had called early in the morning and told him it was crucial they meet as soon as possible.

"What's up?"

"Sit down. We need to talk," Nick told him, eager for the confrontation.

"Fine, but I've only got about fifteen minutes. The jet's fueled and the pilot's almost ready. I'm going to Scottsdale for a few days."

"No, you're not."

Greg didn't know what to think. "You can't - "

Nick interrupted, holding his temper. "Both pilots are instructed to clear all flights with me. Including yours. If you want to go, take a commercial flight."

"Commercial? We have a jet. Why would I take a commercial flight?"

"I've got news for you, Bordeaux - you're cut off here!"

"Are you nuts? You can't tell me what I can and can't do."

"You've been buying time with me for years now. The business has gone to hell. I can tell you what you can and can't do from now on and it starts today. Sit your ass in that chair and be glad I'm not calling your father in on this."

"My father? What the fuck?"

"I'm so furious I don't know where to begin."

"Look Nick, don't worry about the finances. I know we're having a slow quarter, but it's going to be fine. We'll make up for it. People are just stalling - sitting tight. They'll spend money before the end of the year to get the write-offs," Greg said, referring to clients who would qualify as active investors in the eyes of the IRS. "They're just waiting until the last minute. And we'll generate plenty from the Scottsdale auctions. Trust me."

"Trust you?"

"Sure. Trust me," he said as he stood up. "Look, I've got to go. Call the pilot back."

Nick held back from reaching across the desk and grabbing Greg's collar. "I said, sit your ass down."

"What are you so upset about?"

"The banks sent a notice informing us that they're not going to be buying our contracts anymore. They see the business as too volatile. Clients are already defaulting. Our corporate offices sent a report - there's an increasing number of clients that aren't able to fulfill their commitments," Nick said, referring to the promissory notes Vintage held because the clients didn't qualify for bank financing.

"I can't control the clients."

"I know you can't, but this is serious - this, combined with the lack of sales is bad enough. Now I find out that trusting you has become my next biggest problem."

"What are you talking about?" Greg said, a lump quickly forming in his throat.

"Shut the hell up. I'm fed up with you and your superior attitude. You're making deals behind my back - making sales you're not reporting to the company."

"I...I..."

"Damn you. Who do you think you are? Clients approached me at the show to tell me you're skimming sales behind my back."

"How else am I supposed to come up with the money to buy you out? Where would I get the money if I didn't..."

"I'm not dealing with you," Nick said. "You've got sixty days to buy me out, or I'm putting the company into bankruptcy. My lawyer has started the paperwork. We'll be ready to file in sixty days, if we need to. I'm not dumping another dime into this sinking ship."

"Sixty days?"

"Yes."

Greg could smell defeat, and it sickened him. "You can't file for bankruptcy."

Ron grinned as he listened to the encounter through the interoffice intercom system. His scheme to buy Vintage and L'Equest for pennies on the dollar through the bankruptcy courts was coming to fruition. Soon, he would enjoy the elevated position he was entitled to.

"If you fight me on this, I'll have you arrested for criminal fraud and a host of other charges. Clients are so angry at how you've treated them, they've said they'll testify against you."

"How can they be angry? They agreed to the deals."

"They're finding out how you've been double dealing on them and how you go behind their backs and - "

"That's bullshit! I haven't done a damn thing wrong."

"Take your chances then. I'll call my lawyer and call the police, and you can just take your goddamn chances if you're so sure of yourself, you arrogant, self-serving son-of-a-bitch," Nick shouted.

"Hold on. You're getting out of control."

"You're the one who's out of control. I'm not the problem."

"Screw you!" Greg yelled.

"Screw me? Yeah - that's what you've done."

"I haven't done anything to you."

"You'll be sorry if you don't get the money together. I'm washing my hands of you, one way or another."

"Call your lawyer. See if I give a shit. You're a crook calling the kettle black."

"Get out! Get out of this office right now."

Chapter 30

Greg stormed out of the meeting with Nick. He drove to Johnny Pallinto's, hoping to let off some steam. Johnny wasn't there, so Greg went home to Bordeaux Hill. As he pulled into the circular drive, a servant was loading luggage in the glistening black Rolls Royce.

Several years before, Bill Ronstadt, a publicity hound and wheeler-dealer client from Florida, offered Greg the black Rolls in trade for a mare he wanted to buy at a Vintage auction. Ronstadt offered to bid the mare up to $300,000 under the condition that no cash would change hands. Ronstadt had already traded a yacht for five of Matt Robard's horses in an auction, so, Greg decided to get Marcie the car she had always wanted.

Greg always preferred a sure thing to speculating on larger profits. He offered the PenDennos, the mare's owners, $75,000 cash, plus ten breedings to a stallion Greg had imported for his own private program at Bordeaux Hill. He emphasized that the value of the breedings was $100,000, but omitted the fact that no one had ever booked a breeding to him. Greg convinced them to keep the arrangement confidential - the publicity they would garner for getting a mare they personally bred into a Vintage auction would be priceless to their breeding program. It was common knowledge among Vintage's high-rollers that it never hurt to do Greg favors.

Marcie didn't recognize the Rolls as an extravagance. She easily justified the price tag of only $75,000 – after all, that year, Vintage racked up more than $40 million in sales. Greg was on top of the world. Why shouldn't she be?

"What are you doing home?" Marcie asked.

"Problem with Nick. We're not going to Scottsdale."

"What's going on?"

Greg told her most of what was happening with Nick, and what the month's final disappointing sales figures were.

"We've got a lot to deal with right now."

"I'm not selling my jewelry or my cars," Marcie said as if everything was about her.

"I didn't say you should, but if we need to later, that's what we'll have to do. We definitely need to take a better look at our finances and see what we can do to cut back. I'm serious this time. We have to cut back."

Tears filled her eyes as they turned red. "Cut back? Everything was going so well."

"It doesn't take more than a bad year to get in trouble in this business."

"Our bad business year still makes more money than any other farm in the country. Probably the world," she said, forgetting that there were other breeds of horses.

"I know, but the money goes out as fast as it comes in. Nick gets share of the proceeds, and the sales support us, my parents, Patrick and Liz, the entire staff – we've gone from nine employees to over three hundred. We pay our expenses for the development, the limos and drivers, the jet and the pilots. The Prevost. It goes on and on."

"But our sales were outstanding last year. There's got to be plenty of money until these next sales in a few months."

He tried to explain, but she wouldn't let him.

"I don't want to hear this. You'll make things work out. I know you will."

"I will," Greg said. "Things will work out, but I don't think they're ever going to be like they used to be."

"Used to be? The money we've made has been a dream. It still is."

"Money isn't going to keep pouring in like we're accustomed to. You saw how bad the Yearling Sales were, and we hardly sold anything this month. October is always a great month, between private treaty buyers and selling breedings and syndicate shares. Things aren't looking good. We have to accept it and make the best of things."

"I'm not accepting anything. You'll make things happen – that's who you are. That's who I love."

"I can't control the tax reform or the stock market. That's what's killing us."

Marcie looked bewildered. "I don't understand how things could get so bad."

"Never mind. I don't want to get into it. I've got a lot to deal with. Bear with me and put the brakes on spending."

"That's fine. I've got more than I've ever dreamed of anyway. I just don't want to lose it."

"We're not going to lose anything. Don't worry. I've just got a lot to deal with."

"Call Ron. He'll know what to do," Marcie said.

"Yeah."

As the mare loped around the indoor arena, Greg didn't care that she was dropping her inside shoulder and wasn't flexing into the bend. He rode so naturally, the methodic cadence of her stride eased his tension, and that was all that was important right now. Riding provided him the mental clarity he needed.

Ron entered the arena carrying a dripping wet umbrella. When the mare turned the corner and saw him shaking the rain off of the loud round tan monster, she bucked, twisted and snorted in one swift movement.

Greg rode it out then laughed. "That was an E-ticket ride! Your umbrella works as well as the fire extinguishers."

"Want me to chase behind you with it?"

"Not now. I'll have the guys do it for the next photo or video session, though. How did she look? She felt all puffed up."

"I wasn't really paying attention. All I could think about was how you stayed on her like it was nothing."

Greg cracked a smile for the first time in weeks. "She was just scared."

"She's pretty lathered up. Are you finished with her?"

"Yeah. I'll get Jose to cool her down and clean her up. Be right back."

Once in the house, Ron poured a couple glasses of Cutty with a splash of water while Greg washed his hands.

"You sounded pretty disturbed when you called," Ron observed. "What's going on?"

"Nick's upset about how bad sales have been. He's insisting I buy him out within sixty days. He says that if I don't, he'll file bankruptcy. I believe him. I really believe him," Greg said, horrified at the notion.

"He can't just file for bankruptcy. You have until June. We'll get things done by June."

Greg shook his head. "No. I have sixty days. He's not changing his mind this time. I'm sure there won't be any more extensions."

"Because the sales have been off?"

"Yeah, and personality conflicts."

"That's all there is to it?"

"More or less."

"He can't just change on a whim," Ron said. You have a contract for June 1. He can't just arbitrarily change the date. Don't worry."

"He said he is, and I've got to go by what he's saying."

Ron looked into his drink glass. "There something more to this?"

"Kind of, but I don't want to discuss it. Bottom line is, we need to figure out a new game plan and get moving on it. I thought we'd have a decent fourth quarter and that the next Scottsdale sales would enable us to get this deal done with him."

"We should call an outside attorney that doesn't know Nick. I know someone we can use. He's in California - we can probably call him now." Ron had already contacted the lawyer and prepared him for the inevitable call.

"Do you have his number?"

"In the car. I'll go get it."

Ron couldn't look as if he knew the extent to which trouble was brewing. When Greg called him and asked him to come over, he didn't indicate there was a problem.

By the time Greg went to the kitchen, emptied a jar of salsa in a bowl, and grabbed a bag of tortilla chips, Ron was back with his phone book, a leather bound note pad, and his Mont Blanc pen.

With his Hermes satchel at his side, Ron ate a few chips and sipped his scotch. Greg slouched into the sofa, rested his head back, and closed his eyes, unready to face the world.

Ron spoke calmly. "Have you ever thought about simply selling out of the big game and starting over on your own with a modest size program? Right here at Bordeaux Hill? Life would be so much simpler, and you wouldn't need to answer to anyone."

"Never gave it a thought."

"Maybe you should. You've spent your entire life proving yourself to your dad and brother. You've done what you set out to do. You deserve a rest - a relief from the pressure of spinning so many plates."

"Spinning plates. That's a perfect term for my life."

"I know. When I think of you, I think of the guy at the circus, spinning plates. Your image is the center plate - people have to trust you and believe in you. One plate is the Scottsdale operation, one plate the auctions, one plate the operations here, one plate the real estate development, one plate your own program and one plate the Medallion Stallion program."

"I get it," Greg said, his head spinning like a plate.

"To do it without destroying the spinning plates, you need to keep them in balance and all going equally well, or everything is going to fall apart."

"In this business, if the center plate falls, it'll take everything down with it. Everything. Shit - I'm the center and things are spinning out of control."

"Right," Ron confirmed. "So if you get out of this while you can, you'll keep your sanity and move toward a simple life where you can enjoy the horses again. And your wife."

"The world wouldn't lean on me anymore?"

"Nope. Neither would your family."

"I'd start sleeping at night again?"

"You would," Ron said.

"Sounds like a dream. Definitely on the opposite end of the spectrum of anything else I've ever dreamt about."

Ron stoked his cohort's ego. "You've become the biggest and most powerful. Is it everything you thought it would be?"

"Some days - yes. Others - no. Lately, no."

"You've got a lot on your shoulders - tax reform killing the big investors, the Medallion Stallion program is turning into a nightmare."

"Please - don't remind me. It's all I think about. But if I can run things my own way - without Nick, I think I can keep everything going. We'll get rid of the jet and the limos, radically cut back on the cost of producing the auctions and lower the land prices at L'Equest."

"It makes sense, but do you really want everything falling on your shoulders still?"

Greg shrugged.

"Even with Nick out of the picture,everything would still be on your shoulders. You know that, don't you?"

"What alternative do I really have?"

"Let Nick file for bankruptcy and you can start over with a clean slate. You can blame everything on him."

"That's no alternative," Greg said without hesitating. It would be like admitting failure to his father and everyone who knew him.

"You won't be the only one. Believe me."

Greg was indignant. "I won't be humiliated by a bankruptcy. I can't do that to myself or my parents."

"You might not have a choice," Ron said realistically.

"It won't come to that. I won't let it."

"It's come to that already from what Nick is saying. He's drawing money out of his own account to maintain Vintage and L'Equest. Do you have any idea how much personal liability Nick has?

"He took that risk when he wanted controlling interest."

"I know," Ron said. "But who knew the market would do this? He certainly didn't know any more than we did."

"That's his problem."

"It's not just his problem. You and your parents are draining money from your accounts, also, just to keep things afloat."

"We are?"

Ron poured another drink. "Yes. Didn't you realize that?"

"I didn't think about it. I have bookkeepers and an accountant. I don't even pay my own bills."

"If I were you, I'd let Nick file bankruptcy and start over. That's my opinion, as a friend," Ron said.

Greg was getting pissed off. "I'm not doing that!"

"Fine. If you can buy out Nick, then you need to sell off

as much as possible to get the debt paid down and reduce overhead. Once you do that, maybe you can find someone to buy you out and let you run your own operation."

"Who would buy me out? There's no one that can handle everything I do - or knows everything I know. My name and reputation are what makes all of this work."

"Made. Past tense - I hate to remind you," Ron said, glad to remind him.

"Who would buy me out?"

"Sell the buyer on the idea that it's the Vintage name, the herd of horses and the real estate that have the real value. Get a consulting contract and hire me as management. Larry will probably still want to do sales and keep living in his house."

"You've thought a lot about this already, I take?"

"I have," Ron said. If Greg only knew how much he had thought about it.

"What about my father?"

"He'll get his prorated share of the proceeds from the sale. He can decide if he wants to continue in his capacity as a breeding consultant. That's up to him."

Greg grinned in spite of the conversation. "Patrick can get a job with someone else. Or start his own place. That's his problem. I've carried him long enough."

"Right."

"The thing is, most of the time, I thrive on having so much going. When times are good, it's what I live for. I think I should just try doing it all on my own after Nick's out of the picture. I'll see what happens, and if it's too much, then I'll go with your idea."

"You're not really completely on your own, you know. You've got corporate advisors, and I'm always here for you. You know that," Ron said.

"I'm canning most of the so-called corporate advisors and shutting down their business offices in Scottsdale. Did you know that office costs us $350,000 a year now?"

"That's excessive," Ron agreed. "There's no sense in being in a corporate office park."

"That was my father's doing. Not mine. He's the one who said he'd just need to sell a couple of syndicate shares a year to pay for it."

Ron understood the reasoning at the time. The image seemed important when dealing with big business people - then it turned out that hardly anyone even saw the corporate offices anyway.

"I'm surprised Nick didn't close the corporate office already," Greg said as an afterthought.

"We couldn't get out of the lease."

"Shit! The waste..." Greg said, his words trailing off at the thought.

Ron shook his head. "It's easy to get carried away with financial commitments when you're making so much and need the tax deductions."

"Things add up. Like when I took a mortgage to build my place, I didn't think much of a $25,000 monthly payment. It was just selling a couple of breedings or a mediocre quality suckling each month. It didn't even phase me to spend a million bucks on decorating this house. Now, I could kick myself."

"So, make the adventure a big lesson and rewarding experience. Move on by simplifying."

Greg tensed. "Why are you pushing this on me?"

"I don't mean to. It's just that I can see what all this is doing to you, and you shouldn't have to live with the problems and the pressure when you have a choice. I just want to help."

"If I sell out, would you commit to signing on with a new owner?"

"Sure," Ron said without hesitation.

"My dad and I would probably have to commit to consulting, too. It's probably the only way I could get a sale."

"Talk to your dad. I've brought it up with him and he says he'll do whatever it takes to keep you all from losing everything."

Greg raised his brows. "Losing everything? Is that how he sees it? That we might lose everything?"

"To be honest, it's how everyone around you sees it. You're the only one with blinders on. The only one who sees a bright future," Ron said.

"Seriously?"

"Seriously."

There was a long pause as Greg thought about how over the years, Ron had become a confidant, the unofficial partner with big ambitions.

"I've got a lot of thinking to do."

"You do," Ron agreed.

"We should call that lawyer. No matter what I decide, I've got to get Nick taken care of."

Using the speakerphone, Ron got Glenn, the lawyer, on the line. Greg painted the broad strokes about his problem with Nick and asked his advice.

"You were right not to use an attorney that Cordonelli uses," Glenn assured them.

"That's what I thought," Ron said.

"I would advise you to put me on retainer, and come to my office as soon as you can."

"Sure. But is there something we can get started on right away? Like tomorrow?" Greg said.

"Certainly. First, see if your partner will walk away from everything with a down payment. If he will, you can liquidate company assets to pay the balance. That way you don't have to come up with all of the money through personal funds. A down payment will help you to buy time."

"He's always said he wanted a lump sum," Greg said.

"But, it's been years, and he hasn't gotten what he wanted," Ron told him as if this was the first time they had spoken about it.

"Make him an offer," Glenn said. "He'll probably at least seriously consider it if he's ready to go to the extreme of filing bankruptcy."

Greg felt hopeful. "Good idea. How much do you think I need to offer as a down payment?"

"Maybe five million," Glenn suggested.

"I don't have five million bucks liquid," Greg said. He had no intention of spending his rainy day fund. That money was being accumulated in the event things became desperate.

"I'm sure there's something you could do to raise it. Maybe your father could lend you the money. It would be short-term, if you start liquidating assets after you get Mr. Cordonelli out."

"I won't have a liquidation - I'd ruin myself and the business. I want the business intact, with me and my parents owning it outright."

"You seem like a creative and resourceful young man. I'm sure you'll work something out."

"Sure. We'll work something out," Ron said before Greg could respond.

The following morning, over strong Columbian coffee and homemade New York style chocolate raspberry swirl cheesecake,

Ron reported to Nick what Greg and he had discussed, and what the lawyer from California had advised.

Later, Ron found Greg in his barn at Bordeaux Hill. Greg had expected him, but not at any particular time. Just as Ron walked through the covered arena and into the barn, he heard Greg yelling at Danielle, an apprentice rider for the Bordeaux Hill program.

The most talented people rode for Vintage East or Vintage Scottsdale. Those that didn't make the cut, but had marginal talent, were occasionally hired to work at Greg and Marcie's private operation, which really only existed to keep Marcie away from Vintage as much as possible. Danielle had all the makings of a talented rider, but not the confidence that she needed to ride spirited young horses. With enough mentoring, Greg was confident that she'd be able to work her way up to riding for Vintage.

Greg spotted Ron out of the corner of his eye and signaled him that he'd be with him shortly.

Furious, Greg continued the angry tone with Danielle. "Is this the second time or the third time that I've told you?"

"Second," she said with a snippy tone, knowing it was the third time she had been caught. Luckily, Greg wasn't around his own training barn as much as he was at Vintage's.

Greg put a hand behind his neck and started rubbing the tension away. "I'm serious, Danielle. I'm going to have to fire you if you keep doing dangerous things. I don't want you hurt, and I don't want the liability."

"We were just walking - and I bent forward. I'm not even tall enough to hit my head on the doorway," she said with no show of respect.

"That's not the point. Besides, I do have taller horses than Status. She's one of my smallest horses, in fact. Anyway, the mare could have slipped on the concrete or startled at something around the corner that she couldn't see - any number of things could happen that could get you seriously hurt," Greg said.

She looked away and rolled her eyes as if her parents were scolding her for staying out past curfew.

Greg continued. "Why do you think there are signs posted that say 'no riding in the barn aisles'?"

"I wasn't riding in the aisle. I was just riding from the indoor arena to the outdoor arena."

"Unless you and the horses can fly, you had to have

ridden on the concrete through that corner to get out the door. I saw you ride out the door. Don't deny it."

Danielle smirked. "They do it all the time at Vintage, and no one's ever gotten hurt." She hung out there on her day off so she could learn more about riding, and because she had a crush on a trainer she wouldn't believe was gay, no matter what his friends and co-workers told her.

"First of all, you follow my rules at my barn," Greg said, calming down. "Second, the doorways are a hell of a lot taller at Vintage. You never know what's going to scare a horse. I've told you a dozen times. You're only to ride in the arenas and with the gates latched closed. There are mounting blocks in both of them. No excuses. I mean it."

"I quit," she said abruptly.

"You're quitting because you don't want to hand walk a horse from the barn to the arena?" he asked incredulously.

Danielle thought about how absurd it sounded. "Well, no. I'm quitting because I'm sick of you always nagging. If things aren't perfect, you act like it's the end of the world."

"I'm concerned about your safety," he reminded her.

"You act like this about everything. You always want everything immaculate and everything put away all the time. It's stupid. And it's a waste of time and energy," she said.

"If you're going to work for me, you'll do things the way I want. If you don't like it - leave."

Danielle regretted what she had already said, but couldn't remain silent. "Nobody even comes to your stupid barn anyway. Why do you care how it looks as long as it's clean and the horses are taken care of? No one's going to buy any of these horses," she said, making a sweeping motion to include the entire barn.

"Just leave. I don't need someone with an attitude like yours here," Greg said.

"Write me a check and I'll be on my way."

Without another word, Greg walked into his barn office, unlocked the file cabinet with the Bordeaux Hill business checkbook, and wrote her a check on the spot. "This is money for the rest of the month. I hope you learn a lesson from this. You're a nice young woman at heart. You just need to learn that certain people are authority figures, and you need to learn how to be respectful and follow rules, whether you agree, or not."

Danielle grabbed the check out of Greg's hand and walked off in a huff without another word, even ignoring Ron as she walked by him.

Ron overheard most of the heated discussion. The barn wasn't that large and he knew Greg wasn't expecting privacy.

"You did the right thing," Ron said.

"I know. But I could have used her help still. She's the last rider I had left," Greg said regretfully.

"Really?"

"Marcie caught the other three riders smoking pot in the barn a few days ago. She fired them on the spot."

Ron raised his brows. "Pot?"

"Yeah. Of course, they needed to be fired for smoking in the barn anyway, but it being pot made the violation worse."

"That's all you need. People creating a fire hazard smoking around dry hay and dry shavings - and people too stoned to use good judgment handling the horses," Ron said sympathetically.

Greg thought for a moment. "You said you were going to need to cut back on man hours at the training barn, didn't you?"

"Yes. Why? Do you want to see if a few people want to work part-time for you and part-time for Vintage?"

"That's exactly what I was thinking."

"Fine with me," Ron said.

"Good. Anyway, I called MacDermott last night. He offered to co-sign on a loan for $6 million if I'll put up collateral," Greg said, referring to clients who lived in Seattle and owned a chain of upscale department stores.

"What kind of collateral?" Ron asked.

"Our stallions and our syndicate shares, and all other financial interests we have in stallions."

"Hopefully it will go through. You need it."

Greg nodded. "I put in a call to Darrel Desmond, too, but he's out of the country. I doubt if he'll call back, but who knows," Greg said.

"I wouldn't hold my breath," Ron said.

"Why don't I make the offer to Nick, contingent upon my being able to make a deal with MacDermott or Desmond?"

"You can't. That's still using corporate assets to pay him."

"Can you secure a short-term loan and use the sale as collateral? Then, we can postdate one contract for the sale and have another contract..."

"Stop. Now you're getting into doing a fraudulent transaction again," Ron said, hoping that eventually Greg would see his only real option was agreeing to a bankruptcy filing.

"What's the difference of timing if Nick doesn't find out?"

"For one - it's fraud whether Nick finds out or not. Second, now he knows more about how you operate - he's savvy enough to dig deep into what you're doing. You've got to find another way. A legal and ethical way."

"You knew I was calling them. Why didn't you say something before?"

"I thought it was obvious you were putting out feelers for verbal commitments. That in itself would be in a gray area, just to know where we'll stand if we can get Nick to agree to a down payment to walk away."

"So, you're saying I can't get a contract until after Nick is gone?"

"You know that," Ron said.

"Yeah, don't give me shit right now."

"I'm on your side. Don't get mad at me," Ron said.

Greg stood and paced the room. "Actually, I do know someone who will let me float a loan, if I can do all of this quickly enough."

"Great. Who is it?"

"Don't worry. I'll handle it."

Ron was leery of the evasive answer. "I'll draw up the paperwork."

"I'll handle it. This guy is cool. We've done things on a handshake before."

"$5 million on a handshake?"

"Yeah."

"You better get something in writing, Greg. That's a lot of money, especially lately."

"I'll deal with it. I appreciate your concern, but I'll deal with it."

Ron shook his head and wondered what Greg was up to now. He couldn't imagine Greg would use any of the cash he had been stashing away. Ron wouldn't touch his own at this juncture.

"Fine. But be careful that you don't do anything to make things worse."

"Trust me," Greg said as he had dozens of times before.

"It's your life. My career, but your life."

A half hour into the meeting, things worsened by the minute.

"You've been double talking since the first word left your mouth," Nick said to Greg. "Ron, what's he trying to get at?"

"I'm not sure. I'm just here out of curiosity, to be honest."

Greg ignored Nick's attitude, his face set in a mask of indifference.

"I've had it with you Bordeaux. You think I don't know you? Just make me an offer that's cut and dry and I'll answer you."

"I'm just trying to feel you out," Greg said, not inclined to explain himself.

"Stop it. I'm not playing games. Is your point that you want me to accept a down payment instead of the $15 million outright?"

"Yes. That's it in a nutshell. I don't know how I can swing it otherwise."

"Why didn't you say so? Quit beating around the bush with me."

"Sorry."

Then to Ron, Nick asked, "Have you arranged to get everything refinanced? My name's not staying on one single loan or mortgage." To Greg, he added, "I'm not going to be liable for anything. Do you understand me?"

Greg shuddered. "Yes. I understand you won't be liable for anything."

Ron jumped in. "I've been working on locating lenders, and things look good, but I was hoping interest rates would go down. I haven't secured anything. Until yesterday, we didn't need to have this done 'til the summer."

"Can you get on it today?" Nick asked Ron.

"I've already placed some follow-up calls and told my people that I need to act quickly."

"Good. Keep me informed. Nothing's happening until I have written loan commitments in my hands."

"We understand," Greg said.

"So, how little of a down payment do you expect me to settle for?"

"What's the least I can get you to take?"

Nick thought about what Ron had told him. "A third. Everything's to be paid to me in one year. Including interest at twelve percent."

"One year? Twelve percent?"

"Yes. No negotiating," Nick snapped.

"And I'm taking back my Ocala farm. It's only fair, given the compromise I'm making. Besides, then you won't have to absorb the overhead there, too."

"I'll see what I can do," Greg said, not caring about the Ocala operation. It had never made a profit anyway, and it was really Nick's stomping grounds."

"Can you get $5 million cash or not? I told you to stop jerking me around."

Greg swallowed hard. "I think so, but I'm not sure. I'll have to let you know."

Nick looked at him sharply. "I spoke with my lawyer yesterday. If you don't get this done before the end of the week, we're filing bankruptcy for Vintage Incorporated and L'Equest. I'm not pouring another dime into this sinking ship. I need to get back to my own life."

Several replies occurred to Greg. He remained silent. He knew that anything he would say would make things worse.

Chapter 31

When the Windsor family met Marcie in Louisville, they told her about Lily being her biological mother. Marcie was beside herself. Once over the shock, she cried when she found out why she had been given up for adoption. During the same visit, Garth told her he was handling the money Greg had been secretly squirreling away. By her reaction, they thought she was going to have a breakdown. It was a lot for one person to handle in a day. Garth said he'd like to protect her if she would accept his help. Since then, Garth and Marcie talked on the phone at least once a week.

Marcie called her brother from the barn office at Bordeaux Hill.

"Why are you so upset with him today?" Garth asked with comfortable familiarity.

"I can't take him anymore. I feel like I'm living with a stranger. Yesterday, he came back from a meeting with Nick and wouldn't tell me a thing," Marcie said. "He barely spoke to me all evening, then, this morning he didn't even wake me up. I guess he was trying to avoid being with me."

Garth didn't know what to say. He wasn't used to

having a sister to advise. "Is there anything I can do?"

"Yes. I want the money he's been hiding. I want it all. That bastard would leave me penniless if it meant he could keep his stupid horse business," Marcie exclaimed indignantly.

"Fine with me," Garth said. "You're my sister. It's the least I can do."

"What are you going to tell him when he wants the money?"

"I'm not sure. He hasn't indicated that he needs it yet. In fact, I just got another check from him about a month ago," Garth pointed out.

"Good. All I know is, I need to start a new life," she said, looking out the barn office door and making sure no one was around.

Garth felt like a conspirator. "With the man you told us about?"

"Yes. With Bob. I'm in love with him," she said sadly.

"Where did you meet him?"

"He's the maintenance guy at the farm next door," she said, referring to Johnny Pallinto's. "I know it's not much of a job, but he treats me well and he loves me. He wants children, too. With the money you're giving me, it won't matter what kind of work Bob does."

"I don't mean to sound judgmental, but if you love Bob, why are you drinking so often?"

"I can't stand the guilt of cheating on Greg. I do love him, you know. And he's never physically hurt me. It's just that he's shut me out over the years, and he refused to let me have a baby. He's broken my heart - we've drifted so far apart. I'm sure my drinking hasn't helped, but I don't know how else to handle things when I'm stuck in this stupid hick town with nothing to do. Greg won't even pay for the country club membership anymore. Bob and I have fun just being together."

"I understand the need for companionship," Garth said. "But a farm maintenance man?"

"Don't think of him as a blue-collar worker. Think of him as someone who treats your sister like a queen. He adores me. I need that."

"I'm glad he's giving you what you need. What I can't picture is how you can transition from the world of glamour and wealth with a powerful and influential husband, and jump into the arms of someone like Bob. But if he makes you happy, that's all that matters."

"I'd rather be with Greg. Believe me. But we haven't been happy together since the legal problems Alec started. We've spiraled downhill ever since."

"I hope Bob isn't after your money," Garth said.

"He can't be. His boss told him that Greg's going broke. Bob has no idea Greg was hiding money, let alone that you're giving it all to me. He loves me for me."

"I'm glad. But maybe when you take the money, you shouldn't tell Bob until you know things will really work out."

"I've thought about that. It's a good idea. We'll have to move out of Kentucky right away though. I can't stand living with Greg and loving Bob. That's why I want the money now. I'm ready to make the break."

"I can have it to you in a couple of days."

"How much is there?"

Garth smiled to himself. "Just over $7 million."

"Are you serious?"

"Yes."

"In that case, leave a million for him. I don't want him flat broke if he loses everything else."

"If you're sure."

"I'm sure."

"Fine. I'll do it."

"I can't wait to celebrate with Bob."

"I thought you weren't going to tell him yet."

"I'm not going to tell him about the money. I'll tell him we're celebrating that I'm making a promise to leave Greg by the end of the week. He can walk out on his job, and we'll drive off into the sunset. Maybe we can go to your parents' place for a few days so I can get to know them better - other than as clients - and so they can meet Bob."

"Sounds good to me. Maybe I'll join you."

As soon as Garth hung up from Marcie, he called his parents and told them what was happening, including that he was giving Marcie over $6 million, thanks to Greg's scheming. They worried for Marcie, although they thought she was making a sound decision to be with someone for love rather than money. Looking forward to spending time with her, Davis said he'd prepare the guest cottage.

Garth's next telephone call was from Greg.

"Listen, I need $5 million of my money. Is there any way I can get it right away?" Greg said, calling from his kitchen at Bordeaux Hill.

"Is this for buying out Nick?"

"Yes," Greg said, not liking being questioned, but he wanted to be cordial. "He agreed to accept a down payment."

"Well Greg, I'm sorry, but the funds aren't available."

The color drained from Greg's face. "What do you mean 'not available'?"

"It turns out I was scammed," Garth said. "The whole thing about this futuristic communications system using the telephone lines and computers was just bullshit."

Greg thought he was going to pass out. "No way! That was my money - you didn't get scammed out of my money. This has got to be a joke. You're joking, right?"

"I'm not kidding. Believe me, I feel horrible. I put every penny you sent me into the deal."

"You're going to sue them, aren't you?"

"I can't. These crooks are nowhere to be found. And on top of that, even if I could find them, you used scammed money to pay for your investment."

"That has no bearing. I trusted you. You said I could trust you."

"I'm sorry. Believe me. I feel terrible about this," Garth repeated.

"I ought to sue you."

"Right. Tell the judge how you got the money you sent me. And explain your way out of all of the recorded telephone conversations you've had with Alec and me about the money."

Greg felt like his world was ending. "You recorded telephone conversations? I can't believe..." he trailed off.

"Believe it. We had to protect ourselves from you," Garth said, proudly knowing Greg believed the fabricated stories about the lost money and the recorded conversations.

"What you did is illegal - helping someone hide money. You'd be in big trouble, too."

Garth smiled. "That's the beauty of all this. There's no way either of us will be doing a damn thing about what happened."

Greg slammed down the phone without another word. Garth didn't care. It was worth it to give his sister $6 million and have $3 million for himself. She didn't need to know he was holding back $2 million dollars for risking his license to practice law. He'd sleep just fine tonight knowing that Greg was likely to end up a broken man without the million his wife wanted for him. He deserved it.

Garth's next phone call would hopefully be his last for the day.

"This is it. Greg's penniless. I gave the money he's been hiding to Marcie - "

"To Marcie?"

"Yes," Garth said without further explanation.

Ron didn't find the claim plausible. "We agreed to split the money. It wasn't yours to give away. It was my idea about the telecommunications scam - "

Garth cut him off. "Things change. Shit happens. Sorry."

"Did you give Marcie the money yet? Maybe we can split it in thirds. That's only fair. She deserves something, putting up with him. But I'm the one who made it easy for him to skim all the money. I didn't do it for nothing."

Garth grinned. "I know you wanted Greg's money, but you also wanted to force the companies into bankruptcy. You've got half of what you wanted," Garth reminded him. "I assume Nick will file."

"He'll file. I made sure of it. Today, I told him I can't find any lenders willing to refinance or let him off the notes. I've got funding arranged to buy everything out of bankruptcy when the time comes. Thomas and I will continue the business one way or another," Ron said.

Greg hung up from Garth, panicked his world was crumbling around him. Within an hour, the negative thoughts subsided. He couldn't allow himself the luxury of not remaining focused. There were always options. He had to consider his options. He refused to be shoved into his deepest nightmare without going down knowing there was nowhere else to turn.

He could clear his mind and think creatively when on the back of a horse. He rushed to his barn. All of his barn help were out mending fences in the woods, so he tacked up the mare for himself. *So this is what it would be like if I started a small operation of my own. Marcie and I would help clean the stalls, groom and feed the horses. We'd do all the training ourselves - we wouldn't be so big we'd need assistant trainers. A hot walker and a treadmill would be all the assistance we'd need.* For a fleeting moment, it sounded like a good life.

On the packed dirt path just outside of the barn aisle, Greg swiftly mounted Alexandria and rode her to the outdoor arena, shielding the descending sun from his eyes. The mare refused to let him open the gate while he was mounted. Each time he laid the rein across her neck and put pressure behind her girth to move her over, she stiffened, rounded her back and raised her head. He tried turning her the opposite direction and she did the same thing. He dug in a little with the heel of his boots - he didn't wear spurs. She twitched her tail and threw her head in the air. He tried backing her up and starting over several times to no avail.

Finally, he dismounted, led the mare in large circles from the ground in order to gain her trust, and then remounted. Once again, she refused. Alexandria flicked her ears back and forth in agitation. This time, when Greg dug in with his heels to give her a clearer signal, she flinched, abruptly turned around and bolted back to the barn. Greg kept his seat without a problem.

He would have been just fine if he hadn't caught a glimpse of something out of the corner of his eye. As the mare ran at a full gallop to her barn, Greg inadvertently spotted Marcie in the arms of a man. He thought they were kissing, but it happened so quickly he wasn't sure. Without his realizing it, the mare ran through the double sliding doors of the barn with no regard for how tall her rider was. Greg's head hit the steel beam of the header and the wooden sign of the Bordeaux Hill logo. He was knocked off the mare and fell onto the concrete aisle, his head hitting first. Scarlet red blood poured from his right ear staining the concrete.

Marcie and Bob walked around the far side of the building with smiles across their face.

"You really think I should just leave right now?" Marcie asked Bob.

"If we're going to do it, let's do it right now, while you've got the nerve. Who knows how long it will take before Greg even realizes you're gone."

"You're right. I love you. There's no sense in waiting. Let me pack a bag real quick and get my purse. We'll take the Mercedes. It's in my name and it's paid for."

"My car's only worth a thousand bucks. I'll just leave it at the farm. We've got a million dollars, thanks to your brother. We'll buy everything brand new and start a new life."

Marcie grinned. "We can't go overboard. A million dollars won't last that long if we're not careful. I'm hoping I won't have to get a job after we have a baby."

"You won't," Bob said. "I'll get a job and take care of us,

but the million we'll be starting our lives together with will really help."

"I know. I want to put money in a college fund first thing before we spend a dime."

"I can't believe Greg scammed that much money from the farm without anyone knowing."

"Me either," Marcie said. "It must have taken him years to accumulate a million dollars."

"I hope you know I loved you before I knew you would have that money."

"I do. I know it in my heart," she said with a smile.

"You'll leave Greg a note, won't you? You can't just disappear into thin air."

"I already wrote it. I can't face him to tell him it's over."

Later that afternoon Ron flew to Scottsdale. Thomas picked him up at Sky Harbor International Airport.

Thomas invited him out to dinner because Fiona was playing bridge with her friends. Mother Tucker's Restaurant sat high on a hill overlooking jutting red rocks with cactus sprouting out from the crevices. The Valley of the Sun was incredible when the light hit just right. The food at Mother Tucker's was nothing to rave about, but the view was fantastic and the prices reasonable.

The men drank a couple of bottles of beer while Ron disclosed limited information to Thomas about what was happening with Nick and Greg in Kentucky.

"You've been like a father to me," Ron began.

Thomas tingled from a twinge of guilt. "I think of you as my third son, Ron. So does Fiona, even if she doesn't always show it."

"With everything going on in the business and our world's being turned upside down, I've spent a lot of time reflecting about my own life. I was wondering - would you like to tell me anything you weren't prepared to tell me before?"

Thomas turned pale. He didn't respond, other than quickly blinking his eyes, a nervous habit he acquired in the military.

Ron took a deep breath. "Thomas - I know you're my biological father. I had hoped you'd tell me yourself someday," he said thoughtfully.

Thomas felt a rush of affection. He smiled a smile that

was painful and pleasurable at the same time. Part of him was bewildered to be facing the moment. The other part was overjoyed.

"I'm sorry I wasn't man enough to tell you myself. I've always wanted to."

"I know," Ron said. "I think I've sensed that you started to dozens of times over the years. I'm sure it would have been very difficult, but I wish we could have been honest about this since I was a boy. My mother told me when I was old enough to understand. I grew up knowing you're my dad."

"You did?" Thomas said, remembering the exciting affair he had when they lived in Seattle. It was the only time he had cheated on Fiona.

"Yeah."

Ron's mother, Linda, had an affair with a young Marine. One night, after Linda and her lover had an argument, Linda seduced Thomas. When the Marine moved overseas she pursued an affair with Thomas.

"I'm so sorry. It must have been difficult for you to keep it a secret. Believe me, I regret it," Thomas said. Overwhelmed with emotion, he had a hard time swallowing. "I don't mean I regret fathering you - I mean I regret not owning up to it."

"You owned up to it in your own way. You've been in contact and caring all of my life. You've helped me and my mother every way that any father would. You've always been there for me. It just would have been so different if we had both been open about your actually being my dad."

"Well, thanks to you, we've got this moment and forever. I do love you, Ron."

"Me, too," Ron said with the ghost of a smile. "Does Fiona know?"

"No. She doesn't. That's why I never told you. I was afraid it would break her heart if she knew about your mother and me - and about my fathering a child. Fiona and I were married at the time."

"I know. Mom told me. And I know how old Greg is."

"Of course. I wasn't thinking. That was stupid of me."

"Don't worry about it. You didn't expect to have this conversation," Ron pointed out.

"May I ask, why did you decide to bring this up right now?"

"I had to get it off my chest. The more problems there are and the more I see you worried, I wanted you to know I'm here for you because I want to be, not because I'm on the payroll."

Thomas wished Greg and Patrick would talk to him so candidly. They always showed respect for him, but rarely showed emotions after they were in their teens.

"I have to tell Fiona. And the kids. I'd better tell Fiona first and give her time to adjust. Will you come to the house with me?"

Ron hesitated, wondering if he should tell him that Patrick already knew they were half brothers. "I think you should tell her alone. It's going to be shocking enough without her worrying about how to act in front of me."

"You're right. Why don't you go to the barn lounge? When I think Fiona is ready to see you, we'll come out or I'll call you to come to the house."

"That's fine. But don't rush telling her on my account. I just felt like I had to talk with you about it at this point."

"No. I want to tell her. I've wanted to tell her since the day I knew your mother was expecting. It'll feel good to get it off my chest."

"Do you think she can handle it with all the business problems happening at the same time?"

"She doesn't really care about the money. She just cares that we have a roof over our heads and food to eat - and we're all happy and healthy. I'm the one driven by the money. Fiona's simply along for the ride."

"If you think she can deal with it, let's go."

Ron walked around the barn rather than going to the lounge. Just because he didn't care to know much about horses didn't mean he didn't feel good being surrounded by them. Smelling them. Hearing them. Admiring their beauty.

Thomas was glad Fiona's bridge group had left. He could talk with her immediately while he had the nerve.

"You're back early. Did you even eat?"

"Come to think of it - no, we didn't. We just had a few beers. I came home to talk to you."

Fiona looked at him with a questioning expression.

"Sit down."

"Fine. What's going on?"

"I'm not going to beat around the bush. I just want you to know I've never spent a day without loving you in every way possible."

"It sounds like you're beating around the bush," she said

calmly.

"Okay. Here it is: Ron is my son. My biological son," he said nervously and proudly as he waited for a dramatic reaction.

Fiona put her arms around his neck and whispered two simple words: "I know."

Thomas almost fell over. "You know?"

"Yes. I've known since Ron's first birthday."

"Why haven't you said anything?"

"Why haven't you?"

During the short ride on the golf cart to the barn, Fiona told Thomas she had read a legal document that had come in the mail for him. It had something to do with Thomas providing for his son, Ron McGill, born in Seattle, Washington.

"I've tried a million different ways to pry it out of you. Including trying to make you mad, like when I said we should fire him because he doesn't come here often enough to work. Nothing sunk into your thick head," she said.

Thomas felt twenty years younger with the burden of keeping the secret lifted. "I guess I'm not as smart as I thought. Ron's known all of his life, too. We'll need to tell the kids sometime soon."

"Should we talk to them one at a time or as a family?"

"One at a time. I've thought about it plenty, and every time I come up with the same answer. We'll tell them one at a time."

Thomas parked the golf cart outside to avoid making tracks in the freshly raked barn aisles.

"I thought you were going to call," Ron said when he spotted them.

"The phones are out at the house. Let me check and see if they work here," Thomas said as he reached for the phone in the aisle way. "This phone is out, too. We'll check on it later."

"No tears, Fiona?" Ron said softly.

"No tears," she said, her lips turned up. "I'm glad the two of you have come out of the closet!"

Ron looked at his father, pleading for an explanation with his eyes.

Thomas grinned.

"What did you tell her?"

"That you're my biological son."

Fiona put her arm around her husband's waist. "I mean out of the closet in that both of you have known the truth all your life and neither of you would talk about it. It was a turn of a phrase."

"Oh. And you're all right about this?" Ron asked tentatively.

"Ron - I've known since your first birthday. What I want to know is why you've picked today to tell Thomas."

Horses whinnied for attention in the background, but with the intense conversation no one noticed.

"To be honest, it's because I really think Thomas should either take control of the business himself, or let me take control. I'd be happy to do it."

"This again?" Thomas said, slightly aggravated.

"Yes. Nick will walk away with a down payment of $5 million. If you can pay it, we can take over the business ourselves. Otherwise, he's filing for bankruptcy in sixty days," Ron told them, then described the details.

Thomas felt defeated. "Chapter 7 or Chapter 11?"

"I don't know. He says his lawyers haven't decided," Ron said.

"I can't believe it's come to this," Thomas said.

Fiona walked to the nearest stall and began to cry at the thought of them being bankrupt, even if it was only the business, and not personal bankruptcy. How had Greg let everything get so out of hand?

"Do you have access to $5 million?" Ron asked.

"I'll have to think about it," Thomas said. "I don't have a dime of liquid-cash after all the money we've been pouring into the development. My gut instinct is to trust Nick's judgment - if he wants out that bad, I don't think I want to risk borrowing the money to buy him out, even if it's only the down payment."

"I understand," Ron said. He smiled in spite of himself. He didn't want them to think their relationship was about the money.

"You've already arranged for the refinancing at a good interest rate?" Thomas said, referring to getting Nick out from any liability.

"I've got written loan commitments, but if we're in bankruptcy, it's a moot point," Ron said.

Thomas hated the idea of a cloud over their head, but reality was reality. "We'd be better off filing, wouldn't we?"

"It's not really our choice. It's Nick's choice," Ron reminded him. "Although, I guess that if there's a way to get him out of the picture before he files, it would put the decision in your hands. Otherwise, I can come up with the money to buy it out of bankruptcy. I'll own half of the business," Ron said.

Fiona didn't give Thomas a chance to respond. "Thomas is too old to take over again. If you really think Greg will run the business into the ground, you should take control," she said to Ron, as hard as it was to admit.

Thomas agreed. There was no way Patrick and Liz would be capable. Patrick never got involved in the business, even after he and Liz got married. If anyone could save the business, it was Ron.

"I hate to admit it Fiona," Thomas said, "but, I think you're right. We've got to give Ron the chance to turn everything around. Greg's not on the right track. He's not capable of dealing with the adversity."

They returned to the house and discussed the details of the transition in the kitchen as they nibbled on leftover citrus grilled shrimp, spinach quiche, fresh sourdough bread, goose liver pate, Brie and fresh papaya.

Over coffee and fruit torts, they agreed it didn't seem likely that Greg would be able to put everything together in time to stop the bankruptcy.

Ron handed Thomas an outline of his plan. Thomas positioned the paper where he and Fiona could read it together.

"So, as you can see," Ron said, "we can make this business worth operating once our expenses are radically reduced. As I told you earlier, Nick's keeping the Ocala farm for himself, which is only fair under the circumstances. It's actually to our benefit to be rid of the loss there.

"We'll close the California operation immediately. It's not worth the headaches anymore. We can sell the L'Equest land to various developers who want to build subdivisions with large lots. I've already put some feelers out - I think we'd be able to accomplish it and make a little money, depending on what we pay for it in bankruptcy. And, we can sell the sales center to some type of business that doesn't need a liquor license."

Before Ron continued, Thomas said sadly, "We can't afford to stay on this property anymore. I can see that."

Ron nodded. Fiona cried more.

Thomas continued. "We're always getting offers for this land. I've been fighting off the developers, but their offers are tempting. They all want to build condos and a commercial development. Maybe we should sell this Scottsdale property and move to Vintage East."

This was the first Fiona had heard of this. "You can't be serious," she said to Thomas.

"From what realtors are telling me about the value of the land, I wouldn't mind. It's getting so built up around here anyway," Thomas said, not admitting they wouldn't really have a choice when it came down to it.

Ron didn't think Thomas and Fiona would consider moving voluntarily, so he hadn't thought about it. "I would imagine we could clear up all of the Vintage debt with the sale of this property," he said, not referring to the L'Equest debt.

Fiona couldn't imagine moving anywhere else. "You mean we'll be losing our home?"

"Don't look at it that way," Thomas said.

"But that's what's going to happen. No matter if we're bankrupt or not, whether we sell or not, we're losing our home?" she said. The tears continued.

"It's just a building, Fiona," Thomas said, not admitting that he felt the same way. It wouldn't change anything. One way or another, they'd be losing their home and their oasis from the rest of the world.

"Let's look into it further," Thomas said.

"Anyway," Ron said, "as you'll see on the outline, we'll get rid of the jets, the motor coach and the limo's. We'll sell all of the truck and trailer rigs except for the eight-horse set up. When we put on the auctions, we won't pay for celebrity entertainment and we won't have catering. We'll limit the alcohol to beer and wine. People will understand - in times like these, everyone will be cutting back. And of course, we won't need elaborate auction catalogs or as much advertising. Two-page spreads will work as well as the ten-page spreads we've been doing in the trade publications."

Fiona wished these ideas were Greg's, rather than Ron's.

Thomas nodded in agreement. "We could probably sell the horses for a quarter of what we've been averaging, and still be able to make it."

"I think you're right," Ron said. "And, if you want my opinion, we should stop holding consignment auctions. Let's sell our own horses. We need to make all the money from the sales, not just a commission."

Thomas shook his head. "I don't know. I think we should at least hold one or two consignment sales. We can't just stop supporting our clients, even if we're legally a new entity."

"Fine," Ron said.

Ron assured Thomas and Fiona that he would be able to come up with the money to buy everything out of Chapter 7 or Chapter 11.

Father and son would continue the horse business, but this time with Thomas and Ron at the helm.

The hardest part will be telling Greg, Thomas thought.

The best part will be telling Greg, Ron thought.

I can't believe we're going bankrupt, Fiona thought.

Marcie was long gone with Bob. The Bordeaux Hill barn crew that had been out repairing fencing never returned to the barn. One of the bitter workers suggested they all walk out on Greg and teach him a lesson for how lousy he had been treating them lately. Over the past year, his temper flared and nothing was ever done to his standards. Christmas bonuses were eliminated, and he stopped providing coffee and donuts in the morning and sandwiches with chips for lunch. "Screw him," the ringleader said. "I'm walking. How about you?" A rally began. "He can feed the horses tonight!" the oldest man said. "And clean the stalls," the youngest man said. The entire crew followed and drove off without stopping in the barn.

Greg was still unconscious on the concrete floor.

The following morning Ron received two phone calls. Nick called from Florida to tell him he had decided in the middle of the night to return to Ocala. Greg hadn't returned his phone calls the previous day or evening. Nick was so fed up he had directed his attorney to file the paperwork for the bankruptcies immediately.

The second call was the hospital letting him know his mother was hospitalized with a serious case of pneumonia. He took the next available commercial flight to Seattle.

Ron talked to the doctor before he entered her room and discovered that his mother had very little chance of surviving for more than the night.

"Son," she said with just barely a hint of life in her eyes.

"I got here as quickly as I could, Mom."

He held her thin wrinkled hands between his. They were cold as ice.

"I know."

"Are you in pain?"

"My heart is aching, but my body is being sedated."

"Don't be afraid to die, Mom. Heaven's a better place, and if it's your time, it's your time. I'll miss you, but like you've always said, death is part of the cycle of life."

"I need to tell you something," she whispered.

Ron acted as if he hadn't heard her.

"I should call Thomas. He would want to be here for you," Ron said.

"No. Please, don't."

"But Mom, I know him. He'd want to be here to say goodbye."

"That's what I need to talk to you about."

Ron looked at her curiously but didn't speak.

"Thomas is not really your father," she confessed as tears filled her eyes.

A searing pain shot through his chest. "Not really my father?"

"I'm sorry. I'm sorry to both of you. I shouldn't have lied, but it's what I thought I had to do at the time."

"I don't understand," he said gently as his thoughts began spinning. He had spent his life idolizing Thomas Bordeaux, believing he was his biological father.

"I'm sorry, but he's not your father..." she trailed off.

When Linda discovered she was pregnant by the Marine, who had since moved overseas and didn't keep in contact, she immediately pursued an affair with Thomas. She then told Thomas she was pregnant, carrying his child. Linda tried to convince Thomas to leave Fiona, but he refused.

"Mom. You're on medication. This can't be true."

"It's true. I swear to you. I don't know if you should tell Thomas, but I had to tell you," she said, her voice weakening more. "You need to know the truth. You can handle the truth," she whispered her last words before she slipped into eternal rest.

Chapter 32

Ryan Sanders fled the rat race in Manhattan. He was psyched up to spend a couple of quiet weeks at his farm in Santa Barbara. Shawna, who had very little interest in trying to join him, couldn't get away from the network. Ryan arranged to meet with his finance people in L.A., and arranged time with Karla, the casting agent in Santa Monica. She offered to meet Ryan in Santa Barbara - they had worked there together on projects in the past.

Karla, an intermediate rider who grew up in Montecito, boarded her cross-country gelding at Ryan's. Dan, Ryan's partner and trainer, specialized in Arabians, but the farm boarded and trained a dozen horses of other breeds to accommodate Ryan's friends and business associates.

When Karla arrived at the barn, her 16.2 hand gray Hanoverian, named Per Soghare - which means *'to dream'* in Italian - was being tacked up by a Mexican groom. Ryan was feeding fortune cookies to Brimsome, the 15 hand bay half-Arabian gelding he would be riding.

"By the way, I never did get a chance to tell you - the actress your friend Ron hired for the practical joke was totally freaked out by the job."

"Freaked out? Why?" Ryan asked.

Karla led Soghare to the mounting block, mentally preparing herself to ride the rambunctious beast. "When I first called Torrie and told her the job was for a practical joke, she asked how much it would pay. Since I was doing a favor for you, I said she could negotiate her own rates. I passed along Ron's phone number and let them deal directly."

Ryan swung his leg over Brimsome who started to walk off before Ryan was situated. "Right," he acknowledged as he gently bumped the snaffle bit to stop the horse. He slid his boots into the stirrup irons and centered himself in the slippery new saddle. He'd have to remember to ask someone to oil it and rub old denim on the seat before he rode in it again.

"Anyway," Karla continued, "Torrie met with Ron. He had a rough script written, and they role-played. She knew the real thing with your friend would actually be improvising, but Ron wanted her to know the general idea of where the subject needed to lead, and what she had to admit..."

At their rider's cue, Soghare and Brimsome walked off toward the lake.

Ryan cut in. "Had to admit?"

Soghare bucked playfully when he spotted three deer on his near side. Karla tightened her reins and reprimanded him with her crop. He bucked harder, swinging his hips right, then left, then threw in another bold buck. Karla stayed in the saddle, accustomed to his antics. He threw his nose in the air as he wrung his tail with each additional step.

"Loosen your reins. Relax your seat and move with his stride. He'll feel it, and he'll settle down," Ryan said.

Karla followed his suggestion. Soghare responded by lowering his head and stretching out his neck.

"Thanks," Karla said. "Anyway, when Torrie found out the role wasn't what she was led to believe, she got worried and questioned Ron. He convinced her to go along by tripling the amount of money she originally agreed to. She was skeptical and apprehensive, but she was past due on rent and her car payment, so she still agreed to do it."

"Backtrack here," Ryan said. "What was she admitting?"

"Something about murdering someone. Trust me, I was pretty freaked when I heard about it myself."

"Murdering someone? Why didn't you call me?"

"I did," she said. Before she could elaborate, a flock of birds flew close overhead. Soghare grew anxious and broke into a canter. She abruptly pulled back on the reins and squeezed her legs to hold on. He ran faster. She pulled him into a circle to slow him down.

"Take the pressure off of his sides and gently bump him with the bit - lean your upper body back a few degrees. You're just making him worse the way you're responding to him," Ryan yelled. He was surprised she didn't know to ask her horse to half halt.

Karla bit her lip as she followed Ryan's instructions. Within a couple of strides the gelding reverted to a relaxed walk.

Ryan didn't want to insult Karla. He weighed his words and used a friendly tone. "Have you read 'Centered Riding' by Sally Swift?"

"No."

"We've got an extra copy in the barn lounge. Have a look. If you like it, take it and read it before you ride again. I think you'll get a lot out of it," Ryan suggested.

"My riding instructors always told me not to let him get away with anything. He's rowdy, but apparently that's part of what makes him a good cross-country horse. His energy level and such."

Ryan shook his head, feeling sympathy for Soghare. "A horse can be energetic and maintain their manners at the same time. You just need to learn to handle him in a way that he knows you're alpha, but that you respect him enough not to inflict discomfort. If you communicate with him in a kind way, he'll be obedient and become fond of you. Horses want to like people. You just have to give him a reason."

"I really ought to have someone ride him regularly for me. Coming up here to ride on weekends isn't enough. Sometimes I even miss a weekend or two. He gets so excited when I finally ride him, it's more like a battle of wills."

"Talk to Dan," Ryan said, hoping he wasn't offending her. "He'll have someone ride him for you during the week, and maybe you could take a few lessons. I know Soghare's well trained and behaves beautifully when he's handled right."

Karla didn't plan to join Ryan for a riding lesson, but she knew he meant well.

"Fine," she said, referring to the book and his advice.

"I'm sorry I interrupted. So, you called my office?"

"Yes. They said you were on location and that they couldn't disturb you unless it was an emergency. Even though I was worried, this wasn't an emergency - so I just left a phone message for you to call me as soon as you had a chance."

Brimsome extended his stride and picked up his pace to keep up with the long-legged tank of a horse.

"Shit," Ryan said. "It's been so long ago, I don't even remember if I got the message. I obviously didn't call. I wish you had tried back."

"I was swamped with that Oliver Stone movie. Anyway, it just slipped my mind and I didn't think about it until a couple of days ago. I'm casting a film for Spielberg, and I thought of Torrie for one of the smaller roles. When I called her about it, she said the last thing I got her still gave her the creeps."

"Shit. I can't believe this," Ryan said.

"What?"

"It's a long story."

Ryan trotted Brimsome until he was shoulder to shoulder with Soghare. On his refined half-Arabian, Ryan felt like a midget on a pony. Once at Karla's side, he told her that the real Morgan Butler was arrested for the murder of George Finn. He explained the relationship between Sonia and Morgan - and told her some of the other background.

He continued, "Sonia loved Morgan's stallion. She bought him so that Morgan would have the money for a defense attorney and keep up the expenses on her house and everything - she's single. Morgan's in jail, claiming her innocence. Her lawyer is appealing the verdict - it was a totally circumstantial case."

"How do you know all of this?"

"Shawna's kept up on the case. That's how I know about the appeal. And, Sonia told Dan because she wanted our farm to stand Ambiguous at stud. Her farm doesn't have a breeding lab or the trained staff to handle a stallion."

"May I ask what she paid for the horse?"

"Sonia said she paid $1 million and Morgan retained breeding rights. Marty said the insurance application she saw showed that the horse was insured for $2 million, with Morgan as the loss payee for half."

Karla raised her brows in amazement.

"When we get back, I'm making some calls. This doesn't fit together - Ron hires Torrie to meet with Greg and admit she murdered Finn. That's supposedly a joke on Greg? Then, Morgan gets tried and convicted on circumstantial evidence. It doesn't add up," he said, recalling Shawna said the case against Morgan was weak. She said the authorities didn't care about anything other than having someone behind bars, so the good citizens of Beverly Hills could sleep at night.

"I bet it was a set up," Karla speculated.

Ryan told her what little he knew about Ron, and told her about the Bordeauxs. They spent the remainder of their ride speculating about everyone's motives and never did end up talking about his film.

After their ride, the first call he made was to Shawna, who immediately insisted he contact the District Attorney or Detective Harman. She asked him to call her after he'd talked with one of them. In the meantime, she'd be arranging to leave town with an investigator and a camera crew - she wanted an exclusive on the story.

The following morning, Ryan found himself telling the D.A. and Detective Harman what he suspected.

"To be honest, Mr. Sanders," the D.A. said, "the only evidence we really had against her was a weak motive, an audio recording of a confession and the testimony of Ron McGill and Greg Bordeaux. The video wasn't close enough to tell exactly what the woman looked like. Now, from what you're telling me, if it's correct, we've prosecuted the wrong person."

"I can't believe Ron would set someone up."

Harman swallowed the last of his coffee. "You said you don't know him to speak of. It's hard to judge someone's character under the circumstances."

"I know. But I just can't picture his setting up someone else for murder just because Greg was a suspect."

Harmon looked down at his notes and hiked his shoulders. "What makes you think that Ron and Greg weren't in on the charade with the actress together? Seems to me, Ron tried to protect Greg because Greg solicited his help."

"But Ron told Karla the joke was on Greg," Ryan said, not wanting to believe Greg was capable of murder.

Greg was the mastermind of the horse business. Why not of the murder of Finn and the set-up of Morgan?, Harman concluded. He couldn't see why Ron would try to protect Greg without a solid reason.

Harman tapped his pen on his desk. In his experience, people were capable of just about anything. "Can you stay in town? I'm not sure if we'll need you for anything else."

"I'll be in Santa Barbara," Ryan assured them.

~ ~~

Greg laid in the barn entry with fragmented thoughts swimming around his head. He was unable to tell if he were conscious or not. The wind was knocked out of him, and his body and head ached like never before. When he mustered the will to open his eyes, it was almost dark outside. Alexandria stood with her saddle slipped to the side, the left stirrup iron dangling below knee level, and her braided leather reins dragging the ground. She kept close to the horse in the stall across from where Greg fell. The mare heard him moan. Avoiding stepping on her reins, she took small steps until she could nuzzle Greg's head.

At least I have sensation, he thought, still not having moved.

He opened and closed his fingers. Then he wiggled his toes in his boots. Those parts still working, he gently moved his head to see if his neck was sore. It seemed fine. He eased himself into a sitting position, unaware of anything abnormal. His body ached, but no worse than it did from any other bad fall he had taken. As he started to stand up, he felt unsteady and nauseous. Each breath hurt his ribs, but again, no worse than any other accident.

Suddenly, he was aware of the dried blood caked on his face. He rested on the ground until he felt steady enough to attempt standing. Taking it slowly, as he finally raised himself to his feet, he noticed the pool of dried blood on the concrete floor. The sight made him vomit without warning. The smell made the mare back away, but she kept her eyes on him, obviously concerned.

Pain seared through his body. After managing to hobble a few steps, he steadied himself on the nearest stall wall. His right ankle was sprained -it throbbed when he applied weight.

Finally, he called out into the barn. "Hello. Is anyone here?" he said weakly. He couldn't call loud enough to be heard from outside. When the horses heard him, they began whinnying - some banged on their empty grain buckets. Greg realized the horses hadn't been fed. The racket from the horses got louder. He knew he wouldn't be up to walking to the feed room at the far side of the barn, let alone, up to carrying all of the hay and grain around. He summoned the strength and pain tolerance to walk outside and call out for help.

No one answered.

No one came.

The horses got louder. Creatures of habit, they wanted to eat. Alexandria followed Greg outside and started eating grass. While removing her saddle, Greg felt a searing pain as he raised his arms. He accidentally dropped the saddle to the ground - frustrated, he just left it there. Walking with an unbearable limp, he led her into the nearest pasture and removed her bridle.

He didn't have the strength and pain tolerance to lead each of the stalled horses outside. Grateful to have both interior and exterior doors, he managed to open the back doors of the stalls so the horses could eat and drink in their pasture.

With all of the horses out, just as he wondered what time it was, the automatic lights on the barn exterior came on. When the mosquitoes started biting him, he made his way to the house. He opened a cold can of Budweiser and washed down six Tylenol and three Darvocet.

He collapsed onto the sofa, untied his boots and slipped them off, then laid there waiting for Marcie to come home from wherever she was. As he waited, the painkillers knocked him out.

The following afternoon, there was pounding on his front door. Greg, fast asleep, didn't hear it. Then there was pounding on the kitchen door. Again, Greg didn't respond. His friend, Johnny Pallinto, tried the door handle. It wasn't locked. He took the liberty of entering the kitchen door. He found Greg on the sofa, not responsive to his name being called out. Johnny bent down and shook him, noticing the blood on Greg's shirt.

Startled, Greg opened his eyes.

"Are you okay? You're a mess," Johnny said.

"I'm hurtin' for certain," he moaned.

"What happened?"

Greg told him everything he remembered.

"We better get you to the hospital. You might have a concussion."

"Let me see how I do by morning. I can't even think of moving right now. Between the fall and the painkillers..."

"I'm sorry about Marcie. Is there anything I can do?"

Greg looked at him questioningly.

"Marcie - your wife," Johnny said. "Remember her?"

"Of course, I remember my wife. What are you sorry about?"

Johnny cleared his throat, wondering what to say. "You don't know?"

"Know what?"

"The word spread at my barn like wild fire that she ran off with Bob, my maintenance man. He told everyone she left you a note."

"What the fuck?" Greg said, suddenly having a flashback. Right before he hit his head on the barn door, he thought he saw Marcie kissing someone.

"You didn't get the note?"

"No. I don't know what you're talking about," he groaned.

"Stay here. I'll look for it. Where do you think she would have put it?"

"On the kitchen table, probably."

The note was there. Greg's head ached. He asked Johnny to read it. How much more personal could it get at this point?

As Johnny read the note, Greg cried inside, but was too macho to let himself go in front of his friend. "If she was going to leave me, the least she could have done is take that goddamn painting of herself."

Johnny smiled. At least Greg still had a sense of humor. "The light's flashing on your answering machine. Do you want me to play your messages?"

"Go ahead."

There were messages from Nick from the previous day and evening - the last one was apparently the last straw. He said he was flying back to Ocala, and his lawyers were going to file the first thing in the morning.

There was one more message from this morning - it was Nick. They were now officially in bankruptcy.

"I need to be alone," Greg said.

"What about the horses?"

"What about them?"

"All the horses are in the pasture," Johnny reminded him. "Where's your barn help? I looked for you in the barn before I came to the house and there wasn't a soul around. The stalls were dirty and the horses were outside. There aren't any cars outside either - cars for the help, I mean."

Assuming everyone had quit, Greg said, "The horses have grass and water from the stream. I can't deal with anything else right now."

"Do you want me to send my crew up to clean the stalls? It looks like you've had a walk out. Whatever I can do to help."

"That would work. I can't think. Whatever you want to do."

Johnny checked to make sure the gates to Greg's pastures were secured before he returned to his own farm.

Chapter 33

Ron followed his mother's wishes and had her cremated. There was only a private funeral service since they didn't have family, and his mother had no close friends.

From a pay phone in the Seattle airport, Ron called Nick in Ocala. Nick told him the bankruptcies had been filed. Ron hung up and dialed his next call.

"Well, I'm finally going to own L'Equest and Vintage," he said, not feeling as excited as he had anticipated.

The original plan was that he'd be the savior son who could give Thomas what he wanted, while Greg was the son who screwed everything up and Patrick was the son who didn't care much either way.

"I'm not paying you the rest of the money until Morgan loses her appeal," Sonia said.

They had agreed that he would be paid all of the money

when Morgan was convicted. Later, Sonia convinced him to wait for the majority of the money until he needed it - otherwise, it might look suspicious that shortly after her husband was murdered, she took out a loan and couldn't account for the funds.

"I can't control how long the system takes," Ron said impatiently. "You're not a suspect. You've got control of George's companies, and you've received the insurance proceeds."

Sonia thought for a minute. "I suppose that means you want to meet?"

"Yes. I'm at the airport now. I'll call you when we land."

On the flight from Seattle to LAX, Ron ordered a Cutty and reclined his first-class seat. He closed his eyes and thought back to the day the wheels were set in motion that would ultimately change his life forever.

The vivid memory played like a motion picture: A few days after Greg made the proposal to George, Ron had called Sonia and pleaded with her to convince her husband not to buyout Nick. He warned her that the business wasn't as profitable as Greg had made it appear, and swore that Greg wasn't telling George everything he needed to know in order to make a sound decision - a decision to turn down the supposed opportunity.

Before she would consider his request, she wanted to know his motivation for sabotaging Greg's goal.

Ron flew to LAX to meet her before her flight to Greece. Sonia sent her nanny and the kids to eat lunch while she talked with him.

"I don't want anyone to buyout Nick," he remembered telling her. "We work well as a team, and I don't know if I could get along working with anyone else. I know Nick's ways. He knows mine."

"What makes you think you wouldn't like working for George?" she had asked.

Ron remembered pausing as he decided how candid to be. He labored to maintain an even tone. "It's not that. In all honesty, no one knows it, but I'm trying to raise the money to buy out Nick's interest myself."

"Where would you get the money?"

"I've got someone who will co-sign on the bank notes, and I've got some cash accumulated, but I'm not sure how I'll get the rest," he remembered admitting. It was embarrassing.

Sonia excused herself to use a pay phone. When she returned, Ron was shocked when she said, "I have a plan - you kill George."

Sweat instantly darkened the fabric under his arms. He wondered for a moment if he had misunderstood her - she uttered the words so quietly.

She leaned in close to him, the need for secrecy critical. "You kill him - or have him killed. If they suspect me, you set up Morgan Butler."

Ron looked at her with an expression that said the idea was absurd.

Sonia kept glancing around, making sure no one could hear them. "If it becomes necessary, make it look like Morgan did it so I would buy her breedings. Then, I'll offer to buy Ambiguous - as a friend doing a favor - so she'll have money for bail and a lawyer. I love that horse, and I know she'd never sell him unless she absolutely had to."

Shocked, Ron, now on the edge of his chair, reached for his cup of coffee and spilled it. Sonia ignored the mess and made him an offer he couldn't refuse. Ron recalled the slight tremor in her voice as she made a proposal.

"If you do it, I'll give you the money to buy out Nick. If George doesn't have enough cash, I'll take out a loan against his business - and I'll have the life insurance proceeds. There's a double indemnity clause on his policy - there will be plenty of money to go around. We'll both get what we want."

When the image of the words burned themselves in his mind, he was sickened - and intrigued. In that moment, he found he didn't even care to know why Sonia wanted her husband dead.

Ron sipped his Cutty.

The pilot made an announcement about the altitude and weather conditions.

Ron found himself wondering why he didn't ask Sonia, "What about Morgan? You don't want to send an innocent person to prison, do you?"

He supposed neither of them felt as if they had an alternative.

Chapter 34

Three cars with blue flashing lights pulled into the driveway at Bordeaux Hill. The sirens didn't wake Greg, who remained on the sofa with a bottle of Darvocet on the table next to him.

The police rang the doorbell. No answer. They banged on the door. No answer.

Johnny had seen the police cars with their lights on pass his property. He immediately jumped into his car and followed them, worried something had happened to Greg - perhaps an ambulance was on its way.

Johnny rushed up to the police, who were conferring near the front entry.

"Excuse me," Johnny said. "I'm a friend of Gregs. Can I help you?"

"Do you know if he's home?"

"I'm not sure. Have you checked the barn?"

"We've got officers checking now."

"May I ask what this is about?"

"No. But you can help us. Do you know if he has a weapon in the house?"

Johnny hadn't thought about it before. "I know he doesn't hunt. He said he could never kill an animal, but I have no idea if he has a gun for personal protection. I can't imagine that he would, but I have no idea."

Before anyone responded, Johnny scooted between the bushes and looked in the front window. "He's passed out on the sofa. He got hurt and took some Darvocet. They must have knocked him out, again."

"Do you have a key?"

"No. But the back door - the kitchen door, was open yesterday. That's how I got in, and I don't recall locking it when I left."

Within five minutes the police were at Greg's side pulling him up from the sofa. He was out of it, unable to comprehend what was happening."

"Greg Bordeaux, you're under arrest for the murder of George Finn. You have the right to remain silent..."

Chapter 35

In New York City, Ryan sat in the control booth watching his wife doing a live feed in the newsroom studio.

The teleprompter rolled:

I'm Shawna Sanders with breaking news.

Garment industry mogul, and collector of Champion show horses, George Finn would turn over in his grave if he knew why he was fatally shot at the front door of his Beverly Hills mansion.

Ron McGill, of Scottsdale, Arizona, was placed under arrest at his home after returning from his mother's funeral in Seattle.

Inside sources have disclosed that McGill entered into a plea bargain by giving testimony about his employer, Greg Bordeaux of Vintage Arabians.

McGill has admitted that Bordeaux paid him to hire a hit man to slay Finn. McGill says Bordeaux wanted the Greek tycoon dead as retribution for a business deal gone bad - and perhaps as an unspoken warning to other clients of Vintage Arabians.

McGill will be placed in protective custody until he testifies in court that Bordeaux was furious with Finn for having backed out of a deal to buy a 45% interest in his exclusive Kentucky equestrian development and to buy a 30% interest in the lucrative horse breeding operation and auction business.

McGill will also testify that Bordeaux masterminded a scheme whereby horse broker, Morgan Butler was convicted of Finn's murder. Butler has been serving time in prison while awaiting an appeal.

Stay tuned for more details on this twisted crime and the warped legal system where McGill will only serve 90 days of jail time in exchange for his testimony about Bordeaux.

I'm Shawna Sanders in New York. Thanks for tuning in.

"Cut. That's a wrap," said the show's director.

Cali Canberra's
emotionally charged tale
is a
crime story
that revolves around the
moral and ethical issues
of selling high-end horses
for record prices.

Criminal behavior, greed, jealousy,
betrayal, seduction, friendship and
even romance inhabit the pages of this
unpredictable
no-holds-barred story.

9th Annual (2001)
Writer's Digest
National Book Awards
Mainstream/Literary Fiction
Honorable mention
8th place out of 350 entries

Rene Killian, a female bloodstock agent, plays by her own set of rules in her continuous pursuit of the almighty dollar. Trying to claw her way to the top, she's caught in the political crossfire between some of Southern California's most influential breeding farms and her own investors. Jared, one of her biggest spending clients, has threatened to destroy her. Now, she'll go to extreme measures, including blackmail and extortion, to get Jared out of her life. In the midst of her problems, she has an affair with a respected equine attorney who discloses confidential information about his own family and wealthy clients, in order to win her affection.

Cali Canberra
takes us on a wild ride of
intrique, murder, manipulation,
corruption and suspense.
Trading Paper discloses the
inner workings of the
exclusive horse business
through an entertaining
character driven story.

An unparalleled
insight
into the lives of some
of the
top players in the
horses business and
what made this
unique industry tick.

At the peak of the Arabian horse industry in the 1980's, St. Louis businessman Johan Murphy takes time out of his stressful life to meet with his unscrupulous new lawyer. Caught between a rock and a hard place, Murphy's finances prohibit him from making the upcoming installment payment on his champion mare, *Love Letter*, a horse that he recently acquired at a prestigious Scottsdale, Arizona auction. Murphy's problem sets the stage for the demise of an entire industry. The legal entanglements catapult into motion a chain of events that impact the entire Arabian horse industry in a way in which it will never recover.

Excerpt from Never Enough!

In a flash, the exuberant bay stallion hit a lick at a full extended trot, making his bold entrance into the preview ring with Luke Remmacs on the end of the lead line. The pounding of the horse's hooves kicked up emerald green pine shavings.

Henry Copper, the professional announcer, fell silent, knowing he could not be heard over the whistling and applauding of the crowd - which was Freedom's cue: as a natural response to the attention he knew was just for him, he lifted his tail, pranced and popped his ears forward as he snorted through his enormous masculine nostrils.

Seasoned Arabian lovers in the audience whistled and stood to cheer the stallion on as if he were Elvis in concert. The enthusiasm was contagious. Newcomers followed along, surprised at their own reaction to the charismatic animal. Luke deftly removed the thin gold filigree and patent leather halter, swung it in the air and turned a thousand pounds of testosterone loose in the ring to strut his stuff.

"What is everyone so excited about?" Ron practically screamed to Rene.

"The horse! Isn't he spectacular?" Carol answered before Rene responded.

"Yes," Rene said. "This is exciting. It's how the farm gets you all pumped up and wanting to buy at the auction."

Freedom seemed to be living for his audience, showing-off his unbelievable cadence - then, every once in a while he reared high into the air and followed up with a buck. When the crowd cheered, he took several strides at a canter. Just to make sure people were still paying attention, he abruptly stopped, stood perfectly squared facing the bleachers, then promptly swung his head high in the air and whinnied, announcing that he was the King. Every rock hard muscle in his body was flexed: the snort from his oiled air passages sent the crowd into wild excitement as the band played *Chariots of Fire*.

Rod wasn't impressed, which disappointed Carol.

"I saw that horse earlier standing in his fancy stall. He's just a horse. What's the big deal? And what's with these people?"

"It's just meant to be fun and make the event exciting," Rene explained.

"I think this crowd is ridiculous if you ask me. It's just a horse! And that stall of his - the woodwork is as nice as what I have in my den - and the custom wrought iron stall grates - and engraved silver name plates - come on!"

"Well, just keep quiet and let me have fun, honey," Carol told him.

"Fine. This is your day. I'm going to get a drink. You ladies have a good time."

"We will. Bring us some wine," Carol said as she winked at him.

Rene hoped he wouldn't walk back by the preparation barn. He was obviously a sharp man, and would pick up on all the artificial things they were doing to make the horses look better than usual. Applying oils as makeup highlighters, putting ginger in the rectum of the horse so they would keep their tails high, spraying a light coat of glitter on the hair, and everything else they do to make horses look fantasy-like.

When Carol and Rene looked back out toward the preview ring,

Freedom was rearing up and playfully striking out while on his way back to the stallion barn. Aston was next, acting just like Freedom, and the crowd remained just as enthusiastic.

Without delay, a silvery-gray mare was turned loose in the ring. Carol was observant and asked why there were four men in with the mare. Rene explained that they were controlling the movement of the horse as much as possible by shaking small plastic containers with tiny rocks in the bottom; the sound imitates a rattle snake. She told her how the response of the horse is to move away from the sound. If the men didn't urge the mare, she may just stand around sniffing the colored shavings - certainly not the best way to show off a beautiful horse.

Rod didn't come back with wine, which was just fine - champagne was being served in the stands and around the ring.

"These horses look so much better than the ones in the pastures," Carol observed.

"These horses are all conditioned, and about a week ago, the horses had all of their hair shaved off."

"That must take forever. I know how long it takes me just to shave my own legs."

"It takes about 3 hours. Then, they rub mayonnaise into the skin to prevent it from getting dry. By today, the hair has grown back just enough to show the color. Probably starting at about five this morning, the horses were bathed with expensive shampoos and deep conditioning treatments, then they were sponged down with a very light coating of a mixture of Shapley's Oil and warm water, then allowed to dry again. That's how you're able to see so much of their muscling."

"Wow. What a production. And look at their manicures."

Rene laughed. "I guess that's what you could call it. They lightly sand the hooves using three different grains of sandpaper, then black or neutral shoe polish, then they buff the hoof before they paint it with a clear glossy sealant."

"Sounds like the pedicures I get at the salon. Now that Rod and I are together I go in for the whole treatment. They do my hair and make-up and everything."

Rene acted as if she was amused by Carol's attitude. "Same with these horses. An artful groom applies special highlighting oil around the horse's eyes, on the muzzle, on the cheek bones and inside their ears. It's like make-up on women. The oil either highlights the good features of the horse, or the groom can distort what the horse actually looks like if they needed to. If the horse's shoulder doesn't have enough angle to it, they put oil near the shoulder line of the horse to make it look like that is the real angle of the shoulder, when it really isn't. There are lots of other tricks too. Like letting feet grow longer than they should, especially the toe, and then putting weighted front shoes on. The weighted shoes make the horse trot higher than what is natural."

"How did you find all of this out? It's amazing."

"Experience. And time in the business. Being an insider. New people don't have a clue. That's why they use me to help them buy their horses."

Rene and Carol talked through the entire presentation of another thirty-two horses.

After the preview, across the expansive lawn, the buffet tables were covered with fabulous gourmet food. Portable bars were close at hand, no matter where you were.

"Let's find Rod and get a table to eat at," Carol suggested to Rene.

"Sure. Will you need to ask him if you can do business with me, or can you just buy through who you want?"

"I'll just tell him that I'm going to let you find me a horse. He won't care, especially after I tell him how much you taught me. I had no idea there was so much to knowing a great horse and identifying what you like about a particular horse," Carol confessed.

"Most people don't know what they don't know. That's why I can be of such an important service to you. The main thing right now is that you'll need to decide if you want to be able to ride the horse you buy, or if you'll just pay to have a trainer ride and show - or if you'll want to buy a broodmare, and of course, you'll have to decide how much money you can spend."

Carol bit her lip. "The amount of money doesn't really matter. A couple of months ago Rod sold a division of his company for just under a half billion dollars. I think I'll tell him I want a broodmare *and* get a show horse that will stay with a trainer. It would be fun to have a foal and watch it grow up, and it would be exciting to watch my horse be shown."

I've got a live one.

"That's a good idea…plus, while your show horse is being trained, you can take riding lessons, and eventually get good enough to ride your own horse."

"Oh my God! I'd never be good enough to ride a horse that costs that much money! I'd be afraid I would do something wrong."

"Don't worry," Rene said. "Take lessons from a top notch instructor, and she'll talk to your trainer and let you know when she thinks you're ready. The trainer will be there with you to coach you on how your horse is cued. No one will let you do anything harmful."

"I don't know. Lets take one step at a time. This place is so breathtaking, isn't it?"

"I can't say that I'd mind owning a place like this," Rene said, hoping to plant a seed in Carol's mind.

If he has that much money, maybe I can get them to buy a big farm and start a long-term breeding program. They could be a gold mine. All those commissions and markups…

Newchi Publishing

11110 Surrey Park Trail ~ Duluth, GA 30097
770-664-1611
Toll free phone: 866-314-1952 Toll free fax: 866-314-1950
calicanberra.com

Books - $14.99 each + $3.95 s&h for the 1st book & $1.95 for each additional book

Qty:

__ ISBN# 0-9705004-0-8 (Trade Paperback) **Trading Paper** by Cali Canberra

__ ISBN# 0-9705004-2-4 (Trade Paperback) **Never Enough!** by Cali Canberra

__ ISBN# 0-9705004-3-2 (Trade Paperback) **Buying Time** by Cali Canberra

Beautiful Note Cards & Stationary packaged in imported Organza bags

$12.99 per set ~ 3 sets: $30 ~ $1.50 per set s&h

Qty:

__ Oil painting of bay stallion from cover of Trading Paper
Note Cards - Set of 8 w/ envelopes 4.5" x 5.5" full color

__ Water color of white mare from cover of Buying Time
Note Cards - Set of 8 w/ envelopes 4.5" x 5.5" full color

__ Oil painting of bay stallion from cover of Trading Paper
Stationary - 24 sheets w/ 12 envelopes 5.5" x 8" full color image

__ Water color of white mare from cover of Buying Time
Stationary - 24 sheets w/ 12 envelopes 5.5" x 8" full color image

Visit calicanberra.com for additional images & products.

We accept checks, Visa, MC, Discover & American Express

Name on card:____

Billing Address for card: ______________________________________

____

Shipping address if different:___________________________________

Phone #:____________________ e-mail:_________________________

Card#:______________________________ Expiration date:__________

Type of Card (Please Circle): Visa / Mastercard / American Express / Discover

About

The Author

Cali Canberra researched various profitable industries and the law - including issues about money laundering, asset protection, securities violations and ethical dilemmas faced by attorneys. But, Cali didn't have to research the horse industry to write her novels. Canberra, like other successful writers, writes about what she knows and what she has a passion for.

As a lifelong equestrian and businessperson, Cali chose to share her experience and insider knowledge. Fiction is the most entertaining way to tell her stories, but she insists the books are inspired by the way the horse industry actually operates and real things that happen in a variety of industries and professions.

Cali always has characters that earn their lucrative living outside of the horse business, making her stories entertaining to mainstream readers. The series characters in all three books are Ryan and Shawna Sanders. Ryan is an enormously successful movie producer - his wife is the nation's highest paid television news journalist. Other fascinating characters include both civil and criminal attorneys, brothers who import and export produce, an international weapons broker, a mogul in the garment industry and a domineering real estate developer.

Canberra has loved horses her entire life. She grew up riding her neighbor's pleasure and show horses, although she didn't buy her own horse until she was an adult. In Scottsdale, Arizona, she bought her first Quarter Horses and Thoroughbreds to ride for enjoyment, train and sell. The Arabian market was growing by leaps and bounds at the time, which caught Cali's attention. She then focused her entrepreneurial skills and horse sense on buying, selling, brokering and breeding high-end Polish Arabians. In the early 1980's, it didn't take many clients or many horse sales to make a good living doing something she loved. She traveled throughout the USA and to Poland, studying horses and building up a small client base, as she enjoyed her husband and raised her daughter. She sold some of the most expensive horses in the breed. It was the lifestyle she dreamed of.

Cali says that in retrospect, there was very little of the 1980's she would repeat if she knew then what she knows now. She was caught up in making money - and spending money, with little regard for her future or a spiritual life. Then, when the market crashed and it was clear there was no hope for recovery, Cali went on to write fiction about the turbulent era and is loving every minute of it!